HIGH MOON

AIMEE EASTERLING   JENN STARK   B R KINGSOLVER

MARINA FINLAYSON   DALE IVAN SMITH

N. R. HAIRSTON   JENN WINDROW   BECCA ANDRE

Wetknee Books

HIGH MOON

First edition. September 14, 2021.

Written by Aimee Easterling, Jenn Stark, B R Kingsolver, Marina Finlayson, Dale Ivan Smith, N. R. Hairston, Jenn Windrow, and Becca Andre.

Cover Design by: Heather Hamilton-Senter

Contents

Fox Hunt

AIMEE EASTERLING

Chapter 1

A WEREWOLF howl curled across the dappled shade sheltering musicians and concertgoers alike. I frowned and reassessed. No, that wasn't a howl. Not in broad daylight in a city park full of smiling humans. The undulating tone had to be the result of one really badly tuned violin.

Still, I started counting heads anyway. First my ten-year-old sister Kira—half Japanese like me, and also the only other one in the crowd who wasn't rich and white as Wonder Bread. Next, I moved to the students three years older who were paying top dollar for this summer enrichment opportunity. As long as all twenty were present and accounted for, there was no point in worrying about whether that sound had been more than a strange violin.

"Stay away from wolves." Dad's warning whispered in my memory as I continued eying students. Twelve, thirteen.... Drat. I was 100% certain I'd considered that towhead before. Someone must have switched places on me.

Meanwhile, one half of the inseparable Raven twin duo popped up to hover at my elbow. "Ms. Fairchild?" she started, ignoring the glares of audience members who would have preferred she remain seated. The stage was slightly elevated, but the rest of us were lounging—or, in Charlie's case, standing—on blankets spread across the grass.

Which meant Charlie was now obstructing the view of approximately a dozen people arrayed behind us. A dozen people who were rustling and murmuring their dissatisfaction. Well, I'd fix that public-relations issue as soon as I finished my count.

Eighteen, nineteen....

Charlie's next words filtered through the music just as I ran out of students. "Jessie's been in the bathroom an awfully long time."

Ah. So my math hadn't been off after all. And the absence of a sister to finish Charlie's sentences also explained why the curly-haired and snub-nosed teenager had taken so long to get to the point.

I lurched to my feet, ignoring the increased griping behind me. I'd check the bathroom, then....

I didn't do any of that. Instead, I froze as the crescendo of percussion gave way to a momentary silence.

Silence from the orchestra, not silence from somewhere just outside the assemblage. There, an unmistakable howl barreled into the musical gap so obviously that it caught even my charges' attention.

"What was that?" Kira asked, dark eyes widening. She abruptly looked every bit the younger tagalong...a tagalong aware of the secrets we both hid.

"What?" Charlie, less tuned in to sounds, scrunched up her freckled nose in confusion.

"The..." Kira met my gaze then trailed off.

A snooty woman behind us muttered something about children needing to be seen rather than heard. Ignoring her gripes, I donned my best teacher voice. "It's just a dog," I told my students. "I'll check on Jessie. The rest of you, stay put."

Charlie subsided but I knew my sister would be far less malleable even though she lacked the twin's years. Sure enough, Kira met my gaze head-on, her mouth flattening until she looked like a small, female clone of our father. Dad had been tenacious to a fault. Had to be as a human raising two girls with magical abilities after our mother died.

Today, Kira's tenacity seemed inclined to get us both killed. She was already halfway to her feet when she spat out: "I want to see it."

I shook my head, hating to pull rank but having no other option. Teacher voice wouldn't work here, but threats might. "You promised not to be a hindrance. Do you want this to be the last summer session you attend?"

Kira winced, and rightly so. If she didn't follow me to work, her other option involved sitting around our tiny apartment with nothing other than a book to amuse her. Our computer was so slow you could barely use it to play solitaire. I couldn't afford to pay for a second cell phone.

No wonder my sister subsided after one tense moment. "I'll keep count," she promised, squaring her slender shoulders. As if she thought it was no problem to put herself in charge of kids three years her senior.

Her senior, but more innocent of the dark nature of the shadow world. I nodded acceptance. Then I strode away toward the source of the howls.

INSTINCT TOLD ME TO HURRY. But my job required me to make a pitstop before I could deal with the larger issue of *werewolves*. I couldn't leave a ten-year-old solely in charge of nineteen middle schoolers after all.

Instead, I stalked past the point where my nineteen-should-be-twenty girls ran into Tony's seventeen boys. I pretended not to notice the PDA where the sexes came together, averting my eyes and continuing on to the math teacher who was as human as his charges.

Tony was an ultra-pale redhead who'd been known to burn in the middle of winter, but still he lounged with his face upturned toward July sunshine. His eyes were closed and a blissed-out smile sweetened his angular face.

"Can you watch my girls for a few minutes?" I murmured, ignoring the bawdy joke one of his students made in response to my ill-chosen words. I'd learned over the years that if I left any opening for innuendo, teenagers would run through the gap with cheerful abandon. The best response to such a misstep was to ignore, ignore, ignore.

Which was what my co-worker appeared to be doing to me. I would have been annoyed if I didn't know that his math mind considered classical music an inspiring puzzle. "Tony," I repeated, louder this time.

"Quiet." The same woman who'd muttered at me earlier was angry enough now to call her chastisement down the row of fidgeting students.

Ignoring both the snarky woman and the raised hairs on the back of my neck, I waited for my counterpart to blink his way out of a musical reverie. Finally—

"Problem, Mai?" Tony asked at last. His volume, unlike mine, Charlie's, and Kira's, was concert appropriate. Still, the woman behind us huffed yet again.

And Tony turned clear blue eyes away from me to assess the audience member in question. She was dressed to the nines, as if she'd expected plush velvet chairs in an air-conditioned concert hall rather than the chance to sprawl ourselves out beneath maple trees. And Tony's words came out so smooth it took a moment for either of us to realize they represented a verbal slap.

"Behaving appropriately for the space you find yourself in is a very difficult skill to master, isn't it?"

Leaving the overdressed woman to mull over the implications, Tony turned to face the next disrupter, the boy who'd made reference to my breasts. This time, my fellow teacher didn't even need words to get his point across. Instead, he raised one eyebrow and waited until the kid dropped his gaze to the grass. Only then did he turn back to address me.

"Sorry about that. You were saying?"

Right. As amusing as it was to watch Tony deal with the unruly,

I had more important issues on my mind. "Jessie's been in the bathroom quite a while. I need to check on her. Can you...?"

"Take care of your hooligans as well as my delinquents? Sure."

My co-worker's quick acceptance was followed by a reassuring touch of three fingers to the back of my hand. Or was that gesture meant to be reassuring? I blinked, reassessing the way Tony's gaze bored into mine, the way his pupils expanded despite the stark sunlight.

Tony wasn't acting like a friend and colleague. He was acting like someone who wanted to take our relationship to a new level.

Unfortunately, I had far too much on my plate at the present moment to even consider dating. Problems like students with no interest in learning. Bills that stubbornly refused to pay themselves. A kid sister for whom I was the legal guardian...and who shared the same heritage that would make werewolves consider us prey.

Plus, Tony was so very, very human. There was no spark when his skin grazed mine.

Still, I thanked him. Smiled even though I didn't feel like smiling. Managed not to flip off the woman fuming behind us as I momentarily obstructed the view of an entire row of audience members.

Only once I was out of the press and past a row of trees did I clench my fists and break into a run.

Chapter 2

SLIDING my hand across the rough brick wall of the bathroom exterior, I paused to take in the rush of water in an endlessly running toilet. The squat, dark structure was just as ordinary as I remembered, making me doubt my own conclusions. Would werewolves really come here?

Still, my skin prickled as if a predator was watching. And my muscles tightened when Jessie didn't answer my call.

I didn't take that silence as definitive, however, despite the itch in my feet begging action. Instead, I swept through both the women's stalls and the men's stalls, straining my ears for a howl that failed to repeat itself. Equally telling was the other absence—any whiff of Jessie's scent.

Alright. Now it was time to stop sleuthing and start acting. I slipped into one of the stalls to take advantage of the barest modicum of privacy, stripping out of my clothes then letting the magic werewolves lacked suffuse my entire body in one overwhelming wave.

Tingling, prickling. My body shimmered while a loop of magic squashed my clothing inside a newly created fanny pack. Because even though Kira's and my heritage could be hazardous, it had fun benefits as well.

Benefits like creating a physical something out of nothing, then still having enough energy leftover to turn fox. Fast as sunlight flickering through tree leaves, I shifted into my alternate form.

Shaking dainty black paws, lack of shoes made the puddle of I-didn't-want-to-imagine-what on the floor even more disgusting. The urge to lick myself rose in my gorge.

But I wasn't an animal even if I looked like one. So I focused on Jessie's absence while sidestepping puddles. Then I leapt to the top of the stall divider, slunk out the gap below the roof, and landed fox-silent in the bushes outside.

Sniffing the ground in an ever widening circle around the bathroom, my tail fluffed out even more than usual. Here at last, my sensitive animal nose had picked up signs of not one but several werewolves, the scent both like and unlike that of me and my sister. Equally furry but considerably wilder. Rougher. Less reminiscent of playful antics and more suffused with the hunger for blood.

Their presence, while daunting, wasn't all that surprising. In the big picture, werewolves were far more common than fox shifters. Only, they didn't come *here*. This city was on the edge of Atwood territory, far enough from the pack's center of operations so anyone with the right to be present seldom passed through.

These wolves, I suspected, didn't have the right to be present. So why were they invading territory that had seemed safe enough for an under-the-radar family of three foxes—whittled down to two when our mother died on Kira's zeroeth birthday—to settle within?

The issue of why would have to wait. Because I caught the odiferous thread of Jessie's strawberry shampoo at last and followed it away from the bathroom in an odd direction. Not toward the concert and not toward the nearest row of shops, the obvious location where a thirteen-year-old might play hooky.

Instead, she'd passed deeper into the trees, through a wilder part of the park where the understory wasn't mowed and manicured. Thorns grabbed at my fur and triple layers of leaves dimmed afternoon into twilight. Here, predators might stalk without danger of being sighted...until, that is, they were ready to pounce.

I heard the result before I saw it. Not words but swords. The clang of metal against metal that had been music to my ears ever since my father let me pick up a practice weapon nearly as long as I was. That first sword had been a grounding in the human world, a way to grow a new identity after the only adult fox shifter I knew— my mother—had died.

Swords were my salvation.

Now, though, the harmony of swordplay turned harsh. Because scent promised Jessie was on the receiving end of the metallic clashes. And, having had the girl in class for one tripping-over-her-toes semester, I knew she couldn't stand up against a serious fighter.

I didn't bulldoze forward however. Instead, I stuck to the cover of undergrowth, padding a loop around the battle. A fox knew how to scout rather than rage in with sword raised.

And, as I poked my snout through a gap in the leaves, this didn't appear to be the time for rage after all. Sure, Jessie's cheeks were red with effort, sweat plastering her bangs against her forehead. Plus, she wasn't wielding a practice sword but rather an edged weapon— and where had she come across that?

Still, this wasn't so much a battle as a courtship. Swords slid past each other elegant as dancing. His blade grazed hers not to attack but to buoy her up.

The result should have been beautiful. Would have been too...if the participants hadn't been a human girl and a bare-chested werewolf.

Jessie didn't understand the danger, so her eyes were wide with attraction. Plump lips parted as if she hoped for a kiss.

And no wonder. Her opponent was handsome if you liked pretty boys with hair that swished back and forth across mahogany eyes with each sword stroke. I got the distinct impression the young man —nineteen maybe, or eighteen or twenty—hadn't lost his shirt while shifting but had instead removed it to show off his ripped abs.

Clothes. Focusing on his lack of shirt made me realize that I'd shifted back to human form and now stood in the park buck naked save for my fanny pack. Unleashing the magic that had brought my jeans, shirt, and boots along with me, I quickly dressed while the human girl and the handsome werewolf continued to cross swords.

I intended to be ready in case their bout devolved into more than courtship. But, so far, the back and forth seemed innocent enough. Jessie tried to parry and instead lost her footing on wet leaves. That prompted her opponent to drop his sword and scoop her up to lie panting against his hard, bare chest.

"You're phenomenal," he lied.

Or maybe it wasn't a lie. Maybe he was referring not to Jessie's so-so swordsmanship but instead to the way she peered up at him as if he hung the moon.

"I...." The girl was breathless, words stuttering nonsensically. "You...."

"We," he replied, the faintest curve to his wide mouth either adorable or menacing depending on your perspective. His head dipped down, not toward her lips but toward the soft curve between shoulder and neck.

For my part, I summoned a cold trickle of magic, the same magic that had allowed me to shift earlier. All it took was a moment of focus, then my hand clenched down around a sword hilt that hadn't existed a moment before.

After all, Jessie was my responsibility until parent-pickup hour. And the teenagers' banter no longer appeared innocent in the least.

Not when this werewolf was about to bite my student's neck and claim Jessie as his mate.

Even by human standards, their age difference was too great to be kosher. Add in the fact that Jessie had never even heard of werewolves....

"If you can't stay away from wolves," Dad had warned, *"strike first. They're too dangerous to treat respectfully."*

I'd never before met a werewolf, but if Dad considered them dangerous then I agreed with him. Now it was time to rage.

Chapter 3

BARE-CHESTED Wannabe-Biter dropped Jessie on her butt the instant my sword flicked toward him. Proof that he hadn't been lost in the same haze of pheromones and puppy love that consumed my student. Instead, he'd likely heard me approach. Smelled me just like I'd smelled him.

Perhaps assumed because I was female that I was irrelevant? You know what they say about assume—makes an ass of you and me.

The truism had me smiling as I lashed out, aiming for that broad target of exposed skin with my sword tip. Unfortunately, I didn't manage to make contact. Not when the pesky werewolf wasn't even trying to move at human speed.

"What's going on?" Jessie yelped as the werewolf slid sideways faster than her eyes could follow. He danced away from my sword as ably as I dodged student blows, my own fox-assisted eyes barely able to keep up.

Swooping down to retrieve his weapon, he came up behind me next in a manner that would have been frowned upon in fencing class. After all, stabbing someone in the back was far from polite.

We weren't fencing however. We were brawling. And I knew how to fight dirty too.

So I let my sword drift out of lax fingers, mimicking Jessie who had frozen like a deer in the headlights. She was bamboozled by the speed with which her wannabe-lover had turned into a to-the-death fighter, and it didn't take much effort to don her slack-jawed gape. I needed this werewolf to think I was confused about where he had disappeared to. Confused about what to do next.

Then, as a rush of air promised a blade was aiming for my unprotected spine...I dropped. Flat onto the ground, right foot sweeping up to hook around his legs and toss him off balance. Rolling, I landed on top of someone twice as large as I was, my weight insufficient to keep him in check.

He bucked and I struggled not to relinquish my grip on his shoulders. Our bodies tumbled sideways, away from my sword.

The werewolf, darn him, had accidentally gained an advantage he wasn't even aware existed. Because my sword's magic was part of my being. Distance seeped strength out of my muscles, an effect that would worsen quickly as the space between me and my magic grew.

But I wasn't extending that separation. Instead, I glanced at Jessie to make sure the sword was out of her sightline. Then I sucked in a breath and called the weapon back, smiling as it thunked into my waiting palm.

The werewolf beneath me surged yet again, trying to dislodge my stranglehold. But this time my blade proved to be a more than adequate deterrent. Snug as a kitten, I nestled its edge just shy of cutting into the soft flesh beneath his skin.

Now, finally, he stilled.

"What did you think you were doing?" I demanded, pressing hard enough to make sure the werewolf knew I meant business.

He swallowed, or tried to. My sword prevented the bulge of his throat from traveling down and his eyes widened. One hand rose as if to stop me, then he reconsidered that course of action and went limp.

I'd won, but I didn't let my opponent go. Not with Dad's warn-

ings echoing in my memory. Instead, I sawed until the faintest trickle
of blood materialized beneath my blade. "Well?"

This time he answered, his voice a growl. "She smells good."

"It's body wash." Jessie had found her feet and was now skittering in a circle around us. "Strawberry Sensation. Isn't it
delicious?"

She was missing the point of the werewolf's declaration...which
was probably a good thing since the reality made me shiver. Jessie
smelled good to a randy werewolf because she'd showed up this
morning in an outfit that didn't fit the school clothing policy. I'd
given her a used t-shirt out of my own gym locker rather than
making her face the principal.

In other words, the randy wolf wasn't talking about fake straw-
berries. He was talking about the residual scent of fur.

A scent of fur that would fade from Jessie but was impossible to
wash off myself...and my little sister. The thought of Kira made my
sword dig in deeper. The werewolf's eyes bulged but Jessie was the
one whose voice turned strangled.

"Ms. Fairchild, Shane wasn't going to hurt me! You need to let
him go!"

The girl didn't comprehend the thinness of the ice she was
stomping on, and I wasn't about to clue her in to the supernatural
bits. Still, she needed to come to terms with some fragment of the
seriousness of the occasion. "He was heading," I said, sticking to an
explanation humans would be familiar with, "toward statutory
rape."

"No! You don't get it!" Jessie's babbling veered off into a disser-
tation on love and soul mates. Which was handy. The stars in her
eyes would prevent her from seeing what was right in front of her
nose.

So I let her talk while I lowered my voice to a register wolves
could hear but humans couldn't. "Jessie is under my protection."

As I spoke, I turned the sword until the flat lay against my opponent's skin. Pressing now wouldn't risk permanent damage, but it
would cut off his airflow. With wolves, Dad had informed me, you
had to be firm if you wanted to be understood.

So I pressed. *Hard.*

Unfortunately, Jessie caught on before I got my point across. "Ms. Fairchild!" She clawed at my shoulders with soft human fingers. "You're hurting him!"

I let her fight me for a slow count of three, then I released the pressure. "Do we understand each other?" I asked Shane, ignoring my student.

For a long moment, he lay there, sucking in great gasps of oxygen. Then he nodded once, very slowly, the tightness of his mouth suggesting he expected the sword to bite again.

When it didn't, his head bobbing turned frantic. "Yes," he answered before tacking on an honorific. "Ma'am. I understand you."

Young wolves, unlike young humans, apparently knew how to accept when they'd been bested. Because Shane's eyes stayed on the ground even as he tacked on a quiet question. "May I leave now?"

"Go," I answered, ignoring Jessie's huff of annoyance. Keeping my eyes trained on Shane, I waited as he collected both his sword and Jessie's. The shifter didn't so much as glance at my student before disappearing into the undergrowth.

Chapter 4

THE ISSUE WASN'T SETTLED, but the rest of the concert went as
smoothly as could be expected. One of Tony's charges shook up a
soft drink then opened it, squirting everyone within a twenty-foot
radius with the sticky fluid. The snooty woman behind us got a dose
to the face, which I really shouldn't have laughed at but did.

Later, while filing out of the park, two of my girls somehow
ended up knocking a very large drum off its stand. There was
swearing aplenty as the musician chased after his instrument,
catching it just before it rolled into traffic. But, afterwards, he was
more polite than expected about the blunder. I attributed his
forbearance to the way my skirt-wearing students rolled up their
waistbands to bare the better part of their thighs.

So, par for the course when dealing with middle schoolers.
"Nobody dead," I observed as Tony, Kira, and I stood on the steps
of the school watching the last parental car carry away the last day
camper. My sister was glued to my side, which I hoped meant she'd
take what I was soon going to tell her better than she usually might
have.

"No bones broken," Tony agreed, oblivious to the undercurrent
between me and Kira. "Definitely a good day."

His cheeks were mildly sunburnt, or maybe that glow to his skin had more to do with the way his hand was inching toward my fingers. Our skin connected and I flinched nearly as obviously as Shane had done.

"Gotta go," I gulped. "Kira needs a snack."

Mention of food sent my sister sprinting toward home and calories. I followed, glad of the excuse to leave without really saying goodbye.

Tony didn't let the moment pass however. Instead, he called after us: "I'll drive you."

I waved a "thanks but no thanks." Which didn't stop him from taking yet another stab at it.

"See you tomorrow?"

I was already half a block away and I could have pretended not to hear him. But I *liked* Tony...just not in the way he apparently liked me.

So I turned around to walk backwards. "See you tomorrow," I agreed.

"MR. MURPHY WANTS to take you out on a date," Kira observed as she blew in the door of our apartment, shedding shoes, backpack, and water bottle in random locations she'd never remember when she wanted them again.

Following behind, I nudged belongings into their proper cubbies while evading Kira's conversational gambit. "He's a nice guy." Then, before my sister could shift and start dancing on the countertops, I caught her in a one-armed hug. "Hey, slow down for a minute. I need to talk to you."

Her back immediately tensed. "But I stayed *put*."

"You were great," I agreed. "That howl, however...."

"Was a wolf." Kira raised one eyebrow at my silence. "You think I never heard you and Dad talking? Wolves are serious bad news. But I have a solution. We'll chase it out of town!"

I could just see her trying. Kira was like one of those chihuahuas who faced down a rottweiler, instigating a fight she was certain she'd win.

Unfortunately, the hypothetical rottweiler could swallow a chihuahua in one gulp, and a wolf could eat a fox just as easily. "I'll deal with it," I promised her. "But you're going to have to stay home for a few days until things are settled. It's not safe to be out and about right now."

I waited for Kira's sunny disposition to cloud. But she surprised me. Maybe she was growing up, or maybe she'd just been more spooked by the howl than she let on. Because she nodded. "If you get me the gear you promised, I'll stay put."

Of course Kira would jump at the opportunity to turn the thumbscrews about this week's coveted acquisition. A pet-agility track would take up our entire living room...a space which doubled as my bedroom. It would also set my finances back so far that I might have to beg for an extension on the rent.

But if the purchase kept Kira busy running through in-apartment tunnels until the werewolf threat blew over, it would be well worth it. I squeezed shoulders that had loosened into their usual gangly suppleness and promised the moon to my only living family member.

"It's a deal."

∾

UNFORTUNATELY, I hadn't thought through the problem with pet stores when I left Kira stirring boxed macaroni into boiling water. Hadn't considered that wolf shifters likely found the commercial establishments just as useful as fox shifters did.

After all, dental-health dog bones prove awfully useful when you don't feel like going two-legged to brush your teeth. Or at least so Kira told me when she added them to my shopping list.

To cut a long story short, my wince at the price tag on dog-agility equipment turned into a full-on shudder when a whiff of fur carried toward me from the next aisle over. This wasn't Shane, either, who I could have slapped down without breaking a sweat.

Instead, the scent came from the same direction as two voices, both older and male.

"Cooperation is key." The first speaker's words were full of the same sort of heady dominance that had drawn Jessie toward Shane. But this was the more mature version. Deeper. More growly. I was struck with simultaneous urges to swoon and to run.

I did neither. Inside stores, air movement was governed by fans, so there was no danger of the wind shifting and revealing my presence. If I was cautious, I could sneak out before either of the werewolves knew I'd been present. So I selected the cheapest box from the display in front of me and started manhandling it into my cart.

The second voice still wasn't Shane's, but it had more in common with that teenager than the first voice did. "Cooperation is key for you, maybe," the younger shifter complained. "All I want is a neighborhood."

"This city won't go by neighborhoods." A footstep. A gasp. Deep Voice was doing something intimidating or painful. His voice lowered into a growl as he continued. "After the fight, you'll either be with me or against me. Think on that then show up at the Arena tomorrow by high moon."

The Arena. I winced. The werewolf's reference to the under-the-radar venue where I fought in exchange for much-needed supplemental income slowed my attempt to push my cart without letting the wheels squeak. I was supposed to take part in a match tomorrow. The money I hoped to make was already spent in my mind.

Spent on the bulky box I was even now wheeling toward the checkout.

I couldn't attend, however, if werewolves planned to use the match to duke out ownership of the city. This safe harbor was safe no longer. Kira and I would have to flee.

But flee to where? Every inch of land around us was owned by a wolf pack. Finding another unused territorial edge where I could make a living and Kira could get a quality education would take time while opening up additional dangers for my sister.

Would it be safer to hunker down and wait out the current intrusion? Hope the werewolves growling in the next aisle over tore each other to shreds and left no survivors to threaten Kira and myself?

I was deep in planning mode when a hand landed on my shoulder. I didn't even have time to create a sword before I was spun around.

"And who are you?" asked the growly, deep-voiced werewolf who'd taken advantage of fan-assisted air patterns to sneak up behind my back.

Chapter 5

"LOSE YOUR FRIEND?" I retorted, scanning what I could see of broad aisles jam-packed with over-priced pet toys. There was only one werewolf present. One werewolf with hair long enough to be curly and a muscle shirt outlining his better-than-human physique. He was ten times more handsome than Shane...if I ignored the acquisitive gleam in this werewolf's eye.

Ignored that and the way he sidestepped my question. Holding out the same hand he'd used to halt my forward momentum, he graced me with a breathtaking smile. "I'm Jackal."

Something about the force of his grin had me reciprocating before I thought better of it. I took the offered palm in mine then shivered as a tremor of attraction spun through me.

The response was as purely physical as the goosebumps that rose on my arms when I dove into the public pool every summer for the first time. Tony had been sweet yet elicited no chemistry. Jackal was the opposite—alpha hotness wrapped around deeply bad news.

So I didn't offer my name. Instead, I released the handshake as quickly as I'd accepted it, sidestepping Jackal and pushing my cart forward. With no need to silence the squeaking, I was able to progress much faster this time.

Jackal, unfortunately, paced me step for step as he murmured slippery pleasantries. "What a surprising treat to find in my city."

I didn't glance sideways, but I could feel his eyes gliding across my body like acquisitive fingers. The sensation was approximately as welcome as a root canal.

Perhaps that's why I let my tongue sharpen. "*Your* city? I wasn't aware the Atwoods had started hiring carcass-eaters."

An abrupt tartness in the other shifter's scent suggested my blow had landed dead center, but he didn't address the dig about his name. "The Atwoods aren't doing anything with this city," he growled instead. "Not while their alpha lies dying. I expect it to take months for the son to bring his pack to heel. By that time, everything around you will be mine."

Jackal was probably right about that, unfortunately. Territories didn't last forever. A weakness in the center allowed neighbors or lone wolves to nibble away one edge at a time.

Still, the Atwoods' trouble was none of my business. An ungreased wheel whined complaint as I gave the cart another heave.

Jackal's fist on the wire side stilled my forward progress. His face was so close I could smell the remnants of Doritos. "Mate with the winning wolf," he informed me, voice level, "and you'll be taken care of."

My eyebrows rose. That was a turn I hadn't expected. "Is this your way of saying you find me attractive?"

Jackal snorted a not-so-soft puff of air out his nostrils. "No. This is my way of saying that I'm making you an offer that's in both of our best interests...."

His voice trailed off as his eyes lit on the side of the box I'd chosen. I'd grabbed the cheapest setup, the one intended for canines under thirty pounds. Which meant the tunnels would be too small for a full-grown wolf, even a female one.

My breath caught. Getting roped into a werewolf territorial battle was bad enough. If Jackal realized my true form....

Chest tightening, my lungs stuttered to a halt. Jackal's smile widened, his eyes gleaming with predatory glee. "You have a pup? I can be a stepdaddy."

Breath wheezed out and in again. He'd jumped to a conclusion that was both right and wrong. The box I'd chosen was for a pup, just not a wolf pup.

The beep of a scanner interrupted our fraught moment. We'd ended up in the checkout line and a human worker had come around to scan the box too large to fit on the conveyer belt.

"Who's paying?" she asked, popping her gum.

JACKAL TRIED to swipe his credit card, but I insisted on my independence. And he laughed like a hunter who knew his prey had no way out of a box canyon. A hunter who was ready to let that prey run just a little longer before he pounced.

"I'll be at the Arena tomorrow at high moon," he told me, then rephrased when my brows wrinkled in confusion. "The time when the moon reaches its peak. Right now, that's sunset. Either come as my mate or be prepared to lose your pup."

His threat was ominous both in tone and lack of details. No wonder my heart rate increased, instinct warning me to abandon the agility equipment and make a run for it.

But Jackal would simply follow my scent back to Kira if I didn't accept his ride. And wouldn't it be better to make him think I was obeying? Playing along should win me another twenty-four hours at least.

So I let him toss my purchase in the back of a jacked-up pickup. Let him drive me all the way to the front of the apartment complex where Kira and I lived.

"Until tomorrow," he repeated as I slid out under the shadow of our shabby high-rise. The words were a warning. The eyes on the back of my neck as I manhandled the box down from the pickup raised warning hairs.

He didn't follow me, though, as I laboriously bumped the box up the steep, dark stairs inside. And Kira, thankfully, was too gleeful over assembling her long-sought toy to notice my worry that evening. The next morning, she was too excited about running through the course for me to think she'd break her vow not to set foot outside the door.

So I headed to the school as usual even though my head spun with worries and possibilities. There had to be a way out of the trap Jackal had set for me, if only I could find it. I ushered kids through the local science museum, my thoughts on wolves instead of dinosaurs. And when my fencing students assembled in the gym after lunch, for once I was too frazzled to take attendance.

Because the conclusion I'd come to was as unsavory as it was inevitable. We'd have to flee. I'd pack up Kira and take her...somewhere. After that? Who knew.

Charlie was the one who broke into my planning by alerting me to an even more pressing problem. Charlie who, I noticed, was wearing the friendship bracelet her twin usually had wrapped around her wrist.

"Ms. Atwood, can I talk to you?" The girl was almost in tears, so I set the others on a series of drills that were unlikely to result in eyes getting jabbed out. Then I led Charlie over to the bleachers and sat us both down.

"What's up?"

"It's Jessie."

I scanned the wannabe fencers, searching for the other Raven twin. Jessie wasn't present. I frowned. "Is she sick?"

Charlie shook her head, wordless. And I put the pieces together.

"The bracelet. You're covering for her."

"We're in different morning classes," Charlie confirmed. "I pretended to have a stomachache and asked to go to the nurse's office. Then I apologized for being late when I showed up to Jessie's class."

"Where is she?"

I somehow knew the answer even though Charlie was silent, eyes down as her toe traced the streak made by a skidding gym shoe. The scent of fur on my old t-shirt rose in my memory as if it had just been struck by the sun.

"You can tell me," I prodded, using my gentle teacher voice this time.

Charlie swallowed, her eyes watery. Then she admitted, "I haven't seen Jessie since dinner yesterday. She's been gone all night."

Chapter 6

I LOCKED the students in the gym for their own safety and leaned my head against the cool metal of a locker in the hall. The main doors beckoned, my fox nature twitching at any delay in rescuing Jessie. But the students in the gym were also my responsibility. I'd need the help of an ally if I didn't want my rescue mission to leave havoc behind.

Unfortunately, my only ally on campus was Tony. Tony, who I usually met in the staff room for a snack and grouse session during our shared planning period. Tony, who'd sent me a text to make sure I was okay after I stood him up this morning, a text to which I'd replied with a single word: *"Fine."*

I'd been avoiding him all day so I wouldn't have to say things that would risk our friendship. Unfortunately, making sure we were in different places at all times until Tony got over his ill-conceived crush was no longer going to work.

So I headed around the corner to his classroom, peering in the open door at a hive of enthusiastic activity. Tony was in his element, arms waving and students hanging on his every word, the hubbub reminding me why I'd initially befriended him. How could I not admire a teacher who drew youngsters toward the delights of the mind?

Hoping our fellowship could survive current events, I knocked on the side of the door jamb. "Hey, can I talk to you for a minute?"

Tony's gaze rose to meet mine, his eyes squinting with pure pleasure. "Sure." He murmured a bit more mathematical mumbo jumbo then came out to join me, pulling the door closed behind his back. "What's up?"

There was no time for verbal foreplay so I launched right into it. "Your aunt's cabin. Is it available this weekend?"

The cabin was the carrot Tony had been holding out in front of all of his students this summer. Up in the forest, with a big pond and trails and the promise of campfire stories. Anyone who behaved at least moderately well would be invited to take part in a big end-of-summer sleepover. Before I'd realized what was boiling up between us, I'd promised to be the female chaperone.

Now, the cabin was the safest place I could think of to stash Kira while I dealt with werewolves. Plus, Jessie's parents could rest easy thinking their kids were on a school-approved field trip. Hopefully that would prevent them from calling the cops.

I didn't say any of that, however. No wonder Tony's eyebrows drew together. "Sure. Do you and your sister want a weekend away?"

I shook my head. "No. I need you to take Charlie up there tonight, along with any other student available on short notice. Kira too. Don't leave the property until I call."

I was already scribbling a note to my sister on the back of a receipt as I debriefed Tony and ran ahead in my mind to the tasks awaiting me. Find Jessie, deal with Jackal and the Arena fight, then go from there.

None of which I could do while herding youngsters. Speaking of which: "I locked my class in the gym. Can you keep an eye on them until the end of the day? Maybe let everybody play volleyball while you call parents to expedite permission slips? Make sure the Ravens send two sleeping bags."

Their parents would assume the second was for Jessie, thus covering for the missing twin's absence. Meanwhile, Kira would need bedding since we owned nothing portable. Two birds, one stone.

My feet itched to be gone, but I paused, meeting Tony's eyes. He was usually malleable but now he frowned, shaking his head.

"That won't work. Issue one: short notice means most kids won't be able to come on a trip I've been promising for weeks. Issue two: I can't take a mixed-gender class on an overnight field trip without a female chaperone."

Really? The roadblock was school policy? "Pretend I drove up early and came down with a stomach flu," I suggested. "Is there a room with a door? Kira can check on me a few times. Bring ginger ale. It will work."

I expected Tony to say yes immediately. Sure, he'd be risking his job if anyone called his bluff. But he was always offering me rides and other favors. He'd left little doubt that if I needed a wingman he was ready and willing to be on call.

Now, he took a step toward me until we were just a little closer than was really appropriate for co-workers. "And after this is over, you'll tell me what's going on? Over dinner?"

I'd thought I could ignore Tony's gentle flirtations until they subsided. That we could skirt an overt conversation that risked our friendship. Apparently, I'd been wrong about that.

But the safety of Kira and my students now trumped loss of friendship later. So—

"Dinner," I promised. "Tomorrow night."

Getting help from Tony had been easy enough, if I ignored the potential repercussions. Tracking down Shane and Jessie, on the other hand, required a trip to a shadier part of town.

In broad daylight, the outside of the Arena blended in with all of the other abandoned buildings in the Warren. The big, blocky structure had once been a factory, but the sign above the main door had faded so much that words were now impossible to make out.

Not that the Arena needed a sign. Locals knew to cluster around when the windows lit up like eyes glaring into the night. As soon as the doors opened, spectators streamed inside to fill the concentric rings of stadium-style seating, pressing close to the dented cage of a platform promising that the only thing produced here was fights.

Or that's what the interior usually looked like. Today, the clang of metal on metal wasn't swords but something different. Stepping through the front door, I found three burly bouncers unscrewing seats off the concrete floor then hauling them away to stack in a back room.

Meanwhile, their tiny, seventy-something boss pointed and ordered and ensured that no one even considered taking a break. Ma Scrubbs' eyebrows shot up, however, when she saw me. "Mai. Didn't you get my message? Tonight I don't need you. The idiot who rented us out has bad credit, so I made him pay double in cash. Your gain. Paid day off."

She started peeling bills off of a huge wad, pausing only to flick a middle finger at someone who'd huffed out a complaint behind her back. I didn't blame the guy for his assertion of unfairness either. I was even less of an employee than he was and none of us merited vacation time. Plus, despite her name, I was no relation to the Arena's boss.

But Ma Scrubbs knew how close my finances hovered on the edge of zero and she owed some sort of favor to my dead father. Dad had never spelled out the specifics, but he'd left me a list of people I could count on to help—once. Ma Scrubbs was at the top of that list, and I suspected Dad's favor was the original reason she'd hired me on.

Dad's favor was likely also the reason I was suddenly being graced with a paid vacation, one I couldn't afford to turn down. "Thanks," I said while the Arena's owner continued peeling off twenties. "But that's not why I'm here."

The helper who'd complained now took advantage of Ma Scrubbs' lack of attention to drop into a seat for a breather. The action had taken place outside her sight line, but somehow Ma Scrubbs knew what was happening anyway. Whirling, she pointed one bony finger at the errant employee. "You! Did I say it was nap time?"

"Eyes in the back of her head," muttered a guy who was on his knees ratcheting big bolts out of the concrete. "I warned you." Rather than replying, his friend shot out of the seat so fast it would have fallen over if the base hadn't been attached to the floor.

I scratched my cheek in order to hide my smile. Ma Scrubbs was entirely human and had no supernatural eyesight or hearing, but she sure managed to give that impression. Mimicking her had turned into my MO on the first day of school every year. The result was startling. Students stepped into line so fast I was able to treat them gently for the rest of the term.

Ma Scrubbs, in contrast, never went from harsh to gentle. Now, she glared at the mutterer. "Is there something you want to say to me?"

The recipient of her glare weighed three times as much as his boss and had all of the extra weight in height and muscle. Still, he shook his head vigorously then returned his gaze to his task.

One long moment of silence followed, during which Ma Scrubbs stared and her employees worked faster than ever. Finally, she turned back to face me. "As you can see," she snapped, "I'm busy. Can your problem wait?"

Despite the terseness of her words, she didn't outright dismiss me. This is what my father's favor did and I was loathe to lose it. Plus, I'd promised Dad that I wouldn't call in Ma Scrubbs' boon unless my sister or I was in imminent physical danger.

Still, my father had treated his students like family. He wouldn't have hesitated to use whatever tool he had at his disposal to keep Jessie safe.

Or at least that's what I chose to I believe.

So I shook my head. "No. I'm calling in my father's favor. I need your help."

Chapter 7

FOR A MOMENT, MA SCRUBBS' face softened and she almost appeared grandmotherly. "Is your sister bleeding? Did she swallow poison? Call an ambulance. You don't want to waste your favor today."

I lowered my voice just in case the guys behind us were listening. "I need to know where someone new to town is staying. He goes by Shane. Late teens. About yay high." I reached up a foot taller than my own crown to demonstrate. "Puffs out his chest like a rooster. Thinks he's hot stuff."

Ma Scrubbs shook her head slowly, and for a moment I thought she either wouldn't or couldn't help me. Then she put that worry to rest. "Last chance to hang onto your favor. Fighters without favors don't get paid days off. They don't get called in to fight if they're not making me money. Think of your sister. You won't know how good you had it until the kid gloves come off."

I hesitated, my certainty shaken by the mention of Kira. Was a student's safety now really more important than my sister's safety later? Didn't family always come first?

And, as usual, Dad provided the answer. Not in specific words this time, but in the memory of a time when I'd been just a few years older than Kira was now.

A bad day at school, my new buds of breasts drawing the attention of the loudest bullies. One boy had tried to snap my bra strap and had instead found the back of my shirt underwear-free.

I've since forced myself to forget the exact words he'd thrown at me. But their bite. The twist of my stomach. The cruel laughter of his friends. All remained as fresh as if I was still that thirteen-year-old underdog.

I'd maintained a stiff upper lip until the last bell rang, but then I'd run home and made a beeline for Mama. She'd fix the problem, I was positive. No matter that my mother was eight months pregnant with Kira, her eyes perpetually worried and her energy levels sagging to an all-time low.

The light in her bedroom was off when I slammed in the front door, but I headed in that direction anyway. Mama had taken to resting in the afternoons. I knew where to find her.

Only, Dad stepped into my path before I could achieve my destination. He'd been juggling teaching full time and fighting in the Arena along with handing me lunch money and checking over my homework. Now, clean laundry hung from his calloused fingers as he asked, *"What's up, kid?"*

"You can't help me."

"No? Wanna talk about it?"

"Absolutely not."

And, somehow, Dad had ended up canceling his evening match so he could take me out for hamburgers. The grease did its intended job, lubricating my tongue and warming my stomach. I admitted my embarrassment, then we headed to the store so I could try on bras.

Bra shopping with my father should have been as mortifying as the event that preceded it. But Dad ended up charming the saleswoman and customers alike, turning himself into the life of the party rather than the odd man out in the lingerie department. Between all of us, we selected bras so perfect I later passed two down to Kira. I've grinned every time I thought about our cackling joy since.

That wasn't the end of it either. After a good night's sleep, Dad called both of us in sick so we could hop in the car for an impromptu road trip. I got to choose every stop and direction, leading us in a wiggly loop around the city and the surrounding countryside.

Back at the edge of town, a giant ice-cream sculpture had proven irresistible to my vulpine nature. Dad—the guy who lacked an inner fox and preferred everyone keep their feet firmly planted on the ground—let me clamber up the side.

"I'm going higher!" I'd exclaimed, switching my melting ice-cream cone to the other hand as I worked my way up the hot metal. A slop of chocolate slid off my confection to drip directly into Dad's eyes.

And he'd smiled, snapping picture after picture. By the time I slid back down the spoon to land erect and unhurt on the pavement, we were both laughing so hard that we barely made it out of the parking lot before the proprietor called the cops.

"A woman," Dad told me when we paused at the next stoplight, *"chooses her own adventure. Congratulations on your first step into womanhood."*

Rather than answering, I'd raised my hand to smooth a twisted bra strap. My new breasts felt like a badge of courage instead of a curse.

And when Mama died a few weeks later, I clung to that sunny memory of me alone with my father. Only later did I realize he'd known how much I'd need remembered sunshine. Only later did I realize how hard he'd worked to squash his worries about Mama in order to give me that one perfect day.

So, yes, family always came first. Ma Scrubbs was right.

But a woman also chose her own adventure and sacrificed to look out for those who depended on her. Even if it meant spending a day away from an ailing spouse whose time was limited. Or, in my case, putting off Kira's needs until they actually exploded in my face.

Doing the right thing was the true way to honor our father's memory. So I hardened my voice until it cracked nearly as whip-like as Ma Scrubbs'. "Shane?"

The old woman eyed me for a moment then shrugged, tucking the money she'd been about to give me away in an interior pocket. "Your funeral. Check the pay-by-the-hour motel at the edge of the Warren. Room 17. Last I heard, he's still asleep."

The pleasure of knowing where my quarry denned curled my lips upward. I turned away, but Ma wasn't done with me yet.

"You! Go with her. Do what Mai says."

I'd barely noticed the third chair-hauler before I turned back around to see who Ma Scrubbs was addressing. He was bigger than the other two, like a Mr. Clean with lots of tattoos and no smile. His inability to be stealthy proved itself as he stomped toward me in steel-toed boots.

"No thanks," I started, but Ma spoke over me.

"Favors don't come in halves, girl. Might as well take everything I'm offering. This will be the last freebie you get."

I hesitated. Ma Scrubbs had her finger on the pulse of the Warren, as evidenced by how easily she'd recognized my description of Shane. If she thought I needed help, I might as well take it.

"Okay," I agreed reluctantly. "Thanks."

MR. CLEAN HAD his own set of wheels, something flashy that shouldn't have stood a chance parked on a Warren street. The vehicle hadn't been vandalized, however. And, as I waited on the passenger side for him to push the button on his key fob, he shook his head at me. "It's unlocked."

The door was unlocked...and those were the last words Ma's employee graced me with until we arrived at our destination. "I don't think I caught your name," I offered halfway through the commute down winding alleys and up a hill so steep we couldn't see over the top. His answer came out as a grunt.

Well, we didn't have to be friends. If all went well, Mr. Clean and I wouldn't be spending more than an hour together. Plus, I was quite capable of amusing myself.

So I pulled out my phone and tapped in a request for information from one of Dad's old students. His letter of recommendation had gotten Sarah into Cornell's computer-science department despite grades that ranged from bad to awful. Then, when she dropped out halfway through her second semester to learn gray-hat techniques on her own, Dad had called Sarah up to tell her how proud he was that she understood her own needs.

Like many of Dad's students, Sarah didn't precisely owe me a favor. But I had a feeling she wouldn't mind doing a little sleuthing on the side anyway. Because something Ma Scrubbs said had suggested....

Mr. Clean's door slammed before I realized we'd stopped in front of a seedy motel. The single-story building consisted of one long wall broken by a row of evenly spaced doors. If I remembered correctly, each rental had a matching window around the back.

Shotgun rooms would make for an easy capture. "Wait here for five minutes, then kick in the door," I told Mr. Clean. As he jerked his head in a gesture that might have been agreement, I counted room numbers to make sure I'd end up at the proper window. Then I trotted around to the back.

Every shade was drawn and no wonder since this side of the motel overlooked a sewage-treatment plant. The smell wafting off settling pools scraped at the inside of my throat, but I ignored the discomfort. Ignored my cell phone, also, when it vibrated with an incoming phone call. Instead, I glanced in both directions then materialized my sword directly into my fist.

By my count, I had two minutes left, but I doubted Mr. Clean took numbers seriously. So I positioned myself outside the proper window...one second before a thud followed by a squawk emerged from inside.

Mr. Clean didn't bother speaking and Shane didn't ask for an explanation. Instead, the latter dove through the shades and screen as if he thought he was in wolf form. I let him land on his hands and knees in the gravel before pricking the space between his shoulder blades with my sword. "We meet again."

The werewolf whimpered and I revised his age downward. Maybe Shane wasn't seventeen. Sixteen? Fifteen?

What was life like for a teenage wolf lacking a territory? Maybe not much better than the fate of two fox shifters lying low.

Remorse prompted me to withdraw my sword and nudge him with my toe more gently than I might have done otherwise. "Roll over."

Shane obeyed, the gesture giving the air of a wolf displaying his belly to a stronger canine. His submission was complete enough that I risked calling a question to Mr. Clean over the werewolf's prone body. "Anybody else in there?"

His grunt was followed by the crash of furniture being upended. Mr. Clean's upper body emerged in the window. "Nope."

Nope? Okay, forget remorse and empathy. It took an effort not to slice at Shane with my sword.

Meanwhile, my phone vibrated again, which made me distinctly twitchy. Few people called me and never twice in quick succession....

Still, my student was my top priority at the present moment. I waved the blade in front of Shane's nose. "What have you done with Jessie?"

The young werewolf's response was a babble of vague information. "He told me I'd be safer if I threw in my lot with him. Said I wouldn't have to fight tonight if I proved myself. All I had to do was call her and ask her to meet me. I didn't even have to show up."

The *her* was obviously Jessie. The *he*.... "Who told you?"

Shane peered up at me with watery eyes. "Jackal. The...." He slid a glance at Mr. Clean then lowered his voice to a husky whisper. "The alpha."

Jackal. Of course.

Chapter 8

KNOWING who held Jessie should have been a win. But how exactly would I find the troublesome werewolf in a maze-like city famous for the pair of tourists who'd spent ten hours hunting each other after getting separated one fateful summer? When the newspaper interviewed the duo after the fact, it turned out they'd never been further than three blocks from each other. Despite that, they might have kept wandering indefinitely if the wife hadn't had the clever idea of asking the police for help.

In the modern day, cell phones expedited tourist reunions. But I didn't know Jackal's number and he was unlikely to answer if I did call him. Meanwhile, summoning the police wasn't an option when dealing with wolves.

What I knew was Jackal's planned location at sunset. A location that was a last resort since it involved giving in to an ultimatum I very much hoped to avoid.

That thought trail didn't help solve the larger problem, but it did remind me of the relentless buzzing of my own cell phone. I twitched my sword in preparation for sheathing it...and Shane yelped as if I was about to slash his throat.

"You're free to go," I told him, overtly swinging the weapon further away from his sensitive organs.

"Really?" The werewolf looked even younger now, eyes widening. Had he never been given a second chance?

"Really," I agreed, releasing eye contact. Shane scurried away the second my gaze slid to my phone, and I only granted him the bare minimum of attention after that. Instead, I blinked at the sheer quantity of messages cluttering my screen.

All were from Tony. Without bothering to check either texts or voice mails, I called my co-worker back.

"Problem?" I opened, watching Shane slink back through his window. Then I lost interest in the werewolf as Tony replied.

"Mai?" His voice was tense, I noted. And, unlike his usual MO, he didn't dive right into conversation.

"Yes," I said into the silence. Silence that wasn't so silent as a car started up on the other side of the motel. The engine gunned and I knew without peering into Shane's room that the space now held only its original occupant. Mr. Clean had completed his task and headed back to his usual job.

Which was fine. I could handle myself in the Warren. However, I was no closer to retrieving Jessie...and apparently I had a more immediate disaster on hand.

Because Tony finally found his voice in order to relay a story that tightened my throat. Charlie had been the only kid able to attend his sleepover on such short notice, so he'd let her tag along as he swung by to pick up Kira at our apartment. Everything had seemed fine at first. Tony handed my sister the note and she asked Charlie if the other girl would help pick out clothes for their upcoming sleepover. The pair disappeared into the bedroom, closed the door...and never came back out.

"Kira went down the fire escape," I guessed. "With Charlie?" That was the part that didn't make sense. If my sister had gotten spooked by the howl yesterday followed by my note today, why bring along a human when she split? Instead, she should have followed our emergency plan—go fox and head to the cemetery to hide inside the massive weeping willow that marked our parents' final resting place.

An emergency plan that had sounded better before werewolves invaded the city. Before the residual aroma of fur on a t-shirt became enough to nearly get a human teenager's neck bitten.

I only realized I was squeezing my phone so hard I obstructed the speaker when the mumble of Tony's words came out too soft to hear. Loosening my fingers with an effort, I cleared my throat. "Could you repeat that?"

Tony's voice was still tense, but he showed no impatience at my request. "When I barged in, I didn't see either girl. But, yes, the window was unlocked."

"Okay. I'll find them." I pressed my face against Shane's window screen to make sure the young werewolf wasn't going to cause any additional problems. Luckily, like any teenager woken before he was ready, Shane had sprawled back out across the bed, his eyes veering to mine but the lids already sagging. I had a feeling as soon as he heard me leave he'd begin to snore.

"I appreciate everything you've done," I continued, leaving the werewolf and making my way around to the front of the motel. Could I afford to call an Uber? With the deadline of sunset looming, could I afford not to call one? While debating, I salved my co-worker's delicate conscience. "You're off the hook."

Tony released a huff of laughter that didn't have any real pleasure in it. "Mai. I'm not going to leave you in the lurch. Where are you? I'll pick you up and we'll track down the girls together."

I frowned, not understanding. "You've already done me one favor."

For a long moment, Tony was silent. Then he used the same gentle schoolteacher tone I brought out for kids afraid to spill their guts about parental trouble. "There's no such thing," he explained, "as favors between friends."

~

I PACED FOR A WHILE, then called Tony back with another request. And he broke school rules yet further by reading Charlie's cell-phone number off the permission slip she'd filled out an hour ago. "She didn't answer when I tried," he warned.

So I was surprised when my student picked up on the second ring. "Hello?"

"Charlie. This is Ms. Fairchild. I need you to tell me where you are."

A honk came through the speaker. The dull hum of tires on pavement. If I had to guess, the girl was riding a bus. The question became—a bus heading where?

My student's voice turned coy. "I can't really...."

She was about to hang up, and that wasn't acceptable. "Charlie," I barked out, mean-teacher voice in full effect now. "Put my sister on."

Charlie was used to obeying me. So I wasn't surprised by the rustle as the phone changed hands.

Kira, in contrast, was a fox to her core. She sounded distinctly uncowed as she chirped out a cheerful, "Hello."

Cheerful was good. Cheerful meant my sister might slip up and keep the line open long enough for me to ferret out some sort of identifying information.

"Kira." I kept my voice low while relaying information not approved for human ears. "You know why you can't be out in the city right now. Don't draw Charlie into something that will get her hurt."

Kira blithely ignored the werewolves I was reminding her of. "I'm not drawing Charlie into anything. It was her idea. She said you're hunting Jessie. We're going to help."

I winced. When my sister helped, plates broke. Windows shattered. On one memorable occasion, a riot had been sparked.

"Maybe helping isn't the best idea," I started, only to pause as Tony's car pulled up beside me. My co-worker reached across to push open the passenger door, then flushed as it became clear there was nowhere for me to sit.

Not because of empty fast-food containers or similar debris. No, the space was full of textbooks, academic journals, geeky measuring tools I didn't know the name or purpose of.

No wonder Tony's face reddened, the color emanating from embarrassment rather than attraction this time. "Try not to be such a nerd, Tony," he muttered, low enough that a human wouldn't have caught the self-slander. Scooping up armloads of mathematical debris, his gaze lowered as if his eyes and mine were similarly charged magnets physically unable to meet.

Which wasn't fair. Tony was helping me. He shouldn't be beating himself up for being *smart*.

I covered the microphone with one hand while touching his shoulder with the other. "Kira and Charlie are on the line," I murmured. "I'll put them on speaker phone. See if you can hear any clues I've missed about where they are."

My gesture worked. Tony's blush faded and he didn't apologize as I sank into the cleared passenger seat. We both listened as brakes squealed and an engine roared.

"Kira," I started. "How about this: we'll all hunt together."

"Not likely." My sister snorted. "If you find us, you'll lock us away and we'll never get to have any fun."

Werewolves weren't fun. Kidnapping and against-her-will mating weren't fun. But I couldn't say any of that. All I could do was repeat my sister's name. "Kira...."

"Gotta go!" she chirped. "If you find Jessie, text us. We'll do likewise."

"Wait!" One word only, then Kira had severed our connection.

So why was Tony smiling?

"I know," he told me, "where they are."

Chapter 9

WELL, Tony didn't know the girls' exact location. But he'd guessed which bus line they'd chosen. Had extrapolated how far they would have travelled based on the time elapsed since they'd raced down the fire escape. "If we take the hypotenuse, we can catch them here," he observed, tapping a location on the paper map disinterred from the pile of math paraphernalia.

"How can you be sure?" I demanded as he steered toward the spot in question. Not that I doubted his grasp of geometry. But— "You recognized something about the sound of the road?"

Tony graced me with a true laugh this time, his eyes sparkling as he shook his head. "I recognized the brakes. I took that bus last week when I had to drop my car off at the garage. It squealed at every stop. Same register, same intensity, same bus."

In my experience, lots of bus brakes squealed. But we had nothing else to go on. So I didn't complain as we crossed town, leaving the Warren behind and entering a retail district. Shops whipped past, their awnings tattered and streaked with bird droppings yet still managing to shade most of the sidewalk. This was an area where public transportation needed to be, and was, dependable. Sure enough, a bus pulled up to the curb before we could find a parking spot.

I was yanking on the door handle, my seatbelt unbuckled, before I thought to glance at my temporary partner. "Go," he agreed, slowing to a stop despite the horns blaring behind us.

I sprang out, using a little extra fox speed to wedge my foot into the bus door before the barrier could slide all the way shut. "Wait!"

"Make up your mind," the balding driver complained. "In or out." Then as I padded up the steps toward him, he added, "Fare card?"

"I don't have one with me," I murmured, scanning the interior of the nearly empty bus. An old woman sang quietly in Spanish to the toddler in her lap. Two high-school-aged boys with locks swayed to their earbuds. A woman in a business suit sat so erect her back didn't touch the seat.

Kira and Charlie weren't present. I turned back to the driver. "Did you see two girls? The younger one looks like me minus thirteen years. They..."

"You're gonna make me late, lady," the driver groused. "Pay or get off the bus."

No, he didn't just grouse. He was halfway out of his seat, ready to push me down the steps without providing any information about my sister.

Then Tony was there. Out of breath, cheeks red from exertion. "Here you go." He slipped the driver a bill that was far too large to pay for a ride for two. "Keep the change."

"What for?"

"Taking your break now so you can answer a few questions," Tony said, his gentleness defusing the driver's annoyance. "The girls?"

"Haven't seen 'em."

"And your brakes. They don't squeak, do they?"

The driver rolled his eyes. "Nope. I get mine checked, unlike Roy."

"Roy's bus." Tony leaned in a little closer, his excitement palpable. "It's on this route?"

"Half an hour behind mine."

Tony eased back down the steps, waiting at the bottom to offer a hand I didn't need while nodding at the driver. "Thank you for your time."

THE IDEA of cooling our heels for half an hour, hoping Tony's guess panned out, chaffed like the wedgies middle schoolers seemed to think were a fun way of pranking their classmates. I paced for less than a minute, brain moving far faster than my body. Then I smelled werewolf fur on the breeze.

The relief of forward momentum had me spinning toward the alley before I remembered my human investigative partner. He, however, didn't let me go so easily. "Mai! What are you doing?"

"Wait here," I called over my shoulder. "I'll be back. If the girls turn up first...."

Tony sighed. "I'll take care of them. Do what you need to do."

If a shifter had given in so easily, I would have doubted his word. But Tony's footsteps didn't pound after me. When I glanced back, his eyes were on the street, obeying my command.

So I didn't worry about my co-worker as I followed the thread of fur down the alley to the next cross street. There, the scent grew stronger rather than weaker. I was clearly doing the unimaginable—racing toward a werewolf instead of away.

Well, not racing. Werewolf senses were as good as fox senses. I preferred to be the one benefiting from the element of surprise.

So I slowed, following the thread of scent as it turned left onto a major thoroughfare. Left again down an alley. Left onto another thoroughfare. And...left back into the alley I'd started in.

The around-the-block technique was a simple trick I'd used myself to set up ambush. Hairs on the back of my neck rose, but I paced forward anyway. "I just want to chat," I murmured, knowing wolf ears would catch every word I uttered.

No answer. And no movement. But the werewolf reek in this

small space between a wine shop and a cafe had grown as strong as damp, unwashed dog. I continued forward another step....

And only then, when I was fully in shadow, did the predator pounce. Only once I was too far from busy streets to call for help...not that I intended to bring anyone else into this mess.

Instead, I pulled at my magic, forming a sword behind my left leg even as the whoosh of air past my right cheek promised the werewolf was leaping toward me. At first I didn't see him. Then I caught a blur of deeper darkness within the shadows. A wolf, in animal form, lunging for my jugular.

No, not my jugular. Hanging around Tony was making me think in angles, and this angle seemed to terminate at the curve between my shoulder and my neck.

Something about that niggled at my memory. But this wasn't the time to solve puzzles. Instead, I slashed my sword just close enough to the wolf's back to be a warning rather than a wound. A cloud of gray hair spun up to encompass us both.

"My sword is sharp," I observed, dancing lightly on my feet to match my opponent's circle. "Next time, I'm aiming for blood."

The wolf huffed at me and I got the distinct impression he thought my threat was cute. My size and gender meant I got that response often. No wonder I'd learned to turn the tables on those who underestimated me.

The wolf attacked again and this time I used his momentum against him. He was aiming for my legs, not with his jaws but with his shoulder. As if his goal was to trip me up rather than to bite me. To bring me down to his level so he could...what? Rip out my throat? Slobber on my face?

Regardless of his intentions, the wolf was moving so fast a human wouldn't have been able to follow his trajectory. But I wasn't human. I bent my knees to evade before he could knock them out from under me. Then I stabbed my sword through the muscle of the wolf's upper foreleg.

He squealed like a stuck pig, the tone high-pitched and endless. Or, no, that wasn't the wolf squealing. That was brakes in need of replacement.

"Gotta go," I told my opponent. Leaving him there, I sprinted toward the noisy bus.

Chapter 10

"GOOD TIMING," Tony noted as I slid to a halt beside him. The bus had stopped but the doors hadn't yet opened, which meant I couldn't see inside. I rose onto my tiptoes, trying to catch a glimpse...and Tony's hand settled around my wrist.

His grip was gentle, yet I still had the distinct urge to yank myself free. My fox nature hated being restrained.

Then I was given a different reason to evade as Tony dipped a finger from his free hand into the blood splattered across my forearm. "What happened?"

"It's not mine," I answered...which, I guess, wasn't the right thing to say. Because Tony's orange eyebrows drew together and I suspect he would have finally demanded answers if the whoosh of hydraulics hadn't promised the bus doors were opening up.

Charlie was the first one to hop off. She'd clearly already seen me and Tony because she smiled and ran toward us, almost as if she hadn't just been responsible for a wild-goose chase that sidetracked us from hunting her sister.

No, I corrected myself, Charlie wasn't responsible for our dogleg. Kira had almost certainly been the main instigator and also the one who understood the full stakes of the matter.

I peered over Charlie's shoulder, trying to decide how hard to crack down on my sister for something I likely would have done exactly the same way in her shoes. Then I frowned as a different girl followed Charlie down the steps. "Jessie?"

The twins were genetically identical, but I'd never had a problem telling them apart. Charlie's face was just a little sharper, Jessie's gentler and rounder. Now, the two looked even more distinctive since Jessie's clothes and hands were embedded with what looked like long smears of dirt.

Tony's tensed jaw suggested he saw the same things I did, likely also noticing the way Jessie flinched when a random stranger brushed past her along the sidewalk. The girl was traumatized. No wonder my co-worker pulled out his phone. "I'm calling the police."

"No." I barely managed to restrain myself from knocking the device into traffic. Instead, I lowered my voice to last-chance-to-listen teacher mode. "You don't understand the big picture. I swear to you, police will make everything ten times worse."

"That's what Kira said too," Charlie observed, slipping her hand into her sister's. She tugged Jessie forward until all four of us were out of the flow of foot traffic, shielded by the outdoor seating area for a restaurant that didn't appear to be attracting any business.

No one offered further explanation, but Tony humphed and subsided anyway. Which gave me leeway to peer over the girls' shoulders once again. Kira would come prancing down the steps of the bus any second now. She'd be proud and sassy, her dark eyes sparkling with glee at having saved Jessie and one-upped me....

Instead, the hydraulics hissed and the doors eased shut.

I was running past the girls before anyone could stop me. Pushing through a crowd of tourists who were gawking at something I didn't care about. The bus picked up speed as I shouted, "Stop!"

The vehicle didn't stop, but its acceleration was slow enough for me to catch up with the door anyway. I pounded on the glass, repeating my command louder and more forcefully. But the bus driver just rolled his eyes and slammed his foot down on the gas.

In a puff of exhaust, the bus was gone. And so was any chance Kira would disembark.

I only realized I was standing stock still in the middle of an active lane when someone screamed obscenities at me. In a daze, I stepped back up onto the curb.

From the restaurant seating area, the twins peered at me wide-eyed. Okay, so maybe it wasn't ordinary human behavior to run after a bus and bang on its side, screaming. So sue me. My sister was missing the same way Jessie had been missing an hour earlier, and of the two Kira was in considerably more danger from wolves.

With an effort, I urged my feet to carry me back to the only available source of information. Then I forced a single word through lips so tight they felt like overstretched rubber bands. "Kira?"

Charlie winced but answered. "Someone called me from Jessie's phone with the offer of a swap. Kira agreed to trade herself. We bought a tracker first so it'd be easy to find her later. But we didn't think of the subway. The guy took Kira down the stairs and the app hasn't been able to locate her since."

I SQUASHED my emotions long enough to listen to Charlie's description of the kidnapper, one that matched up perfectly with Jackal. Blood pounded in my ears. My sister was in the hands of a werewolf —the one thing both our father and mother had repeatedly warned against.

My teeth tried to sharpen, but I closed my eyes and forced calm to blanket me. None of this was the Raven twins' fault. They didn't know the danger they'd pointed toward a ten-year-old child.

Focusing with an effort, I used all my senses to take stock of the situation. Jessie was no longer wearing my t-shirt. Flaring my nostrils, I sniffed as surreptitiously as possible. Yep, the scent of fur had also faded from her person.

"Take them to the cabin," I ordered Tony. "Or clean them up and send them home. Whatever's easiest. I'll deal with this."

They didn't move. Instead, all three humans peered at me like I was crazy. Tony was the one who voiced their answer. "That would be an infinite amount of no."

Jessie's cheeks lifted into the barest hint of a smile at the geekiness of his answer. Which was good. I wanted the kid not to be traumatized.

I wanted more to find my sister. "Jessie." It took a crazy amount of effort to keep my voice gentle, but I managed. "Do you know where he held you?"

"No," she murmured, voice mouse-meek. "He taped my eyes shut and put sunglasses over them to hide what he'd done. Then he warned me not to make a sound or he'd stab me. I felt the knife so I didn't say anything even when someone came up and asked if we needed any help. I crawled down a tunnel and let him lock me in some sort of underground dog kennel. I was an idiot."

"You weren't an idiot," Charlie countered, eyes flashing and sisterly devotion in full effect. "You survived a bad situation."

"It was idiotic to trust Shane," Jessie shot back, her voice firmer even though she was beating herself up verbally. Then she turned to me. "You were right, Ms. Fairchild. Shane was using me."

"A lesson we all have to learn the hard way." I took her hand and squeezed it even though everything inside me was screaming *"Go, go, go!"* I couldn't rush off and save Kira if I had no clue where she was being held.

I did, however, have a clue as to where she'd turn up. Yesterday, Jackal had threatened my sister if I didn't join him at the Arena by sunset. I eyed the sun, already dipping below the tops of the tallest buildings. If I had to, I'd march into the repurposed warehouse and trade myself for Kira just like Kira had traded herself for Jessie. But there had to be another way....

Then I realized what had bugged me about the wolf fight a few minutes earlier. That shifter had been lunging for my neck, but not as if he intended to kill me. Had he instead been trying to force a mating like Shane had initially planned to do with Jessie? Was there more to tonight's territorial battle than I currently understood?

I pulled up the bus system's app, swiping through options with increasing annoyance. I'd have to make three transfers on my way back to Shane's motel if I wanted to ask another round of questions. By the time I arrived, I would have used up all of my buffer time before Jackal's deadline.

I squared my shoulders. So I wouldn't follow this thread of sleuthing. Instead, I'd go in blind and defenseless—well, not quite literally. Not like Jessie had done. Unlike the human girl, I possessed a glowing ball of magic which I was able to turn into a sword at a moment's notice. And, if it came down to Kira's life versus our secrecy, I had my inner fox ready to scratch and bite.

Mind made up, I considered the public-transportation route to the Arena. It was just as circuitous as the one to the motel, but I could get there in time.

Or at least so I hoped.

The air suddenly felt cold against my skin, and this time I didn't shake off Tony's hand when it fumbled for my fingers. "Hey, we'll figure this out," he promised. The words were meaningless since he didn't know shifters existed. Still, his next question wrung a nod out of me. "Want a ride?"

Chapter 11

I WASN'T SURPRISED to find the door to Shane's motel room open a crack. Likely after Mr. Clean kicked it down, the latch would never close properly again.

What was more surprising was Shane's activity when I pushed the door open. The werewolf was up and packing, and as we entered he straightened and met my gaze head on. "I got a call that Jackal has your sister. I'm sorry. I didn't intend that. She's just a kid."

Was he apologizing for fear of my sword, now disintegrated back into raw energy? I didn't think so. *"Second chances,"* Dad once told me, *"sometimes have profound consequences."* Sure enough, Shane's body language suggested he'd done an ethical about-face.

I softened...but Charlie didn't. I'd told Tony and the twins to stay put in the parking lot, but I wasn't particularly surprised when feet slapped the pavement and Charlie pushed into the doorway beside me. "And my sister isn't a kid?" The corollary—that Charlie was also a kid—wasn't apparent in the flashing of her eyes.

Then Jessie was there too, wriggling between us and charging into the room. She didn't look like a kid now either. More like a whirlwind of rage as she barreled toward Shane, stopping just in time to slap him across the face.

Well, not really the face. My student was shorter than her target by a considerable margin, so her fingers only made contact with Shane's chin and mouth. Still, my sword was in my hand and I was between the two before either could blink twice.

After all, it's not wise to slap werewolves unless you're ready to back up that show of force with something pointy. Luckily, I was properly prepared.

Only, Shane didn't attack. Instead, he cupped his chin and nodded. "I deserved that," he told Jessie, leaning around me so he could meet her gaze. "I'm sorry I lured you in yesterday. It was a dick move."

I only realized Tony had joined the twins in the doorway when he started making guesses. "So why did you do it? Is this a gang hazing ritual? Has organized crime moved into town?"

Shane's gaze slid to mine and I shook my head almost imperceptibly. In response, he cleared his throat and evaded the question. "Something like that. But I swear I won't repeat my mistake."

His words shivered through me as if they held werewolf power I hadn't formerly been aware of. Whatever that tingle meant, I found I believed the young shifter. Shane really hadn't intended for Kira to be kidnapped. He was now ready to turn over a new leaf.

And Tony must have believed him also. Because my co-worker pulled out his phone and tapped out a text. He waited a moment then offered Shane a lifeline.

"I have a friend out in New Mexico," Tony observed. "He's running a regenerative-agriculture operation in the desert. It's long hours of hard work in hot sun with very little pay. But if you're serious about keeping your nose clean, he'll take you on. A bunk and food are included. No one will find you there."

Again, Shane glanced at me, eyebrows rising. He likely wanted to know if this farm was within peak werewolf territory. But he was more likely to have that information than I was, so I just shrugged.

And Shane made his choice. "Yes, sir. I'd be in your debt if you'd recommend me to your friend."

Which was all well and good. A change of heart. A werewolf rising above his predatory nature.

But that didn't help my sister.

"In the bathroom," I ordered Shane. "You and I need to talk."

I HERDED him into a space so small he had to back into the shower to make room for two. Shutting out the humans, I turned on the sink faucet just in case one of the twins got the bright idea of pressing her ear up against the door. "Now," I demanded, "explain about the neck-biting thing."

Because I'd only assumed it was a werewolf mating ritual. Had read that once or twice...in paranormal novels. Here in the real world, it might make sense that a lonely youth like Shane would seek out a human life partner. But that wolf in the alley—he'd had no reason to want to mate with me.

Unfortunately, this was apparently information all werewolves should have sucked up with their mother's milk. Shane's brows drew together. "I mean, it's obvious, right? Neck biting is the old way of forcing a mate bond. What do you want to know?"

"Start at square one," I nudged, hoping he'd assume Kira and I were orphans who hadn't had access to shifter culture up until this point. I was walking a fine line here, teasing the reality that foxes were unlike wolves. But I had to hope Shane would be too concerned about his own skin to do the more advanced math. "Why does everyone want a mate so badly?" I continued. The yearning obviously had nothing to do with love.

"Our women stay in packs," Shane said after a moment's consideration. "There aren't any lone-wolf females. I mean, not counting you, of course."

"Of course. Let's not talk about me. Let's talk about you. You wanted to mate with Jessie because...?"

"I thought she was like us. A true mate boosts our dominance."

"True mate?" I lifted my eyebrows and Shane's chin drooped.

"Yeah, I know she wouldn't have been my true mate. But even

just looking like you have a mate helps. Half the battle is posturing. Wolves who appear stronger don't have to fight so much. I needed all the help I could get."

That I understood. The same was true during sword fights. Mess with your opponent's mind and you didn't always have to be more skillful with your blade.

"Jackal wanted Jessie for the same reason?" I guessed.

"Yeah, until he figured out she was human. Then he wanted your sister. Having a mate will make him seem more like an alpha." Shane's voice dropped even lower than it already was. "He's not, though. I thought I could pretend this was a pack he's forming, but I can't. A pack is a family. This is just a power struggle. A war like the rest of outpack life."

"Okay." His explanation was bad news for me and, I hoped, good news for Kira. Jackal wanted the mate who would make him look like the biggest wolf possible. So he'd traded up from a human to a shifter child. Surely that also meant he'd trade up from Kira to me.

Or at least so I hoped.

Either way, I needed to get to the Arena fast and deal with this werewolf war I'd stumbled into. First, though....

I leaned into Shane's personal space, not bothering to raise my sword but putting its bite into my words instead. "You will never again attempt to mate with someone against her will. If you do, I will find you and I will skewer you. Do we understand each other?"

"Yes, ma'am," Shane replied, his nod reminiscent of a bobble-head doll. "I swear! I—"

Before he could add to his promise, a knock on the bathroom door interrupted us. I turned off the sink. "What?"

"The app," Charlie called, louder than she really needed to. "It pinged me. It's showing where Kira is."

Chapter 12

THE RED CIRCLE on the map pulsed above the Arena's location. No wonder when I looked out the door and saw the horizon beginning to glower with orange and red.

And above the descending darkness, the moon. A sharp crescent, like a curved sickle blade.

High moon—sunset—had snuck up on us. The fight would be starting momentarily. And Kira was in the middle of the mess.

This time, I was the one who asked for help. "Tony, I need to be there *now*."

"On it."

We piled into the car with a minimum of discussion. Tony drove. Shane took shotgun because I wasn't about to cram him in the back with the twins. Then Jessie, Charlie, and I plopped down amid the textbooks and pointy math debris. It was a tight fit, but the ride was short.

And I was focused on my sister rather than on any current physical discomfort. By the time the Arena came into view, I'd worked out a plan.

"Wait here until I send out Kira," I instructed. "Drop Shane off at the bus station, then take the girls somewhere safe. I'll contact you when I'm able to pick up my sister. Please and thank you."

The car screeched to a halt. I flung my door wide...and all the other doors popped open as well.

Tony met my eyes across the top of the car. "We're coming in with you."

"You are not," I countered, voice harsh. "And I have no time to explain."

The air hummed with disagreement. Shane was the first to fold, taking one look at me then disappearing back into the car. The twins, on the other hand, watched Tony, waiting for a cue.

And Tony wavered. Didn't reiterate his offer, but didn't obey me either. I frowned. *Now* he'd decided to stand up for himself? To stop letting me captain the ship?

"Tony," I hissed. "I'm serious. This is life or death. I need you to get in the car and wait for my sister to come out this door."

"I'll get in the car," my co-worker countered, "for ten minutes. Then I'll drive both you *and* Kira to safety, or I'll come in and get you both out."

I swallowed. Tony was purely human. He possessed no supernatural reflexes and he couldn't even use a sword. The protractor that had poked into my butt during the ride over was his best potential weapon, which wouldn't go very far against an Arena full of shifters.

But I didn't have time to argue. Had no hold over Tony that would force him to obey me. So I nodded. "Ten minutes then Kira and I will both come out. Be ready."

My words lingered in the air as I turned away and headed into the Arena to deal with wolves.

ON ORDINARY FIGHT NIGHTS, the doors would have been blocked by Mr. Clean and his fellow bouncers, who collected cash and made sure no troublemakers made it inside. But Jackal had rented out the entire space and Ma Scrubbs had given all of her employees the evening off as a result. So there was no one to stop me as I stepped in through a side door.

This was where I usually entered in the evenings, trotting down the stairs on my left to check in with Ma Scrubbs before heading back up then opening the door on the right to dive into the Arena itself. Just as it had on other fight nights, the pulse of voices and scents pressed against my skin through the tightly shut Arena door while the route leading down was quiet and dark.

I glanced at the tracker app that Charlie had added to my phone during the drive over. The pulsing dot suggested Kira was on the far side of the building but it gave no indication of elevation. The question was, upstairs or down?

I wavered, trying to guess how Jackal would play this. He could tie Kira up in the stadium itself, using her presence to boost his alpha status. But a girl held against her will wouldn't be good for optics...assuming Jackal hadn't forced a mating already.

"I'll be at the Arena tomorrow at high moon," he'd told me in the pet store. *"Either come as my mate or be prepared to lose your pup."*

Why threaten me if he intended to settle for Kira as a consolation prize? No, Jackal would be holding the line until the last minute, expecting me to appear.

That hope led me down the dark stairs that opened onto Ma Scrubbs' office and the changing rooms. As I descended, sounds and scents dampened. Soon, my whispering footfalls were all that broke the silence.

Which was a bad sign. A trapped Kira wouldn't be silent. Unless she'd been knocked out or gagged, my sister would be biting and screaming. She'd once caught a trailing scarf in an automatic door and nearly taken the building down with the heat of her rage.

I swallowed. Maybe Kira wasn't here after all. Still, I'd chosen to head down these stairs. Best check the room at the end of the hallway, the location the tracker seemed to be leading me toward.

I padded closer...and Jackal's voice threaded out toward me. "Cutting it close, aren't you, Mai?"

~

I DREW my sword out of thin air, spinning into the cramped changing room. This was the space I was usually assigned to, and was that a coincidence or yet more evidence that my mere scent was a hazard around werewolves?

The possibility didn't matter. All I had eyes for was the sole inhabitant—Jackal. "Where's Kira?" I demanded.

"Safe." His grin was sharp-toothed, his eyes sparkling with pleasure at having won this first round. "And she'll remain safe as long as you join me above as my mate."

"Assuming you win," I countered, buying time. If Kira wasn't here, why had the app pinpointed this location? My eye lit on the little black box resting on the chair beside Jackal. "Did you strip my sister to find that?" I demanded.

Jackal snorted. "Please. She stuffed it down her sock. It was evident at a glance."

I doubted my sister would be so obvious, but there was nothing I could do about the past. "And where is she now?"

"I'll bring her to you once I've won," Jackal promised. "Of course, if I lose, no one will ever find her. Poor child, withering away without her sister. She'll..."

The mental image bit like wolf fangs. I broke into his mind-warp with a warning of my own. "If Kira and I aren't out of here in ten minutes, you'll have humans intruding with 911 on speed dial. Is that how you want to begin your reign as alpha? Dealing with police?"

"The fight could be over in as little as thirty seconds," Jackal countered, taking a step toward me. He raised his hand to the level of my face and it was all I could do not to flinch as he teased a finger across my cheek. "The timeline depends upon you," he continued. "Bare your neck and let's get this over with."

The moment had arrived when I had to choose between my own future and the safety of those I cared about. Unfortunately, Jackal's touch—unwanted, unasked for—made it hard to think.

So I focused my breathing the way Dad had taught me to. In for four, hold for four, out for four, hold again. *"Center on what's important,"* he'd admonished. *"Choose a signpost and follow its lead."*

Dad had been my signpost ever since Mama died. He stood between our family and the wider world, protecting me and Kira with broad shoulders that were entirely human. Even while doing that, he'd still had the energy to take students under his wing when their own parents proved worthless, helping dozens of lost souls grow into the strong adults they were meant to be.

Dad would never have considered letting Kira, Tony, and the twins get sucked into a werewolf power struggle. But he might not have barreled directly into danger either. While teaching me to fight, he'd drilled me on evasions long before he'd let me start attacking. *"If there's no obvious way to win,"* he'd said once, *"stall. Serendipity might come to your aid if you wait long enough."*

There was no obvious way to win, so I'd bet on serendipity. Hunching my shoulders to shield my neck, I shook my head. "No bites, but I'll fight at your side."

Chapter 13

I THOUGHT Jackal would reject my offer, but he just shrugged. "Your funeral if you've made the wrong decision." Then, as he pushed past me and started up the stairs, he added, "Or, no, the funeral won't be yours. Can you have a funeral without a body? I guess your sister will find out."

He was trying to mess with my mind, but I'd made my decision. So I ignored his banter as I followed in his footsteps, glancing down at my cell phone instead of rising to the bait. Not to check the tracker app but to consider the clock. Our time in the basement had felt like an eternity, but only three minutes had passed. I still had seven to go.

My feet lifted a little more easily as hope buoyed me. Seven minutes was an eternity in the fight ring. While I'd often drawn battles out to please the crowd—and Ma Scrubbs—I usually knew within the first thirty seconds who would be the winner. With my sword clenched in one fist, I was confident I could end things quickly tonight.

Was confident...until Jackal eased open the door to the stadium. Only the emergency lights were on, but my eyes had already adjusted to the similarly dim lighting in the stairwell. So I could tell there were dozens of people in the Arena rather than the handful I'd been expecting.

Correction: these weren't just people. These were fighters. One leaned into another's personal space and was shoved backwards with a growl. Someone else snapped his teeth challengingly in front of an antagonist's nose.

The overwhelming scent of fur and the grace of each motion suggested none of these people were hired human fighters. Meanwhile, the layout of the space—wide open now that the chairs were removed—left no doubt that everyone present was here to fight.

It was less clear whether there were alliances or whether the upcoming fight would be a free-for-all. No one so much as glanced in our direction as we stepped into the room.

Still, Jackal's back tensed in front of me. So I sidled around him to find the focus of his glare.

The shadowy figure leaning against a wall slightly outside the fray didn't look particularly problematic from a distance. He wasn't any taller than average and his left arm was fixed close to his body using a piece of cloth turned into a sling. In fact, when someone tried to provoke him by pushing into his personal space, he just smiled and shook his head.

Still, something about his posture radiated danger. Power.

Sure enough, Jackal growled out a warning. "Blackout is the one to watch. He'll...."

Whatever Jackal intended to say about the other werewolf trailed off as Blackout's gaze slung around to meet mine. While I was sure shifter senses had alerted the other werewolves when we entered, no one else seemed to care about our presence.

Blackout cared. In fact, his reaction seemed disproportionate to the gentle simmer of aggression filling the Arena. He bared wolf-sharp teeth, lank hair not quite obstructing our view of eyes that had widened along with his nostrils. His undamaged hand slid a sword out of the sheathe at his waist.

Then he charged.

～

THE LOW-LEVEL AGGRESSION in the room stilled in ripples as Blackout pushed past other fighters. But I barely noticed. Instead, I had eyes only for the charging werewolf.

The charging werewolf...who appeared to be aiming not for Jackal but for me.

"You bitch," Blackout snarled, his sword slashing toward my chest. Or, rather, toward where my chest had been one second earlier. His rage meant he signaled every move in plenty of time for me to parry, so his sword met my blade instead of my flesh.

"I don't think we've been introduced," I countered, dancing aside as he roared out ire that seemed far out of proportion to me stepping into the room beside Jackal. Blackout was so furious he'd be easy to vanquish. If this was the worst these werewolves had in store for me, I'd be able to tell Tony to stand down long before my time was up.

Blackout growled something wordless and infuriated in response to my banter, which is when I made the connection. "Was that you in the alley?" I asked, letting amusement color my guess. "I hope you got that arm looked at. You never know where my sword's been."

As I spoke, I opened myself out of a defensive posture, tempting Blackout to once again slash at my unprotected front. The move was an easy way to disarm an inexperienced opponent, or an opponent too angry to use his brain.

Sure enough, Blackout lunged in, and I pivoted...straight into Jackal. My supposed mate hadn't trusted me to take care of myself. Instead, he'd managed to dive directly into my path.

Which meant Blackout wasn't the one disarmed; I was. Jackal's elbow slammed into my sword hand. My magical weapon spun away, my energy draining alongside it. The blade clattered against the ground...and the tense *waiting* in the air of the Arena broke.

It was almost as if our audience had been holding its breath until it became clear which way the power flowed. My collision with Jackal must have proven we weren't mates. And now, it appeared from the abrupt clang of swords, many were choosing to bid for the role of alpha themselves.

"Shift," Jackal barked as he parried a blow from Blackout. His command made sense given his assumptions about my nature—with my sword lost in the darkness, wolf teeth would be an adequate defense.

Fox teeth, on the other hand, would turn the tide of this battle in a very unfortunate direction. So I shook my head. "No."

Jackal growled by didn't press the issue. Instead, he slammed his sword into Blackout's, the reverberation harsh in the air. "Get behind me then."

This order I obeyed. Not because Jackal had told me to, but because the distance between me and my magic dragged me down more than if I'd run a marathon without eating any breakfast. My legs wobbled and threatened to give out.

But it was dark enough in the Arena that no one would notice if my sword slid toward me. Or at least I could hope that was the case.

So I guarded Jackal's back from the encroaching fighters while drawing my sword along the concrete floor inch after inch. Time, which had flowed so slowly when my weapon was in my hand, now seemed to be sliding like water through my fingers. How many minutes were left before Tony would storm into the Arena with the Raven twins beside him? Or were we down to seconds now?

I kicked out at a shifter who'd thought it was a good idea to stab Jackal in the back while he was otherwise occupied. Our opponent's blade spun away into the darkness. He growled then retreated and I was able to once again focus on my sword.

It was almost close enough to grab now. Once the weapon was back in my possession, I could do more than kick at opponents who impinged on my personal space. Perhaps I could even prevent Jackal from trying to fight on two fronts at once.

"Stay in your lane!" I barked when the male I was allied with swiveled to slash at another backstabbing werewolf. The gesture could have been considered chivalrous, if he hadn't had an opponent of his own to contend with. As it was, the opening nearly allowed Blackout to slice off Jackal's ear.

As Blackout's blade whistled close, I shoved Jackal sideways. Both of them roared fury at me and the world.

Jackal added in a growl of rage at the sword his knees had come down on. *My* sword. It didn't cut him, but Jackal's flesh halted its forward momentum. And now I was facing Blackout, who appeared to have finally found his words.

"He lied, didn't he?" the other major contender for the role of alpha prodded. His smile was wide and his teeth were pointy while he waved his sword slow as a pendulum before me. "You're not mated to that idiot. Choose me and I'll protect you from the rabble."

His sword arm opened out to encompass all of the shifters fighting in the dim sprawl of the Arena. Some had gone furry while others lay on the ground moaning. There was blood in the air.

Still, everyone was aware of us. The battle slowed and eyes snapped to me and Blackout.

This moment, not a sword stroke, would determine the winner of the match.

Two days ago, I would have said that one alpha was as bad as another. But Jackal alone knew where Kira was located. I couldn't change my loyalties now.

Instead, I dropped to my knees beside the asshole who'd drawn me into this mess. The werewolf who had once provoked a quiver of attraction but who I now found revolting.

Our mouths slammed together like enemy swords.

Chapter 14

TWO SETS OF TEETH COLLIDED, my lip caught in the middle. The pain brought tears to my eyes.

That wasn't the only source of discord either. Jackal tasted foul. Not from garlic or other food particles but from an overbearing dominance and a profound lack of compatibility. He tasted like the end of my independence, the loss of any hope of a true romantic relationship, the cessation of my ability to pass for human with a simple teaching job.

Still, the gesture did its work. Our kiss wasn't a mating bite, but it was a claiming. The mood of the room shifted a second time, and I could tell without looking that the battle would end quickly now.

Or maybe not. A shout. A flicker of incoming danger caught out of the corner of one eye.

Not everybody was ready to throw in the towel. Someone thought it was a good idea to cut down the competition while he was engrossed in a kiss.

I pushed away from Jackal, swiping my sword up off the floor as I scrambled to get my feet under me. But I could tell it was too late to stop Blackout's weapon. My blade wouldn't make contact before his sword slid straight through Jackal's heart.

"Jackal! Move!" I shouted. Not that I cared about his life. But I cared about my sister's. If Jackal died now...would I ever find her? Or would Kira rot in some dark hole, dehydrated and starving and thinking I'd abandoned her to her fate?

Jackal, darn him, didn't respond to my order. His eyes remained closed, his face dreamy. As if that kiss had been much better for him than it was for me.

I tried to force more speed into my pretzel-mode limbs. But even shifter muscles are still just muscles. Blackout's sword was six inches from Jackal's breast and closing fast while I'd only made it up to my knees.

Still, I swung as high as I could. Maybe, if I was very lucky, I could at least partially deflect the blow.

I wasn't lucky. And yet...Blackout grunted once, short and surprised. His sword clattered to the ground beside me. Blood spurted as his body fell like an oak beneath a forester's ax.

Jackal and I were in the path of both body and bodily fluids. The gore was overwhelming, like nothing I'd seen in previous fights. Blood splattered my eyes, my cheek, my gasping mouth.

Meanwhile, Blackout's dead weight pinned me to the ground. Not a metaphorical dead weight. A literal dead weight. Panicking, I pushed upward with little success.

Then Jackal was yanking me to my feet, his face glowing with satisfaction. "My new beta has proven himself!" he roared, releasing me so he could clap the back of the shifter who had slaughtered our opponent and apparently won a leadership role as a result.

I swallowed down bile that I hoped was my own rather than the dead man's. Saving us had been appreciated, but there were non-lethal ways to end a fight.

And this backstabber was being honored with the role of second-in-command? "Jackal," I started.

"Quiet," he snapped without even glancing in my direction. His grip on the backstabber turned hard and demanding as he continued. "Do you accept your role? Do you vow allegiance?"

The other shifter didn't hesitate to seize the offered power. "Yes, alpha."

A sigh from the crowd. Now the battle really was over.

Well, nearly. Jackal eyed each shifter in turn, measuring, testing. "My pack will be strong, my territory large," he intoned. "If you prefer not to join us, I recommend you run fast and keep on running. At dawn, you'll either be with me or you'll be dead."

~

WHILE JACKAL GATHERED allegiances like deadfall apples, I pulled my phone out of my pocket with bloody fingers that refused to swipe it awake. Only after scrubbing both phone and hands against a small square of unblemished jeans was I able to check the time.

Eleven minutes had passed. If Tony saw this carnage....

I spun for the door, and once again Jackal's hand clamped down on my shoulder. "Where do you think you're going?"

"To call off the cavalry."

For a long moment, he simply eyed me. Was this to be the first test of our mating? Jackal would bark out an order in front of his pack and I'd either have to obey him or lose the protection I'd just sacrificed my honor for?

Instead, he nodded. "No heel dragging. I'll meet you on the balcony afterwards to discuss your sister."

And terms. We'd discuss terms too.

But I didn't want to get into that with shifter ears perked all around us. Instead, I agreed then sprinted for the entrance. Bursting outside, I was surprised to see that it was dusk rather than midnight. The past eleven minutes had felt like an eternity, but out here birds twittered their evening chorus as if death hadn't struck the Arena moments before.

Well, not everyone was fully oblivious. Tony strode forward, shoulder to shoulder with Shane. The pair took one look at me and froze.

Then Tony blinked, swallowed. "Let me guess. Not your blood?"

"Right," I agreed. "We'll talk later...."

I was already turning back toward the Arena when Tony spoke again. Unlike Jackal, he didn't sling me around with a hard hand on my shoulder. Instead, I was paused by the wistfulness of his words. "You're going back in there."

His tone made it clear that Tony was starting to understand the distance that lay between us. Not the specifics of the situation but the gist of why his world and my world had no intersection point.

I didn't turn back to face him. Couldn't afford to when the gap between his straightforward protectiveness and Jackal's manipulations was laid out in such stark contrast. Instead, I managed only one word. "Yes."

"Okay." Tony's sigh of acceptance, I thought, was the end of it. As I'd suspected, I was losing his friendship, even if the reason for that loss wasn't unrequited love but rather my choice to run with wolves.

However, as I walked off, he called after me. "We'll be out here waiting. If you need help, just call."

I wouldn't though. I made the decision never to draw Tony into supernatural awfulness even before I joined Jackal on the Arena's balcony and was instructed in my duties as alpha's mate.

Duties that involved quitting my job and losing every shred of normality I'd created. Binding myself for life to an egomaniac and accepting that my days would be ruled by shifter brutality. All to win a tiny pocket of safety for myself and my sister. All to make sure my only surviving family member would remain safe.

I stood firm, though. I didn't bow my shoulders at Jackal's harsh words, just nodded my acceptance. And when he left to collect Kira, I sank down into the dim corner at the back of the balcony and mourned the independence I'd just lost.

Chapter 15

MY PHONE PINGED me out of my misery with a message from a source I'd forgotten: the former student of my father's who excelled at financial sleuthing. I'd dropped Sarah a line after Ma Scrubbs mentioned Jackal's lack of solvency, and her response now made me hoot in delight.

"Everything alright up there?" one of Jackal's new pack mates called from the Arena floor. He was scrubbing away blood, both living and dead bodies having already been moved off the premises. After all, werewolf warfare wasn't reason enough to forfeit the damage deposit.

"Fine," I answered, scrolling through the information. Then: "When Jackal returns, tell him I'll meet him downstairs."

"Yes, ma'am," the werewolf replied. But I barely noticed. I was speed walking and reading at the same time, a huge grin unfolding across my face.

Jackal had a *family*. Well, an ex-wife who'd sued him for unpaid child support. A mate who, if the divorce papers were any indication, had been the one filing for legal separation in the first place.

If claiming me with a kiss was enough to turn this battle of lone wolves in Jackal's favor, learning he'd been kicked to the curb once already would surely have the precise opposite effect. "Thank you, serendipity," I murmured, ditching my bloody clothes on the floor of the downstairs bathroom. For the first time since entering the Arena at sunrise, I relaxed enough to stand under hot water and let the flow pound away both worries and gore.

Because I'd stalled just long enough to build the winning hand. No need to kowtow and beg for scraps at Jackal's heels any longer. No need to regret tying myself to a werewolf whose touch made my skin crawl.

I was drying off with Ma Scrubbs' skimpy excuse for a towel when footsteps sounded in the hallway. Wrapping my torso, I stepped out...and opened my arms as Kira scampered into view.

"Mai!" She barreled into me the way she used to when she was knee-high and traumatized by kindergarten. Like Jessie, dirt streaked her body. But she was fine. She was *fine*.

So I didn't succumb to the urge to run my hands across every inch of her body then dig into the dark recesses of her psyche. There might be damage there, but if so we'd deal with it later.

Later when we were alone. And safe.

Now, I stuffed my sister under one arm, unfolding us out to form a united front against the so-called alpha who'd tried to claim me. The werewolf whose eyes currently checked out the hint of cleavage above my towel.

"Eyes up here, pervert."

Jackal blinked then barked out a threatening laugh. "I think perhaps you need a lesson in obedience."

"Do I?" I cocked my head, ignoring the way Kira's hug had turned tight and frantic. "Or perhaps you need a lesson in how to keep a mate. Carla and Corey." His ex-wife and child. "Do those names ring any bells with you?"

"Who told you?" Jackal took one menacing step forward.

"Does it matter?" I stared him into stillness even though he outweighed me significantly. "Just think what your new pack would say if they learned you had a mate and lost her. Not wolf enough to make her stay, I guess."

"Carla was a bitch...." he started.

I silenced him with a slashing hand motion. Then I laid down the law. "You'll pay off your child support so no one else connects the dots I did. And our mating will be in name only. I'll join you for one appearance per week, PDAs going no further than hugs and hand-holding. Kira and I will live in our apartment and go about our normal lives with no shifter visits. There will be no hunting in animal form." I took a step forward and held his glare with a stare-down I'd learned from my kid sister. "In exchange, you'll ensure no one in your pack ever forces a mating, that my students and my sister are protected like honorary members of your clan. Do we have a deal?"

Jackal wavered. A true alpha, I suspected, wouldn't have let me dictate changed terms less than an hour after we'd made our initial agreement. A true alpha also wouldn't have been a dead-beat dad.

He was silent for so long that I wasn't sure my blackmail held the weight I thought it did. Then he nodded...before slapping me with demands of his own.

"I can work with that," he growled. "But our mating will be believable. No sidepieces like the one hovering in the parking lot."

"Sidepieces?" It took me a moment to realize what and who he was talking about, then I hastened to correct the misapprehension. "Tony isn't that kind of friend...."

Jackal leaned in closer, the reek of fur choking me. "I want him gone. Break up or I'll break him up."

And that was reason enough to sever my friendship with Tony. To protect the gentle math teacher from an underworld both wild and dangerous.

So I nodded, accepting the loss of my only adult ally as the consequence of my decision. "Alright."

SHANE'S BUS wasn't due to leave for another hour, so after I pulled on spare sweats we all squeezed into Tony's car and headed to a nearby diner. "Order enough to keep you fed for the whole bus ride," Tony told the young werewolf. "It'll be safer if you don't get off until you arrive."

"Yes, sir," Shane agreed, sliding into a booth beside Kira. And I let him, even though he was a werewolf and she was the youngest of the bunch. Because since hugging me in a death grip in front of Jackal, Kira had bounced back enough to step on the pseudo-alpha's toes accidentally-on-purpose. She'd taken over the conversation during the ride here, turning her time underground into a grand adventure. When push came to shove, I trusted my little sister to keep everyone else on track.

Meanwhile, Tony and I had issues to discuss in private. So we chose a booth within eyeshot and out of earshot of the younger set. Then we waited until our server had taken our order before getting down to business of our own.

"Tony," I started, not quite sure how to break up with someone when we'd never been a couple in the first place. The best way, I decided, was to rip off the bandage quickly. "I'm not interested in a romantic relationship with you or anyone else."

For a minute, I thought he hadn't even heard me as he fiddled with the jam packets. His eyes stayed down as he nodded. "I figured as much, but that's not what I wanted to talk about. You came out of that building covered in blood. You're in more trouble than Shane is."

Tony was just so *good*. In that moment, I regretted both my lack of attraction to him and the deal I'd struck with Jackal which made further time together impossible.

Shaking my head to dismiss might-have-beens, I shut down Tony's line of questioning. "I'm not in trouble anymore."

"My friend has room for you and Kira both," Tony continued as if I hadn't spoken. "He's a nice guy. You'd be safe and happy there."

A farm in the desert? I'd find the lifestyle relaxing for approximately ten minutes then stifling when there was no one present to cross swords with.

And while I could handle being stifled, Kira would dwindle away without friends to bounce off of. My social-butterfly sister was currently chatting up a storm on the other side of the dining area, every head bent toward her. This city and the people in it were her element.

I was willing to slog through eight years of pretend mating while Kira grew the rest of the way up.

So I swallowed and told the truth. "Kira wouldn't be happy there."

"Maybe, maybe not." Tony decanted the jam cubes, added in the salt and pepper packets, and started building a tower. This, I realized, was his way of dealing with the discomfort of our conversation. So I didn't try to make eye contact as he told the inanimate structure: "I was homeschooled on a farm and I was happy." His cheeks reddened. "But I'm not exactly socially well adjusted. I see your point."

"Hey." I waited Tony out, until the blotchiness faded from his pale skin. "Being socially well adjusted isn't everything. You're dependable and smart and honest and kind. Don't beat yourself up just because I'm a mess."

And now, finally, I had to finish ripping off the bandaid. I cleared my throat, trying to loosen a tightness that only clenched harder the longer I waited to say what had to be said. "This dinner. Tonight." I sucked in a breath then spat out words that sounded even harsher in the air than they had in my imagination. "It's the last time we can hang out together."

At last, Tony's blue eyes rose to meet mine. His jaw was firm, the condiments forgotten. "I can handle a friendship, Mai," he promised. "I was out of line, pushing the boundaries of our relationship. But I don't want to lose you. We can turn back the clock...."

I swallowed, hating that I had to say this. Hating Jackal and werewolves and, yes, even my own fox blood. "No," I told him. "We can't."

Epilogue

LIFE SETTLED down after werewolves took over our city. Money grew tighter and fights grew tougher without Ma Scrubbs' promise to my father to fall back on, but Kira and I got by.

At the end of the summer, Tony took all the kids from the summer enrichment program up to his aunt's cabin with one of the bus drivers as the second chaperone. Then...he was gone. I dug frantically at first, certain Jackal had decided to do away with the human math teacher despite our complete lack of contact. But, no, it turned out Tony had merely moved on to a bigger and better job.

For his part, Jackal more than toed the line of our agreement, buttering me up with sweet nothings that might have worked if he hadn't threatened me at our first meeting. I smiled and ignored the words...then spent an entire weekend stealth-trailing him. On Sunday, he wandered into a Walmart garden center, fingering plants while he waited for the staff to look in the other direction. Then he pried up a flagstone to reveal a hole in the ground.

I watched as he crawled inside and dragged the stone back over the entrance. Had Jackal stashed someone else down there in the interest of blackmail? I tightened my fist around the newly material-ized sword, straining my ears and considering slithering in after him. But after a few minutes, a hint of music too faint to be noticed by a human emerged along with the barest thread of cigarette smoke.

So perhaps this was Jackal's top-secret man-cave as well as his holding cell. The reason for his visit wasn't relevant at the present moment, but if Jackal ever considered hiding another prisoner in that hole I'd be prepared. I made a mental note of the location, then beat a hasty retreat.

And the Raven twins? They'd watched from Tony's car while werewolves bearing weapons streamed out of the Arena. They'd digested the helplessness engendered by Jessie's time spent trapped underground. Then they decided as a pair that the solution was private lessons in swordsmanship.

"You're sure?" I asked when they came up to me after class the following week with their proposal. "A course in basic self defense would be more time effective. It wouldn't hurt to carry around pepper spray either."

The pair, I was glad to see, had returned to their usual tactic of finishing each other's sentences. "No, we want..." Jessie started.

Charlie: "...To be menacing. Our parents can pay."

Jessie again: "Will you teach us?"

What answer was there other than yes?

I was beginning to breathe easy again by the time Kira emerged from her room tentatively rather than in her usual whirlwind of joyful chaos. During the last two weeks of summer school and extracurricular sword lessons, my sister had spun through life with her usual exuberance. But now she dragged her heels, her chin tucked into her chest.

The reality of her past captivity, I suspected, had finally hit her. Well, we'd work through the issue together. Slay the demons, even if they were only in her head.

I tugged my sister down onto the couch beside me, tucking a strand of hair behind her ear. "Do you want to talk about it?"

Her brow furrowed. "About Dad's letter?"

Okay, now I was thoroughly lost.

Only after I pushed her back to arm's length did I notice the paper clutched in my sister's right hand. No, not a flat sheet of paper. An envelope with two words marking the intended recipient.

Dad's handwriting, unlike his sword fighting, was a hurried scrawl that few people could decipher without assistance. I was one of the few. And how could I not recognize the letters that made up my own name?

"He said to give it to you once you stopped banging things with your sword every night," Kira admitted in a mouse voice. "But...I forgot."

The fact my sister had lost track of our dead father's words came as a relief, actually. It was proof that she'd bounced back from being made an orphan. That I'd managed to recreate security in her ten-year-old world.

Not that I needed further proof. I saw it every day when she joined in the Raven sisters' lessons and bested them with facility despite the age difference. When she argued me into spending money on things we didn't really need.

Like the pet-agility equipment which Kira had gotten sick of immediately after its purchase. I really need to package up that gear and sell it on online....

But first, I had a letter from Dad to consider. I turned the envelope over, brought it to my nose and inhaled nothing other than paper and sister. Any lingering aroma from our father was long gone.

Inside, though, his words were as fresh as if they'd just been written. *"My dearest Mai, my oldest child."* I could hear Dad's voice in my head as I deciphered his chicken scratch. *"I've left you with a lot of responsibilities. Your sister. Fox secrets. I suspect you've turned these burdens into the center of your life."*

I paused to swallow down the lump in my throat. Dad knew me better than anyone. Even dead, he could see into my heart.

And, as always, he pushed me past self-imposed limits. *"There's more to life,"* he admonished, *"than responsibility. Someday, you'll be drawn in a different direction. Maybe you'll decide to put yourself first and follow a new career path somewhere that offers less safety for your sister. Or maybe you'll find a person who tempts you to go out on a limb and share secrets you thought were sacrosanct. I've been grateful every day for your mother's fearlessness in choosing to share her life with me. Be equally fearless. Your gut will tell you when the time is right."*

I shook my head. Dad had no clue what he was asking of me. Had no clue about a not-really-alpha who'd mandated a no-friendship policy in exchange for his protection. No clue about the way our lives were more penned in than ever by the scent of shifter fur.

"In the meantime," Dad ended, *"please know how proud I've always been of you and your sister. You are the best parts of both me and your mother with none of our faults."*

I ran my thumb over the professions of love that finished the page, imagining Dad writing these words in between bouts of chemo. About one thing at least, he'd been right. We were all better for the way he'd made Mama's secrets his own. Without Dad in our lives, Kira and I would have lacked so much.

Stability. Love. Challenges to be our better selves.

I'd lost track of Kira's presence until she took the paper out of my hand, folding it as carefully as if it was a holy relic before returning it to the envelope. "Then," she said, "Dad told me my job was to cheer you up." Her eyes sparkled and she kicked out of her shoes as she challenged me. "First one to shift and make it through the track gets to choose dinner. If *I* win, we're eating ice cream for the main course *and* for dessert!"

My sister was already shimmering down into fox form, pointy nose poking out of the clothes she hadn't bothered removing. My body felt too heavy to join her, my limbs as exhausted as if I'd gone ten rounds with a superior swordsman.

But this was my sister. She needed me...and I needed this.

So I followed suit, although I did strip first. By the time I had my paws under me, Kira was waiting by the ramp leading up to the first tunnel. She chittered a challenge and I puffed up my tail in response.

What was the girl thinking? I won physical challenges for a living. I'd make her eat brussels sprouts. Broccoli. Spinach.

And she was a little cheater. Kira bit my ear on the swinging bridge, which slowed me down a little. But I leapt straight over her back and scrambled up the ladder before she reached the first rung.

We tumbled into a snarling, not-really-biting embrace as we whooshed down the final slide together. Then we shook ourselves back to humanity, her hair sticking straight out and her eyes sparkling. My features, I was sure, looked exactly the same.

"So, ice cream?" she demanded. "My toe crossed the line before yours did."

"And my nose," I countered, "crossed the line first. So...carrot sticks and chicken nuggets, *then* ice cream."

Kira stuck out her hand in a cute rendition of the shake I offered at the end of my more formal matches. "You have yourself a deal."

Later, I'd mull over Dad's words and accept that I had no way of following his advice. Later, I'd regret the agreement I'd made with Jackal...but not quite enough to risk my sister's skin by upending those terms a second time.

Later, Kira would run smack-dab into a different sort of alpha and our lives would change irrevocably. But I didn't know any of that at the time.

Instead, Kira and I tugged on pajamas while the oven preheated. Then we shook frozen chicken nuggets out onto a tray and quibbled over whether to keep the pet-agility track.

As usual, Kira won.

I HOPE you enjoyed Mai's first adventure! If you'd like to see what happens when she and her sister meet another alpha werewolf while deep in the shadow of a magical mystery, you won't want to miss Wolf's Bane, FREE on all retailers.

Or prepare to dive into two free novels plus a slew of exclusive extras when you sign up for my email list.

Thank you for reading. You are why I write.

Wereabouts Unknown

JENN STARK

Chapter 1

"LADIES AND GENTLEMEN, the Flamingo Casino proudly presents your newest *Queen* of the *Strip!*"

Lights shot up from the stage, crackling across the walls and ceilings with white-hot brilliance. Cheering and applause surged up from the hundred or so cocktail tables scattered through the Flamingo's second-largest auditorium. The woman on stage grinned and waved to the crowd with pure, unfettered joy...but it was never the sight of a pageant winner's jaw-cracking smile that made Nikki Dawes's heart thump hard enough to hurt.

No. Nikki leaned back against the bar, crossing her long legs as she settled her elbows on the counter. She studied the contestant who twirled and posed, fluttering her long, satin-gloved fingers. Past the feathers and wigs, the platform heels and sequined gowns, it was the eyes that told the true story of the beautiful starlets strutting the stage. Eyes that had seen too much, lost too much, that stared out, wide and disbelieving, savoring the crowd's favor half in wonder, half in vindication, but always with just the *tiniest* shred of doubt woven in. Like all this might be pulled away as quickly as it had been showered over their Aqua-netted heads.

Nikki had been running the Flamingo's Queen of the Strip

beauty pageant for going on two months now, and she didn't think she'd ever get tired of it. From the laughter and chatter of the full auditorium, she suspected the Flamingo's patrons wouldn't either—at least not anytime soon.

"We've got a new one, boss."

Speaking of eyes that saw too much, Glinda Wren sidled up to the bar beside Nikki, her pink confectionary-style Good Witch of the North regalia billowing out around her as she seated one impressive hip on the next barstool over. Beneath her strawberry colored bouffant wig and sparkly crown, Glinda's golden arched brows peaked impossibly higher as she glanced toward the back of the room, where the front doors opened out onto the main casino area. "Whoops, false alarm. No we don't."

Something tingled at the back of Nikki's neck as she turned to peer into the depths of the Flamingo's auditorium. They had custom retrofitted this room for the twice-weekly pageants that had become famous on the Strip in no time flat, and the tables were alight with multi-colored lamps pulsing in time with the music. Nearly every table was filled with locals and tourists alike, while Nikki's team of competing showgirls worked the space alongside the cocktail servers, each more fabulously dressed than the last.

Nikki didn't see anyone out of place, but there was no doubting Glinda's instincts. The indomitable Miss Wren had a good eye, and she'd grown up on the mean streets of southern L.A.. She didn't miss much.

"A runner?" Nikki asked as the bartender handed her a large crystal flute filled with champagne. Runaways were more frequent these days, now that the show had gained some notoriety. Word had gotten out in Vegas that if you could get to Nikki Dawes, she'd help you get clear of whatever hunted you. Most times, the predators were the traditional sort—the strong subjugating the weak in a story as old as time. Sometimes, those predators hunted psychics.

And Nikki knew psychics. She'd been working the Strip for over ten years, and she'd seen a lot of Connecteds stream past the glittering lights and clattering slot machines. Some played, some stayed, and the most powerful of them all soared high above the city, running an entire magical empire that, until recently, Nikki had only experienced in limited quantities.

The Arcana Council were the physical representation of the Tarot; demigods who'd been kicking around earth since the dawn of recorded history, with a charge to keep the balance of magic in the world. Nikki'd fallen in with them as a part-time chauffeur and informant on all things magical in the city. And when they'd started working with small-potatoes Tarot reader with big-spud abilities, Sara Wilde, Nikki was all in. She and Sara had instantly clicked. After that, all Nikki had ever wanted to do was to stand strong for her bestie…a life choice that had reaped her a whirlwind of trouble of the very best kind.

Now a totally different kind of trouble was hunting the Connected community. And to help her gear up for that fight, Nikki had unexpectedly found herself in her own glitter-bombed seat at the high table of the Council…a development she was still trying to sort through. Her whole life she'd insisted on presenting herself as a larger-than-life superstar, and now she was the straight up *Moon* of the *Arcana Council*.

She needed a complete wardrobe overhaul, STAT.

Beside her, Glinda gave a short, contemplative hum, refocusing Nikki's attention to their more immediate problem. In this light, Glinda appeared to be maybe half of her fifty years, a combination of expertly applied cosmetics, a dedicated yoga practice, and sheer, iron will.

"The girl I saw was definitely a loner," Glinda decided. "But maybe not a runner the way we usually get. She wasn't terrified so much as searching for a way out, and not finding it through here. Young, presents female, presents older than she probably is. She wasn't unsteady on her feet, so I don't think she was using, but there was something about her that just read off to me. She was too tight, too pissed. And now she's gone."

"Well, that's no good," Nikki muttered, and Glinda lifted her glass.

"Figured you'd think that. I'm also figuring you won't be presenting the Queen's sash tonight, yeah?"

Nikki'd already laid her glass down on the counter, untouched, and edged off the stool. She was wearing a blue sequin pageant gown slashed up to her hip bones on both sides, enough to show off her white, patent leather thigh-high boots, and she flipped back a stream of fire-engine red curls as she winked at Glinda. Fortunately, her gown was well-suited for whatever the night threw at her, with its shoulder-baring bodice wrapped tight over her breasts, the waist cinched in with a white leather girdle. Ordinarily, she'd have paired the ensemble with forearm-hugging white gloves, but sometimes, a girl just needed to be able to reach out and touch someone.

Especially if there was a runner somewhere close, needing help.

"I think I'm just going to have a walk around, check in with folks, see what I see," Nikki said.

"I've got the bar," Glinda nodded, flexing her fingers as she winked at their shared joke. "It's about time for a new manicure anyway."

"Your tips *are* looking a little tired," Nikki agreed. Though neither had expected it when they'd started the Queen of the Strip pageant, brawls among the guests and quite a few of the pageanteers broke out at the Flamingo with cheerful regularity. It was a good thing the club's owner was unconcerned with property damage—and that he liked a good fight.

Tall, dark, and devilishly handsome, Aleksander Kreios was nothing if not a fully hands-on manager of his smokin' hot establishment. He was just that kind of a stand-up demigod—and, as it turned out, he was Nikki's new boss on the Council as well, the Devil of the Council in the very fine flesh. Nothing like keeping your W-2 situation tidy.

Nevertheless, tonight the Flamingo didn't have the feel of fight night. The energy of the room was carefree, redolent of dark whiskey, cheap wine, and fancy beer, along with the infectious joy of the pageanteers competing on stage. Her troupe of performers never failed to entertain, except when someone came into the bar determined *not* to be entertained. And they'd been running the show long enough that most of those assholes simply stayed away.

So why had the girl Glinda had seen split so quickly? What was she looking for—or scared of?

Nikki moved through the room with the ease of long practice, navigating through the precisely situated tables—close enough for sociability, distant enough to allow each attendee to enjoy the show in whatever way they chose.

She picked up her shadow almost immediately and smiled, deliberately not looking back at the bruiser who'd latched himself to her side. He and his hundred-strong pack were her guardians, kind of a gift with purchase when she'd become the Moon. Nikki was never one to say no to an entourage, but their leader, Torsten,… went above and beyond.

And if he wanted to tail her tonight, he'd have to keep up.

She pushed out the door as a small group of college kids entered the Flamingo, the last one a girl whose worried expression caught her attention. Nikki brushed against her, drifting a hand along the girl's arm, which caused the other to flinch.

"Sorry, darlin'," Nikki said. The girl glanced up, blinking fast as she took in Nikki's costume.

"Oh! It's no problem," she blurted. Then she was gone, leaving Nikki with a raft of near-term memories to sort through. Up until recently, Nikki's abilities had been pretty modest—they'd almost had to be, she'd always reasoned. Combined with her outsized personality, and considering the kind of magic her bestie flung around on the regular, if Nikki had been a monster-truck-level wizard, she'd have flattened everyone within a quarter-mile radius.

Instead she'd honed her skills more quietly, particularly during her years as a beat cop in Chicago, well before she'd had the guts to move to Vegas and let her own star shine more brightly. Some police officers were Connected without even knowing it, the cop intuition that was so important to the job seeming to come to them naturally.

Nikki's intuition went a little farther. She'd always known she was different, of course—on multiple levels. But it was her ability to pick up the most recent memories of anyone she touched that had proven to be invaluable in questioning suspects and witnesses. It's where she'd also learned how easy it was for people to lie to themselves, bending the reality they'd seen to fit their world view.

Like the girl she'd just cozied up to, who had seen *something* not right in the street outside. It'd flashed to her left, barely catching her notice, a blur of black on shadow, moving too fast to seem natural. The way a young woman might be yanked off street and into an alley—only that couldn't be right, could it? That didn't happen in Vegas. The Strip was safe, everyone said so.

And so the college co-ed had hurried on with her clutch of her pals, leaving the question of who or what she'd seen in the alley to slip away into nothing.

Nikki heard the soft footfall on the sidewalk behind her, noticeable only because she was expecting it. She stopped. "You know, sugar lips, you're really starting to cramp my style."

"You're tracking someone. It's a skill I excel at."

Torsten melted out of the shadows, giving Nikki the opportunity to more fully appreciate the features and attributes of her newest tagalong. Rugged, towering, and rippling with muscle, Torsten was the defacto leader of the guardians of the Moon, which apparently made him Nikki's new number one fan. With his dark mane tumbling down to his neck, his flashing black eyes and sensuous mouth permanently set in a scowl, he was also so damned earnest about protecting her that she couldn't bring herself to send him off, even though he and his crew had plenty of work to do that didn't involve babysitting detail.

More problematic, even though she'd tangled with guys every bit as big and strong, Nikki admittedly felt a little out of her depth with Torsten. I mean, how exactly were you supposed to on-board a werewolf? Were there special HR manuals for that?

"Shouldn't you be back with the others trying to shake your family tree?" she asked him now, if only to cover her nerves.

The previous Moon had fled earth with only half her pack, way, *way* back in the day. Now that the Council member and her guardians had returned to the fold, one of the most important tasks they had was to see who—if anyone—was left of their former full guard.

Apparently, that task didn't rate with Torsten. "That will require researching six thousand years of history," he countered, reasonably enough. "It's not urgent. What you do is urgent. And my place is with you."

The flood of pride, possessiveness, and loyalty flowing from the guy was so strong that Nikki blinked hard, jostling one of her false eyelashes loose. It wasn't that she wasn't used to backup. She had *Sara*, after all. But Sweet Mother Mary on a *Tricycle*, the way Torsten stared at her made Nikki's heart shimmy like a showgirl on Seventies Night. His intense focus might eventually become a problem—but not yet, she decided. Definitely not yet.

"Okay, love chop, here's the deal," she said, her words a little more brusque than she intended. "A runner I'm interested in showed up at the back of the bar. Short, dark hair, thin."

"The female," Torsten confirmed, with such certainty Nikki leveled him a sharp glance.

"You saw her?"

"Of course. She looked like a thief, but she was too skinny to be a good one. She didn't make sense. Also, she had no pack."

Nikki smiled a little sadly. "There's a whole lot of people on this rock who don't, sweet pea. It's a problem. What else did you notice about her?"

"She was touched by the gift," he said, so nonchalantly that Nikki swiveled toward him.

"Whoa, whoa, whoa. How do you know that?"

Torsten raised a dark, heavy brow. "I told you, I'm a tracker. What good would a tracker be, if I couldn't tell when someone had been touched with magic?"

Nikki rolled her eyes. "What you don't know about this earth is too long to work out, but let me tell you, most folk who are touched with the gift don't know it, and sure as shit don't know how to use it. What about our girl? Turn here."

As she spoke, she gestured Torsten down the street where the corners matched the intersection she'd picked out of the college student's memory.

"Her gift...it's difficult to say if she knows its full strength,"

Torsten hedged. "She was mostly afraid. She should have been, given the three who tracked her."

Nikki's stomach plummeted. "She was being tracked."

Torsten nodded. "They didn't enter the bar with her, but their energy was all around her. So much so that I expected to sense her relief at reaching freedom, but that wasn't there. She appeared more disoriented, jostled by the crowd, and she fled again almost as soon as she arrived."

"And you didn't go after her?" Nikki asked, only to be on the receiving end of Torsten's silver-eyed censure.

"My place is with you," he said again. "Unless and until you send me elsewhere and even then—"

"Yeah, yeah, got it," Nikki said, waving him off. She peeked down the alley. It was disappointingly empty, but Torsten surprised her by moving down it anyway. He reached back and grabbed her hand, and Nikki jolted at his warm, vital touch. It unnerved her in a way she didn't want to explore too closely, but she let him tug her along down the dark street, his preternaturally soft voice drifting back to her.

"She's this way, and she's not alone. If it's a fight you want, Mistress Moon, you shall have it."

"She's hurt?" Nikki asked quickly, and Torsten's chuckle was low and grim.

"No. But she's about to be."

Chapter 2

THEY'D ONLY MOVED two blocks more, down the skinny alley and past a service courtyard, when Torsten slowed again. By now, Nikki could hear the voices too. Her neck prickled again, less a magical reaction than good old fashioned cop instincts kicking in.

"How many?" she asked.

"Three, beyond the girl," Torsten murmured. "Two men, one woman. Skilled, older. Mercenary. They know they have something, their excitement betrays that, but they don't know what. They want to hurt the young woman, torture her. They have a harsh mistress."

Nikki tightened her jaw. "Fucking Dixie," she muttered, her mind immediately jumping to the most likely asshole in charge of this hit, a woman who knew the Connected community like the back of her hand, and who had, once upon a time, been a friend to Nikki herself. But Dixie Quinn had fallen a long way from the days of her being the den mother of the Las Vegas Connected community, ready to welcome the skilled and the savvy into the rollicking world of the magical Vegas Strip. Now she was potentially one of the biggest problems the Connecteds faced on this earth. "If that's where this leads..."

She broke off as Torsten lifted a hand. They edged around the corner, and sure enough, a slender girl in beat-up, loose-fitting clothes stood in the center of three grown-assed adults. They were shoving her from one to the other, smacking her on the head and the shoulders, and when they spun her to the right, catching hold of her shirt to expose her belly, Nikki's hands balled into fists.

"Don't you *dare*," she whispered, the words little more than a thought. A flash of moonlight shot across the shadows, making the three adults jerk as the girl collapsed to the ground. Had she caused that? That'd be pretty cool.

"Is there a plan?" Torsten asked, but Nikki was already moving forward to draw the attention of the mercs.

"Right," she barely heard him mutter behind her. "So no plan."

"What the *fuck*?" The merc closest to Nikki whirled to face her as she strode up, his lip curling as he took in Nikki's outfit. Given his total sartorial fail of a way-too-pricey leather jacket, a Henley the color of sadness that stretched over his spark plug shaped belly, artfully battered jeans and scuffed high-end shit-kicker boots that he could in no way pull off as a fashion statement, he really needed to show more respect. Then again, haters gonna hate.

"You mind telling us why you're picking on a kid?" Nikki asked, noting the not so subtle shift in the trio toward their weapons—clunky box-like tools instead of guns or knives. She lifted one ring-bedecked finger. "You pull a weapon on me, ferret balls, I guarantee you're not going to get out of a cage for a very long time. And when folks inside find out you were abusing a kid, let's just say you're gonna wish you were dead."

"She's no kid," the black-clad woman spat, giving Nikki her first burst of useful information that she hadn't already figured out herself. A rush of heavy perfume followed hard on her words, strong enough to make Nikki's eyes water. "She looks like a kid, but she's obviously a *mutant*. Couldn't figure out how to grow up, huh?" the woman jeered, and Nikki's gaze jerked to the runner again.

There was no telling what the female merc was mocking specifically, or how well she actually knew the body that lay beneath the kid's loose, dark clothing, the rough-cut hair, the large bruised-looking eyes and sullen mouth, but Nikki didn't need to see the girl to know the heart inside. Even without touching her physically, she could feel her energy, her power, and her inherent goodness. And she thought she understood a little bit more about why these three mercenaries had come out to tango tonight with a kid who looked barely old enough to drive. They were being careful. They didn't have knives in their grips, after all. They didn't want to carve up the merchandise.

"Who are you working for?" Nikki demanded.

No answers were forthcoming, and Nikki sidled over, widening her stance. Like most of her gowns, this sequined masterpiece was equipped with a quick release waist that would leave her in tight shorts that were definitely Down To Fight—though she didn't much care to leave the beautiful material of her skirt decorating this shitty back alley. Still, the mercs weren't new at this game, which made Nikki all the more unhappy, because she didn't recognize them. Las Vegas was her turf, and protecting the Connected here had been sort of a sideline for her since her earliest days on the Strip. She'd gotten distracted of late, and she'd worried that that was going to come back to bite her in the ass. It looked like her concerns were valid.

"Okee doke. If you're self-employed, then you don't have any vested interest in this particular product, and I do." Nikki tracked Torsten moving around the perimeter of the courtyard in the opposite direction. The kid—and whether she was an adult or not, she definitely looked like a kid—slanted Nikki a new and resigned glance. This was someone who'd gotten used to not trusting anyone. It was a hard lesson to learn so early, but it would serve her well.

"Bullshit," the nearest man said, a thug in a two-hundred-dollar hoodie and thousand dollar jeans who somehow hadn't gotten the memo that Vegas was still hot AF at night in the summertime. "We've been tracking her for ten days."

"This little bitty thing?" Nikki mocked. "Now you're just making me feel cocky."

Despite Hoodie Guy's bravado, Leather Jacket Guy was the biggest problem, she decided, the most volatile, and the most amped. Nikki didn't know what he was on, but she suspected it wasn't just garden variety meth or even heroin. No, by the cut of their clothes and the quality of their tech, these mercs were well outfitted, all the way to their addictions. They were mainlining technoceuticals. Had to be.

The second before he moved, Leather Jacket Guy's gut twitched, which was a little easier to tell given how tight his Henley was. With a skill that Nikki had developed not on the streets of Vegas but flat-footing it through Chicago's worst neighborhoods, she struck.

Whether he was uniquely attuned to her or merely as good at fighting as he wanted her to believe he was, Torsten moved, too. Unfortunately, they both went for the biggest threat.

"Dammit!" Nikki could see in a flash that Torsten wasn't going to back down, and to be fair, he barreled into the heavyset man leading with his shoulder, aiming for Leather Jacket Guy's solar plexus. The result was quick and devastating, and the two of them went flying back in a flurry of fists and kicks. Torsten's impressive growl was punctuated by zap of electricity, and Nikki shuddered in solidarity even as she shifted direction to pile into Hoodie Guy, keeping Chanel No. 5 in her peripheral vision.

Torsten had been stuck in a hole for going on six thousand years, so he probably wasn't super familiar with getting tazed. Hopefully, he was a quick study.

Hoodie Guy sized up the situation with credible efficiency and didn't even bother putting up a fight with his fists. Instead, he brought up both hands, double pumping the electrical shock devices at Nikki. She'd anticipated that, which was the only reason why she was able to dance out of range in time, using her momentum to throw Perfume Girl into the stream of electricity.

Perfume Girl wasn't the only one in for a shock. These devices weren't Tasers, not exactly. The female merc lit up from the inside out, and she screamed with unholy outrage as something hot and white flared above her shoulder, a living spark of energy. In the brief instant that Nikki had laid hands on her, she'd figured out the woman's secret, only now her partner in crime knew it too.

"You've got the *gift*," he snarled, making it sound like a curse. "Stronger than that little bitch, I bet. You lied!" He lunged at the woman, who hauled up a huge arcane black-market blaster gun and leveled him. The merc didn't glow, he incinerated. A second later he was little more than an oily smoking smudge against the back wall.

The woman turned instantly to Nikki, only to be met with a roundhouse punch that knocked her out cold.

Nikki dropped her large hands to her legs, lungs bellowing as Torsten dragged the second unconscious merc to her side. Merc number three wouldn't be going anywhere ever again, and the girl was long gone.

"What the *fuck* was that about?" Torsten demanded, dumping Leather Guy beside the female, whose perfume was still kicking it even if she wasn't.

Nikki gave him a lopsided grin, tucking a red curl behind her ear. "Glad to see your language skills are coming along. You've got the kid lo-jacked?"

He blinked, then tilted his head and gave her a quick nod. "She's about two blocks away, not moving as fast as she should. She's been hurt pretty bad."

Nikki nodded, straightening her gown and scraping something questionable off the sole of her boot. "Then we shouldn't have any trouble tracking her down."

Chapter 3

"I DON'T KNOW what it is you think I'm going to be able to do here."

The detective who sat opposite Nikki at the Boomtown Deli scowled from her to the kid and back again, but Brody Rooks was full-on human, which Nikki figured was a good thing for keeping the young Connected woman stable. Nikki had deliberately kept Torsten out of direct contact with the girl. He was still outside, bringing in reinforcements, but she already had a plan worked out.

Now she returned her focus to Brody, one of LVMPD's finest, despite his perpetually battered faded brown suit and the suspicious-looking bruise that currently shadowed his jawline right along with the two-day-old beard. "You're a detective. You're assigned to special victims." She punched a finger at the young woman. "That's what she is."

"You're an idiot," the girl muttered. Swimming a little in her own oversized black jacket, her shoulders hunched forward to frame her ratty gray tank top, she stared across the table at nothing in particular, ignoring the food though her fingers twitched like quivering antennae toward the utensils. Nikki didn't want to think about how long it had been since the kid had last eaten, but there was no doubting that it'd been awhile.

"She should be with child services," Brody countered, slinging one arm over the back of the booth as he settled deeper in his seat. "I'm not a babysitter."

Nikki arched a brow. "You're not, but you used to be less of an asshole. More to the point, she's not as young as she looks, and she's your newest snitch."

It always did Nikki's heart good to watch a cop stiffen in surprise, and even more so to see the kid straighten up. She addressed the girl head-on for the first time.

"You shook those people for ten days, or at least that's what I picked up from you. How'd you pull that off? Brody here has already run their sheets. They're professionals, but not criminals, not in the usual sense. They got a system all their own. They hunt psychics."

The young woman didn't say anything. Nikki placed her age at early twenties, despite her slim build. She'd probably—no, she'd *definitely*—had a rough go of it her whole life, but she'd maybe not really dialed in to her Connected abilities until recently.

"When did your magic first show up?" Nikki asked, and the girl froze up. Nikki saw Torsten enter the diner. Their gazes connected and he immediately ushered his fellow pack member to the bar. Good man. Wolf. Whatever.

"I don't know what you're talking about," the girl answered sullenly, and Nikki waved a lazy hand.

"Oh, sure you do. I don't care how many shitheads you had to fight off growing up. You don't hold off three mercenaries with the skill set of these guys without having special abilities. And that kid I saw in your memories, the young teenager you saved from the dark room with the cage? That took balls *and* power, my friend. You've got magic, and a hell of a lot of it. How does it manifest? "

The girl remained staring at her food, but her energy had picked up, and Brody jumped in with his trademark good cop role. He hated playing "good cop", but sometimes a man had to stay in his lane. "Don't let her bully you," he said, rolling his eyes. "She gets on her high horse and it's hard to knock her off. You don't have Connected abilities? That's okay with me. Not everyone can read memories like Nikki here. She kind of corners the market on that."

The girl glanced toward Nikki without meeting her eyes. "That's bullshit."

"Hate to break it to you, kid—"

"Stop calling me that," the girl snapped. "My name's Sierra."

"Okay, Sierra, thanks for that. But my skill isn't bullshit. It's also not as useful as you might want it to be, because people tend to remember things somewhat differently than the way they really went down. For instance, you walking into my club a few hours ago? You locked eyes with a woman dressed like the Good Witch of the North and thought the place wasn't safe. Everyone scared you, but especially her. You picked up on her aura, and I gotta tell you, Glinda Wren's aura should be registered as a lethal weapon. She sensed you too, sensed your abilities, and you couldn't have that, so you split."

Now Sierra was staring at her, and Nikki winked. "Here's the thing, buttercup. Glinda wouldn't hurt a fly. She hits like a kitten, no matter how hard I try to teach her. If she'd bothered you, you'd have twisted her into a knot. And it's too bad she spooked you— you'd already shaken your tail when you slipped into the Flamingo. It was the wrong move to slip back out again."

"You're making all of that up. You're guessing."

"Let's just say for the sake of argument, she isn't," Brody put in, drawing the girl's attention back to him. "That doesn't change the fact that you had three professional operators on your ass, who we've now identified as seriously bad news, and you nearly got the jump on them. Would have gotten the jump on them except there was something about that courtyard you didn't plan on. What was it?"

"It wasn't the courtyard," the girl grumbled, grimacing. "I was stupid. They had a jammer. They were higher up on the food chain then I gave them credit for."

She finally sat back in a chair and picked up her coffee, taking a long draft. Nikki could see the hollows in her cheeks now, the bruising under her eyes.

But Sierra was apparently ready to spill. "I've been doing this for a while, running the streets, drawing off the worst mercenaries from their targets, until the targets could get to safety. I've gotten pretty good at it. Unfortunately, especially recently, it's gotten tougher."

Now Brody was starting to get interested, Nikki noted with satisfaction. As a special assignments detective with the LVMPD, he had a long history of working with the slightly off-kilter community of Las Vegas. He came by it honestly, having been tagged in his rookie year with a smart-mouthed Tarot-reading teenager back in Memphis, Tennessee—the same star-crossed teenager who'd grown up to become Sara Wilde. There'd been a lot of water under the psychic bridge since then, but Brody knew a thing or two about the Connected now, that's for sure. And he had his finger on the pulse of the arcane black market.

"Who?" he asked now. "Who were those mercs working for?"

Sierra lifted her coffee mug toward Nikki. "You mentioned a woman's name when you first hit the courtyard, but you're wrong. They're old guys. Brothers or cousins, some family shit like that. It's usually family with these people. They target kids, I mean who the fuck doesn't, but these guys are particularly interested in those who've just come into their powers, or who are right on the cusp. Like they're hunting them down, wanting to take them out of commission."

"Uh-huh," Nikki drawled. "And you just happen to show up in time to keep that from happening?"

Sierra smiled back, all teeth. "Something like that. Believe me, if I understood what was happening to me, I'd stop it. But I go to sleep every night—and when I wake up, I know in a hurry whether or not I've been tapped to help out someone being hunted. Mainly because I wake up somewhere different. After that, it doesn't take long. Maybe I have time to find a bathroom and a cup of coffee, maybe not, but then I'm off again, hunting. It's not all that hard. When these kids go through the change, it's obvious to anyone with eyes to see. All you gotta do is look."

Nikki smelled bullshit, but she wasn't sure what part of the girl's story wasn't tracking.

"You're summoned," she clarified, "but you don't know by whom? Like, are you some kind of guardian angel?"

The kid snorted, but something in her expression shifted, a flinch she probably didn't know she revealed. "If I am, I'm the runt of the litter. All I know is that I go to where the trouble is, whenever and wherever it calls. Once I'm there, I do what I can to help."

Nikki peered at her more closely. Still no mention of her working for someone, but *someone* was paying the bills for this girl, even if not very well. "When's the last time that you got a full night of sleep?"

"Who knows?" the girl shrugged. "When you show up in different time zones every day, everything starts to blur together. The only way I know for sure where I am is through my cell phone. And even that isn't foolproof if the networks don't recognize it right away. But, you do what you can."

"Uh huh." Nikki lifted a brow. "Well at least that explains why you're not all that concerned about getting flagged by Brody here. You don't think you'll be around for long."

The girl smiled wearily. "Probably just as long as it takes me to fall asleep," she agreed.

"Well, I'm not gonna fight with you," Brody said abruptly, surprising Nikki. He had his hand in his pockets, jingling his keys with an odd metallic clatter. "I'd like you to put my number in your phone, though. That's it. Any help you can give me, anything you see in the city while you're here, I'd appreciate. You've got skills, you've obviously got Connected ability, and you're used to working alone. I can respect that. But I'm up to my ass in hunted Connected, and I don't have your skills or your ability."

She flipped him a glance. "You have some. Not a lot, but some. Most cops do, whether they're crooked or straight." Fair assessment, Nikki thought, but Sierra seemed to otherwise buy the line of bullshit Brody was selling her. She leaned forward and pulled her phone out, setting it on the table. She swept it on and pivoted it toward him. "Program it in."

She watched him closely as he keyed the number in, but he did nothing but punch the digits and push it back toward her. "Call me or don't. But I promise I'll pick up if you do."

Nikki put on her best judgmental frown. "I'm not feeling as good about this exchange as you two apparently are," she said, but the girl edged forward in her seat, finally willing to eat. Excellent.

Nikki and Brody exchange a glance, and she scooted out of the booth. "Take it easy, Sierra." She stood, extending her hand to Brody. He shook it, barely able to hide the roll of his eyes, while Nikki grinned at him as his most recent memories filled her mind.

"That's it?" Sierra asked, around a mouthful of waffle. "You're done with me?"

"Not hardly." Nikki winked. "In fact, while I'm here, lemme make a couple of introductions." She waved over Torsten, along with the tall, angular warrior he'd brought in with him. A female, Nikki noticed with satisfaction. The woman strode over easily as both Brody and Sierra looked up—and the girl froze.

"What *are* you?" she blurted, then blushed hard. "Oh my God. I'm sorry."

"Don't be," the female warrior shook her head, her silver eyes narrowing. "Your senses don't deceive you. I'm different, and I work hard to ensure people know it. That works better for me. My name is Magritte." She held out her broad hand to Sierra, who took it, her eyes widening in undeniable alarm as she straightened.

"No, you don't understand," she looked around furtively. "You're the real deal. They'll figure that out—my tracker is going berserk. You've got to get out of here."

She reached into her jacket and pulled out what looked like a fancy metal tire gauge. The compass-like dial at its tip was spinning crazily, jerking back and forth between Torsten and Magritte as Sierra started speaking fast.

"When I'm sent to—I mean when I'm summoned to help a Connected, it's only half to get them out of danger from whoever is hunting them. I get a finders' fee for anything that trips this trigger. It's only happened a couple times before this week, but the monitor has been going bananas since I showed up in Vegas a few days ago.

I assumed the thing was broken, but it's pretty much on the verge of exploding now. You have to get out of here. The guys I work for, I don't lie to them. I can't. It's important. So I'm going to have to report you sooner or later."

"Well, then, things are already looking up," Magritte said with a smile. "Maybe you can tell us a little of what we need to watch out for?"

Torsten stiffened, then glanced toward the door of the deli. "Someone's here for you," he said to Nikki. "A car just drove up, and the driver has you on his mind."

Nikki chuckled, but she wasn't surprised. "If I had a dollar for every time that happened," she cracked, glancing over to Brody. "Mind if I step out for a second?"

"Take your time. We'll get Magritte and Sierra acquainted," he said, pointedly ignoring the girl's phone that still sat on the deli table as he met Nikki's gaze. Detective Delish had an in with the Arcana Council when it came to tech. He'd done something to Sierra's phone, no doubt about it…Nikki just didn't know what. Hopefully it would be enough to keep eyes on her.

She'd have to trust him on that score—she had other mackerel to fry it looked like. She swung back to Torsten. "Alrighty, sweet lips, we've been tagged. Let's go make a deal with the Devil."

Chapter 4

THE LIMOUSINE WAITING for them on Las Vegas Boulevard was a long gray SUV as big as an Airstream, making Nikki grin. "Well, looks like we rate a party bus. I approve."

The door swung open as they approached, though there appeared to be no one in the front of the vehicle driving. Torsten made an almost instinctive move to block her at the last second, but she slid into the limo without batting an eye. "Don't you worry your pretty little head," she said, patting the seat beside her. "I get the feeling this is gonna be an amusement park ride to nowhere."

"I didn't see the need to waste your time,"

With those laconic words, one figure appeared in the front of the SUV, while another materialized in the bench seat opposite them, sprawling in leisure as the vehicle pulled away from the curb. The fact that both figures appeared to be the same man only deepened Nikki's amusement.

"I've always known that two Devils were better than one."

Aleksander Kreios nodded at her, then his attention fixed fully on Torsten, who hissed in feral warning between his teeth. "The former Moon held you in Atlantis for six thousand years," Kreios said. "Did she ever talk to you about her responsibilities to the Arcana Council?"

Nikki could sense the anger simmering off Torsten. "She had no responsibilities to your Council," he growled. "And I don't answer to you."

"Technically true," the Devil agreed, equitably enough. "You answer to the Moon, who is now Nikki. The Moon is not merely a goddess, however, she's a critical member of the Arcana Council. A Council I now run. With me so far?"

Torsten rumbled, and the Devil smiled, all teeth. "Good. Our job here is to keep magic from going off the rails, and that job has become appreciably more difficult of late. We set out looking for the Moon to help us with that."

"You didn't find her," Torsten retorted, his big hands balling into fists. "You killed her. Only Nikki attempted to defend Celestine against her enemies, and she nearly died as well while you all stood by and *watched*."

Nikki thought for a second about calling the wolf off, but the Devil seemed to be holding his own. He leaned forward, fixing Torsten with a hard glare.

"Celestine left half her pack behind, Torsten. She left them to survive on their own in an uncertain world, and then *abandoned* them for six thousand years while she hid from her responsibilities. Do you deny it?"

"I don't." Torsten curled a lip, baring teeth that were elongating into fangs. "She fled from your precious Arcana Council and your approach to managing magic. She disagreed with you. That doesn't make her wrong."

"No. It only makes her weak," Kreios countered, making Nikki blink. "And we don't have time for weakness. There are certain matters that the new Moon is going to have to take on right away, to protect the greater Connected good. I'm trying to figure out how helpful you will be to that process, or if you will just remain a pain in the ass."

"You have no dominion over me," Torsten insisted, but the Devil cut him off with a sharp wave.

"I don't, in point of fact," he said, his voice a low and dangerous purr. "If you choose to serve Nikki, however, if any of your pack remain allied with her, that dominion is something you're going to have to accept."

Torsten slanted Nikki a dubious glance. "You're bound to him?"

"Only when I'm very, very lucky," Nikki returned, not missing the flare of possessiveness that sparked in Torsten's eyes, or the glint of amusement in the Devil's.

"But here's the skinny, hot stuff," she continued. "I'm brand spanking new to the job, and we're in a shit pile of trouble. I need your help, and that means that what the Devil here says, goes. I can't be worried about you running rogue if I'm on an assignment and I need you to step up."

Torsten bristled. "Of course I will always serve you. The entire pack is dedicated to you. We have remained the constant guardians of the Moon for six millennia."

"Then, arguably, you might be ready for a break," the Devil pointed out, and if he was looking to needle Torsten, he succeeded.

"*Never*," the wolf snapped, his tone steel-sharp. "The Moon suffered greatly when she left Earth for Atlantis. She found safety there, solace, but she was never quite the same. That said, we remembered the wars. We remembered what it was to fight for our right to exist. We continued to train, and it didn't take long for others to come to Atlantis. A host of angels and their equal and opposite shadows, demons from the upper realms. Their war was constant, and should we ever feel the need to do battle, they would turn on us with equal ferocity if we poked them hard enough. Trust me, we had plenty of opportunities to sharpen our skills."

He raised his hand to forestall the Devil's next question. "But you don't want to know if we can fight, you want to know if we can listen. We are pledged to the Moon, once and ever more. We will honor that pledge. If your order is her bond, then we will follow you, unless she is at risk."

Nikki pulled a face. "Hold up there, Sparky. You may not have all the information you need when you make your call on what's a threat to me. I can assure you, it's far less than you think."

To her surprise though, Kreios waved off the concern, his smile deeply satisfied.

"I accept your terms, Torsten. I also accept the fealty of your pack within the constraints of Nikki's safety as you see it. Your link to her will help protect her, and we are entering dangerous times. In fact, we need more of the protection that you and your kind can offer the Connected of this world—and we need it in the open. Nikki tells me you have a hundred-odd wolves that remained here on earth when Celestine fled to Atlantis. Where are they?."

"Nowhere," Torsten said. "We've sensed none of our kind since we've returned."

"And that surprises you."

Torsten scowled. "Yes. Celestine spoke often of the pack she had left behind, insisting that the warriors she'd called to her we're only half her domain. The other half she had left to their fates, as you say. The guilt she carried for that was strong, but she believed they remained behind. She always believed that."

Nikki frowned. She'd gotten distracted with Torsten's reference to the Moon's power. She'd been on the job barely a week, but she still didn't have a sense of how her own abilities were going to evolve. She'd just assumed it would be obvious, but clearly she needed to ask her second-in-command about them. For now, though, something else caught her attention.

"Half her domain? How many wolves did she bring to Atlantis?"

"Two hundred," Torsten said. "Ours is not a race that evolves the way humans do, or even wolves. We are, we were, constructs of magic born in fire and smoke. The original 400 split off into various packs, two hundred traveling with the Moon, and two hundred remaining on Earth. Over time, our numbers dwindled to one hundred in Atlantis, but we believed—we'd always thought there were others who remained on earth."

Nikki grimaced. "And you haven't been able to find any of them so far."

"We haven't," Torsten said heavily. "When the demons arrived in Atlantis a generation after we did, the angels following behind them, they carried tales of the world to us. Your Arcana Council had driven all those with Connected abilities into hiding for their own safety. Those who didn't hide were, more often than not, killed by the ordinary humans who didn't accept them. We discounted the stories from the demons, but when the angels spoke of the same, the Moon wept."

"She wept," Nikki said drily, unable to keep the sarcasm from her voice. "It didn't occur to her that she might have done more for her people if she hauled her own ass out of Atlantis and helped them a little bit more directly?"

"Her tears were truly a sight to behold," Torsten continued steadily, and Nikki glanced at him. His face had gone a little slack, his eyes unfocusing, and she drifted her hand to his meaty bicep, laying the gentlest finger on it.

Through the contact, she could see what he saw: Celestine, her predecessor Moon, with long white blonde hair spread over her shoulders, and her perfect, petite hands cupped into a bowl. She wept into those palms, and as the tears overflowed, they poured in silver streams into a mist-shrouded well.

"She said her tears would reach the pack, but that we could never travel through that portal. We would die in the transfer, unless she was with us."

Kreios regarded him steadily. "Yet she never left Atlantis, not once in all that time?"

Torsten shook his head. "Celestine lived as a goddess, and we remained to protect her. She sang and drifted through starlight, muddling the skies. And when she slept, Atlantis was dark and full of danger. We had our hands full. "

"For six thousand years," Nikki deadpanned. "She never got bored."

Torsten flashed her a weary smile. "Perhaps immortality will teach you patience, as well."

"Yeah. Don't hold your breath."

"We *have* found a few possibilities of living pack members, based on some renewed searching we have undertaken," Kreios began, and Torsten stiffened.

"That's not possible," he insisted. "We would sense our own. They are not here."

"Perhaps," The Devil allowed easily. "But given the tracker that young Sierra was carrying, it appears that *someone* is looking for werewolves—and they apparently are about to find you. Wouldn't it be handier if we found them first? Or, at the least, arrange the meet-up according to *our* terms?"

A slow smile spread across Torsten's face. "I understand what you're saying," he allowed. "And I think your suggestion is sound."

"Good." The Devil leaned forward. "Then this is what we're going to do."

Chapter 5

"I DON'T LIKE this plan at all. In fact, your plan totally sucks. It's stupid."

With this declaration, Sierra shoved her hands in her pockets and scowled at the newest addition to their crew at the deli, a tall, gangly man with a mop of curly black hair barely constrained by his Where's Waldo style knit cap. With his long-sleeved-t-shirt-covered elbows on the table, his fingers fluttering, Simon hunkered over her werewolf-sensitive tire gauge with undeniable fascination.

He paid no attention to Sierra, who huffed out a breath in frustration. "How about I tell my clients that I ran into you, and that something about you set the gauge spinning, but that you left after that and I don't know where you went. That's much better. You don't want to mess with these guys."

"You do, though," Nikki pointed out. "You mess with them on a regular basis."

"That's different," Sierra insisted, pushing her inky dark hair out of her face. "I get to help people who need it, people I was going to be pulled in to help anyway. My clients pay me for my time, and they never seem pissed off when I can't find their magical

MacGuffins. But when I do find them—I don't know what they do to them."

To Nikki's ear, Sierra didn't sound worried about the plight of the souls she turned over to her employers, so much as indignant. Interesting. But Sierra jolted as Simon turned the gauge upside down, then scowled at him. "Hey, be careful with that. It's the only one I have, and if it breaks—"

"I'm not gonna break it," Simon assured her. He peered more closely at the device. "There is definitely something hinky with this design. The external structure is nickel plating. But this face here, it's some kind of a radiated silver, like a tuning fork set inside of a compass. I don't think it's meant to ping off a particular person, just to go haywire when one's in the vicinity. Which is a little questionable, if Sierra's job here is to track down people."

Simon the Fool was the gearhead of the Arcana Council, and there was no gadget on the planet that he couldn't figure out with enough time. Unfortunately, they didn't have a lot of time right now, not if Sierra might get sucked out on another Connected-finding adventure at any moment, a Connected who may or may not also be a werewolf.

"They don't really care about the Connecteds I help," Sierra said, shrugging. "They only want to know when this thing goes off."

"Which they'd know automatically," Simon said. "This thing trips, there's no *way* it isn't connected to some sort of receiver on their end."

Brody turned toward Sierra. "If that's the case, what do they need you for?" he asked, reasonably enough.

"To confirm the identification," she said grimly. "If it goes off, it's still got a margin for error. Certain kinds of Connecteds trip it up. Illusion magic can do it, and so do Connecteds with a lot of anger on board."

"Anger?" Brody asked. "That's a Connected skill?"

"Like a wilding rage, I bet," Simon said, his head coming up as his eyes fixed on Sierra again. "That's what you're talking about, yeah? People who get so angry it affects the people around them, causing their attackers to back off from the rage?"

Nikki watched Torsten's scowl deepen as Sierra nodded.

"Exactly like that. Doesn't usually happen with the kind of folks I go after, but it has happened. Particularly if they're, like, teenage guys who feel cornered. But sometimes girls too, though almost always teenagers. The older a Connected on the run is, the more they're able to police their emotions. But not the kids."

Nikki grimaced at the irony of Sierra's words. She was barely more than a kid herself, but Nikki knew she didn't feel that way. She'd probably seen enough pain for a lifetime. Unwanted, the image of the girl in a cage Sierra had saved flitted through Nikki's mind. She'd definitely seen too much pain for someone so young.

"The rage business means something to you?" She asked Torsten, but his gaze remain fixed on the tire gauge, and Nikki peered back at Sierra. "How long after you make contact do they respond? And what usually happens?"

Sierra shrugged. "Honestly, I've only had to do this part a couple of times before, and it didn't end well. My runner barely hung in there long enough to get tagged by Romero's agent, and I didn't see him again after I left the bar. The agent gave me a new gauge, which made me think that the one I had was faulty, but he never said a word to me."

"Interesting." Nikki didn't need to glance at Simon to know he'd picked up on the girl's slip. So the family who hired her was named Romero. Common enough name, but it was a place to start. "You got a name on that runner?"

"Gabriel Finch," Sierra supplied, and Simon cocked his head, clearly memorizing that name as well. "It was maybe two weeks ago, in a redneck town outside of DC. I didn't hear about it again, even though I scanned the news looking for a mention of him."

"Why do you do that?"

"Just a bad feeling." Sierra sighed. "It's just—like the energy is shifting. But that time like every time before, my account gets a cash deposit simultaneously, every time I alert them of a potential hit, whether it pans out or not. It's not like I see anyone from the family, usually."

"Usually," she murmured, and the way Sierra flinched, she knew she was on to something. "What does the family really want from you, Sierra?"

"I don't know," Sierra muttered, her face shuttering. "And I don't care. Their money keeps me going as I help people, and whenever I find the people they're looking for, that's just more cash for me to survive." She pointed to Torsten. "You should get out of here before I have to report your whereabouts. Because believe you, me, I'm going to confirm that you're worth them checking out."

"Ordinarily, I'd suggest that be a shitty idea," Nikki commented. "But what the hell. We can keep you safe, and frankly we need you as bait."

The girl's lip curled. "I think you've got our roles a little confused."

"Not even a little bit," Nikki said. "Are you going to get in trouble if we know they're coming? Will they know that you've talked to us?"

Sierra shrugged one narrow shoulder. "They never told me not to tell the marks of their interest. And they would have. They're as arrogant as you people are, it looks like."

"Excellent," Nikki grinned. "Make the call and let them know you have a live one. This will be fun!"

"You people are freaks." Sierra took out her cell phone and keyed in a number. When the line picked up, a soft series of chimes rang. She waited it out, grimacing as the voice came on the line. It was a cold, feral-sounding female. "Press One for routine drop. Two for discovery. Three for assistance."

Sierra reached out and stabbed the number 2. There was a brief pause and then the recording continued. "You'll receive a text." The transmission was broken and her phone buzzed simultaneously. As the Fool leaned close, she swiped to her text screen.

"Blackjack Bills?" Simon asked as Nikki made a face.

"That place is a shithole," she groaned, while Brody grunted in agreement.

Sierra recovered her phone and studied the screen. "Well, it's also the rendezvous point. The game is, I'm supposed to ask you to go there with me, promise you money, safety, a getaway vehicle, or whatever I think will get you there. The Romeros never actually seemed to care. I got the impression that they'd know everything they needed to just by talking to me."

Torsten blew out of breath. "Then we go to this Blackjack Bills, and we wait?"

Sierra just waved helplessly, and Simon blew out a long breath. "There's no way it's going to be this easy," he said.

"In that I agree with you," Torsten grimaced. "This is quite clearly a trap."

"Excellent." Nikki stood, clapping her hands together. "Then let's go spring it—right after I freshen up."

Chapter 6

"YOU SURE DO you know how to pick your shitholes," Nikki observed, while Sierra shifted on her bench seat, rolling the glass bottle of Mexican beer in her hand.

"I don't have a good feeling about this place, either, if that's any consolation."

Nikki nodded, flicking a dust mote off her black long-sleeved shirt. She'd gone full-on SWAT black, with a jaunty camo patterned scarf at the neck, and steel-toed boots that were dying to get a stomp on. Sierra still looked like she'd stolen her clothes from the homeless, but Nikki would have time to work on the girl's wardrobe later.

"You got anything on our flown finch?" she subvocalized to Simon, holed up in some command vehicle with Brody, well away from the bar.

"I'm working on it, but nothing yet," Simon returned. Not helpful.

The doors opened, emitting a rush of cool air and the sound of motorcycles. Nikki looked up as a trio of thugs entered the bar, noted the parade of slapping shoulders, the familiar calling out of long-time regulars. Then she felt the thugs' gaze settle on her, and shift to Sierra.

"I don't suppose…"

Sierra snorted. "Let me tell you, you'll know the Romeros or any of their pack when you see them. They're about eighty-seven rungs higher on the social ladder than these guys. But these guys are probably going to be trouble. They seem a little…angry."

"Probably," Nikki agreed.

The men justified Sierra's suspicions a moment later as one of them blustered up and stopped right in front of them, his heavy fists dropped onto the table, making their drinks jump. The man leaned toward Nikki, whiskey on his breath.

"You're new," he mouth-breathed onto her, and she lifted a brow.

"Just passing through," she assured him. "You seem to be a regular. I can see why. It's a nice place."

The guy narrowed his bleary eyes on her, but before he could say anything further, the door opened again and Torsten, Magritte, and a third wolf Nikki had only met briefly entered the bar. They were dressed tough, decked out in their Harley gear that they'd somehow managed to scuff up enough so they didn't look like they were fresh off the assembly line. But they still were nowhere near as weathered as the majority of the bar.

"Gordy," voice spoke from the darkness, and the bruiser in front of Nikki turned.

"Yeah, yeah," he muttered. But before he left he swung back to Nikki.

"We don't *like* your kind in here," he muttered to her, and she gave him a wide smile.

"I promise you, sunshine, the feeling is mutual. I won't be staying long."

She watched Gordy as he swung away to join his cronies at the other table, picking up on the tightening energy. A quick glance around the bar didn't yield any more answers.

"You see your contacts?" she asked Sierra, whose hand had tightened on the bottle of beer so hard it now shook in her hand.

"I don't," she muttered. "And it's been too long. These guys don't wait. They come in, they assess, they leave. But it's only happened twice so maybe——"

"Let's see what you got," one of the men at the bar shouted out of nowhere, and he slapped his hand down on the counter and rose. Nikki tensed instantly. The shirt that stretched over the man's shoulders was a deep blue Tom Ford, the pants were dark red Versace. He turned, and his preternaturally beautiful face creased into a smile. Sierra stared at him, transfixed, but not with recognition, Nikki thought. Or not quite recognition.

The man tossed a coin up in the air.

Feeling suddenly caught in some kind of heavy thrall, Nikki stared at the coin flipping end over end, everything going still around her as her eyes tracked the shimmering bright flash of silver. It spun around once…twice…

Chaos broke out.

Half the bar burst out of their seats, lunging not at Nikki and Sierra, but at the three members of her pack who'd barely cleared the door. In that same moment, her guardians leapt forward, more than happy to pile into their nearest attackers. This wasn't at all what the plan had been, but Nikki figured she'd roll with it.

Sierra sprang away from the bar, but Nikki circled her wrist with a vice grip. When she did, she got a flash of other men, different men—attractive beyond reason, well-dressed, hard eyes.

"Wait, you *know* Versace Guy? He's one of these Romeros or whatever?" But the girl shook her head violently, and when her gaze connected with Nikki's, her eyes were fully dilated and practically spinning with fear.

"I've got to go, I've got to——"

She yanked hard, and Nikki saw a new, far more terrifying vision. "I have to *go!*" Sierra cried again, and then she was gone—disappearing into the shadows.

"Shit!" Right before their hands had parted, Nikki'd gotten just a quick glimpse of what the girl had seen, barely registering it as it passed into her short-term memory. Teenagers in decent clothes—looking haggard but not abandoned or abused—huddled in front of a fire, some kind of burned-out building sparking behind them. And two groups with guns rushing in from either side to attack them.

And that was it. That was all Sierra apparently had to go on, before getting sucked into another fight not her own.

Unfortunately, Nikki couldn't go after her, or at least not yet. She had her own fight to manage.

She jerked back in surprise as the original thug, Gordy, crashed into her table, half landing in her lap.

"You!" he screamed, spit flying. He reached for her as if to choke her, which was all the invitation Nikki needed.

Throwing up her left arm to block his lunge, Nikki delivered a powerful right hook to the man's prodigious belly. The satisfying rush of air he expelled made her grin, her pleasure diminishing slightly when she fully registered the stench of rotting meat and rancid cheese that accompanied it.

"Bless your dumb ass, you have some serious health issues you need to look into, Gordy, assuming you walk out of here on your own two feet," Nikki advised, cracking him hard against the jaw has he tried to regain his feet. He groaned and tumbled onto a seat, sprawling backward. "Trust me when I tell you that you do not want to get up again, not while I'm here."

"Fucking freak," Gordy managed, fumbling to right himself and take another swing.

"Well, now you're just hurting my feelings," Nikki deadpanned before delivering a punch across Gordy's temple strong enough to send him over the other side of the table and crashing into the far chairs. She looked up to see Torsten wheel around abruptly, his apparent attempt to help her having been deemed unnecessary at the last second. Good. He was starting to become a pain in the ass about that.

Nikki straightened and peered around the room. The Versace-clad bar patron remained pressed back against the bar, just out of the fray, his eyes focused sharply on a certain sector of the fight.

Nikki didn't need a road map to find what had attracted his attention. A full half of the bar appeared to be fighting just for the sheer hell of knocking each other around, but the other half were piling on the three members of her pack. Torsten, Magritte and a young wolf she believed was named Rogan were making a fight of it —but as much as Nikki enjoyed letting them get their exercise, enough was enough.

Brushing off her black tactical pants, Nikki ducked another punch, kicking the asshole to the side as she made her way to the bar. Versace Bob seemed so entranced with the fight, she thought he didn't see her at first, but at the last minute he turned so quickly that she almost lost sight of him, his right elbow jutting out, clearly angling for her throat.

Nikki jerked back and down, then piled her shoulder into the guy's chest, driving him off the edge of the bar and into the stools.

"You know, that's just not neighborly," she began to chide him, but before she could get the words out fully, she had to flinch again, as with an inarticulate roar, the man rushed her.

Sweet *Christmas*, he could move.

It was like getting hit by a linebacker, and even for somebody of Nikki's size, it was way more than she could handle. She went flying backwards, reaching out at the last minute to haul the guy with her, using his momentum to roll them halfway across the room, the sound of rattling change dimly registering in her mind as she clamped down hard on his bare wrist.

The scream of memories—years, decades, *generations* worth— was so intense it nearly blinded Nikki, and her moment of hesitation was all the guy needed. He flung back a closed fist, cracking it against her jaw, sending her spinning. By the time she righted herself, it was too late. The man was gone, though the fight continued on around her.

"Nikki!" Torsten was at her side, his roar incomprehensible as he lifted her to her feet, grunting with exasperation as she twisted away to grab for the prize that Versace Bob had left behind.

"What were you *thinking*?" Torsten demanded, sweeping her up into his arms as she blinked at him bleary-eyed, her tongue probing the slightly loose teeth in her jaw.

"Y'know, you go' some kind of hero complex, don' you," Nikki began, then her mind cleared just enough for her words to sharpen to a snap. "You left the *others*?"

"They're fine," he grunted, tightening his hold around her as he stomped towards the door. "They'll fight until we get free and then this will be done."

"But how do y'—" Nikki's head lolled against Torsten's broad shoulder as he hustled her out of the bar. He had a very nice shoulder, it had to be said.

The night was surprisingly quiet this far out of Vegas, without even the fleeing tail lights of Versace Bob breaking the night. Where did he go, anyway?

Nikki stared down the empty stretch of highway, half-imagining that she saw them. "You get a load of the guy at the bar?" she asked, squinting as Torsten paced up and down in front of her, muttering to himself like a caged, well, wolf. "Shouldn't you get back in there and help them fight?"

"They're done," he grunted. "It wasn't a fair fight. Humans are smaller than we remember."

He huffed a laugh, but his attention wasn't on her. She was still feeling a half step too slow, and when he nodded as if to himself, that clinched it.

"Are you talking to them?" she demanded. "Like in their minds?"

He glanced at her. "Of course. All guardians have that ability, just as you do."

Nikki grunted a laugh, pushing her fall of auburn hair off her shoulder. She should have gone with the blonde, she decided a little woozily. "Not exactly, honey fangs. Full Moon abilities didn't convey with the sale. But maybe eventually, yeah?"

Torsten frowned then his gaze drifted up. "The moon isn't full," he murmured.

"Far from it," Nikki agreed, peering upward, still trying to get her bearings. "But while we're on the subject, what other psychic abilities do you have that I should know about?"

He turned to her more fully now, frowning in earnest this time. "You don't know?" he demanded, and then he shook his head. "It doesn't matter. You are new to the role, but you were made for it. I and my pack are proud to serve you."

"Well, that's good to know," Nikki tried to give him a winning smile, then winced in pain. She lifted her bunched-up hand, intending to test her jaw with it, to see how badly she'd been cracked, then realized she was still holding something. She narrowed her eyes in confusion as she uncurled her fingers, but she wasn't prepared for the sharp huff of surprise from Torsten as he leapt toward her, knocking her prize out of her hand.

"Where did you get that?" he demanded, before stooping down to pick it up himself. In his grip it burned bright silver, and Nikki squinted at it.

"Um...the floor?" she hazarded, her mind going a little fuzzy. "Why'd you *hit* me, you overgrown stuffie? Why's everyone trying to hit me tonight?"

Torsten blinked hard at her, looking lost, then shook his head. "I'm sorry. It's just... " he held up the coin. "These were made by Celestine's tears, the gift she fashioned from her own sorrow. She intended them for the pack she could not take with her. Each coin was purest silver, which could cause grave danger to my kind if it were to pierce our skin, but was still the highest grade of metal she could produce to help her guardians survive without her."

He spoke with a hushed wonder, and Nikki frowned at the coin.

"What's the big deal about it then?" she asked, her words still a little slurred. "It just looks like a fancy coin."

"It's a coin only a few can lay claim to, unless their magic is very strong," Torsten said. "That man in the bar who dropped it? He was a werewolf."

Chapter 7

SIMON SAT BACK from the conference table at the Arcana Council's headquarters above the Luxor Casino. He held the silver disk up to the light, grinning like, well, a Fool.

"Your wolf man is right, this is high quality silver. And it's a coin that was minted before we were using silver regularly in commerce, which was maybe three or four thousand B.C.E." Simon said, rolling the disk in his fingers. The crescent moon image stamped into one side flashed to become a full moon on the other, so the effect of him running it through his fingers created an illusion of a waxing and waning moon.

"How in the hell did we not know of the existence of these things before? Have you ever seen anything like it?"

Nikki addressed her question to the two figures at the top of the table, the Devil dressed more typically in his Mediterranean playboy attire of choice, a long linen shirt and slightly baggy trousers, cut off with a ragged hem that fell just above his scuffed sandals. But it was a different Council member who answered her, his eyes glittering black and gold as he watched the Fool twirl the silver disk.

"There is very little that we haven't seen, Miss Dawes," Armaeus

Bertrand said quietly. "The question was merely identifying the provenance. I confess this was not a provenance I had considered."

The Magician of the Arcana Council was dressed in his most preferred attire as well: Billionaire financier, all ten-thousand-dollar dark blue suit and crisp white button-down, platinum gold at his cuffs and neck, and leather loafers that Nikki suspected played angel's choruses when he walked. He drifted his hand over the table, causing a small wooden box to appear with a latch that sprang open after he made another gesture. Inside the box lay six silver disks identical to the one that Simon had. "Admittedly, coins created from the tears of a goddess would have improved their resale value a great deal, but they weren't cheap to begin with."

"*Excellent*," Simon crowed, tossing Sierra's coin to Armaeus even as the Magician slid the box his way. Simon picked up one of the other coins, peering at them closely.

"These are *exactly* the same," he said, sounding slightly awed. "You'd need a numismatic guide to say for sure, but—"

"But these coins are identical to each other," Armaeus finished for him. "Pristine, in fact, showing none of the wear that you would expect from currency, even currency that was minted for the sole purpose of display and not commercial use. The fact that these coins have lasted as long as they have, six thousand years according to carbon dating, and have gone through as many hands as they doubtless have, or coffers, storage containers, pockets or bags of gold, they should have picked up normal wear and tear, but there's none. Not on this coin," he held up the one Simon had given him. "Or the others. Which begs a very important question."

Nikki had already gotten there. "Why did Versace Boy leave it behind?"

The Magician cocked an elegant brow at her, and she bowed modestly. "I didn't just fall off the glitter van yesterday, Crumpet," she said. "He wanted to drop it, he wanted me to pick it up. He arguably would have been detained by Torsten if he'd made another grab for it, but he easily could have been waiting for me outside and put a hurting on both of us if he'd wanted to snatch the thing back. So what do you figure? They've got some kind of tracker magic on it?"

"If so, he's discovered his mistake by now." The Magician raised his shoulder in an elegant shrug. "As a member of the Arcana Council, Miss Dawes, it takes a very special kind of technology to track you. Technology that for all their vaunted abilities, the Shadow Court does not possess, at least not yet."

Nikki made a face. If the Arcana Council's M-O was to ensure that magic stayed balanced and hidden away, the Shadow Court had an equal and opposite mission: all the power funneled to the magical elite, and may the whole damned world know about them. Though the Arcana Council had blocked the Shadow Court's bid for global domination so far, their adversaries had become a total pain in the ass, and showed no signs of letting up. "You think that's how these Romeros swing? Torsten thinks the guy with the coin was a werewolf."

The Magician grimaced, but before he could speak, Kreios huffed a droll laugh.

"It *is* possible, Armaeus," he pointed out. "You can't see what you don't look for, and we haven't been looking for shifters who are not human hybrids. But Nikki's pack are clearly not hybrids. They are creatures unto themselves."

"Which means that they are made of magic," the Magician countered. "Magic is my domain, last I checked."

"Yes, *and* they were created at the dawn of the council by a member of the Arcana Council," the Devil argued right back. "Celestine's abilities certainly went above and beyond. Regardless of the wear of time on her soul, when she formed these creatures and then left them, it's reasonable that she would have put protections in place to keep them safe, even—*especially*—from a newly created Council that she did not trust."

"So where did you get these?" Nikki asked, gesturing to the silver coins in Armaeus's velvet lined box. "Seems to me, when you track down who has them, you can determine whether or not they ping your human radar, yeah?"

"A reasonable approach," the Magician agreed. "Unfortunately, most of these coins came from, shall we say, anonymous or perhaps worse, recently deceased sources. And I've been collecting them for the past eight hundred years."

"Deceased," Simon mused, looking up for the first time from his study of the coins. "Why did I think that werewolves couldn't die?"

"You're thinking vampires," Nikki told him, but he shook his head.

"I mean, they're super strong right?" he said, casting his gaze skyward as if trying to recall the werewolf Wikipedia entry. "They're fast, tough, and they heal, like, right now. Other than silver bullets, I didn't think anything ordinary could stop them."

"At least these six were stopped by something," Armaeus offered drily. "Though I tend to agree with Nikki, this seventh token was left behind quite deliberately. And while it failed in its likely intended purpose to track us, that doesn't mean it hasn't served some other purpose. You say the man who dropped it watched the fight of Torsten and his team members?"

"Oh, yeah he did. He was all over it," Nikki said. "Probably wouldn't take a hell of a lot of effort to figure out that Torsten and his buddies are currently based in Vegas. And there are enough folks out there who know that it's also Council headquarters."

"If these guys are any good at all, they'll have already figured the connection out," Simon agreed. "It's not like we've kept ourselves a secret from anyone who cared to look."

"And yet *they* have kept themselves a secret, which is curious, isn't it," the Devil asked. He lifted a hand, and one of the slender disks disappeared from the box and appeared a moment later in his fingers. "All these years the Romeros and their line have stayed in hiding, yet now they choose to reveal themselves. Why? What has changed?"

"What hasn't changed," the Fool said derisively. "Nikki's the Moon, and she's brought a pack along with her. If these guys are Celestine's renegade werewolves, they're going to notice that."

Nikki rubbed her jaw. It was still a little tender. "Beyond that, we helped one of their operatives, at least for the hot minute that we could keep our hands on her. Maybe that counted for something?"

"Speaking of Sierra, I've got some news on that," Simon said. "Brody gave me her tracking coordinates left over from the finger-print transfer he was testing out on her phone. Worked like a charm, I'm happy to say. Let's see where she netted out."

He swiveled his chair toward the laptop set up beside him, pulling it to him with a practiced gesture. Then he scowled. "Southern California? Seriously?"

"The fires," Nikki blurted. "The image that I got from Sierra was that there were fires, but it looked more like a blown out build-ing, not like a wildfire. And what were the *kids* doing there, for the love of Christmas? That doesn't make any sense."

"There's a lot about California that doesn't make sense," Simon offered, but it still didn't track.

"What else did you see, Miss Dawes," the Magician asked. "Was there anything unusual about the teenagers?"

She frowned, shaking her head as, unbidden, another set of chil-dren flashed in front of her eyes, an image from another time, another place. She stuffed it down as quickly as it surfaced, but she could feel Kreios's attention focusing on her. There was nothing the Devil enjoyed more than learning the secrets that humans tried to keep from him, but Nikki didn't mind so much as she let him plumb her thoughts. In a mighty show of discretion, he kept his focus on her recent memories. Whoever had coined the phrase the Devil is a dumb spirit didn't know Alexander Kreios.

He nodded to her, then glanced at the Magician. "It's almost certain that those are the targets of our intrepid young Connected hunter. And it's at least theoretically possible they may be were-wolves as well. Do we have a location for them?"

"Yup," Simon said. "Looks like it's some kind of old festival town that's being used as a movie backdrop? Maybe these kids are tourists or, like, extras on some video?"

"That tracks," Nikki nodded. "Those fires behind them looked too violent to be straightforward fires. Whether the buildings on that street were blown up on purpose, I don't know, but they don't look right to me."

"Santana City," Simon said, typing furiously on his keyboard. "And if our girl's been there now for the better part of two hours…"

The Magician stood. "Then we'd best be getting there."

He looked at Nikki. "I know you're used to traveling with Justice Wilde…"

Nikki grinned, flipping her Valkyrie-style braided blonde hair back over her shoulders, doubly happy that she'd taken the time to change her do when she'd had the chance after the bar fight. "Darlin', I'll take whatever wings you've got. Let's go save some kids."

Chapter 8

TRAVELING AIR ARMAEUS had its benefits. Taking the Magician's hand had almost been surreal. Despite all their interactions over the past few years since she'd started working more closely with the Arcana Council, she'd rarely touched the guy, and now she chuckled to realize that he had effectively blocked his memories from her.

"Not that you would pry," the Magician murmured, his voice wry as they dissolved into a puff of quickly scattering molecules, reforming a moment later on the edge of a blighted town.

"Who else do you need?" he asked, and Nikki blew out a breath, choking a little on the acrid air.

"If those kids are wolves in the making, or if even just one of them is, I'll need Torsten and Magritte," she said. "More than that, they might get spooked, and I don't want to risk anyone I don't need to. I've only got a hundred of them, and a third of that number are kids, not fighters."

"Agreed. Take this."

Armaeus handed over one of the silver medallions and she took it with some surprise. "They can't track me, right?"

"They cannot. But this was clearly left behind as your contact's calling card, so you may discover a use for it."

Nikki stuck the medallion into her bra as the Magician whisked into a puff of smoke again. She didn't know how long he would be, but she didn't need him to start her survey of the scene.

The scene…was a deathtrap. Fire still smoked in several of the buildings, every one of which had been blasted through. No roofs remained, just the burned out hulls of a one-time boomtown, now rendered into a post-apocalyptic movie set. It also appeared abandoned, but as Nikki surveyed the street, she felt eyes on her. As much as she wanted the souped-up tracking abilities that Torsten seemed to rock, those skills hadn't come down to her. But the extra sensory awareness, the feeling of knowing everything that lurked both in the light and the shadow, persisted.

Was she simply drawing on her experience from being a cop, or had she been gifted with some extra ESP after all? If Torsten was to be believed, she wouldn't know until she danced naked under the full moon or some shit. Then again this was Torsten talking, and he really was a dark wolf at heart.

Nikki smirked, then caught the movement she was waiting for. A step past an open doorway, darkness silhouetted against shadow.

She frowned as she glanced around. The Magician had not yet returned with her pack. Was that on purpose? Did he feel like she could get further on her own? Or was he simply watching and waiting, wanting to see what might happen before he made his move? Her money was on the latter. She had watched him enough with Sara to recognize that Armaeus was above all else, an accumulator of information. There was always more he wanted to know before he made a decision or acted. And he wasn't above pushing things beyond normal limits to learn it.

That had never been the way Nikki handled things, of course. For good or bad—and there was plenty of bad—she tended to jump first, ask questions later.

She decided to see what she could shake out on her own.

"It's no fun being hunted is it?" she called out at the top of her voice, calling up the images of the scared looking teenagers and imagining them as about-to-turn werewolves. "I'm being hunted right now, but I know a little bit about that. In one way or another,

I've been hunted for most of my life. But this isn't the life you signed up for is it? These weird changes, the pain, the dreams. There you were, as normal as can be, living your life, having fun with your friends. And then this shit hits you like a wallop to the jaw. And now you don't know who to trust."

The strangest blip of emotion zinged out across Nikki's senses, coming from further down the street. Young. Afraid. Angry. Torsten had seemed particularly interested in the rage reaction that Sierra had mentioned, and it made sense that an emerging wolf would have some anger issues. Was that what she was dealing with here? Celestine had only left two hundred of her werewolf guardians behind. Even though these Weres were supposedly extremely long-lived, how many had survived down the long years? Even the pack protected in Atlantis had dwindled to only a hundred-strong.

"I could tell you that I could keep you safe, but I don't expect you to believe that," she continued. "So I'm going to make a different offer for you. For you, and you alone. Your friends will be fine. Those I'll keep safe. But you, I'll teach *you* how to be strong. How to be different without hating being different. I don't know what anybody promised you, or if they've gotten that far yet. Could be all they've given you are threats. But I'm not here to threaten you. I'm here to—"

"Shut *up*!" Nikki almost sighed with relief when a taut, angry voice cracked out from one of the burned-out buildings. It was about time. She was running out of bullshit fast. "Get out of here! Just leave us alone!"

Nikki pivoted slowly, her arms still down by her side. That was a female, young, and not a Connected one, so far as Nikki could tell. Just brash and stupid the way teenage girls could sometimes be when they were scared. The girl didn't say anything more, and Nikki imagined her friends shushing her with glares and tight-lipped gestures. Poor, stupid kids. How many more were like them, their recessive werewolf genes coming to the fore out of nowhere, turning them into something they never wanted nor expected to be?

"Others are going to come," Nikki said. "They're probably already here. You've seen one tough young woman. She's got an unfortunate taste in clothes, but she looks like she could roll hard in a fight and still come up swinging. Her, you should trust."

A zip of attention focused on her from on the other side of the street, and Nikki nodded to herself, triangulating her position. Two parties accounted for, which meant there were two others. Mercs who clearly had more patience than the idiots she'd run into in Vegas, and maybe whoever was behind the silver disk.

She remembered Torsten's odd reaction to the coin, his shaky explanation about its pull. Werewolves couldn't resist the tears of the moon, whether they'd been shed a second ago or six thousand years. What about wolves who'd never *seen* a coin, wolves who maybe didn't even know who they were yet? Would they react the same? Or, if they knew what they were, if they were fully developed and part of the pack that was hunting these kids down potentially to protect them, would they not be able to resist the coins' call, either? Versace Bob had left the coin behind, but maybe he had access to more of them whenever he wanted. Maybe that wasn't the case for every wolf out there.

It was worth a shot.

"You wanna know what I found?" Nikki drawled, pitching her voice even louder. "Something I think you might want. Something I might want if I were in your position, anyway."

She pulled out the coin, even as her ears picked up a stran-gled, masculine, '*No*,' which frankly surprised the shit out of her, but it was already too late. She tossed the coin up in the air, and screams of rage, need, fear, and excitement filled the air from all sides.

A half-dozen figures stormed into the street.

"That's *mine!*"

To Nikki's shock, it was Sierra who bolted into the street first, her eyes wide and wild, desperation on her face.

"They promised me, they promised!" she howled, and Nikki understood that the payment this girl wanted from the elusive Romero family was only partially about money. Was she actually aware that she was an emerging werewolf, or had the family she worked for kept that information from her as well?

Nikki wheeled around as a second rush of bodies barreled into the street. The kids from Sierra's vision.

"Jack, no!"

This was the same voice that Nikki had heard before, a goldenrod blonde who was racing after a pale young man who seemed to be more arms and legs than body, his thick dark hair flying, his large clear blue eyes wide and almost crazed. Power rippled off of him, and he reached for Nikki at the same time that Sierra did.

Nikki reached out and wrapped her arms around both Sierra and the boy she thought was named Jack, barely keeping her balance as she absorbed their forward movement. She sensed more than saw the next players emerge in two tight clusters, both of them jacked up with excitement—too much excitement, frankly, for them to be the owners of these coins. Which meant said owners weren't here yet. Which meant she was screwed. *Great.*

"Hold up, hold *up*," Nikki shouted, grappling with Sierra and Jack even as she could have sworn she heard the sound of a gun being lifted. Though how she could hear such a thing—

A cascade of gunshots rang out down the long street, clearly not intending to kill, not yet. Nobody could be that shitty of a shot.

"Everybody *down*," Nikki roared, taking the two teenagers to the dirt.

Chapter 9

NIKKI WAS UP and moving again almost as quickly as she hit the dirt. Still trapped in her arms, Jack and Sierra seemed smaller than they should, gangly in the way of the young and not fully formed. Feral, too, as Sierra bucked and kicked, sinking her teeth into Nikki's forearm.

Not a bad move, but an unearthly level of primal energy was pouring through Nikki's body, not at all her own. A second later her pack roared down the street, not just Magritte and Torsten, but fully twenty wolves—some still in their human form, some mid-conversion, some fully rocking their wolf mojo.

Whatever grit the mercenaries hunting the children had, and Nikki assumed they probably had some, completely abandoned them as the wolves split off and entered the burned-out buildings. There were more wild shots, but unless these guys were packing silver bullets, they would ricochet off the tough hide of her pack. Sure enough, human bodies began being flung into the street, and when they landed, hard, they didn't move again. By now Jack and Sierra had both stopped moving. Instead they merely stared as the pack rounded up the bad guys and came bounding out again, seamlessly shifting into their human forms. Or at least it seemed seamless to Nikki, because it happened so fast. She'd always assumed it would hurt more, but the wolves looked like they were enjoying themselves far too much.

"The young are ready to be moved."

Nikki blinked, having momentarily misplaced the other teens in her struggle with Sierra and Jack. But she looked over to where Torsten indicated to see a small huddle of teens partially collapsed on each other, all of them fully passed-out.

She lifted a quizzical brown at Torsten. "They all *fainted?*"

"We gave them a little help," Magritte said, smiling slightly. "It's a lot to take in, and better for their memories to be muddy than their nightmares to be clear."

Sierra pushed away from Nikki, vibrating with anger. "This was *my* job," she grouched. "It's my only job and I had it *handled*. We would have been well away from the mercenaries before they had searched all the buildings. I knew where they were."

"You did, didn't you," Torsten said, his nostrils flaring as he studied her beneath his heavy dark brows. "And there's a reason for that. You should have changed by now."

Nikki expected the girl to bluster, but she didn't. Sierra's shoulders slumped, and she sighed. "It's not my fault," she muttered, glancing away. "I was taken, when I was younger. Held, they—did something to me, stunted my growth. I got out only a few years ago."

Nikki jolted, resisting the urge to close her eyes. Sweet Mother Mary, so *this* is what she had seen in the girl's memory. The cage, the darkness, the torture. Not a child she had finally rescued—but herself. How long had she been trapped until she'd managed it?

"You saved yourself, and were called to save others," Nikki said, her gaze focused on Sierra. "And then what? You were found by somebody else?"

"I knew the moment I met the first of them that we were— connected, somehow. Bonded. But they said no, not so fast. They just wanted to hire me," Sierra said, a little bitterly. "My blood wasn't *pure* enough for them to take me straight out. But they said I could earn it."

Nikki made a face. "These guys sound more and more like assholes every time I learn something new about them." When she would have made a move for the coin, still laying on the ground, Torsten stopped her with a look. Then Jack finally spoke.

"Who are you people?" he asked, his tone low, measured. "What's going on?"

Nikki laid a hand on his arm, just below the singed short sleeve of his shirt. In a flash, his memories scored across her mind.

School, home. Luxury and comfort, friends. The ordinary trappings of a teenage life of what looked like moderate wealth and freedom, privilege even. What would his life be like now, if he continued down the path Nikki suspected he was on?

"It's a lot to take in," she said quietly, when he didn't pull away. "But if you remember nothing else, remember this: Regardless of what you are, *you* get to choose who you are. The heart doesn't change."

At that moment, Sierra's cell phone blared a short, staccato ring. She lunged for it with just enough latent desperation that Nikki's heart tugged hard. Jack may not know what he wanted to be, but Sierra had been denied her chance at who she felt she truly was for too long.

"They're summoning you," Sierra said, her voice tight as she stared at the screen. "They want you to come to them. Only you."

Nikki nodded. "Well, that's a pity. What else did they say?"

Sierra blinked up at her, and Nikki met her gaze. "I don't leave any one of my pack behind, fighter girl. Ever. What else did they say?"

"Oh. Nothing more than that. Just a series of numbers. GPS coordinates, maybe."

She turned the phone to Nikki, and didn't resist when Nikki pulled it from her hand. Nikki heard the soft laughter of the Magician deep in the back of her mind.

"I assume you'll want only your closest companions this time? And young Sierra too, I should think."

Nikki didn't even have time to answer before Armaeus whisked her and her team away in a puff of smoke.

A few moments later, Nikki, Torsten, Magritte, and Sierra stood on the elegant porch of a large stone mansion. It was hot, stickily so, and the air smelled heavy with dirt and growing things.

"Wait, where are the others? Are they safe?" Sierra snapped, her gaze narrow and furtive. "I knew they were based in Louisiana, I absolutely knew it. But if this is their compound, it's dangerous. Where's Jack?"

"They'll be close, but they'll be safe," Nikki assured her. "The Magician will keep tabs on them. Probably a good idea to ease Jack into his new potential community as slowly as we can."

Sierra snorted. "Good luck with that. He's close, way closer than me, and I've been getting closer every year."

Nikki set that comment to the side as she peered up at the broad doorway that had yet to be opened to them.

"Well, this is a good use of our time," she complained, loudly.

"They did say for you to come alone," Torsten said, but Nikki didn't miss the hard glint to his eyes, and she still felt the roil of the emotions flowing from him and Magritte. Maybe she was becoming more sensitive to her pack without the need for the full moon ceremony. She would take it, if it helped her keep them safe.

With that thought, the door opened, and Nikki wondered fleetingly if the wolves inside the house could read her thoughts as well. She didn't think so, and not just because she was the vaunted Moon. There was a strange energy about the mansion that she couldn't quite place; it wasn't Connected energy, exactly, and it wasn't the same energy of Torsten or his team. It was wilder, older, and more primal.

A figure emerged from the shadows of the foyer, and Nikki blinked, suddenly sad that Simon had not traveled with them. It was a robot, like the prototypes she had seen on the news but which few ordinary people had. The android looked close enough to a human without being disconcertingly real looking, but it smiled a mobile smile and gestured with its right hand. "Please come inside. The others are waiting for you."

Torsten bristled beside her, and Nikki could almost feel his and Magritte's hackles rising at the automaton, but Sierra held her surprise at bay. She was doing everything she could to earn the right of inclusion, Nikki thought, her mouth tightening. She knew what it was like to have every day feel like an audition.

She followed the automaton inside, and now it was her turn to cover her reaction. Because Holy Freaking Gold Diggers, the Romeros were apparently *loaded*.

Working with the Arcana Council, Nikki was no stranger to opulent wealth and overstated living conditions, but from the looks of their home, the werewolves of Louisiana would fit right in with the most egocentric of the council. Lavish marble rolled in all directions, across the floor and up the walls, which were hung with heavy gilt-framed paintings that Nikki suspected had to be real. Old masters were lined alongside up-and-comers from the past century, creating the perfect mix of old and new, similar in approach to this old, stately mansion being tended to by a robot.

"Is there any information you've been instructed to give us?" Nikki asked trying to keep her tone conversational despite the fact that she was talking to a computer. She reached out as casually as she could, and tapped the robot on the shoulder—

And felt like she'd been blasted into the next continent.

The robot turned to her, oblivious of her reaction, and smiled broadly, its placid, empty face guileless. "Of course. They said there was an eighty-seven percent likelihood that you would ask," it replied. "Time is at a premium for the family and for you. Ordinarily your interference in family business would not be acceptable, but in this case it is different. The family is honored that you accepted their invitation."

With that, the robot felt silent, and Nikki registered the annoyance of her packmates but shook her head slightly. The Romeros still thought they were in control of the situation, and this *was* their house. Despite the fact that she now knew way more than she could even process, thanks to getting a palmful of I, Robot, she would see how this all played out.

They moved up a short flight of stairs and down another long hallway, this one richly paneled in rosewood flooring, with a long woven runner down the center that probably cost more than Nikki's entire wardrobe. She made a face as she strode along, studying it beyond her steel toes. These guys sure were impressed with themselves.

The paintings gave way to more landscapes, ranging from violent woodland attacks between man and beast to pastoral views empty of any human. She was still working out the meaning of that juxtaposition when the android slowed, pivoting gracefully to show them into a large room where a fire burned. Not truly necessary given the heat of the evening outside, but for the first time, Nikki registered the relative chill in the house. Then again, now that she thought about it, if you had a fur coat available on demand...

She bit back her grin as she stepped in behind the robot.

"Nikki Dawes," the robot announced. "Sierra Haggerty. Guardians," the robot announced.

Nikki hid her surprise and curiosity as she and the others entered the room, but her attention was arrested by the five figures up near the fireplace who turned to face them. Flanked by opulent furnishings, they looked like they had been cut out of a royal portrait. Tall, handsome, well-built, males and females alike. Three men stood in the center, all of them looking roughly around the age of thirty, while one young woman and one older woman framed the trio of males. The Romero brothers? They were big, with dark black hair, dark eyes and Mediterranean features, and they all scowled at her.

The one in the center spoke first. "Welcome, Mistress Dawes," he said. "I am Augustus Romero. Your pack would have us believe that you are the Moon returned, a goddess, come to grace her people once more." His lips curled in a hard smirk as he raked his dismissive gaze over Nikki. "We have no need for goddesses."

"Yeah?" Nikki smiled as well, but she was already done with these assholes. "Well, that's too bad. Because you're the one who summoned me. From where I'm standing, I'd say that means you need me. And because we're all trying to move things along as quickly as possible, let me go ahead and say I'd be willing to bet you need me to recapture the wolf that you lost, the one who's being held in chains, his blood drawn against his will to spike the drugs being made by the agents of the arcane black market." She grinned at the Romeros' stupefied faces, feeling only slightly guilty for having misused their android so thoroughly. "How'm I doing so far?"

Chapter 10

TO NIKKI'S SURPRISE, the older female gasped first, her hands fluttering to her face. Her hair was also dark, but her features were more delicate, Eastern European, maybe. And she was clearly horror-struck.

"Jonathan!" she began as the male beside her turned her way sharply, his face flushing with annoyance, though he didn't stop her outburst.

Fortunately, Augustus didn't feel the urge to coddle his— mother? aunt?—but kept his focus on Nikki.

"My congratulations on your discovery skills," he said. "As it happens, you're right. And we appreciate your aid as well. The young wolf whose welcome you interrupted is one we had concerns about acquiring. Sierra here is one of the best trackers we have. This young man had not realized his nature yet, but others had. He was being tracked. Had you not come with the reinforcements that you did, a second troop of mercenaries waited in the mountains beyond."

Beside Nikki, Sierra stiffened. "Well that would have been good information to have," she muttered, and Augustus sent her a cool look.

"It was information we only discerned after the fact." Sierra flushed, and Nikki narrowed her eyes as Augustus returned his attention to her. "Your skills have proven valuable to us, Mistress Dawes. Your assistance isn't something we ask lightly."

"It's not something I give lightly either, honey pot," Nikki assured him. "But we'll get to that later. The intel I have is that your wolf is held in…some kind of citadel?"

Augustus nodded. "It's a stronghold held by members of the arcane black market."

"The Shadow Court?" Nikki asked quickly, but Augustus merely lifted one shoulder, dropped it.

"Unknown. We don't trouble ourselves with the politics of the Connected." There was no denying the judgment in his tone. Judgment, but not dismissal. Envy, pride, and indignation rolled off the entire family. Interesting.

"Fair enough, but how'd they get to your boy? You guys keep pretty close to yourselves. The Council didn't even know about you."

Augustus curled his lip into what almost passed as a smile. "There have been Councils in the past who have," he said, surprising her. "We learned over time that revealing ourselves was not to our favor. Time is one thing we have an abundance of."

Torsten hooked his thumbs into the waistband of his trousers. "You're strong, long-lived, you heal fast, and are impervious to most assaults. Those are all the powers you have?"

The third Romero brother spoke now, quirking a smile. Nikki jolted, recognizing him as Versace Boy. "Yes," he said. "And we're rich, which also helps."

"Lucian." The young woman beside him bit her lip as the middle brother looked over at his younger brother murderously. Murderous seemed to be brother #2's default expression.

"But you don't have any other skills?" Magritte murmured soft enough that Nikki barely caught the words, while Lucian turned to her, his eyes as bright as Christmas.

"We've got all the senses," he assured. "Sight, hearing, smell, even taste, as weird as that is. We can tell the varietal of any ingredient in our food or drink. Interesting, but not always useful. And touch, too, so that's——"

"Lucian, enough," Augustus interrupted mildly. He focused on Nikki. "But to answer your warrior's question, no. Our goddess, back when we revered her as such, saw fit to drop her tears upon us. She blanketed us with silver, but she took her magic with her, and there was no one left to teach us the ancient ways. We survived by our own wits and skills, our strength and her silver. Which, ironically enough, killed its fair share of our number, before we learned enough to protect ourselves."

"Silver bullets," Nikki mused. "Is that what slowed down Jonathan, how he got trapped?"

"What slowed him down was hitting the concrete after jumping out a three-story building," the second brother said, only to earn a sharp, "Matthias," from his older brother, before he continued to Nikki.

"Matthias is right. Jonathan was overpowered while he was dazed from a fall. The best we can tell, what's keeping him in place is some sort of silver injectable. As long as it stays dormant, there's no problem. But if it explodes and it makes its way to his heart, he dies. Even with the finest surgeons and medicine men in the world, we couldn't act fast enough to save him, and he couldn't heal himself so quickly either."

Nikki grimaced. Sara could help the poor guy, no question. Nobody healed faster than she did. But first they had to get the werewolf out from whatever cage he was trapped in.

"South America?" she said. "I don't suppose you could narrow that down at all?"

"I'd prefer if we explained on the way," Augustus countered, pulling out a sleek looking mobile device.

Nikki made a face. "Not to put too fine a point on it, sugar lips, but I can get there a hell of a lot faster than you can. Trust me on that."

Augustus didn't skip a beat. "You could, but you forget that we are working with members of the arcane black market. They will sense magic as easily as I can sense the quickening of a heartbeat from thirty feet away. Far better for us to take our private jet and use less magical means to evade detection. As you, yourself have pointed out, we've gotten quite good at that over the years."

"*Their terms are acceptable, Miss Dawes,*" the Magician spoke in the back of Nikki's mind. "*With your permission, I would like to keep an open line of communication between us. In the meantime, there is a rich opportunity for discovery here in this quite lovely mansion. I assure you, I will find the opportunity to explore very instructive.*"

Nikki flashed Augustus a broad smile. "All righty, then, it looks like we're off to Brazil. Is the whole famdamily going, or will this be a more exclusive engagement?"

"I'm going," Sierra blurted, making Nikki blink. "I almost had him safe—you didn't act fast enough."

"If we had acted any faster, you would've been in chains with him," Augustus countered. "And the danger to you would have been far greater."

"I don't see how," Sierra said, clearly aggravated.

"Because you are *Connected*, Sierra," Augustus said, and his voice shook the tiniest bit when he said her name. "Your nature as a wolf remains hidden. But it won't be hidden for much longer, and that will make you the rarest of our kind."

"Believe me." Lucian rolled his eyes. "You're lucky he's let you do as much as you have. You're his absolute favorite hunter by a long shot."

Sierra blushed furiously at that, and Nikki stepped into the conversation to give the girl a chance to recover. There was no question that Augustus, asshole or not, had a special place in his heart for Sierra, but she was only going to be allowed to indulge in young love after she kicked some arcane black-market ass. Those were the rules.

"So, what's the story on this Jonathan?" she pushed. "Does he have magical abilities, to your knowledge, or did the bad guys just target him because he's one of your inner circle?"

"He's my son," the older woman said. "If any of our kind were eventually to develop abilities in a full moon ceremony, it would be him. But he was so reckless. So foolish!"

To her surprise, Matthias tightened his jaw and patted her shoulder awkwardly. Was she his mom, too? Nikki didn't understand the family dynamics here, but she was quickly getting forgotten in the shuffle. That was okay by her.

"We can be prepared to leave within the hour," Augustus said. "We did not expect you quite so quickly when we summoned you."

"Yeah well, it pays to have friends in high places," Nikki said.

"And as I think you'll see, it pays to have them in low places, too."

Chapter 11

IT WAS another twenty-four hours before they arrived on the outskirts of the Brazilian citadel. As citadels went, it was…busy.

"I thought you said this place was closed down tight?" she muttered, peering through the long-range binoculars. They had enhanced night vision, which shouldn't be necessary, because it was full daylight. But it was also the deepest jungles of Brazil, and Nikki found she couldn't make heads or tails of anything she saw without them. *With* them, however…

"There's a steady stream of vehicles in and out, supply trucks," she said, pointing to the far end of the compound.

"Yes, but this is where they're keeping Jonathan," Augustus said, gently pushing her binoculars to the right until she saw a separate structure, surprisingly elegant, with wide manicured lawns.

"Getting into the production area of the drug facility gets us on the ground, but the two areas don't intermix. In all the time we've studied it, we've never seen anyone go between the buildings, at least not above ground."

"Are you looking at getting in via tunnels?"

"Sadly, no," Augustus said. "Our kind lose their energy below ground. We get slower, weaker the longer that we're away from the open air. Even if we were to survive traveling a short distance, we likely would not have the strength to rescue Jonathan and pull him back through those passageways. There has to be another way."

Nikki bit her lip, thinking. "Is it any enclosure at all that snuffs out your mojo? Or just literally underground?"

She cocked a glance at Torsten, but he was frowning at Augustus as well.

"It was never an issue for us," Torsten admitted before Augustus could speak. "There are no subterranean passages in Atlantis. Those would flood. The game was always to seek higher ground, not lower. But we can do just fine above or below ground, even if the Romeros cannot."

"Anything above ground works just fine," Lucian said. "The more light, the better, and the more potent we are."

"Got it," Nikki said. She rocked back on her heels. "They're keeping your boy underground until they need his blood, and then they pull him out into open air just long enough to get potent blood when they stick him. Then, in he goes again."

Augustus sighed. "This is what we've suspected, but he's been in that hellhole for three months, and no amount of aerial surveillance has been able to penetrate it. Early on, we tried bribing the help, but not only were they unhelpful, they were killed for their troubles and hung on the exterior wall for wild animals to find."

"Excellent motivational tactics," Nikki said. "These guys should write a business book."

"We abandoned our attempts at getting information that way, I assure you. Not out of any sense of altruism, but simply because Jonathan's captors seemed on to us far too quickly. They somehow knew the moment we made contact with their workers."

"Technoceutical serum, maybe?" Nikki suggested. "Or maybe the help is that loyal?"

"Or maybe what you were seeing wasn't real," Torsten put in.

Nikki glanced his way, but he just shrugged. "You spoke with the help, who gave you vague information. Subsequently you saw them getting their bodies ripped off the wall. This is a very remote location, with highly specialized needs for secrecy. Far more likely that they had loyalists to protect it, and it was just an illusion that you saw getting eaten. Easier to keep your current stooges alive than to train new soldiers."

"Okay, I take it back, *you* should write the inspirational book. So, we need to get in, is all." She rubbed her jaw, peering upright. "Tell me again, how did Jonathan get caught specifically? He was a member of your royal brotherhood or whatever the hell you call each other. How did you lose track of him?"

"We didn't lose track of him," Lucian said. "Sierra was following him, and he knew it. Jonathan liked to enjoy the finer things in life, and we indulged him, especially his mother."

"Uh huh," Nikki said. "And her relationship to you is——"

"Cousin, and the closest family to the central line," Augustus replied. "Purity of blood is important; it was all we have left."

Nikki let that go for now. With the mother not on this detail, she could learn more of the information she really needed to know. "So, party boy Jonathan went out and got drunk, and Sierra here was sent after him? Why her?"

Augustus shifted, a flair of possessive annoyance wafting over to Nikki. *Interesting.*

"He liked her," Lucian put in, while Sierra muttered something dark under her breath.

"Okay, good enough reason. But then the bad guys show up, and Sierra prepares to defend Jonathan. What happens after that?"

Sierra spoke up. "Romero's embedded guard swarmed in, but for some dumbass reason, they took me first before going for Jonathan. And that's all the time the mercs needed. They chased him and he leapt out a window, thinking he could make it, but—he didn't. And they got to him before we did."

"Uh-huh." Nikki thought she understood now. Royal or not, Jonathan had been more expendable than his supposed bodyguard, given her fully-fledged Connected abilities. Augustus had had to choose…and sometimes hard choices sucked.

"He's been in there too long," Augustus said now, confirming her suspicion. "His loss would be…very difficult for us. For all of us."

"Then maybe we propose a trade," Nikki said, sounding the words out in her mind, trying them on for size.

Torsten was way ahead of her. "I say we propose a two-for-one trade," he agreed, his eyes gleaming. "Mistress Moon has some experience working with the arcane black market. And she's dressed for the part."

"That's for sure," Nikki grinned, jutting out her black-clad hip. "I show up on their front porch with two magnificent wolves, and these bad boys have *abilities*. That's way better than what they've got with Jonathan."

Sierra shook her head. "They'll kill you."

"They won't," Augustus, sounding stricken. "But they will take you all the same, and then you'll be as trapped as Jonathan is."

"You're probably right," Nikki said. "But I've had my coffee today, so I'm thinking I'm going to be okay. And Torsten and Magritte love nothing more than to surprise me. We go in."

"We need to go with you," Sierra said quickly, Nikki held up her hand.

"You do that and we'll all be on the inside, with no clear path out. Trust me, I know you guys are going to have your hands full out here. You need to get your team in place," she advised Augustus. "While you, Sierra, are going to be summoned to save our asses. Because I'm going to be sending up emergency wolf flares. When that happens, you're going to have to haul Augustus with you to wherever we are, however you can get that done. I've got a feeling we may end up needing all the paws on the ground we can get."

"We can do that," Augustus said, effectively silencing Sierra, though not for long Nikki surmised. "Lucian will lead the ATVs through the jungle, while Sierra and I stand at the ready to fight with you."

Nikki swallowed her chuckle as the girl blushed again, and Augustus squared his shoulders with fierce bravado. *These two.*

Getting down to the front gates of the compound immediately took on an appropriately dramatic turn as Magritte and Torsten shifted into wolf form, larger than usual, standing with their heads even with Nikki's shoulders.

Torsten bent down, providing an easy leg up, and Nikki narrowed her eyes at him.

"Only until we get close," she muttered. But when she pulled herself onto Torsten's back, he immediately leapt into action, making her yelp with surprise as she buried her hands into his thick fur.

"What the *hell*," she snapped, and she thought she could almost hear his wild, feral laughter deep in the recesses of her mind. Then there was nothing but crashing brush and startled fowl, maybe even a few skittering lizards as they made their way down to the main road.

The walls of the main compound loomed high, but Torsten once again had a twist on the action in mind. He howled, wild and exuberant, and he and Magritte picked up speed as they galloped out of the forest and onto the road. They crested a small rise and then leapt not ten feet away from the gates of the compound, soaring through the air and clearing the high wall. A second later, they landed inside a segmented courtyard of manicured lawns and garden plots. Lights blew up across the space, klaxon bells ringing loud.

Nikki slid off Torsten's back, grinning broadly. "Now that's what I call an entrance!"

Chapter 12

TORSTEN SHIFTED BACK into human form, as Magritte remained a wolf, silvery and proud, standing between them.

"Do you know where we're going from here?" Torsten asked quickly as doors flew open from buildings to either side of the courtyard. Twenty soldiers with guns raised raced through the doors. They immediately spread out and dropped to their knees in semi circles around Nikki, Torsten and Magritte. Once in position, they held themselves perfectly still, their guns trained on the three of them.

Nikki surveyed the rows of gunmen. "I thought we'd just have a little chat, see where their heads are at."

"Right," Torsten said. "So no plan."

The front doors of the main building swept open, and two figures emerged, far older than Nikki would have expected. They looked vaguely Northern European to her eye, but with the glare of the lights it was hard to tell.

"I need to touch them, but I'm not sure how to pull that off," Nikki muttered, while beside her, Magritte huffed a soft laugh.

"I'll help you with that," she promised, the words slipping

through the back of Nikki's mind. That was all the reassurance Nikki needed.

"Whoa, whoa, whoa," she shouted, stepping forward and waving her arms. "You want to call off your firing squad before two of the rarest wolves you'll ever get your hands on get struck by one of their BB guns?"

The man stepped forward, but it was the eyes of the woman that Nikki didn't trust. They were hard, fierce, and pride rippled from them. She was the one in control here. She was the one who called the shots.

"We were not expecting guests tonight," the man said smoothly, taking another step forward. "Where did you come from? And what do you have?"

"I work for the Arcana Council," Nikki countered, making Torsten and Magritte both flinch with surprise, but she could tell from the shuttered expression on the woman's face that she knew the Council well. Jealousy wafted across the open courtyard. "You've got something we want, so we found something you would want more," Nikki continued. "Simple as that."

"She's lying," the woman announced, and Nikki felt it then, the prickly brush of the psychic touch. A mind reader. She hadn't been working with Sara for so long that she hadn't learned how to school her mind into being protected among strangers, but she *had* dropped her guard here. She'd been too cocky, too confident. Stupid.

Still, what had the woman picked up, exactly? What had been uppermost in Nikki's mind?

"She thinks of nothing but love," the woman announced. "Hidden, unspoken love. She wants Jonathan because she's in love with him."

Beside Nikki, Torsten froze, but to his credit he didn't say anything, while Nikki held on to the emotional tsunami she'd picked up between Augustus and Sierra—held on and ran with it.

"It doesn't matter my reasons," Nikki said, as stiffly as she could manage. "You've got a werewolf without magic. He's got strength, he's got guts, he's even got royal blood, but he can't do what mine can."

"And what may I ask, is that?" the man asked, and Torsten turned to the woman.

"I know your every thought, Mistress Elba," he said, with a voice suddenly as smooth as caramel cream. "You are human, and I was made to serve humans. I know the location of your favorite flower, the wine you favor, the last time you experienced pleasure. I know all these things, and more, and I can give you whatever you desire."

As he spoke, the woman's emotions jackrabbited in a dozen different directions. Nikki didn't know if Torsten was spinning bullshit, but it was bullshit this woman clearly wanted to believe. Hell, it was bullshit *she* wanted to believe.

"And the female?"

Magritte extended her neck, her snout lifting up. She howled, and the note was long and beautiful, filled with light and promise. It extended out, out—

Every light in the facility exploded.

Magritte bounded forward, and Nikki flung herself half onto her back, half onto her flank, holding on tight until she reached the caretaker of the citadel. In an attempt to ward Nikki off as she toppled over onto him, the man flung his hands high, allowing Nikki to grab one bared wrist and squeeze tight.

"Jonathan," she snarled, and though the man's expression turned mutinous, his mind flashed to the information she needed; a cave built into the side of a pit, chains dangling from all sides, far too deep to escape...the creature within, close to death.

"Magnus!" the woman screamed, the word cutoff in a garbled shriek. But by then Nikki was up and running, following the path that good ol' Magnus had laid out for her.

Within seconds Magritte and Torsten joined her, pounding up the stairs to the big house, Magritte pausing only long enough to howl one long, vicious note back toward the porch.

Behind them, the entire front of the building exploded outwards into the courtyard, blocking all the gunmen with a pile of rubble.

"*Girlfriend*," Nikki crowed. "You gotta stop hiding your light under a barrel."

They ran on, taking advantage of the chaos to reach the back of the building, which was covered by a series of trellises, artfully designed to make it look like the entire area was buried in deep jungle. Nikki could feel the crackle of magic shooting through the space. No wonder the Romeros had never been able to penetrate this part of the compound.

"Over here," Torsten called, back in human form as he leaned out over the pit. "Something's down there, but it's not good." He swiveled to peer at Nikki. "Whatever is left of that wolf is a broken mess. He may not survive the night and if they've put something in him that has silver...it's already leaching through him."

"I did that to him," Magritte's words were hushed, and her face when Nikki swung to look at her was transfixed in horror. "The bullets in the guns were made of silver. I exploded them, but I didn't think...I didn't think."

"Whelp, looks like our timetable just moved up," Nikki said. "Let's go."

She stepped off the side of the pit. Torsten grabbed for her at the last second, wrapping her in his embrace, and plummeted with her as they dropped down twelve feet.

Not twelve feet, Nikki realized quickly. Try more than fifty.

Magritte cannonballed down beside them and Nikki and Torsten broke apart as they crashed to the floor of the pit. She'd expected Jonathan to leap against his cage in violent rage, but nothing more than a pitiful huff sounded from the hole dug into the rock, while Magritte and Torsten roared with rage. Bounding forward in a blur that was half human-looking, half wolf, they leapt for the gates that restricted Jonathan, shearing off abruptly and circling back as Nikki rushed forward as well.

"Silver on the ground," Magritte cursed in the back of Nikki's mind, lifting a paw that had a bloody mark, while Torsten growled in frustration, shaking out his hands.

"That roar of yours is going to get you in trouble, sunshine, but not today. Let's just get the hell out of here."

She ran forward, and it was her turn to battle through the silver-spiked wall of Jonathan's cage, but given Magritte's efforts, they were in shambles, little more than jagged spikes.

The man who she assumed was Jonathan lay on the palette, barely able to raise his head. He certainly didn't protest as Nikki hauled him over her shoulder, fireman style. She swiveled around, as Jonathan groaned something that sounded vaguely like "danger," but she merely hugged him to her a little more tightly.

"No wolf left behind buddy, that's the new pack motto. Get on board," she ordered.

She lurched back out into the pit, not seeing Torsten or Magritte at first, then finally locating them at the back of another small corridor cut into the side of the pit, leading to God knows where. She looked at them, staggering a little under Jonathan's weight. "We can't go that way. He doesn't have much time."

"Agreed," Torsten said. "Come on."

Nikki stumbled over to him and he switched back into the form of a mighty black wolf, growling with alarm as she laid Jonathan's body over him. She turned to Magritte, who also had regained her silvery animal form. This time, when Magritte lowered her shoulder to give Nikki easy access to her back, Nikki didn't hesitate.

"Oh my God, I love you guys," Nikki breathed as she scrambled up onto the wolf, and then the wind was ripped from her throat as both Torsten and Magritte turned and surged forward, galloping as fast as a train. They broke through to the open air, Nikki barely feeling the chatter of bullets that sailed down over them as Magritte and Torsten leapt up high, their trajectory almost vertical, until they cleared the pit and landed on level ground. There was more running then, a lot more running, but by this time, Nikki was fading in and out.

"Son of a bitch," she muttered. "I've been hit."

Torsten shifted his muzzle toward her, never breaking stride, and sank his fangs into her shoulder.

"You will not die," he ordered as Nikki's sight went white again, and this time his voice rang through her mind with crystal clarity.

With another soaring leap, they were back among the trees, magic rippling like a snapping sheet around them. Nikki vaguely had the sense of people all around her, both new and strangely familiar scents and sounds filling her mind.

Augustus and Sierra were there—and others, too. But Nikki couldn't get a bead on her packmates. Where was Torsten—or Magritte? Had they been hit...was that even possible?

Then, in her delirium, she heard a voice she'd recognize anywhere. Sara Wilde, Justice of the Arcana Council.

"Nikki, what in the hell?" Sara demanded, the pressure of familiar arms circling Nikki tight. "I leave you alone for three days..."

"Dollface," Nikki sighed. "You've got to help Jonathan—"

Then she blacked out completely.

Chapter 13

THE SOUND WAS QUIET, like rain pattering against the glass, the quick, hiccupping breaths sounding almost apologetic in the stillness. Nikki lay motionless, still half asleep, and awash in the tide of a mother's relief and release.

She smiled as she heard Sara's voice over the soft sobs. Lifting herself on one elbow, Nikki squinted against the firelight, which struck her as her head cleared the top of the couch where she had apparently sprawled.

"How can I ever thank you for your help?" The woman asked, over and over again, but it wasn't a legitimate question, and Sara didn't take it as such. She sat back on her haunches, unselfconscious in her typical attire of tee-shirt and jeans, her hair whipped back in a ponytail, her attention focused on the male spread out there, his large chest moving up and down rhythmically as he slept.

"Right now, you just need to focus on getting your son better," Sara said. "They took him apart pretty good, but I put him back together the best way I knew how. I hope I got it right."

"You did, you did," the older woman cooed. "He's perfect. He's alive and he's perfect."

Nikki chuckled to herself as she pulled her own legs over the couch. She was feeling pretty hale and hearty herself, so she suspected that Sara had topped off her tanks as well. She still wore the black fitted shirt and tactical pants that she had shown up in at Werewolf HQ, so not too much time had passed—or no one had had the guts to redress her.

"You're awake."

She blinked, not sure if she'd heard the voice aloud or simply in the back of her mind, but across the room on the other side of her sitting area, she saw Torsten. His cheek was scarred lightly, she realized with surprise, both at the injury as well as her ability to see it in the gloom.

She gestured with a flick of her finger, and he grimaced.

"I didn't even feel it until after it was all over, but Magritte's howl burst several bullets mid-trajectory. Not everyone in that compound was happy to see a full-fledged wolf and weren't afraid to take us out."

"Nifty." Nikki scowled. "You going to be okay?"

He nodded. "Magritte took some silver too, but it appears that six thousand years in Atlantis has improved our resistance against it. That and the ministrations of your best friend took care of the rest."

Nikki glanced over to where Sara had returned her attention to the fallen Jonathan. Her heart swelled in her chest, knocking hard against her rib cage. "A girl's gotta have friends," she murmured.

"You do," Torsten agreed. "And I am honored to serve one as loyal as you are."

The fireplace chose that moment to flare, and as it did, all the lights swept up higher in the room.

Nikki straightened, but remained seated as Augustus Romero strode into the room and gestured her down. Instead, he took a chair opposite her, waving his brothers to other seats around the room. Lucian went directly to the woman sobbing, kneeling down beside her. He was probably her favorite, Nikki thought, though Augustus was growing on her, too. Matthias had too much anger for any one person, but at least he kept his murderous expression composed for the moment. She peered around. "Where's Sierra?"

Augustus grimaced. "Recovering. When she brought me to you,

it swung her into the change completely. For all her preparation, it's still a shock when it happens. And it's never ideal to happen when you're being chased through the jungle with a dying wolf on your hands."

He leveled a look at Nikki. "We owe the Arcana Council and you a great deal,. for coming when we called, and aiding us before we had even struck a deal."

"There are some situations where no deal is required," Nikki countered. "I don't require your service or your paybacks. But we do need your help. War is coming to all of the Connected, all of those who are different in this world. That means you, as well. You can continue to hide, and we will protect you as best as we can—"

"No." Both Matthias and Augustus answered that, and Nikki was gratified to feel the sincerity rolling off both of them.

"The time for hiding is now past," Augustus continued. "We have hidden too long. We have forced the strongest of our kind to live in the shadows, while only the weaker were risked to gain our standing in the world. No more. I have hidden for over five hundred years, and I am ready to fight."

"We're all ready to fight," Matthias said, his gaze shifting to Jonathan as well. Sara had stood now, and was talking with Lucian and Jonathan's mother, doubtless giving them advice on how to care for Jonathan. Nikki grimaced. The fact that he even needed such care after her efforts was telling. He had been very, *very* close to death.

"Okay, what's next?"

Nikki turned as Sara came up, and she made more introductions until Augustus and Matthias moved over to see how Jonathan was faring. Left alone, as Torsten watched from the side of the room, Nikki hugged Sara, hard.

She pulled back and gave her best friend a wide grin. "Look at me rockin' this whole Moon thing. How'd I do on my first job?"

Justice of the Arcana Council gave her a lopsided smile, her pride and relief washing through Nikki so strongly, it almost bowled her over. "You did better than anyone in the world could," Sara said, her voice only cracking a little. "Let's go make the world a better place for magic."

Catching Torsten's eye, Nikki grinned. "Dollface, that sounds like one hell of a plan."

Epilogue

NIKKI STOOD ALONE in the center of the natural stone amphitheater deep in the red rock canyon, staring up at the moon. It was the first full moon that had risen since she had taken on her new role, and she could feel the magic rising with it. Though she'd been experiencing breakthrough moments of communication with Torsten and even Magritte, now she could hear the thoughts of every member of her pack simultaneously.

No wonder Celestine had eventually lost it.

"There are ways of shielding yourself." Torsten's voice sounded in the back of her mind, ever willing to stand in to serve and protect. But Nikki only smiled. She didn't want to stop the flow of connection she was feeling—not yet anyway, not now. The members of the Romero family were moving through the shadows toward her, and her role tonight was one she wouldn't trade for anything.

The Romeros were the first of twelve werewolf families spread across the globe who had endured six thousand years of life without their goddess, their community evolving into an elite aristocracy of the super-rich, incredibly strong, and insanely stealthy. Not every family was willing to step forward, yet, but with the Romeros pledging their fealty to Nikki and the Arcana Council, others would follow.

And given the war on the Connected community that was fast approaching, they'd need every last member of her pack that Nikki could assemble.

But all that was a problem for another day. Tonight, she would lift her hands to the night sky, reveling in the moonlight that poured over her, filling her up, making her shine. She would welcome Sierra Haggerty into the Romero family, where the young Connected could begin to torture the lovestruck Augustus on a more regular basis, and she would allow her own well to be refilled.

But perhaps the biggest task of all now lay before her, as she turned to see Augustus, Matthias and Lucian stride forward, Augustus and Matthias supporting Jonathan between them, while Jonathan's mother and sister hovered just beyond the set, as if to catch Jonathan should he suddenly fall.

He wouldn't fall, though. Sara's healing magic had seen the wounded werewolf through the worst of his trauma, and the care and love of his family would see him through the rest. The pack would stand with him and for him, ever and always.

"Mistress Moon," Augustus called, lifting his free arm to his chest and folding his fist over his heart. "I bring to you the family Romero, your ancient and once more guardians. We pledge to you our service, our support, and our bond."

With her newly attuned senses, Nikki looked at Augustus with eyes that had grown sharp enough to see the faint flush of pride in his cheeks, ears that could pick out his heart's heavy, certain beat, and the accompanying tumble and rush of the emotions swirling through him. Emotions that sharpened to a prism point as she opened her arms wide.

"Augustus Romero and the entire Family of Romero, I gratefully accept your bond," Nikki shouted, sensing their hearts take wing as she called down the very moonlight to do her bidding. "And after far too many lifetimes where you have served with nothing but your strength and your spirit, I am honored to—at last—give you your magic."

A rush of wind filled the soaring amphitheater, a chorus of howls surged up, and the stars in all their heavens shone a little brighter as the mighty werewolves of the Moon finally came home.

~

Thank you for reading, and I hope you enjoyed WEREABOUTS UNKNOWN! To jump into the world of Nikki Dawes, Sara Wilde, and the Arcana Council, check out the entire Immortal Vegas series, starting with the free books One Wilde Night and Getting Wilde!

Elemental Witch

B R KINGSOLVER

Chapter 1

A FRESH START. That's what they told her, and it was true. What they didn't say was that it was probably also her last chance. Everyone admitted that it wasn't really her fault. No one had ever told her she needed to set wards to screen herself from the elementals if she wanted to have sex. It was an accident. On the other hand, she was the one who caused the disaster.

Uncle Teddy helped her move her belongings into the cottage and put things away. She had to admit the cottage was nice and very comfortable, not at all the shack she had feared. A living room and a separate dining room were in the front, with a lovely kitchen behind the dining room, connected to a large workroom with benches, shelves, cabinets, and its own double sink and a gas cook-top. A door from the living room led to her bedroom and bath. The cottage wasn't large, but for one, or even two people, it was fine.

Teddy took her out to dinner, and the following day, he and Rupert Glockner, head of the local Supernatural Council, took her for a tour of the campus and to buy groceries.

The morning after that, Teddy hugged her close, planted a kiss on the top of her head, and said, "I'm not going to tell you good luck. I think you've used up a lifetime's worth of luck. What I will say is, study hard, behave yourself, and set your wards."

"I promise," Joanna said. "Thanks for everything."

"I'll see you next summer," Teddy said. With one last squeeze, he let her go, climbed in his truck, and drove away.

With a lump in her throat, Joanna watched him go, then turned to face Mr. Glockner, her jailer. He seemed nice. Although she had caught a wary look in his eyes, she hadn't detected any animosity or fear from him. But he and everyone else on the local council knew why she was there. The harlot of Oregon. She had felt her face grow warm every time she had to talk to him.

"Joanna," Glockner said with his distinct German accent, "everything will work out fine. If there's anything you need, let me know. And if you just need someone to talk to, or a home-cooked meal, you're welcome in my home anytime. Susan wants you to come to dinner tonight so she can meet you."

Susan was his wife. They had three kids, all much younger than Joanna.

"Thank you," Joanna said. "I'll be there."

She watched him walk down the path away from her. The cottage where Joanna would live and Glockners' home were on the edge of the forest that formed the west boundary of the city. Their house was about half a mile away from hers.

Joanna walked down her long driveway until she reached a foot-path heading in the direction of Midleton College. She had a week before classes started, and a long list of things that needed to be done, from buying her books, to getting her student ID, to simply figuring out where to find everything.

At Oregon State, she had moved into a dormitory as a fresh-man, and everyone around her was in the same boat. None of them knew anyone, and they all were away from home for the first time, which made it easy to meet the other girls and make friends. At Midleton, she would be living alone, and as juniors, most of the people in her classes would already have a circle of friends.

Joanna spent most of the afternoon walking around campus. Some of the buildings reminded her of Oregon State. She also strolled into the area north of the university. Clothing stores, bars and restaurants, and various other businesses catering to students lined the streets. The town looked a lot different from what she was used to on the west coast—older and the brick buildings were narrow, tall, and long. One street that she walked down near the river had stately old Victorian mansions.

Judging from Rupert Glockner's demeanor and dress, Joanna was willing to bet that his wife was a hippie earth-momma, like Joanna's mother. Joanna showed up at the Glockners' that evening wearing a long skirt and a loose, flowing white blouse embroidered with red butterflies.

She knocked on the door, and it immediately opened. A pair of children's smiling faces— probably around ten years old—peered out at her.

"You're Joanna," the boy and the girl said in unison. Then the girl said, "Wow! Your hair is wild! I've never seen hair that color."

"And you're David and Diane," Joanna said to the twins.

"And that's Lizzy," Diane said, pointing to a younger girl who was watching from the other side of the room with her thumb in her mouth. "She's only four."

"Hello, Lizzy," Joanna said. "You know you shouldn't suck on your thumb, don't you?"

"That's what Mom tells her," David said, "but she still does it."

Joanna smiled. "You know that will make you buck-toothed, and you won't be able to whistle," she said to Lizzy. All she got in return was a suspicious scowl.

Joanna started to whistle an Irish jig, and the air sprite hovering over Lizzy's head began to dance and twirl. Lizzy's hand dropped to her side. "Wow!" she said, watching the sprite with wide eyes. "How did you do that?"

"They like to dance," Joanna said, "and they like music. When you learn to whistle really well, you can put on performances with elementals and butterflies that are super neat. But you won't be able to whistle if you continue to suck your thumb."

A pretty blonde woman stepped into the room. "Hi," she said with a smile. "I'm Susan. I'm just finishing up in the kitchen. Can I get you something to drink?" She took Joanna by the elbow and pulled her along. "Goddess, thank you," she muttered. "I'm about at my wits' end trying to keep that kid's thumb out of her mouth."

Joanna looked around the spacious kitchen. Herbs hung from the ceiling, along with copper pots and pans. Jars of home-canned fruits and vegetables lined the shelves on every wall. The room was well-lighted and cheery and cluttered without being messy. Pots on the large stove bubbled, and the smells made her mouth water.

With a questioning look on her face, Susan held up a bottle of white wine. Joanna nodded, and Susan poured a glassful and placed it on the large table in the center of the room.

Joanna took a sip and allowed herself a smile. Susan was dressed exactly as Joanna had imagined. The cozy, welcoming feel of Susan's home caused Joanna to relax for the first time since coming east.

"I'll have to remember that," Susan said. "I can't whistle worth crap, but I'm the only one other than Lizzy who can see the elemental. Will they dance to other music?"

"It's actually an air sprite. When she's older, she may attract elementals, but sprites are much simpler beings. They like clear, high-pitched sounds," Joanna said. "A flute or recorder or even a penny whistle works great." She cocked her head and asked, "You can see elementals?"

Susan smiled. "I'm a hearth witch. Not much power, but anything that has to do with hearth and home and growing things is within my sight. I can't command an elemental, but I can provide an environment where they feel comfortable. And in return, they help me with what I want to do."

"It is comfortable," Joanna said, glancing around again. Maybe this exile wouldn't be so bad after all. "Where's Mr. Glockner?"

"We own a shop in town. Rupert will be coming home soon."

"What kind of shop?"

"A witch supply store," Susan said with a grin. "Herbs and other ingredients, charms, potions, candles, that sort of thing. We also sell stuff I make and bake."

Rupert showed up about half an hour later, and Susan put

dinner on the table. After a week of eating in diners while driving east, Joanna thought she had stumbled into heaven. When dinner was over, Susan sent the kids out to play and then poured wine for the adults.

"Do you like the cottage?" Susan asked as she rejoined her husband and Joanna.

"Yes, it's really nice," Joanna said. "I'm very pleased with the workroom. I'm careful about mixing potions and stuff, but it's nice to be able to keep that sort of work separate from where you prepare your food."

"Do you practice alchemy?" Rupert asked, looking surprised.

"Oh, yes," Joanna said. "I have a spell book that's been handed down in my family for ages, and I've always been fascinated with what you can create."

"Rupert is an alchemist," Susan said. "We built the cottage together when we were first married, and that was his room. I'm glad you like it."

"Did you meet in this country?" Joanna asked. While it was obvious that Rupert was from Europe, Susan had no trace of an accent at all.

Susan gazed fondly at her husband. "No, I spent a summer hitchhiking across Europe when I was in college. Rupert picked me up in a bar in Vienna one night, and by morning, I was in love."

Joanna had to smile at the way Rupert's face turned red, and Susan laughed.

"Oh, my," Susan said, "I've embarrassed you, haven't I? Well, I'm not embarrassed. I'm madly in love with my Transylvanian alchemist and I don't care who knows it."

They seemed like an odd couple. Susan was pretty and outgoing and at least a decade younger than her husband. As short as his wife, with a receding hairline, Rupert wasn't at all what Joanna would consider handsome. But the way they looked at each other left no doubt that they were happy together.

"Joanna," Rupert said, "there are a couple of professors at the university who would like you to stop by this week. Helen Weatherspoon is in the art department. She's also an elemental witch—air and water. Doctor Lance Underwood is the chairman of the ecology department and a fire witch. He has been assigned as your faculty advisor."

"And they're both on the local supernatural council," Susan said. "I think they've been assigned to make sure you don't cause a natural disaster."

"Now, Susan," Rupert said, glaring at his wife, "that's a very inappropriate thing to say."

She laughed. "As if I ever cared about being appropriate. She's an adult, and she has a right to know how things are structured."

Joanna shrugged. "I'm aware that I'm viewed as a walking catastrophe waiting to happen. I've spent the past year and a half with people monitoring everything I do. If I sneeze, everyone around me freezes, waiting for the world to come to an end. I'm just happy that your community was willing to accept me. Everyone in Oregon treated me like a pariah."

"It wasn't your fault," Susan said. "I think everyone understands that."

Rupert cleared his throat. Leaning forward, he fixed Joanna with his eyes. "Yes, people are afraid of you," he said. "And no, from my understanding, what happened wasn't your fault, and no one believes you have any malicious intent. But it is the nature of people to be afraid of someone who holds so much power. Since it slipped away from you once, they're afraid it might happen again."

Joanna felt her face grow hot. "I know better now," she mumbled. "Besides, it's not like I have a lot of opportunity to be in that situation."

"It will get better, honey," Susan whispered. "Don't give up."

Later, Rupert offered to walk Joanna home, but she said, "That's not necessary. The elementals protect me."

Walking Joanna to the door, Susan handed her a small basket. The contents, wrapped in a dish towel, smelled of fresh-baked bread. "Don't be a stranger," Susan said, giving Joanna a hug. "I hope we can become friends."

The moon was high, not yet full, but it supplied plenty of light for Joanna to see the path home. She knew the forest stretched for miles to the west, eventually rising into what easterners called mountains. There was a lot of activity going on in the forest, some that she could hear and some that the elementals told her about. The moon would be full in a few more days. With her new home so close to the forest, she expected it would be interesting.

As if in answer to her thoughts, the trail curved around a large tree, and she found a wolf with a black coat standing in her way.

"Hello," Joanna said with a smile. "You're out a bit early this month, aren't you?"

The wolf growled.

"Oh, give me a break. That's not very friendly. What are you, antisocial?"

It snarled and stalked toward her, gathering its hind legs beneath it as though it might spring. Suddenly, it flew off its feet, blown to the side, as a strong blast of wind swept across the trail. The wolf yelped as it slammed against a tree.

"I don't know why you're being such a bitch," Joanna said, walking past it. The wolf watched her as she continued down the path without looking back.

Chapter 2

"DOCTOR WEATHERSPOON?" Joanna called, looking around the art studio. Other than a desk in one corner, it didn't look at all like a professor's office. To most people, the paintings hung and stacked against the walls might have looked like some kind of abstracts, but Joanna recognized them as paintings of elementals. Some air elementals danced and chased each other around the room creating a slight breeze.

"Over here," a voice responded from above Joanna. "What can I do for you?"

Joanna looked up and saw a gray-haired woman in a paint-spattered smock, hovering in the air near the ceiling.

"I'm Joanna de Groot. Rupert Glockner said that I should come to see you."

"Ah! The elemental witch everyone is so concerned about." Weatherspoon dropped a few feet and moved toward Joanna. "You don't look to me like someone planning the apocalypse. But I could use some help. Come up here and help me look for something I've lost."

Joanna's face burned. Everyone she met seemed to know why she was in Pennsylvania.

Weatherspoon rose back up until her head neared the twenty-foot ceiling. Obediently, Joanna asked a passing air elemental for a ride and rose up to where the professor awaited her.

"What are you looking for?"

"A paintbrush. A small paintbrush about a foot long and a couple of millimeters in diameter. The elementals seem to think that hiding it from me is some kind of game. The trick is to slowly glide around the room looking for it. Can't do it from ground level because they keep moving it around. You go over to that side of the room, and maybe between the two of us we can catch a glimpse of it."

Doing as she was told, Joanna floated slowly to the other side of the room, concentrating on looking below for the missing brush.

"Have you considered asking them to bring it back?" Joanna asked.

"And spoil the game? Admit that a bunch of elementals are smarter than I am? Where's the fun in that?"

"Oh."

After a couple of minutes, Joanna said, "I think it's under that low stool over there."

"And what makes you think so?"

"Because the elemental I'm riding refuses to take me over there."

Weatherspoon started laughing. "So, they've started cheating?" She suddenly dived toward the stool. She landed next to the stool, bent down, and retrieved the brush.

"So, Miss de Groot, it seems that we have been assigned to each other. I'm supposed to teach you to use your talents safely. Do you have a boyfriend?"

"No, ma'am," Joanna cringed and felt her face grow hot again.

"Do you want a boyfriend?"

Joanna shrugged. "Well, I always thought it would be kinda nice," she muttered.

"Do you know what to do if you get one?"

"I-I think so."

"I mean with your wards and that sort of thing."

"Oh, yes. If someone had told me before——"

Weatherspoon cut her off. "Of course. Well, if you have any questions, let me know. What does your class schedule look like?"

Joanna pulled it out and showed it to the professor.

"No classes on Friday morning? How in the world did you manage that? Well, I'll come by Friday at nine o'clock and we'll take a hike in the woods. There's a lake a couple of miles west of campus. It's a good place to practice and play. Okay?"

"Yes, ma'am."

Weatherspoon smiled. "And call me Helen, Joanna. This doesn't have to be painful. I promise we'll have a good time."

Feeling better than she had before going to meet Professor Weatherspoon, Joanna walked across campus to Dr. Underwood's office.

She climbed three flights of stairs and down the hall to the last office. The door was open, so she walked in, knocking on the door as she passed it.

"What?" a low, booming voice growled.

Sitting behind the desk was a huge bear of a man. Black hair swept back from his face and fell around his shoulders. A full beard hid much of his face, but the dark eyes seemed to skewer Joanna and hold her frozen in place. Fire sprites danced around the room, and an elemental burned in a curved ceramic dish in the corner.

"I'm Joanna de Groot," she managed to say.

He stared at her for what seemed like a long time. "You don't look like a spawn of Satan," he finally growled. "Except for the hair, of course. Turn your head."

Uncertain about what to do, Joanna turned her head to the side.

"No points," he said. "You have Fae hair but not the ears."

"No, my ears aren't pointed," Joanna said, turning her head back to look at him. "No one knows where my Fae blood comes from." Her mother always blamed her father, whom Joanna had never met.

"Have a seat," he said, gesturing to a chair in front of his desk. "Did you bring your class schedule with you?"

She handed it to him, her hand shaking a little bit. Up close, he was even larger than he had seemed at first. With him sitting and her standing, he was still taller than she was.

He scanned it for a minute, then looked up. "This is a pretty rough schedule," he said. Opening a folder on his desk, he turned a couple of pages. "Your grades at Oregon State were excellent. Are you studious?"

"I study. Yes," she said. "But I enjoy my classes. I enjoy learning. I'm not sure that I study more than other people."

"Are you saying that you're smarter than most people?"

Taking a deep breath, she considered her answer. "I think I'm smarter than a lot of people. I'm not some kind of genius or prodigy. I meet people smarter than I am all the time. I still have to study to get my grades."

His eyes narrowed, then he looked back at her schedule. "Advanced Principles of Ecology, Biochemistry, Physical Chemistry, Molecular Biology, and History of Supernatural-Human Interaction. A completely full schedule and pretty heavy on the sciences."

"Yes, sir."

"You don't think that maybe you should shed one of the chemistry courses?"

"No, sir. Chemistry isn't difficult. It makes sense. I really don't see this as a difficult schedule."

"Okay," he said, handing the schedule back to her. "We'll meet here every Wednesday at eleven thirty."

"Yes, sir."

"Do you always have such an entourage?" Underwood asked, waving his hand at the elementals that had accompanied Joanna into his office. There were at least four or five of each type—air, fire, and water. Her largest fire elemental had wrapped itself around the elemental burning in the corner, and the resulting flare reached almost to the ceiling.

"Usually."

"They're elementals, not sprites."

Joanna shrugged. "I like sprites. They're funny and playful, but they tend to be intimidated by the elementals."

He nodded. "I'll see you in class on Monday."

She left his office feeling very unsettled. He hadn't said so, but it felt like he didn't approve of her. Walking along, remembering their meeting, she realized that he scared her—his size, his manner, his position both as a professor and as a member of the supernatural council.

Feeling a bit calmer when she arrived home, she ate a light lunch and then decided to find the lake that Professor Weatherspoon mentioned.

She stood in the sunshine in her front yard, enjoying the sounds of birds singing, and watching squirrels chasing each other through the branches above. Reaching out to a large air elemental, she pulled its power to her and rose from the ground. Passing the tops of the trees, she rose until she could see the campus in the near distance. The woods continued past the Glockners' property and onto the edge of the university's land.

She had the elemental take her west, and soon a small lake came into view. The road from the city curved by the campus, passed her driveway, and then dead-ended just past the edge of the woods. A wide walking path continued from there to the lake.

Joanna drifted down to the lake. Kneeling, she put her hand in the water, feeling its cold bite. Then the water seemed to warm, and she felt the elemental of the lake welcome her. Quickly stripping off her clothes, she waded into the water, then dove under the surface, surrendering herself to the elemental.

She swam and played with the water and air elementals and sprites, diving beneath the surface and exploring the underwater world, then riding a cushion of air several body lengths above the surface, and diving again into the water.

It wasn't until she began to grow hungry that she thought about going home. Glancing toward the shore, she froze as she realized that a boy sat on the fallen log where she had piled her clothes. She had no idea how long he had been watching her.

The community of witches she had grown up in had no nudity taboos, and indeed many magic rituals required that witches be unencumbered by clothing. But her time at Oregon State had taught her that humans tended to associate a naked girl with sex.

With his attention riveted on her, she had a feeling that he might think that way, which was terribly inconvenient.

"Hello," she called.

"Hello yourself," he answered. "That's quite a show you've been putting on."

Not being sure if he meant her play with the elementals or her lack of clothes, she said, "I would like to get out and get dressed, if you don't mind."

"I don't mind at all," he said with a grin.

"Perhaps you could be a gentleman and turn around," she suggested.

"I don't think so," he said, his grin growing wider. "I'm not much of a gentleman."

Joanna took a deep breath, and when he showed no evidence of moving or redirecting his attention, she stood and began walking toward the shore. She tried not to look at him directly, but it was hard. He was incredibly good-looking, the kind of guy she always crushed on, but who chose girls who were more normal looking—taller, with curves and normal hair.

"Asshole," she said as she reached the log. Air elementals swirled around her, drying her body and beginning the process of drying the blanket of hair hanging down her back.

"Very nice," he said.

"Very rude," she responded.

Balancing on one foot and then on the other, she put on her panties. Pulling her t-shirt over her head was more challenging, as the elementals weren't very cooperative.

"You've got a lot of hair," he said.

Since nothing she had said so far had discouraged him, she ignored him. She pulled on her jeans and sat to put on her shoes.

"What's your name?" he asked.

"What's yours?"

"Kyle. Where do you go to school?"

Oh, dear Goddess, Joanna thought. *He thinks I'm in high school.* There were two high schools in town, and the college.

She didn't answer him, suddenly humiliated. He was obviously about the same age as she was, but when he looked at her, he seemed to see a little girl. Time to go. She stood and called an air elemental.

"Are you starting at the college?" he asked, correctly interpreting her silence as being offended.

Really looking at his face for the first time, she paused. He was even more handsome than she first thought, with hard, muscled chest and arms. But his yellow eyes captured her attention. He was a werewolf. Weres were even more comfortable with nudity than witches. To shift, he would strip, and so would his pack mates.

It also made him even less likely to be attracted to a skinny little human.

"What's your name?" he asked again. "Come on, you can't be that mad at me for looking. Don't tell me that you didn't think about someone coming along and seeing you when you took your clothes off." He flashed that grin again and she felt a little weak. "I won't tell anyone."

"How old are you?" she said in answer.

"Twenty-one. I'm a senior at the college. Do you come here often?"

"Twenty-one," Joanna repeated. "And you think I'm in high school. I guess that would make you a pedophile, wouldn't it? I guess you won't tell anyone. Maybe I should."

The expression on his face was worth every bit of discomfort he had caused her. She grinned at him and began to rise into the air. His eyes widened as he watched her.

"Wait! What's your name?"

Damn, he was persistent. "Joanna," she called as she rose above the trees to head home.

Chapter 3

JOANNA DRIFTED DOWN to her cottage and saw a large basket with a handle, covered with a blue-and-white checked cloth, sitting in front of her door. Susan was walking away and had just reached the path leading through the trees.

"Susan," Joanna called. The blonde woman turned and looked around.

"Look up."

Susan did, and a smile spread across her face. "That's pretty neat," she said as Joanna reached the ground. She waved her hand in the direction of the basket. "I thought I'd missed you. I brought you some fresh herbs and vegetables."

"Thank you. The stuff in the grocery store just doesn't taste quite right," Joanna said as she landed. "Can you stay for a bit? I can make tea."

Susan's eyes grew wide. "Your hair. Goddess, it's alive." Joanna's flame-red hair with yellow streaks was unusual enough, and she wore it in a tight braid most of the time. Unbound, it tumbled and writhed like a sea of flame in a storm, constantly in motion, falling to her waist and billowing in an enormous cloud past her elbows.

Joanna pursed her lips. "For some reason, the air elementals are fascinated with it. That's why I normally braid it; they won't leave it alone."

Susan came in and sat at the kitchen table while Joanna heated water and put away the bounty Susan had brought her. Most of the stuff stayed in the kitchen—either in the refrigerator or hung from hooks in the ceiling—but some went into the workshop. When the kettle whistled, Joanna poured the hot water into a pitcher over a strainer filled with tea and set it on the table.

"It's cool in here," Susan commented, looking at the steaming tea.

"The elementals cool it off," Joanna said. "It helps on a hot day like this." She pulled the strainer out and set it in the sink. Then she called a water elemental and had it cool the tea until the pitcher frosted. Susan's eyebrows shot up.

"Works better than ice," Joanna said. "This way the tea is not diluted."

They sat at the table making small talk and sipping their tea.

"Are there a lot of weres in the woods on the full moon?" Joanna asked.

"Yes," Susan answered, "mostly college students. Wolves, lynx, and a couple of cougars. Older weres tend to go farther from town where the hunting is better. Most of the deer have been hunted out of this area. It's probably not a good idea to go out on the full moon."

Joanna told her about the encounter with the wolf on the path between the Glockners' and the cottage, then told her about Kyle.

"He's so good-looking," Joanna said, "but he thinks I'm just a little kid. He couldn't possibly be attracted to me."

"Honey," Susan said, "men are idiots. But whether he thought you were sixteen or thirty, if he didn't think you were attractive, he wouldn't have been looking. If he comes around again, flirt with him, string him along, and when he gets to panting heavy enough, let him know that you might be open to a boyfriend, but you don't share."

"What? No! I'm not that kind of girl," Joanna said.

"You don't like boys?" Susan asked with a smirk. "I thought you did."

"No, I mean I can't flirt and do all that stuff. I don't know how. Either I'm completely tongue-tied, or if a guy irritates me enough, I want to just rip his head off."

"You had a boyfriend in Oregon."

Joanna snorted. "Yeah, and believe me, we were meant for each other. He was even more socially awkward and geeky than I was."

Susan got a faraway look in her eyes, then asked, "What are you doing this evening?"

"I don't know. Read, probably. I don't have anything else to do."

"Have you considered going out dancing?" Susan asked. "Hitting the bars on Campus Corner?"

"No. I never do things like that," Joanna said. She thought of what she would be doing at Oregon State the weekend before classes started. Probably going to a party with her friends, but she didn't know anyone at Midleton.

"You weren't twenty-one yet when you were going to school before, right?" Susan said. She shrugged. "I know it's kind of intimidating going out alone, but how are you going to meet people if you stay locked up in this cottage all the time?"

"I walked around there the other day. I'm not sure what bars to go to."

"High Moon is a shifter hangout," Susan said. "The Cauldron, The Spellcaster, and Brews and Potions cater to different groups of witches. Not by the type of witch, just personal preference as far as the crowd and the music. Last Call has a crowd with a lot of vampires and Asuras. You can imagine what a human or a witch going there is looking for."

Her eyes narrowed as she thought. "There are also a couple of coffee houses. Java Joe's is for all ages, and Avalon is for those who are over twenty-one because they do serve beer and wine. Both of them usually have live acoustic music. Of course, there are a lot of human bars also. Really, you should get out. This weekend is your last chance before you have to study."

After Susan left, Joanna fixed a simple supper and thought about what Susan had said. Although Joanna had never been in a bar before, it couldn't be that different than a party, except you paid for drinks. And if she didn't like any of the bars, the coffee houses sounded good.

Parting her hair on the side, she plaited it in a loose braid starting under her ear and falling over her shoulder. Dressing in a pair of new jeans and a green satin top that matched her eyes, she set her wards, closed the cottage, and caught a ride with an air elemental to the other side of campus.

Walking past bistros and pubs full of students eating dinner, drinking, and excitedly discussing their plans for the evening, she was so busy people-watching that she walked right into someone. He was much larger than she was, and she bounced off him, staggering and almost falling. A strong hand reached out and grabbed her arm, steadying her.

"Oh, excuse me," she said. "I guess I wasn't paying attention to where I was going."

She looked up and stared into yellow eyes. For a moment, she thought it was Kyle and felt her face grow warm. His face showed surprise, and he grinned.

"Uh, sorry," she stammered, pulling her arm from his grasp. She ducked around him and walked on down the street.

"Nice looking," she heard him say. "I'll bet she'll be a real heart-breaker when she grows up."

She kept walking and didn't look back.

She had armed herself with every form of identification she possessed, and when she tried to enter The Cauldron, she was glad she had. Oregon driver's license, Oregon State and Midleton student IDs, and her passport were barely enough to convince the bouncers to let her through the door.

The bar was aptly named. Throw some techno music, wild light-ing, a bunch of excited college students, and alcohol together and stir. She ordered hard cider at the bar and then wandered around. Susan was right about it being a witches' bar. There were a few weres, and a few humans, but for the most part, almost everyone she came near radiated magic.

A lot of the girls in The Cauldron were dressed the way she was, in a shirt and jeans, but there were also those with ultra-short dresses and ultra-high heels. No one asked Joanna to dance, but she really didn't expect it. Wallflowers were rarely asked to dance unless they were in a group that attracted attention. She finished her drink and headed down the street to the next place.

The Spellcaster was smaller and a bit quieter, and the music was the classic rock and blues she preferred. She hung out for about an hour and felt a lot more comfortable there.

Brews and Potions was very different, more like an English pub. Dark wood wainscoting contrasted with green wallpaper. The walls were decorated with pictures of Ireland and England, as well as fairy-tale castles and druidic ceremonies. She found a stool at the bar, ordered a drink, and looked around. One room held pool tables and dart boards, another room had game boards, and she saw people playing chess, Monopoly and Yahtzee. Booths were full of people engaged in earnest discussions, and everyone's dress was casual.

"You look like you're having a good night," the bartender said. She realized she was grinning like a fool. She'd found the bar for the geeky kids.

"Yes, I am," she said. "I'm a transfer student and just trying to figure out what's going on."

"We have some acoustic acts in here sometimes," he said, "and trivia on Tuesdays. But if you want loud music and dancing, try the Cauldron or the Spellcaster."

"Any non-witch bars you'd recommend?"

He chuckled. "Depends on your kink, I guess. This is probably the most mixed-race bar on the Corner. We're sort of a non-denominational watering hole. A lot of witches, especially those who aren't 'out,' go only to human bars. That's the nice thing about being a witch—we fit in almost anywhere."

A girl and a guy with guitars set up on the small bandstand in the corner of the main room and started playing. Joanna relaxed and enjoyed listening to the music and watching the people. She finished her cider, and Danny, the bartender, brought her another one.

Someone slipped onto the barstool beside her, but he or she was behind her as she faced the performers.

"You must have the best fake ID in the world," a voice said in her ear.

Spinning around, she found Kyle sitting there grinning at her.

"Well, well," Joanna said, "it's Mr. Erroneous Assumptions, barging ahead without fear or thought in a determined effort to stick both feet in his mouth again."

He stared at her, and she stared back.

"Oh, crap," he finally said. "You really are old enough to be in here."

She let one corner of her mouth crook up in a half smile. "My passport says so."

"I'm sorry," he said.

"For what? For being an ass, or for telling me I look like a little girl? You really know how to make a gal feel special."

Kyle opened his mouth and then closed it. He cocked his head a bit to the side, like a dog trying to make sense of something. "I apologize for being an ass. And for being rude."

"I accept," she said with a smile. "Do you come here often?"

"Usually for trivia nights, and the people playing music tonight are friends of mine," he said, motioning to the couple on the bandstand.

"They're very good," Joanna said. "I like their music."

"I'll introduce you on their next break."

Over the next two hours, Joanna met at least a dozen people. Although Kyle was a were, he was well-known to the witches in the bar. Joanna had a good time, but as midnight approached, she started yawning.

"I'm going to have to call it a night," she said. "Take care, and I'll see you around."

"Where do you live?" he asked. "I'll walk you home, or give you a ride if it's too far away."

Leaning close, she said, "Kyle, remember how I left the lake today? I'll make it home just fine. But thanks."

As she crawled under the covers later, she reflected that maybe she would be able to make friends at Midleton after all.

Chapter 4

WHEN JOANNA SHOWED up at the Glockners' for dinner the following evening, Lizzy immediately ran toward her. The air sprite hovered above her shoulder.

"Can you make it dance again?" the little girl asked.

Joanna pulled a tin whistle out of her pocket and knelt down in front of Lizzy. "I can teach you how to make it dance." Joanna blew a few notes, and the sprite started to twirl and bounce around.

Lizzy's eyes grew wide, staring at the instrument.

Susan looked at them in alarm. "You shouldn't have," she said.

"It's okay," Joanna said, producing a larger tin whistle. "I have another one. That's the one I learned on." She grinned. "Almost drove my mom to distraction until I learned to play it properly."

"Like I said," Susan grimaced, "you really shouldn't have."

"Thumb or whistle?" Rupert asked, and Susan threw him a look that could have curdled milk.

By the time Susan put dinner on the table, Lizzy had learned a simple tune, and the sprite was dancing for her.

"Just send her outside if she starts to get on your nerves," Joanna said as she sat down to eat. "If she's playing, you know where she is, and the sprites won't let any harm come to her. By the time winter gets here, she'll know more than one tune."

Rupert laughed, but Susan didn't look convinced.

As the sun went down, the full moon rose over the university. In the forest, the first howls of the wolves sounded. Joanna didn't take the chance of walking, but called an elemental to carry her home. Classes started the following morning, and she wanted to get a good night's sleep.

She tried to go to sleep, but the wolves kept her awake. She finally got up and set additional wards to block out the noise. In the ensuing silence, she soon fell asleep.

The bed shaking woke her up. In fact, everything in the house was shaking, and the winds outside rose to a moaning shriek that she could hear in spite of her wards. Having grown up on the west coast, Joanna recognized an earthquake.

She leapt from the bed and fled to the front door. When she got outside, the moon was almost directly overhead, flooding the yard with a surreal light. The earth was still rolling, and the trees were whipping about in close to gale-force winds. The last time she had seen the elementals go so crazy was that night when she had her first orgasm. But this was different, and it went on and on and on. Joanna didn't get any sleep the rest of the night.

"I SUMMON THEE, K'LUK'ANGRATHANDUB!" the witch's voice quavered, but his pronunciation of the name was precise. He had practiced the ritual and the name until he was letter-perfect. The flames of the candles flared, and as he dripped his blood from the cut on his arm into the bowls of herbs, they began to smolder, filling the room with scented smoke.

The air itself split with a mind-numbing shriek. The room was bathed in an eerie red glow. He had drawn a pentagram inside a circle. Red and yellow flames blazed through the breach, and shadowy figures darted back and forth.

Suddenly the breach closed, and the demon stood before him. It was seven feet tall, with red skin, and its bony arms and legs had too many joints. Short twisted horns jutted from its forehead. The three-eyed face looked as though it was partly melted, pock-marked, and covered with warts and weeping boils, as was the rest of its body.

It peered around, the three eyes moving independently, then it let out a high cackle. "Fool!" it said in a voice that sounded like a hysterical old woman from a bad horror movie. The salt of the circle and the pentagram burst into flames, and the demon stepped through the fire. The earth shook, and a powerful wind sprung up outside, the sound penetrating even into the deep basement.

The demon's hand shot out and grabbed the witch by the chest, its fingers sinking through his flesh into his lungs. The witch screamed.

"Anyone can perform a ritual," the demon said, "but you have to have the power to hold what you call."

It leaned forward with its mouth open, and the witch felt a searing pain. The demon pulled its head away, chewing on something. The witch could still see the demon, but blood was running into his eyes. He reached up, and his hands felt only slick bone. The demon had bitten his face off.

Fire flowed from the demon's fingers into the witch's body. He screamed again and again as the demon grabbed his arm and ripped it from his body. The screaming continued for another five minutes.

THE FULL MOON SHONE DOWN, turning the forest into a glowing wonderland. It was Shara's favorite time—running free with Bobby in the night, the scent of a rabbit pulling them forward.

It was the only time she was happy anymore. She wasn't sure when it all began to change, but a year before she was madly in love, and she thought that Bobby was in love with her. But gradually he seemed to drift away. He said mean things to her, and nothing she ever did was good enough for him. He never told her he loved her anymore, and the way he touched her had changed, had become increasingly rough. His grades suffered along with her, and he seemed angry all the time, especially when he drank, and it seemed he was always drinking.

But when they shifted and went hunting under the full moon, they connected again. He was still rough when they had sex, but in her wolf's body she didn't mind. He took out his anger on whatever they hunted, and not on her.

Rounding a bend in the game trail they were following, she detected a magical presence ahead of her. A tall figure loomed in front of them. The wolves shied to the sides of the trail.

It was fast, so incredibly fast. It leaped toward her and grabbed her before she could duck away. Her coat burned and she screamed, twisting in its grasp to try and bite it.

Out of the corner of her eye, she saw Bobby shift. She couldn't understand what he was doing. They were far more formidable in their wolf forms. As humans, naked and weaponless, how could they fight whatever was holding her?

"I offer you a deal," she heard Bobby shout.

"What could you possibly offer me?" a high voice that sent shivers through her answered. "I already have the woman."

"I will let you possess me," Bobby said.

Shara's blood ran cold as she realized what they faced. A demon. She knew then that she was going to die, and that Bobby would let her. He was bargaining for his life, not hers. She bit down hard on the demon's arm. It screamed and threw her away across the trail. She heard and felt her ribs crack when she hit a tree.

As consciousness fled, she heard the demon say, "Invite me in, little shifter."

Chapter 5

JOANNA STIFLED A YAWN. She had hoped to start her classes well-rested, especially her Advanced Ecological Principles class with Dr. Underwood. Someone dropped into the seat beside her. She turned around and was surprised to see Kyle.

"What are you doing here?" she asked.

"Attending class," he said. "I'm an ecology major. You?"

"You're stalking me," she accused.

"Guilty as charged," he said, and then yawned. "I changed my major just so I could have the same classes as you do."

She tried to figure out if he was serious, then wanted to slap herself. They had met on Friday, and there was no way in the world he had enrolled in that class over the weekend.

"Well," she said, "don't expect me to take notes for you. Especially when you've been out howling at the moon all night."

He gave her a sheepish smile. "Guilty as charged. For real, this time."

At eight o'clock sharp, Dr. Underwood walked into the classroom, passed out the course syllabus, and began to tell the students what the assignments were for the semester. Joanna noticed that he kept yawning, too.

She managed to stay awake until the class ended. Briefly, she wondered if she might be able to go home and take a nap.

"Miss de Groot," Underwood called, "will you please wait after class?"

"How is the Student Center coffee?" she asked Kyle.

"It will strip paint," he answered. "What does Underwood want with you?"

"Will it keep me awake?"

"Get a large cup. Got a class now. See you later."

Joanna walked to the front of the room. Underwood waited until all the other students left, then said, "Did you notice anything unusual last night?"

She stifled a yawn and said, "Other than howling wolves, an earthquake, and a storm that blew in out of a clear sky? Professor, I've been here only a week. I don't know what you folks consider unusual."

The corner of his mouth twitched, and she thought there might be a twinkle in his eye.

"Other than the wolves, I assure you, the other things are unusual. I've never seen elementals act like that."

"It wasn't me," she said reflexively.

"I didn't think it was. I think an earthquake is a little beyond what you could do. Why don't you tell me about what you experienced last night?"

She told him, and when she was through, he asked, "Do you remember anything else?"

"I remember wondering how I could hear the winds. I know I set my wards correctly, and the wind was the only thing I could hear. When I walked outside, everything got a lot louder, and I could hear all sorts of things banging around."

"Are you sure it was wind you were hearing when you were inside?"

She thought about it. "Now that you ask, it really didn't sound like wind. But what else could it have been? I don't think I've ever heard a sound quite like it. I guess when I heard the wind outside, I decided that must be what I heard. What would that sound have to do with the elementals going nuts?"

"I think there was a breach in the continuum," Underwood said.

"A breach? You mean between here and another dimension?"

"Yes, I think someone summoned a demon. I need to speak with Helen Weatherspoon and a couple of earth witches to compare what they experienced last night with what you've told me."

"Are there any conjurers in this area who could call a demon?" Joanna asked.

His face was expressionless. "That's the wrong question. What you mean to ask is, if there are any conjurers stupid enough to call a demon."

She studied his face and tried to process what he said, then it dawned on her. "You think a student called it."

He nodded.

Joanna left the building with enough adrenaline running through her body that she decided coffee wasn't necessary. A demon. A nightmare personified. She shuddered.

"Hey," a girl's voice called.

Joanna heard footsteps running behind her. Turning around, she saw a girl with blonde-streaked brown hair approaching.

"Hi," the smiling girl said. "You're new."

"Do I have a sign on my forehead or something?" Joanna asked with a grin.

The girl chuckled. "No one takes Underwood's class unless they have to," she said, "and I know almost everyone who would have to. I'm Addie."

"Joanna. Why don't people want to take the class? I think it sounds interesting."

"Because he flunks about a quarter of the class every semester," Addie said. "I struggled to get a B in his intro class. Same thing in the other classes he teaches. Don't you think that's a lot of work he assigned this morning?"

Joanna shrugged. "I didn't really think about it."

Addie shook her head. "I hope you're right, but I know people who have taken it, and they say it's a real bear. Do you have a class now?"

"Not until one o'clock," Joanna said.

"Want to go get some coffee? Maybe lunch?"

Joanna laughed. "Are you the welcome wagon for transfer students?"

Shaking her head and looking a bit sheepish, Addie said, "I'm just nosy. You've got the most incredible aura I've ever seen, so I just had to meet you."

"My aura?" Joanna was confused. She wasn't able to see people's auras, and Addie showed no signs whatsoever of having any magic.

"Yeah. You have an aura that shows you're a witch, but it's constantly in motion. It has streaks in it, like lightning, sorta."

Joanna stopped and stared at Addie. "Streaks?"

"Yeah, like crystal, and blue and red shooting through and around your aura."

Joanna attempted to expand her awareness, and mumbled under her breath a 'reveal magic' spell. Usually, it was used to try and show if an object had been spelled, or what kind of magic a charm held. She had never tried to use it on a person before.

If the spell worked, she couldn't tell. As far as all her senses told her, Addie was human. There wasn't a minute shred of magic in her. Susan was a grand archmage in comparison.

"What are you?" Joanna blurted.

It was Addie's turn to stare. "I—what—" she stammered. Then she shook her head. "I don't know what you mean."

"You're not a witch, and you're not any other kind of supernatural I've ever met," Joanna said. "What are you?"

A look of fear appeared in Addie's eyes. "I'm not anything. I … I mean, I'm just a human. Why do I have to be something else?"

"How can you tell if someone has magic if you don't?" Joanna returned.

"I don't know. I mean, I can see people's auras, and I learned that witches' auras are different than normal people's."

"What about shifters?"

"Theirs are different, too. Like Kyle, the hunky guy you were sitting next to in class. His aura is different than yours."

"What about vampires' and Asuras'?"

Addie shuddered. "Vampires' auras are really different. I don't know what an Asura is."

"A succubus or incubus."

Addie still looked confused.

"Have you ever met a girl or a guy who just radiates sex? Someone who makes you feel like your mind is clouded and your crotch is on fire?"

Joanna could see a look of recognition dawn in Addie's eyes. "Oh, yeah, I know what you mean now. They have a different aura, and there are some other people whose auras are similar but different. They don't make you feel like they're seducing you, though."

"Psyvamps," Joanna said, shaking her head. What was this girl? A thought occurred to her. "What do you see when you look at Dr. Underwood?"

"He has an aura like yours, with only red streaks. He doesn't have the crystal or blue ones. I mean, not exactly like yours. Every person's aura is different."

"I need to go," Joanna said, suddenly afraid. She didn't know what Addie was, but with Underwood talking of demons, Joanna found the unknown frightening. "I'll see you around."

"Okay." Addie looked disappointed. As Joanna turned to go, Addie said, "I apologize. I didn't mean to be rude or to make you uncomfortable."

Joanna turned back to look at her. The girl looked miserable, her eyes about half-filled with tears, and she was biting her bottom lip. Joanna immediately felt sorry for how she'd reacted. Here was someone who had approached her in a friendly manner, who seemed open to being a friend. Perhaps someone who was a little too open.

"Can you feel people's emotions?" Joanna asked.

Addie's head jerked up, and she stared at Joanna like a rabbit facing a snake. The answer to the puzzle that was Addie hit Joanna like a bolt of lightning.

"Dear Goddess," Joanna breathed. "You're a sensitive. What did you feel or see last night?"

"That's what I wanted to ask you about," Addie said, still looking scared. "I know something really bad happened last night, but I don't know what it was. There was an earthquake, for Heaven's sake, and not a word about it on the news this morning."

Joanna reached out and took Addie's arm. "Come with me. I have someone I want you to meet."

When they reached Professor Weatherspoon's office, they checked her schedule on the door. It showed she would be in class for another ten minutes. They waited.

Joanna was lost in thought when she heard Addie gasp. Helen Weatherspoon was walking toward them, accompanied by a couple of air elementals and a water elemental.

"What?" Joanna asked.

"Her aura has those crystal and blue streaks like yours."

Weatherspoon raised an eyebrow at the girls' presence but didn't say anything. Opening her studio, she went in, and the girls followed her.

"Have you talked with Dr. Underwood?" Joanna asked.

"No, I've been in class, but I was going to try and find him this afternoon. Who's your friend?"

Joanna turned to Addie, who was frozen in place, her head whipping back and forth trying to watch the air elementals and sprites flitting around the studio, and also gaping at the water elementals forming fountains from several buckets scattered about the room.

"This is Addie," Joanna said. "She thinks something bad happened last night, and she was hoping I might be able to tell her what it was."

Weatherspoon watched Addie for a minute, then said, "Addie? Is that your whole name?"

"Oh, I'm sorry," Addie said, turning to the art professor. "I'm Adele Fisher. I've never seen anything like this."

"What do you see?" Weatherspoon asked.

"Crystal and blue things. Like the streaks in your aura and Joanna's." She pointed to a painting on the wall. "Like that. They're real, aren't they?"

"What is Professor Weatherspoon feeling?" Joanna asked.

Addie shot her a startled look.

"It's okay," Joanna said. "We're not going to get down on you for being different."

"Surprise, puzzlement, irritation," Addie said. "And an undercurrent of fear. You have an undercurrent that feels a lot the same."

"What did you feel last night?" Weatherspoon asked, her voice quiet and soothing.

"Rage, fear, gloating, terrible things," Addie said, her voice shaking slightly. "I woke up when the earthquake hit, and the world was going crazy. Things were flashing by my windows. Things like that," she pointed to an air elemental, "but larger."

Joanna turned to Weatherspoon. "Is she …?" she asked quietly.

"A sensitive? I think so."

"What?" Addie asked, a note of alarm in her voice.

"Come sit down," Weatherspoon motioned to a table in the corner, next to a smaller table and an old refrigerator.

The girls sat down, and Weatherspoon plugged in an electric kettle.

"Some humans are sensitive to magic," Weatherspoon said. "Some humans are sensitive to emotions. It's called empathy. And some humans are sensitive to both. By humans, I mean humans and witches. We're really the same race, you know. Shifters are human also, but they're sensitive to different things."

"I thought that witches and shifters were different," Addie said. "In school, they taught us that witches only look like humans."

"Don't have sex with a witch without protection," Weatherspoon chuckled. "If you can crossbreed, then you're the same species. Human, Witch, Fae, Shifter. We have a common ancestor. Vampires are truly a different race, as are Asuras. They look like us, but we're fundamentally different. You can feed a Fae, a human, and a Shifter the same diet, but a Vampire or an Incubus would starve to death. They're basically parasites that evolved to feed on humans."

"Addie said there wasn't anything on the news this morning about the earthquake," Joanna said.

"Human authorities don't understand what happened, so they hushed everything up. They're trying to ignore it and hope people didn't notice."

"Goddess," Joanna said. "How can you ignore a five-point-two earthquake?"

"That's rather precise," Weatherspoon said with a chuckle.

"Lots of practice assessing them in Oregon and California," Joanna said. She winked. "Besides, a water elemental told me that's what an earth elemental told it."

"We studied about elementals in my Physical Properties class," Addie said. "You can talk to them?"

"Not talk, exactly," Weatherspoon said. "Communicate, but in a way that's almost impossible to explain to someone. It's a combination of feeling and knowing, and I can't tell you how they impart that feeling and knowing to me."

A knock sounded at the door. The knob turned, and Dr. Underwood stuck his head in. "Helen?"

"Over here in the corner," Weatherspoon said.

Underwood crossed the room, slowing when he saw Joanna and Addie.

"Miss de Groot, Miss Fisher," he said. A slight smile came to his face. "It looks as though I'm in time for tea."

He took the final chair at the table as Weatherspoon poured tea for everyone.

"Adele was just telling us about last night," Weatherspoon said. "She said that the earthquake was accompanied by large air elementals outside her window, and powerful feelings of rage, fear, and gloating. Her words."

Underwood looked thoughtful for a couple of minutes, then turned to Addie. "Rage, fear and gloating? Where do you think those feelings came from? Do you think they were from what you think you saw outside your window?"

Addie shrank in her seat. Joanna could relate. Underwood was an imposing figure.

"From the city," Addie said in a small voice. "Not too far off campus." She pointed to the fire elemental hovering over Underwood. "Those things don't have emotions."

Underwood leaned toward her. "When you feel powerful emotions like that, can you always identify the source?"

"I've never felt anything like that before," Addie said. "It was, well, this is going to sound weird, but it was too powerful to be a human. I mean, I've been around someone who just learned her husband was killed, and someone who watched her baby die. Those are awfully strong emotions, but nothing like what I felt last night."

"Adele, I have heard that strong emotions leave a psychic residue," Underwood said in a voice so gentle that it startled Joanna. "If you are in a place where a tragic event took place, or something very happy occurred, can you feel that emotion if the people are no longer there?"

"Sometimes. It depends on how long ago it happened."

"If we blindfolded you, do you think you could follow Joanna across campus?" Weatherspoon asked.

"Maybe," Addie said. "If she was upset or very happy about something, you know, if her emotions really stood out from everyone else's, then it would make it easier. Why?"

Underwood and Weatherspoon looked at each other, and when they both nodded, it was obvious they shared a thought. Addie looked back and forth between them, and Joanna could see that the girl was very anxious about what was going on.

"It's not fair to scare her and not tell her what we're talking about," Joanna said.

The professors looked at her, and then Underwood said, "Quite right. My apologies, Miss Fisher. We think that some fool summoned a demon last night. If it had simply been a small demon, and if the witch who called it had controlled it, we probably wouldn't have ever known about it. But what we suspect is that there is a dead witch out there somewhere, and a very live demon running around."

Before Addie and Joanna left to go to their classes, the professors took Addie's address and mobile number.

"Adele," Professor Weatherspoon said, "we won't tell anyone about your abilities. I can understand why you would want to keep them secret. All three of us know what it's like to be looked at like a freak. But you're not being very discreet telling complete strangers that you can see their auras. Do you understand what I'm saying?"

Chapter 6

JOANNA MADE it to her first afternoon class with two minutes to spare. Looking around, she didn't recognize anyone. Of course, she really knew only Addie and Kyle. As she fumbled in her backpack for her notebook, someone dropped into the seat beside her. She looked over and saw the waitress who had waited on her at Avalon the day she stopped in.

Tall and slender, she had been wearing a black leotard, black tights, and a black miniskirt at the bar. For class, she wore cargo pants and a pink Hello Kitty t-shirt that might have fit Joanna but barely covered the other girl's chest, leaving her midriff bare.

"Hi," the girl said. "You were in Avalon the other night."

"Yeah, I was. I'm Joanna."

"I'm Bev. You taking this as a requirement?"

"No," Joanna said in surprise, "it's an elective. You?" She had signed up for History of Supernatural-Human Interaction because she thought it would be interesting, but after what Helen had said, she was conscious that the very dichotomy of the title was flawed. Witches were just as human as anyone, but with an added set of abilities. True supernaturals were the vampires, Asuras, and demons.

"I have to take a course in social sciences," Bev said, "and this sounded a lot more interesting than werewolf pack dynamics."

Joanna laughed. "What's your major?"

"Art. I'm a painter."

"Oh? What kind of stuff do you paint?"

Bev gave her a wicked grin. "I conjure strange visions and paint them."

"Conjure?"

"So to speak. I'm a conjurer and an illusionist. I envision things, build an illusion, then conjure a still scene that matches the illusion. When I'm finished with the painting, I banish it."

"You don't ever paint demons, do you?" Joanna asked.

"Oh, hell, no. I don't conjure living beings. That's yucky. I mean, there might be people in the pictures, but I don't conjure real people, only constructs that look like people."

The professor came in and began passing out the syllabus.

"Besides," Bev said, leaning close and speaking softly, "you don't ever conjure any kind of living beings. That's summoning, and it's illegal. And summoning a demon is suicidally stupid."

After the class was over, Joanna noticed a young woman walking past them. "Wow!"

The blonde was absolutely the most beautiful woman she had ever seen, dressed and coifed to perfection. She wouldn't have looked out of place in a movie or on a magazine cover.

Bev turned to look. She pursed her lips as if she'd tasted something sour and said, "Yeah, wow. Donna Collins, campus darling."

"A friend of yours?"

Bev snorted. "Not hardly. She's too good for most people. Junior Class President, Vice President of the Tri-Delt sorority, cheerleader, etcetera, etcetera. Closeted witch. Every man on campus is panting after her, and from what I hear, she's not that hard to catch."

"Closeted? Why?"

"Doesn't want the social stigma. If her sorority knew, they would never have let her in."

"Do you know what kind of witch?"

"Yeah, she's an illusionist. Don't get me wrong, she's a beautiful woman, but she enhances it with a glamour."

"So, are those real?" Joanna asked, motioning to her own chest. She knew that another illusionist would be able to see through the glamour.

"Yeah, they're real."

"I wonder what it's like to carry all that weight around?"

Bev choked, and then started laughing. "Well, you and I will never know, will we?"

JOANNA REMEMBERED the night in Oregon when her dormitory exploded. The council told her later that every witch within a hundred miles had felt the magic blast. Every elemental witch within five hundred miles had felt it. She wondered how far away people felt the earthquake in Pennsylvania .

She grabbed a student newspaper in the student center the following morning and looked through it on her way to class, but the quake still hadn't hit the news.

When Joanna showed up at her Biochemistry class, Kyle was just sitting down in the back of the class. He was yawning, and there were bags under his eyes.

"If you sit in the back, you can't see or hear as well," she told him with a grin. "Of course, if you've been up all night, I guess it's easier to fall asleep up here and not be noticed."

He didn't smile. "I've been out searching for a girl in the woods. She and her boyfriend haven't been seen since Sunday night."

"She's a were?" Joanna asked, suddenly somber.

"Yes. Were you in town Sunday night?"

"Yes. Why? Where were you?"

"A friend and I drove up north where the wilderness is less crowded," he said. "Someone told me there was an earthquake and a storm here, but nothing happened where we were."

"You didn't feel anything where you were?" Joanna asked in

surprise as she slipped into the seat beside him. "How far away were you?"

"About a hundred miles north," he said. "We know a place up there that's off the beaten path, and more importantly, is far away enough that most students won't bother."

"Did you find them?" she asked.

"We found her," he said. "She'd been torn apart, and it looked like some kind of animal had fed on her."

"Oh, Goddess. That's awful. You didn't find him?"

"No trace."

The professor started to lecture, and Joanna didn't have time to ask Kyle any more questions.

After class, she asked him, "When do you have lab?"

"Right now," he said.

"Need a lab partner?"

For the first time that morning, he smiled. "Are you good in chemistry?"

"Good enough to drag you through it even if you do fall asleep."

As they were walking to the laboratory in the basement, Kyle stopped and cocked his head as if he was listening to something. Knowing that a were's hearing was much better than hers, Joanna waited. After a couple of minutes, Kyle turned to her.

"What's up?" she asked.

He indicated three girls standing across the hall. "They were saying a girl was attacked and killed on campus last night." He shook his head. "They're probably talking about Shara. Rumors always get things so screwed up."

That evening when she got home, Joanna discovered that the rumor hadn't confused the two girls. Sitting in a van in her driveway were Rupert, Dr. Underwood, Helen Weatherspoon, and a chubby man she didn't know. She invited them in and set to putting the tea kettle on.

"Joanna," Rupert said as the group sat about her kitchen table, "this is Max Brown. There was a girl killed on campus last night."

"On campus? I heard about a were girl killed in the woods."

"Yes, there's that, too. Both of them were torn apart, and it looked as though a wolf had eaten parts of them."

"If we find the demon," Underwood said, "we're hoping that Max can banish it."

Brown shrugged. "We need a name, or a circle of thirteen. But I probably have the strength to hold it in a circle if we can capture it."

"I talked to a were today, also," Joanna said. "He was a hundred miles north and didn't see either a storm or an earthquake. Is there any way to pinpoint where the breach occurred by how far the phenomena were noted?"

Underwood shook his head. "Not precise enough. We're fairly certain that it happened in the town, and your sensitive friend confirmed that. But we think we know that we're dealing with a fire demon. There were burns on both bodies."

"So how do you fight a fire demon. With fire?"

"No, to defeat the demon, it would take a fire elemental large enough to blast the whole town," Helen said, and Underwood nodded. "The best way is to drown it."

"The largest water elemental around here is the river," Joanna said. "The next largest one is that small lake."

"And either of those are large enough to take out a demon," Helen said.

Max nodded. "We know we're not dealing with a very powerful demon. A Greater Demon wouldn't be attacking isolated students. It would be running rampant through downtown and the middle of campus."

"There's something I don't understand." Joanna looked around the table. "I was always told that demons are like psyvamps. They feed on emotions—primarily anger, fear, lust, greed, stuff like that. Why would it need to eat a person?"

The adults looked around at each other, and finally Max said, "She's right."

"Could we have two different problems?" Rupert asked.

"I don't think so," Underwood responded. "Occam's razor. I think the demon has possessed another being."

"The were girl who was killed in the forest had a boyfriend," Joanna said into the silence. "No one knows where he is."

"Joanna," Helen said, "we would like to ask your friend Adele to try and find where the breach happened. We're hoping that we might be able to discover the demon's name."

Joanna shrugged. "I think she said she lives in a dorm. We just met yesterday."

"She gave us her number, but I think she would respond better to you asking," Underwood said.

Chapter 7

JOANNA DIALED the number Underwood had given her. "Addie, it's Joanna."

"Hi, what's up?" Addie sounded upbeat and happy.

"I'm here with Dr. Underwood and Professor Weatherspoon. Do you remember what we talked about this morning? They're hoping that you might be able to help us find the place where you said the negative emotions originated."

Silence. "I don't know if I could really help you," Addie's voice was hesitant.

"Yes, we know that. But do you think you could try? Addie, two girls have been killed. We're afraid it's going to continue if we can't find whatever is doing this."

The sound of a heavy intake of breath came through the phone. "Okay. Sure, I guess I can try. What do you want me to do?"

"Where do you live? We can come pick you up in about fifteen minutes."

Addie was standing in front of her dorm when they arrived. Joanna opened the side door of the van, and Addie climbed in.

Dr. Underwood turned to her and said, "We really appreciate this, Adele, and it's worth extra credit in my class."

She smiled nervously. "That sounds good."

Underwood returned her smile, shocking both Addie and Joanna. "Good. Now, where did you feel the emotions on Sunday night?"

"North of campus, past Campus Corner," Addie said.

Max put the van in gear and drove north.

"Do you feel people's emotions all the time?" Joanna asked in a low voice.

"Pretty much," Addie said. "I can block them most of the time, or maybe filter them is a better term. When I was young, I used to think I was going crazy sometimes."

"Is there anything we can do that would help you?"

"I don't know." She looked out the window, then around at the people in the van, and shrugged. "I wish I did, but I don't even know how this thing works, let alone anything that would enhance it. I mostly try to block it out."

They drove off campus and past the bars and shops near the university. Max slowed and called back, "Where to now?"

"Northeast," Addie answered. "It was farther than this. Probably ten or twelve blocks, maybe?"

After a while, Addie said, "I don't know. I was on the third floor, and Sunday I knew exactly where it was. But here on the ground, I really don't know."

"Stop the van," Joanna called.

Max pulled over to the curb. They were in a residential area with small older houses. Many of the houses had multiple cars parked in front of them, others had multiple bicycles but no cars.

"Is this a student ghetto?" Joanna asked.

"Right on the money," Weatherspoon answered. "What are we doing?"

"I think looking at ground level is probably the wrong approach," Joanna said. "Can you track me if we look from the air?"

Weatherspoon gave her a grin. "I'm sure the elementals can track you for me."

"Come on," Joanna said, grabbing Addie's arm and pulling her out of the van. Standing in front of Addie, Joanna told her, "This is absolutely safe. No matter what, you won't fall. The elemental won't drop you, and no matter how fast you descend, it will set you down softly. Understand?"

"No."

Joanna grinned. "Good, that means you were listening."

The two girls drifted into the air, rising to a hundred feet above the ground. Addie's eyes looked like they would bug out of her head. Joanna turned until she could see the campus, and Addie turned with her.

"Can you see your dorm?" Joanna asked, trying to pick out the building where they had found Addie.

"How in the hell are you doing this?" Addie shrieked.

"Have you taken Pchem yet?"

"I'm taking it now. We're in the same class, remember?"

"Oh, yeah. Well, when we get to the part where the professor attempts to explain how elementals bind and control the physical world, listen to me instead. An air elemental is wrapped around you. It will take you wherever I ask it to. Now, can you see your dorm?"

"You're an elemental witch?"

"Yes. I thought I made that clear. Elementals are the streaks you see around my aura, the things that were zooming around Weatherspoon's studio. Will you please look for your dorm? I would prefer we finish this before dark."

Addie looked, then said, "Yeah, I see the dorm."

"Can you locate your window?"

"Yeah."

"Okay, so where were the emotions coming from?" Joanna asked, turning to look behind her.

Addie studied the area below her. "I think more that way," she said, pointing farther northeast.

"Okay. Wherever you want to go, just point. Left, right, up, down, wherever."

Addie pointed, and Joanna directed the elementals to take them in that direction. Below them, the van lurched into motion.

They drifted along, gradually dropping lower.

"Can you feel anything?" Joanna asked after a while.

Addie didn't answer, just kept pointing, and they drifted still lower. Suddenly she stiffened. "Oh, my! There! That house!"

Joanna took them higher until she could see the van, two blocks over, and waved to the people following them. Then she lowered herself and Addie to the ground.

"Are you okay?" Joanna asked Addie as she dismissed the elementals who had carried them. Looking around, she saw that a large number of elementals had gathered, and they were very excited.

"Yeah, I'm fine," Addie said. "That was wild! Do you do that a lot?"

"Actually, I do it all the time."

"Totally awesome. Do you think I could do it again sometime?"

Joanna grinned. "Sure. I'll have to take you swimming out at the lake before the weather gets colder."

The van drove up, and the side door opened. The girls scrambled inside.

"She found the house," Joanna announced. "It's on the next street over."

"So, what do we do now?" Rupert asked. "You know there's a possibility the demon isn't in there. And even if the demon is in there, we still can't go breaking in without the neighbors calling the police."

"We need more help," Max said. He shook his head. "I never thought it would be this easy. Young lady, very well done."

"We don't know for sure that's the house," Underwood said. "Adele, is there any chance that you're wrong?"

"I guess," she said. "But something bad happened at that house recently. I don't like being even this close to it. I've never felt anything the way that house feels. It scares me."

"Maybe she's reading the demon," Joanna suggested. "Maybe she's not feeling what happened on Sunday, but what's there now."

"If that's the case, then we really need more help," Max said. He pulled out his cell phone. "Lance, can we get some more elementalists over here?"

Underwood took his phone out of his pocket and started punching buttons.

"Rupert, if we're going to take on a demon, we need to get these girls away from here," Weatherspoon said.

Glockner nodded. "Joanna, you and Adele should go now. Can you take her home? And to both of you, our sincere thanks."

Joanna felt torn. She understood that Addie should be removed from danger, but she herself wanted to stay. Watching the adults all talking on their phones, she decided that it would probably take the reinforcements they were calling some time to get there.

"Come on, Addie. Let's go. Dr. Underwood? I'll send a fire elemental to mark the house." He nodded as Joanna crawled out of the van. When Addie joined her, she called a couple of air elementals. As they rose into the air, she sent a fire elemental to hover over the house Addie had pointed out. Then she directed the elementals they were riding toward the campus.

They landed in the shelter of a couple of large trees behind the dorm.

"Thank you," Joanna told Addie. "You might have saved lives today."

"You're going back, aren't you?"

"Yes."

Addie shook her head. Hands on her hips, she said, "You said you've been here only a week. How do you know all these people? Jesus, Jo, you look like a kid, and you're calm as hell about taking on a demon? What's going on?"

"It's a long story, and I'm surprised I look calm. The idea of a demon scares me to death."

"Fine. You said you owe me one. Tell me the story of how you came here."

Joanna bit her lip, considering the woman standing in front of her. Could she trust her? Would Addie still want to be her friend if she knew everything?

"Come to my house for dinner on Friday and I'll tell you," she finally said.

"I can live with that." Addie reached out and pulled Joanna into a hug. "Be careful, okay?"

"I will. I promise," Joanna said through a throat that suddenly had a lump in it.

Addie pushed her away, and Joanna rose into the air. Below her, Addie watched for a bit, then turned, and walked toward her dorm.

Joanna called Helen on her cell.

"Where are you?" Helen asked.

"Headed toward the river. You said if it was a fire demon, we'd need water. I've been thinking about it, and I think I know how to get water to that house."

"It's almost two miles," Helen reminded her.

"Yeah, I know. But if I can create a waterspout and walk it down the middle of the street to get it there, it should be fairly safe."

Helen was silent for what seemed like a long time. "It might work," she finally said. "If we get to that point, I'll join you. It would be easier to control it with two of us."

"Yeah, it would. Thank you," Joanna said with a rush of breath, as much to the Goddess as to Helen. Controlling a waterspout through the middle of town was her greatest worry. If it deviated at all from the path she set, it could wipe out a whole block in a matter of seconds.

She flew over the house and saw the supernatural force gathering their strength on the streets around it. Then she marked the widest streets leading from there to the river. When she got to the river, she made contact with the elemental there. Compared to the water elementals who followed her around, this being was huge, and its power immense.

While Joanna waited, she practiced directing the smaller elementals in the area to create waterspouts. Careful to control their size, she didn't allow them to grow more than about two feet high.

Soon, other elementals joined the game, and she sat back and watched half a dozen waterspouts whirling around the surface of the river. It looked like a surreal dance as they dodged around and over each other, occasionally colliding.

Chapter 8

AS SOON AS the girls flew away, the members of the council launched into action. The local council only employed a small security force, but they were contacted and ordered to the scene. A search warrant was obtained to legalize the operation, and more than fifty supernaturals were contacted for support. A dozen conjurers rushed to the house Addie had identified. All of them had expected a call since a demon crossing first was suspected.

One of the supernaturals was a strong clairvoyant. When she was driven past the house, she immediately agreed with Addie that "something really bad" had happened there.

Max directed the other conjurers as they created a salt circle around the house. All the trappings of the ritual were put in place. Finally, the thirteen conjurers took their places.

"Suppose there isn't a demon in there?" Helen asked.

Max shot her an exasperated look and shook his head. "We expend a ton of energy for nothing, and all of us," he waved his hand at the other conjurers, "are out of action for the next couple of days until we recover our strength."

"Which means we would be even more vulnerable than we are now," Rupert said.

Max and everyone else nodded.

Lance Underwood walked up, putting his phone in his pocket. "We have confirmation that a student named Mark Frankel listed this as his address when he registered this fall. He's a junior engineering student. When he first came to Midleton two years ago, he registered with the council as a witch and a conjurer. I've contacted his professors, and he hasn't shown up for any of his classes this week."

"So, how do we find out what, if anything, is in there?" Rupert asked.

"Can one of you big strong men throw something through one of the windows?" Helen asked in reply.

"And?" Max answered.

"If there's a way in there, I can send an air elemental in to check. If there's a demon, we'll know very quickly."

Elementals and demons were mortal enemies—one devoted to Chaos, the other devoted to Balance.

Max walked to his van, opened the back, and rummaged around. He came back holding a large wrench. Without saying a word, he heaved the wrench through one of the front windows. The sound of shattering glass drew everyone's attention, and the scene went instantly quiet.

Helen sent an air elemental into the house. Only a few seconds later, a werewolf leaped through the window the other way, bounding across the porch and onto the lawn. Gunshots rang out as the wolf headed straight for the small group of council members, slamming into them like a bowling ball into a set of pins. Almost everyone ducked or dove out of the way, but the wolf hit Rupert squarely, snarling and snapping, and knocked him to the ground.

It didn't stay. Continuing across the lawn, it raced up the street to the north. It took some moments for the supernaturals to react, but a team from the local wolf pack took off after it. Unfortunately, the rogue wolf had half a block head start on them.

Unseen except by Underwood and Weatherspoon, at least a dozen elementals also pursued the wolf.

Max knelt down to check on Rupert and discovered a bloody rip in his shirt.

"Medic! We need a healer over here," Max called.

A man and a woman rushed forward, kneeling down beside the council chairman. The woman tore open his shirt and found a ragged gash in his left shoulder where the wolf had bitten him. The man called on a cell phone, and an ambulance parked down the street switched on its lights and drove toward them.

Soon, the healers and paramedics had Rupert bandaged and loaded into the ambulance, which drove away with lights and a siren clearing the way.

"Did you see his shoulder?" Weatherspoon said to Underwood as they watched.

"Yes, there were burns around the wound. That werewolf is possessed."

The air elemental that went inside the house communicated to Helen that the house was clear, and the rest of the council went inside. Other than a nauseating smell of sulfur and a faint smell of rotten meat, they didn't find anything amiss until they entered the basement.

All the trappings of a summoning ritual were there, but they were burned and scattered. The same could be said for the remains of a human being. Blood splattered all the walls, ceiling, and floor; and body parts were strewn about. A head without a face sat on top of an open spell book. Max picked up the head with gloved hands and put it down next to the book.

"There's a page missing. It's been torn out."

"The page with the name, no doubt," Underwood said with a scowl.

"No doubt. Stupid damn kid. He found a name in a spell book—probably one he bought in a flea market—and tried it. Unfortunately, it wasn't a hoax."

"We don't want to leave that here, do we?" Helen asked.

"No, I don't know if any of it is readable, but we need to lock it away," Max said. The book was soaked with dried blood. "I wonder if there are any trash bags upstairs."

They searched through the house but didn't find anything else of interest. Turning the scene over to the council security forces and the supernatural crime unit of the local police, the council members trooped out to Max's van.

As she clambered into the van, Helen suddenly realized something. "Oh, no. I forgot about Joanna."

"What do you mean?" Underwood asked. "I thought she went home."

"She took Adele home, but she's been waiting down by the river all this time in case we needed water to deal with the demon." Helen dug out her cell phone and called Joanna.

"Did you find the demon?" Joanna asked, leaping to her feet.

"We did," Helen told her, "but it escaped. It has possessed a werewolf. I don't think there is any need for you to stay by the river. Why don't you go home, and if we need you, I'll call. For right now, I need to call Susan Glockner and tell her that Rupert was injured. They've taken him to the hospital."

"Is he hurt very badly?"

"I don't think so. The werewolf bit Rupert on the shoulder, but he should be all right."

"Are you going to keep searching for the demon?"

"Yes. We can't just give up."

"I can go over to the Glockners'," Joanna said. "I'm sure Susan will want to go to the hospital, and she'll need someone to watch the kids."

"I'm sure she will appreciate that," Helen said. "I'll call her and let her know you're coming."

When Joanna knocked on the Glockners' door, an obviously upset Susan opened it and said, "Thank you. I'll try to hurry home."

"No problem. Don't worry about us. We'll get along fine," Joanna said.

Susan gave her a quick hug and sprinted toward her van.

Chapter 9

THE MORNING after the demon search was so busy that it was a relief for Joanna to drop into her seat in Dr. Underwood's class. Getting the twins up and ready for school, dressing Lizzy, feeding them all breakfast, then transporting the twins to school had given Joanna new respect for what mothers went through every morning. Luckily, Helen had agreed to let Joanna drop Lizzy off at the studio. After the flight to campus, Joanna would have had to give the kid a sleeping potion to keep her quiet during class.

Almost simultaneously, Kyle sat in the seat on one side of Joanna, and Addie sat on the other.

"So, what happened last night?" Addie breathlessly asked.

"Hot date?" Kyle smirked.

"Roasting hot," Joanna said, giving him a dirty look. "We were demon hunting."

His eyes, which had been hooded and looking sleepy, popped wide open.

"You were dead on," Joanna said to Addie. "It was in there, but it got away. It's evidently possessed a werewolf, and they weren't ready for that. Rupert was injured and was taken to the hospital."

"A werewolf? Are you sure?" Kyle asked. "I thought a demon couldn't possess someone unless they were willing."

"It doesn't require willing, only consent. Think of all the girls who get coerced into consenting to let a vampire chew on them," Joanna said. "I was told that Shara and the other dead girl had been partly eaten, and the tooth marks were that of a wolf."

"That's impossible!" Kyle said through gritted teeth. His eyes dilated, and his expression seemed very fierce.

Joanna didn't take the hint. "Has your friend shown up yet? Shara's dead, her boyfriend's missing, and the demon has possessed a were. It all seems to fit together."

Kyle surged out of his seat, his face red and his fangs showing. "You don't know what you're talking about. We aren't like humans; we protect our females."

He bolted from the class, brushing past Dr. Underwood, who was just coming through the door. Underwood stared after Kyle with a raised eyebrow, then gave a slight shrug, and continued into the small auditorium.

Stopping by where Joanna and Addie were sitting, he said in a low voice, "Can you both please see me after class?" He walked to the front of the room and began the day's lecture.

When the class was over, Underwood led them to his office.

"Miss Fisher, the Supernatural Council wishes me to extend our sincere thank you for your help last night." He handed Addie an envelope. "It has also authorized me to ask if you would consider consulting with us on an occasional basis. Your talents are something we think might be of use."

"Uh, what do you mean by consulting?" Addie looked thoroughly confused.

"I assume Miss de Groot told you that the demon escaped us last night. We hope we might call on you again in helping us to find this demon. We can also foresee that we might at times wish to employ your talents in other matters. You would be appropriately compensated, of course."

Addie gaped at him.

"Think about it. You don't need to give me an answer now."

He turned to Joanna. "I'm sorry to say that your personal life is going to have to take a back seat for a while. We're going to need your help if we ever catch this demon. So please study while you can, and be available. Okay?"

Joanna nodded. "I can do that."

Addie peeked inside the envelope and gasped. Looking at Joanna, she said, "Do you get paid for helping them?"

"Well, I …"

"Miss de Groot is compensated. She is, shall we say, an employee of the Supernatural Council."

After the girls left Underwood's office, Addie said, "I didn't realize you worked for the Council." She held up the envelope. "There's two hundred dollars here. God, I'm freaking rich!"

"That was a clumsy attempt to cover up my actual relationship with the Council," Joanna said, feeling her face grow warm. "It's more like I'm an indentured servant."

"Huh? Like a student intern or something?"

"More like a military draftee. Come to dinner Friday and I'll tell you about it."

"Okay. Hell, meeting you has turned this into the most interesting semester yet. Where do you live?"

"Do you know the road to Pratt Lake? The last turnoff—about two miles before you get to the lake—is my driveway. It's about a mile from your dorm."

They were eating lunch in the student center when Bev stopped at their table.

"Going to class today?"

"Yes. Just getting some lunch first. Would you like to join us?" Joanna smiled and pulled her backpack off the chair next to her.

Bev said, "Thanks. Let me go get something to eat and I'll be right back." She dropped her pack next to Joanna's and headed toward the grill.

"Another new friend?" Addie asked.

"It seems so. I was wondering how I was going to make friends here, but I guess Midleton is just a friendly place."

"It's the hair," Addie said and winked at her.

Bev came back to the table with a hamburger and fries.

"Bev, this is Addie," Joanna said.

"Hi." Bev gave Addie a quick grin, then turned to Joanna, "Did you hear that there were more killings last night?"

Joanna shook her head.

"They found a werewolf downtown, a student, and he'd been shot. They also found a guy and a girl over by the Art Building. A friend of mine almost tripped over them on her way to class this morning. She told me they had been torn apart. Dismembered."

Joanna and Addie exchanged looks.

"Do you know the werewolf's name?" Joanna asked.

"Robert something. I don't remember. I heard it on the radio just a while ago. Man, this place is just crazy this year."

As they gathered up their trash to clear the table, the girl Joanna had seen in her history class, Donna Collins, walked by.

"Miss Perfect," Addie said to Joanna, nodding in Donna's direction. "That's what everyone calls her."

Bev chuckled. "Yeah, she's in our next class."

"I feel really sorry for her," Addie said.

Surprised, Bev asked, "Why?"

"Because she's so lonely and afraid," Addie said. "It must be hard not having any friends and having everyone be jealous of you."

"And why do you think that?" Bev asked. "She's the campus darling. All the guys want her, the faculty and administration love her. She's got her sorority sisters."

"It's just an illusion," Addie said. "Almost everything about her is an illusion except her looks, and she's scared to death that people will find out."

Joanna watched Donna's retreating back, then looked back at Bev, who was staring in astonishment at Addie.

"She's a sensitive," Joanna said to Bev in a low voice as they walked out of the student center. Then she asked Addie, "How do you know her looks aren't an illusion?"

"I don't know, I just do," Addie said.

Bev suddenly transformed, her clothes changing, and her hair turning completely blonde and longer than it had been. She was also wearing makeup, and instead of a backpack, a pretty purse hung from her shoulder.

"Goddess," Joanna breathed. "That's amazing."

"What is?" Addie asked. She looked back and forth between Joanna and Bev with a puzzled expression on her face. "What's amazing?"

"You don't see anything different?" Joanna asked.

"Different in what way? What's different?"

Bev's glamour changed again, and to Joanna's eyes, she turned into a man with a beard, wearing a tartan kilt.

"You don't see that?" Joanna asked.

Addie shook her head. "I don't have any idea what you're talking about." Irritation crept into her voice. "Jo, you know I'm not a witch. Whatever you two are doing, it's not funny."

Bev dismissed the glamour and said, "You didn't see the illusions I cast?"

"No."

"Bev just cast a glamour on herself. Two of them, actually. It was like she changed into two different people." Joanna cocked her head to look at Bev. "You're pretty good."

Addie shrugged. "Like I said, I'm not a witch. I guess I can't see them."

"Now that is freaking amazing," Bev said.

"I'm a witch, and I can't see through them," Joanna said. "Hey, we have to get to class. I'll see you later."

When their class was over, Joanna asked Bev, "Is it common for someone not to be able to see your illusions?"

Shaking her head, Bev said, "I don't believe her. She's just saying that to mess with us."

"She seemed pretty sincere."

Still shaking her head, Bev walked off. Joanna watched her go, then hurried to her next class. The history class and her chemistry class were almost all the way across campus from each other. She hadn't known that when she signed up for them.

Addie had saved a seat for her, and Joanna flopped into it breathlessly.

"Taking up jogging?" Addie cracked.

"I need another five minutes between these classes," Joanna said.

"You and the professor. He's late again."

"You really didn't see the illusions that Bev cast?"

"I guess I'm just dense, but I don't know what you're talking about." There was a distinct note of irritation in Addie's voice.

Chapter 10

THE FOLLOWING morning was unusual in that no additional deaths were reported. Kyle sat beside Joanna during lecture but was quiet until after class.

"I'd like to apologize," he said as they walked out of the building. "I was out of line."

Joanna shrugged but didn't say anything.

"I talked to the were representative to the Supernatural Council, and he confirmed everything you said," Kyle continued.

"I was just speculating that it was your friend. It just made sense that it might be."

"Not my friend. Bobby was a jerk. But Shara was a friend of mine, and I just didn't want to believe that he would sacrifice her to save his own hide."

Joanna stopped and turned to face him. "None of us know what really happened, Kyle. They're both dead, and we still haven't caught the demon."

"Yeah, you're right." He stood there for a few moments. "What are you doing tonight?"

"Studying, I guess. Why?"

"We don't have class in the morning. Some friends of mine are going out dancing, and I wondered if you'd like to come."

Her heart leaped in her chest, and her mouth was suddenly dry. She looked up at him, and his face seemed open and friendly. Was he really asking her out?

"I thought you might like to meet some people," Kyle said. "Come on. It'll be fun."

"Sure," she managed to say. "I'd like that."

"Great! We're going to meet at High Moon around nine. If you don't like the scene there, we can go over to Spellcaster. Have you been there yet?"

"Yeah, I stopped in last week."

"I'll see you tonight, then," he said with a big smile.

Joanna had three hours until her next class and had planned to go to the library to study. But Kyle's invitation had her head spinning. She tried to caution herself that he hadn't actually asked her on a date. He was just being friendly, she told herself, even as her mind wandered toward thinking about what she would wear.

In spite of the distraction, she still managed to write her lab reports for her two chemistry classes and email them to her lab partners, Kyle and Addie. Then she grabbed a quick lunch before her afternoon class.

After class, she asked Addie, "How well do you know Kyle?"

"He's been in a few of my classes," Addie said. "He was my lab partner for organic chemistry last spring. But I don't really know him very well. He's kind of a chick magnet, as you can imagine, but he never struck me as a player. Why? Are you getting a crush on him?"

Joanna flushed. "He asked me to go dancing tonight."

Addie smiled. "Just you and him?"

"Well, no. He said he was meeting some friends at High Moon and asked if I wanted to come."

"Still. High Moon is a pretty rowdy place, though. Want a wing man?"

"Really? You want to come?" Joanna felt a rush of relief wash through her. "Kyle said that if High Moon was too much, we could go over to Spellcaster."

"Sure, that sounds good. I haven't been out dancing since last spring," Addie said.

Something in Addie's tone rang a bit strange to Joanna's ear.

"You didn't go out all summer?"

Addie seemed to draw into herself a little. "I didn't do much last summer." She looked away, then back to Joanna. "I broke up with my boyfriend at the end of last semester and didn't really feel like getting out and doing anything."

"Been there," Joanna said. "Were you the dumper or the dumpee?"

"I guess that depends on how you look at it," Addie said. "I dumped him after I found out he was cheating on me, but I think he was planning to dump me."

Joanna fished for something to say to lighten the mood. "This is a whole new year, right? Time for us to get back in the game, don't you think?"

Addie smiled. "Damn straight. Dancing with the weres, huh? That will definitely take me out of my comfort zone. Have you ever made it with a were?"

"Huh? No!" The question took Joanna off guard and she realized her reaction was a bit strong.

"Me neither. I've heard some things, good and bad, but never dated one. What time do you want to meet?"

"Kyle said that he was meeting his friends at nine. I can swing by your dorm around eight-thirty."

"Sounds good. Joanna?"

"Yes?"

"Do you ever wear your hair down? I mean, how long is it if you don't braid it?"

Joanna chuckled. "Goddess, if it wasn't for my hair, I wonder sometimes if anyone would ever notice me at all."

Addie waited.

"It's waist length, and yes, I wear it down sometimes, but only when I really want to attract attention." Joanna took a deep breath while she thought about going out to a bar with her hair down. "I'll wear it a bit different tonight, but not loose. Good enough?"

With a smile, Addie said, "Okay. See you at eight-thirty."

After dinner and a shower, Joanna sat down at her vanity. The face in the mirror and the cloud of flame-colored hair hadn't changed much since she was thirteen. Her body hadn't changed much, either. Her hips had filled out, and she now had breasts— small though they were—but she could easily see why Kyle thought she was just a kid. He was a full foot taller than she was, and probably weighed double what she did.

He was just being nice, she decided. What would someone as popular and good looking like him want with a skinny little girl like her? Addie was right. Kyle was a definite chick magnet. With his looks, he could have any girl he wanted.

With a sigh, she picked up her brush and began trying to tame her hair. She planned a double-ladder-rope-braid style that she and her roommate in Oregon had found on the internet. It looked very elegant and managed to corral her hair enough that she could wear it down but not attract every elemental in the neighborhood, not to mention the attention of every person in sight. She still remembered the humiliation of a news photographer for the Oregon State student newspaper following her around one afternoon, and then printing a full page of pictures of her hair the next morning.

The girl in the video on the internet had done her hair in five minutes. Even with her roommate Leila's help, it usually took over half an hour to replicate the style with Joanna's hair. And Leila wasn't there to help. Leila would never be there to help again. Fighting back tears, Joanna began to brush her hair.

She finally wrestled control away from the elementals and managed to get her hair done. They still played with the loose two feet of hair hanging down her back, but they couldn't completely go crazy with it.

Having set her wards, Joanna called an air elemental and had it take her to Addie's dorm. The elemental set her down in the same copse of trees where she had dropped Addie off the night they had found the demon.

She took the stairs to Addie's third-floor corner room, and knocked.

"Hi," Addie said, throwing open the door.

Joanna looked past Addie, out the window that had an unobstructed view of the campus and the town to the north. As she entered the room, she noticed that the beds had been pushed together to make one large bed.

"No roommate?" Joanna asked.

"Nope. Got the whole penthouse to myself," Addie laughed. "Not too many girls over twenty-one want to live in the dorms, and I talked them into giving me my own room."

"Why do you want to live here?"

"Easier. I don't have to buy groceries or cook, and I couldn't afford an apartment by myself, so I'd have to have a roommate." Addie bit her lip and turned away, staring out the window. "Actually, that's not entirely honest. I had planned to share an apartment with my boyfriend. But he's sharing it with someone else instead."

"You're an empath. Didn't you ..." Joanna blurted out before she could catch herself. Embarrassed, she said, "I'm sorry. That was a stupid thing to say."

"I ask myself that question about a dozen times a day," Addie said quietly. "I guess I just didn't want to admit it to myself." She grabbed her phone and stuck it in her pocket. "Let's go dancing! Maybe I'll find a hot were who will wipe that asshole out of my mind."

They had half an hour before they were to meet Kyle, and it was a pleasant evening as the heat of the day died down.

"You came here from Oregon?" Addie asked as they walked across campus. The setting sun bathed everything around them in red and shadows.

"I went to school at Oregon State, but I've been living in northern California for the past year and a half."

"Is that where you grew up? I hear there are a lot of witches there."

"I grew up in the redwoods just north of the California-Oregon border. We lived on the outskirts of a town that was mostly witches.

But yeah, the world headquarters of the Supernatural Council is in northern California."

"What do your parents do?"

It was a question that Joanna had learned was quite natural among most college students, but it still caused a moment of unease in her.

"My mom's a healer," she said, "and I don't know anything about my father."

"A healer. That's like a doctor?"

"It's a witch with an affinity for a certain kind of magic. Some healers are also doctors, but my mother never went to college. She's also an alchemist. She mixes potions and makes charms and sells them."

"Can you do that?"

"I can make the potions and spell the charms, but I'm not a healer. A potion is more than a mixture of ingredients," Joanna told her. "You mix the ingredients, brew the potion, and then at the right moment cast the spell. Anything I do is only going to be a quarter as effective as if my mother had cast the spell. She can lay hands on a broken arm and mend the bones back together. I can't do that at all."

They arrived at High Moon right on time as full darkness fell. A couple of boys hung around outside, eyeing the girls walking by. Campus Corner was busy, but not as much as it would be on the weekend. Joanna and Addie showed their IDs to the bouncer and entered the club.

Joanna wasn't sure what she expected, but the inside of the club took her by surprise. The walls were paneled in wood, and it looked like a western hunting lodge. The heads of deer, elk, bison, and other animals adorned the walls. A stuffed deer—posed as if ready to leap—stood on the edge of the balcony on the second floor, looking toward the room below in obvious fear. All of the pictures on the walls were of wolves or large cats hunting prey.

"A little morbid, don't you think?" Addie asked. "See why non-weres tend to avoid the place?"

Looking across the room, Joanna saw a dance floor at the far end, and off to her right, she saw Kyle standing and waving at her. She nudged Addie. "There he is."

They made their way over to where a group of guys and girls had pushed two tables together. Pitchers of beer sat on the table.

"This is the girl I was telling you about," Kyle said. Everyone turned to look. "Joanna and Addie," he motioned to each of them in turn, "and this is Darcy, Don, Carla, Lisa and Donna. Come on, have a seat."

He placed a couple of clean glasses on the table in front of a pair of empty chairs. The girl he had introduced as Lisa poured beer in their glasses. Through a sudden feeling of numbness, Joanna sat down and watched as Kyle sat back down and Donna—Miss Perfect—folded her hand in his and leaned against him.

Chapter 11

"YOU'RE IN MY HISTORY CLASS," Donna said.

"Oh? The Supernatural-Human class?" Joanna asked, trying to play it cool while she learned to breathe again. Addie shot her a sharp glance.

Donna smiled, an incredible thousand-watt smile. "You're rather noticeable."

"Your hair is awesome!" Lisa said. "Turn around so I can see the back."

Joanna did as requested.

"That's really pretty."

Trying to keep from watching Kyle and Donna, Joanna turned back to Lisa and focused on her. A thick mane of natural tri-color blonde hair framed her face and spilled across her shoulders. Her pale-blue eyes had slit pupils, which were barely dilated in the dimly lit bar. Lisa was shorter and more slightly built than the other girls, and it took Joanna a moment to realize that she wasn't a wolf.

"Thank you," Joanna said. "You have rather unusual hair. Is that the color of your coat?"

"Yeah," Lisa said, shaking her head and making her hair fly back and forth. The movement attracted the attention of one of the air elementals accompanying Joanna, and it started to investigate, making Lisa's hair stir as though a sudden breeze had sprung up.

"Kyle said that you just transferred here," Donna said.

"I used to go to school at Oregon State," Joanna said, "but I felt like I needed a change."

"Hey, another westerner," Lisa said, linking her arm through Joanna's. "We'll have to stick together. I'm from British Columbia."

The band started playing, and Donna leaned over and said something to Kyle. They got up and moved onto the dance floor. The other guy at the table, Don, smiled at Addie.

"Want to dance?"

"I thought you'd never ask," she said with a laugh.

Over the next hour, the bar became louder and more crowded. Don and Kyle each asked Joanna to dance, and the other girls all danced with multiple partners as several guys stopped by their table. It was a delight to watch Lisa dancing as she moved with a flowing, loose-boned sensuality, completely unlike the way a werewolf moved.

Suddenly, after a growling argument between two guys on the dance floor, Lisa came storming back to their table and grabbed her purse.

"Too damned much testosterone in here," she announced. "Anyone want to go over to Spellcaster where things are more civilized?"

Donna stood and said, "I'm with you."

Kyle, Addie, and Joanna also gathered themselves to go.

"No thanks," Carla said with a sneer, directed it seemed at Joanna. "I prefer to stick with my own kind."

Lisa leaned close to her and snarled, "Not a problem, bitch. I've had my fill of dogs for the night."

Carla's eyes widened in fear as she stared at Lisa's fangs, which had suddenly appeared.

"I didn't mean you," she stammered.

"Maybe you should watch your mouth, then. And your atti-tude," Lisa said, straightening and tossing her hair. "Joanna? Addie? Ready to go?"

Without waiting for an answer, she headed for the door. Joanna wasn't able to see Lisa's face, or smell whatever pheromones she was putting out, but the werewolves in her way scrambled to clear a path.

Kyle was chuckling as he followed them out of the bar. "Nothing like a pissed-off cat to get the attention of a bunch of wolves."

Lisa spun around. "Watch your mouth, dog boy!"

"Hey, cool your jets," he responded with a grin. "I didn't step on your tail or stick my nose up your butt."

She snarled again, but whirled and began stalking down the street with a fluid, floating gait.

"What is she?" Addie asked, leaning close to Joanna.

"Lynx, I think," Joanna said.

"Yes," Donna said, coming up behind them. "And very prickly at times, but she's a breath of fresh air. You never have to guess what she thinks or how she feels about you."

"And as good a friend as I've ever had," Kyle said, looking at Donna when he said it—a look that made Joanna's stomach clench.

Don and Darcy had stayed behind with Carla, so it was only the five of them.

"Have you met Carla before?" Addie asked Joanna.

"Not that I remember. Why?"

"The hostility she was throwing off was incredible."

"Yeah," Donna chimed in. "She was looking daggers at you all night."

Joanna shrugged. "I don't know. Maybe a redhead stole her boyfriend one time." A thought occurred to her. "Is her coat black when she shifts?"

They all laughed, and Lisa said, "Yeah, it's black. Ignore her. She's such a bitch. I doubt she ever had a boyfriend longer than one night."

"Meow!" Kyle said.

"Honey," Lisa grinned at him, "every catty female you ever met is just an amateur trying to live up to the standard I set."

A couple of blocks away from High Moon, Lisa turned into an alley. A sign on the corner of the building said, 'No Cars.'

"Where are you going?" Joanna asked.

"Shortcut," Lisa said.

As her eyes adjusted to the darkness between the buildings, Joanna saw that instead of an alley, it was a narrow winding lane. Boutiques, a hair salon, a small bistro, and an ice-cream parlor, all closed for the night, lined the way.

"There are some neat shops in here," Lisa said, pointing to a lingerie shop. "They have some really sexy stuff for more petite figures."

The lane curved around, and with a blast of sulfur, a seven-foot horror stepped from out of the shadows. Addie shrieked, Lisa snarled, and Joanna stood frozen in fear.

Joanna tried to process the difference between how she had mentally pictured the demon and the actual reality of it. Physically, it wasn't built at all like any creature she had ever seen. But she had also always thought of it as male, and that was obviously an error.

"Holy crap!" Kyle swore, and started tearing at his belt with hands growing fur. Lisa, already starting to shift, unhooked her skirt and tore it from her body. She moved in front of Joanna, who noticed with another part of her mind that the lynx's paws were huge and her razor-sharp claws extended like large fishhooks.

"Run!" Donna shouted, pushing Addie, who stumbled, then caught herself, and took off back the way they had come.

Joanna's stunned inactivity didn't extend to the elementals that always accompanied her. A fire elemental became visible as it streaked toward the demon. As it struck, the demon responded with fire of its own, and the narrow street erupted in fire so hot that the windows in the shops on either side of the demon melted. Air elementals buffeted the beast, knocking it off balance.

The action of the elementals shook Joanna out of her paralysis, and she added her will to the elementals' efforts. Directing the air elementals to swirl and hammer the demon from all sides instead of just blowing straight at it, she reached out with her mind, searching the skies above her. She hoped to find a rain-laden cloud but

couldn't find any moisture in the clear skies. She did find a high-altitude air elemental, and a gale-force wind roared through the
narrow space between the buildings and knocked the demon
backward.

More fire elementals shot into the alley from both directions,
hitting the demon from the front and the back.

"Come *on*," Donna said, grabbing Joanna by the arm.

"I can hold it off," Joanna answered. "I can hold it until the rest
of you get out."

"Everyone's out but you," Donna yelled, almost pulling Joanna
off her feet and dragging her back toward the main street.

"What? But …" Joanna could still see her friends, running and
dodging as the demon tried to catch them. Lisa and Kyle in their
animal forms were snapping at its legs. Donna tried to duck past the
demon. Joanna stood in front of it with her arms raised …

"It's an illusion, you dumbass," Donna hissed at Joanna. "Will
you come on?"

"Oh, okay." She shook her arm free and tried to reach into her
pocket for her phone as she trotted after Donna.

"Who are you calling?" Donna asked, obviously exasperated.

"The local Council. They need to know the demon is here."

Donna evidently thought that was a good idea as she let go of
Joanna's arm.

"Susan? It's Joanna. The demon is at Campus Corner," she
gasped as soon as the phone was answered. "It's in an alley at …"
she looked at Donna.

"Cobbler's Lane," Donna said.

"It's in Cobbler's Lane. The elementals are keeping it busy, and
someone cast an illusion that has it confused, but it's fighting back.
There isn't any water here. What we need is a fire truck." She
stopped. "I am such a dumbass," she said.

Donna nodded. "Yeah."

"Is there a fire hydrant around here?" Joanna yelled.

"Right around the corner," Addie shouted back. When Joanna
looked at her, she pointed.

Joanna ran around the corner and fixed her gaze and her will on the hydrant. She called to the elementals in the water pipes running under the streets.

"What are you doing?" Donna asked. Then her face froze when she heard a rumble, then a metallic pop, and finally a muffled explosion. "Oh, crap. Heads up!" she screamed as the fire hydrant shot thirty feet in the air, riding a column of water. It arced away from the fountain and fell to the street, bounced twice, and embedded itself in the wall of a brick building.

Joanna directed air elementals toward the gushing water and began the process of pulling the water into a vortex. When she had a coalesced thirty-foot waterspout, she sent it past herself into the Cobbler's Lane. It roared down the pavement and hit the demon with pounding force.

Water exploded through the lane with a sound of a huge wave breaking on a shore. Steam filled the alley, rising above the rooftops. The hissing and sputtering went on for a very long time, and then things were still.

A coughing snarl sounded from the next street over, and Joanna spun to look as Addie yelled, "It's escaping out the other end."

With a muttered curse, Joanna called an air elemental and rode it past a lynx in a silver t-shirt chasing the retreating demon. She spun up another vortex from the still-gushing fountain of water. It took her too long, and when she rounded a corner a couple of blocks down the street, the demon was gone. She rose higher so that she could see down between the buildings, but no matter how high she went, circling as far as a mile from Cobbler's Lane, she couldn't spot the demon.

She drifted back to the street just as Max's van screeched to a halt, and men scrambled out. Another car stopped behind them, and Dr. Underwood and Professor Weatherspoon jumped out.

"It's gone," Joanna announced. "I was right behind it, then it turned a corner and disappeared."

"Probably translocated," Underwood said.

"It was wounded," Donna said. "It looked as though it was half-melted and it was limping."

"Did you manage to get water on it?" Weatherspoon asked,

eyeing the fountain of water that still shot into the air and filled the street as it rushed toward the river a mile away.

"Yes, the vortex idea worked," Joanna said. "Sorry about the fire hydrant. The elementals created so much pressure that I guess it blew the pipe."

"Pretty damn spectacular," Kyle said, standing there with his shirt on, but no pants. Joanna looked at him, then turned away, her face hot enough to ignite. Lisa sat on the sidewalk, wearing only her silver t-shirt, her legs drawn up in front of her to try and hide her nakedness.

"Do you want me to go look for your skirt?" Joanna asked.

Lisa looked down Cobbler's Lane and shook her head. "It's probably soaked and dirty with melted demon all over it. You wouldn't have a spare pair of panties in your purse, would you?"

"Sorry."

"Kyle," Donna said, "give her your shirt."

"Why is it okay for me to be naked, but not her?" he grumbled as he started to take it off.

"Because people will stare at her," Donna replied. "You don't have anything people are interested in looking at."

"Ha, ha," he said.

Dr. Underwood walked over and handed a blanket to Lisa and another one to Kyle. "What were you doing shifting? Did you think you were going to bite a demon?"

"I shifted because I can run faster as a lynx," Lisa said. Joanna didn't believe her for a second, since the first thing Lisa did after her shift was push in front of Joanna as if to protect her.

"Why didn't you wait until we could get here?" Max demanded.

"Oh, I'm so sorry," Donna said, her voice dripping with sarcasm. She didn't look perfect anymore, her wet hair plastered to her head, bedraggled strands curling around her shoulders, her clothes wet and stinking of sulfur. "Next time we'll just say, 'Excuse us, Ms. Demon. Can you please wait until we call some help before you attack us?'"

"We weren't demon hunting," Addie said. "We were going dancing."

Underwood surveyed the scene, then shaking his head, turned to Joanna. "How did fire work?"

"The demon didn't like it, but it seemed to be a stalemate. It couldn't hurt the elementals, but they didn't seem to hurt it either. Air bounced it around, kept it off balance, but didn't hurt it. It didn't like the water at all."

"Come on," he said. "I'll take you all home."

Chapter 12

ALL USES of magic have a price, and though she normally didn't think about it, the previous evening's activities had drained Joanna. As soon as the adrenaline wore off, she barely had the strength to get undressed before falling into bed. Creating the vortex took a tremendous amount of energy, but the biggest drain had been reaching for the high-altitude air elemental.

Joanna opened one eye and blearily stared at her phone, which was blaring the alarm for her to wake up. She briefly considered asking an air elemental to blow it off the table. She finally got out of bed and walked across the room to turn off the alarm, and as long as she was up, continued to the bathroom.

By the time Helen Weatherspoon drove up the driveway, breakfast and three cups of coffee had Joanna feeling almost human.

"Good morning," Helen greeted her. "You don't happen to have any coffee, do you?"

Helen looked as tired as Joanna felt, so she made two more cups of coffee.

"Bless you. This has been a very tiring week."

Joanna had hoped Helen might cancel their Friday morning meeting due to all the excitement of the previous night.

"I considered postponing this morning's session," Helen said, "but I finally decided that the presence of the demon makes it more important that you continue your training. There's never a good time for a disaster, and we can't really plan them, can we?"

It was a pretty, sunny day, and they took the footpath leading from the rear of Joanna's cottage to the lake. Birds sang and flitted about, and they saw rabbits and squirrels going about their business.

At the lake, they practiced creating and controlling water-spouts. Joanna proved more adept at setting up a vortex and drawing water into it, but Helen was far better at controlling the waterspouts. She also had an easier time taking control of a water-spout that Joanna created than Joanna did in taking control from Helen.

After an hour or so, they walked back to the cottage, and Joanna fixed lunch, then accepted a ride from Helen to campus.

Joanna arrived for her history class about five minutes early. No sooner had she found a seat than Bev flopped into the seat on her left and Donna sat on her right.

"How's it going?" Bev asked.

"Sorta strange," Joanna said. "We ran into the demon last night at Campus Corner."

"You're kidding. What happened?" Bev said, sitting upright and turning to Joanna.

"No kidding," Donna said. "Scared the hell out of me."

"Do you two know each other?" Joanna asked.

Bev shrugged and said to Donna, "I've seen you around."

"Donna Collins," Donna said, extending her hand.

"Bev Turner."

"The painter?" Donna asked.

"Yeah, I paint," Bev said, looking a bit puzzled.

"I love your work," Donna said. "That painting you had in the exhibition in the student center last spring, *Sky Castles*? I tried to borrow the money from my dad to buy it, but by the time I talked him into it, it was already sold."

"You like my work?" Bev asked.

Before Donna could reply, the professor asked for quiet and

started lecturing. Joanna noticed that Bev kept glancing toward Donna throughout the class.

When the class was over, Bev immediately turned to Joanna and Donna. "So, tell. What happened?"

"Donna saved my life," Joanna said. "Saved all our lives. She created an illusion that confused the demon enough that we could get away."

Donna laughed. "Oh, yeah, I'm such a hero. Joanna and her elementals beat the hell out of it and drove it off. Man, you should have seen Cobbler's Lane. It looked like Armageddon in there."

"Okay, now I really need a blow-by-blow," Bev said. "Let's go someplace and I'll buy the drinks."

"I can't," Joanna said. "I have another class, and I have stuff to do this evening, but you two go ahead."

"Brews and Potions?" Bev asked, looking to Donna, who nodded.

An idea occurred to Joanna. "Hey, you know what you could do? Donna, do you think you could create an image of the demon?"

"Sure."

"And if Bev could draw it, we'd have a picture we can give the council. Our group last night are the only people who have seen it and survived."

"Yeah, I can draw a picture from an illusion," Bev said.

On her way home after her class, Joanna stopped by a market to buy fresh fish and a bottle of wine for her dinner with Addie that evening. Arriving home, she took a shower and washed her hair. She was sitting on her front porch letting her hair dry and reading when Addie walked up the drive.

"Hi," Addie called with a smile.

Joanna set her book aside and stood up.

"Oh, my God," Addie breathed, staring. "Your hair is unreal."

"Unfortunately, it is. Welcome to my everyday reality. Would you like something to drink?"

Joanna led the way into her house and showed Addie around.

"And this is where you do witchy stuff?" Addie asked when she saw the workroom.

"This is the place," Joanna said with a chuckle. "It helps to have a room like this. That way I don't have to worry about keeping the arsenic separate from the salt in the kitchen."

Addie shot her a look. "You're joking, right? No?" She tucked her hands behind her back. "Okay. I consider myself warned."

Joanna led her friend back to the kitchen and opened the bottle of wine. Addie sat at the table and watched Joanna prepare their meal.

"So, am I going to hear the story about how you came to Midleton?" Addie asked. "You promised."

Joanna had her back to Addie, which seemed to make it easier. Taking a deep breath, she said, "Okay. I guess the best way to start is to tell you that I'm a virgin."

Silence greeted that revelation, but after about a minute, Addie said, "Okay. I think everyone has had that condition. And?"

"I don't know how much you know about elementals, but I was born with an affinity for them. We communicate, though how we do it isn't something I can explain." Joanna turned and touched her hair. "See? My hair doesn't do this by itself. It's an unusual color, but it's just hair. Air elementals are playing with it."

She turned back to preparing the fish. "My mom is kind of a hermit, and she doesn't like men. She had sex one time when she was sixteen and got knocked up. So, in spite of the fact that she's a healer, I didn't get very much in the way of sex education. I mean, I got what everyone else in school did, but no one told me that an elemental witch had to take extra precautions."

"I don't understand," Addie said. "Like, are you super fertile or something?"

"No, nothing that mundane. But the elementals feel my emotions. When I get upset, or really happy, or afraid, they react to that. So, to have sex, I need to set special wards—protective barriers —to block the elementals out. You know, to keep them from getting excited."

"Like what? Do they go crazy or something?"

"Yeah, they go crazy. When my boyfriend in Oregon gave me my first orgasm, they destroyed the dorm we were in."

Addie laughed.

Joanna left what she was doing and went to her bedroom. When she came out, she handed Addie a photograph.

"You saw last night in Cobbler's Lane what elementals can do. Imagine what it could be like if some really large elementals got so excited they lost control. That dorm was about the size of yours, three stories with two hundred rooms."

Addie stared at the picture showing the debris from completely flattened buildings spread over a half-mile radius. The smile on her face faded.

"What do you mean by 'really large elementals'?" she asked.

"The Jet Stream, Pacific Ocean, and Willamette River."

Addie stared at her, then said, "I don't understand."

"Elementals are a form of life that control the world and how it works," Joanna explained. "They are entirely alien to us. They're intelligent, but they don't think the way we do at all. They don't have emotions or thoughts that we can recognize or understand. I've heard people say that there are elementals in a river, or in a fire. That's not correct. The river is an elemental. The fire is an elemental. The ocean is an elemental. Some are very small, and some are huge, but they provide the balance in the world. They are what makes everything work. They hold the world together."

She put the pan with the fish in the oven and placed the steamer with the vegetables on the stove.

"I have some magic that I use to cast spells. I'm not a particularly strong witch, but I know a lot about potions and charms and stuff. I study and learn and get better at it. That's completely different than being an elementalist. We're kind of rare, and to have an affinity for three elements is even rarer. There are only about a hundred elementalists in the world with an affinity for all four elements—air, water, fire and earth."

"So, you have enough power to control the Pacific Ocean?"

"No, we don't control the elements, but I am able to communicate with it, and I can ask it to do something. Depending on how important it thinks what I want is, it might agree to do it. The smaller ones," Joanna waved her hand at one that was swirling her hair about, "enjoy playing games and having fun. So, asking them to fly me someplace is just a game to them."

"And fighting a demon is just a game?"

"Oh, no, not at all. Demons are agents of Chaos, while elementals are dedicated to Order, to Balance. Demons are their natural enemies. I don't have to do anything to make elementals attack a demon, but I can provide some intelligent direction in how they do it. Their innate nature is very direct, but strategy and tactics and working together aren't something that's natural to them."

Addie looked at the picture. "Was anyone killed?" she asked softly.

"No, thank the Goddess, and no one was seriously hurt. But forty-seven people ended up in the hospital with some kind of injuries. My boyfriend had a concussion and a broken arm. I walked away without a scratch. You saw last night. Donna was standing beside me, and she got soaked and blown about, but my hair wasn't even mussed."

"So, what happened afterward?"

"The same thing that's happening now with the demon. The Supernatural Council covered it all up. Everyone who knew me was spelled to forget me—to forget they ever met me, that I even existed —and it was all chalked up to a freak natural disaster. Then they took me away for seventeen months of intensive training and psychological evaluation. They finally decided that it was safe to let me out in the world again, that I hadn't done anything maliciously or carelessly."

Joanna leaned against the counter and took a sip of her wine. "It took a while to find a community willing to take a chance on me, but the local council here agreed to allow me to come and finish college. Under strict supervision, of course."

"But it wasn't your fault," Addie said. "How could they just decide to take control of your life? It sounds like they're treating you like a criminal."

"The fact is, I did cause a lot of property damage and hurt a lot of people. From my point of view, I'm just grateful they gave me choices. I get a house, tuition, and a living stipend. The alternative was to put me in jail forever, and that would make them feel guilty and cost about the same." She shrugged. "Or, I guess they could give me a lobotomy."

Addie stared at her. "They would really do that?"

Joanna began setting the table. "Do you remember your history about the Supernatural Wars?"

"Yeah, sorta. Why?"

"You might have learned it differently than I did." Joanna said. "In the Middle Ages, the church began a systematic campaign to exterminate witches. That led to five hundred years of war, which was settled only after the destruction of Rome in 1756."

Addie chuckled. "I learned that the witches tried to take over the world and they were stopped only through the valiant efforts of the dedicated and holy warriors of the Church."

Joanna snorted. "To my knowledge, we didn't go around burning priests at the stake. Anyway, there are still a lot of people who are afraid of supernaturals. The idea of a single girl creating a natural disaster isn't something the Council is anxious to publicize. Just like now. There are those who would jump on the fact that a witch brought a demon into our world. Neither the Council nor the human authorities want to have TV cameras and anti-supe agitators running around stirring up more trouble."

"Okay, I get it. But what does all that mean as far as having a boyfriend?"

"It means that I can't just spontaneously jump a guy. Setting the wards is a pretty exacting ritual that takes about five to ten minutes and the proper tools. Not terribly romantic. And I've had my one screwup. I won't be forgiven again."

Chapter 13

THE FOLLOWING three weeks were surprisingly uneventful, with no reports of demon activity or additional deaths. Joanna thankfully immersed herself in her schoolwork, training with Weatherspoon and Underwood, and getting to know her new friends.

She saw Kyle in class on Monday and Wednesday mornings, and he had asked her to go out with him and his friends several times, but she always told him she couldn't make it. Her heart always pounded in her chest when she saw him, but it was too painful to see him with Donna.

That didn't keep her from becoming much closer to Donna, however, or to Lisa, who Kyle called one of his closest friends. The two girls were very friendly, but were somewhat closed about themselves. Finally, she asked Kyle about them.

"Yeah, there's a difference between the private Donna and the public one," he said. "But you'll have to ask her why. I'm not comfortable sharing her private life."

"Maybe you can tell me something about Lisa, then," Joanna said. "She seems to have two completely different sides. She's friendly and really nice to me and Addie, and it's obvious she

considers you and Donna close friends. But she's kind of nasty to a
lot of weres, and they act afraid of her."

One side of Kyle's mouth quirked up in a half smile. "That's
easy to explain. She's a cat."

"Oh, come on. That doesn't explain anything."

"But it does. Wolves are pack animals, whereas werecats are solitary. They don't mate for life, and fathers don't stick around to raise
the kittens. And cats and dogs, or lynxes and wolves, are enemies in
the wild."

"And? You're not telling me anything I couldn't find on
Wikipedia."

"Do you understand mass and shifting?"

"Mass? You mean size?"

"Yes. I weigh about one hundred eighty pounds. When I shift, I
still weigh the same. But in the wild, a wolf that large is a really big
wolf. Don is a giant compared to wild wolves."

"Okay. So, what does that have to do with Lisa?"

"As I said, lynxes and wolves are enemies. They're close to
evenly matched, but a wolf is much larger and stronger. Like you,
Lisa is a small woman, and some weres tend to be aggressive in their
human forms. The largest wild lynxes go between twenty-five and
forty pounds for a female, maybe sixty for a male. Lisa is a little over
a hundred pounds, and her claws are as long as her fingers when
she's in human form. She could probably kick ass on a small pack.
As a result, she doesn't feel as though she needs to take any crap
from anyone. And with Kaylynn backing her up, she's probably
right."

"Kaylynn?"

"Her roommate. The werecougar."

"I haven't met her."

"She's got a new boyfriend, so she hasn't been around a lot.
About six-foot-one, maybe six-foot-two, long blonde hair, looks like
a Nordic goddess. She's really hard to miss."

"Oh, yeah, I've seen them together a couple of times, but I've
never met her."

"They came here from Canada. Believe me, no wolf wants to mess with either of them, let alone the two of them together."

Joanna never had close friends her own age when she was growing up. In the small village where she and her mother lived, there weren't any other kids her own age. She didn't really know what she was missing until she went to Oregon State and met Leila and the other girls in her dorm. During her time between schools, she discovered that she missed having friends more than she could have ever imagined.

Determined to get to know her new friends better, she decided to throw a small party. So, she invited Lisa, Donna, Addie, Bev, and Susan to dinner on a Saturday evening.

Susan declined. "Any other time I'd be glad to get away from the kids for an evening, but with the demon still on the loose, I think I should be home if there's an emergency and Rupert has to go out."

Joanna asked Lisa if she wanted to bring Kaylynn, but the were-cougar had a date. "She's madly in lust," Lisa laughingly told Joanna. "She'll get over him sooner or later, and then she'll be around more. As it is, I barely see her myself, and we theoretically live together."

For dinner, Joanna fixed coq au vin and a salad, opened tiramisu mini-cakes that she bought for dessert, and chilled four bottles of white wine. Addie and Bev showed up separately on their bicycles while Donna and Lisa came in Donna's car.

"This is really nice," Donna said, looking around Joanna's cottage. She wandered into the workshop. "Oh, this is *really* nice." With her hands clasped behind her back, she inspected the room, then turned and asked, "Do you suppose I could come over and use it sometimes? I have a spell book, but I never get a chance to try any of the stuff in it. I feel so ignorant sometimes."

"Yeah, we can work something out," Joanna said, secretly pleased. "I know when I lived in the dorms, there were a lot of spells, especially potions, that I couldn't practice. It gets kind of frustrating to read about them and wonder if you can make them work."

Bev said, "Yeah. I have a book that my mom gave me for my

sixteenth birthday, but it's just the standard harmless spells. I have the space in my studio to work magic, but I don't have a kitchen. I have a sink, but you never have open flame in a painter's studio, so potions are impossible." She walked over to where Joanna's spell book sat. It was the size of an encyclopedia and almost four inches thick. "This is really old, isn't it?"

"The oldest spells were written around 1100 A.D.," Joanna said. "My grandmother gave it to me, and she said the cover is demon skin. There's a spell in there for skinning and preserving the skin of a demon." She shuddered, and both of the other witches looked a bit sick.

"There are some spells in my book that I wouldn't ever try," Donna said. "Really grisly stuff. Mine dates from about 1700, when the wars were still going on."

"Are there any transmutation spells in your book?" Bev asked.

"Yeah, there are," Joanna said. "I'm not a conjurer, so I never paid much attention to them."

Donna nodded. "Same here."

Bev stared at Joanna's book. "Mine doesn't have anything for a conjurer. I've added those I've learned, but it's only half a dozen spells. I've never had a chance to study with a conjurer."

"Well, maybe we can look through mine and find some you want to copy," Joanna said.

"I've never seen a spell book," Addie said. "Can I see?"

Joanna smiled and reached for the book. "Yes, but don't touch."

"Oh, I wouldn't," Addie said. "I bet something that old is really fragile."

Donna and Bev giggled.

"No, not at all. Almost invulnerable except to witchfire," Joanna said. "But it would give you a hell of a shock if you tried to touch it."

"Because I'm not a witch?"

"Because Joanna's still alive," Bev said. "Even a store-bought book like mine is bound to one user. For me to use her spell book, she has to be here to turn the pages, and I won't be able to read any spells I don't have the power to do."

Joanna turned to a page and held the book so Bev could see it. "Can you read that?"

"Yeah. It's a summoning spell," Bev said. She studied it a bit more. "Damn! It's a spell to call a Grand Arch Demon! Half of the first page is a warning against using the spell."

"Then why have it?" Joanna wondered. "What's the date on it and what language is it in?"

"It's in Latin, and the date is 1755," Bev answered.

"I think we have a good idea what happened to Rome," Donna said with a chuckle.

Joanna served dinner and the conversation was light and comfortable. Everyone got along well, and Joanna relaxed. Donna in particular was in a great mood and told one funny story after another.

After dinner, Joanna opened the third bottle of wine, and the group moved to the living room.

"I'm going to say something," Bev said, looking at Donna, "and I don't mean to be offensive, but if I am, I'm going to blame it on the wine. I had never talked to you until we took this class together, but you are so different than I always thought."

"Yeah, she fools people that way," Lisa said with a sly grin. "They always seem shocked to discover that she's really a gorgeous, snooty, overachiever instead of the meek little mouse she presents to the world."

Donna straightened in her chair and gave Lisa a haughty sneer. "It's not easy to be Miss Perfect," she said. "People aren't born snooty, you know. It takes constant practice." Then she started to giggle. "Damn wine." Lifting her glass toward Bev, she said, "We'll all blame it on the wine."

With a smile, Bev toasted her back.

Donna took a deep breath and turned to Joanna. "I don't know if you follow politics, but my father is a senator. And since a witch has as much chance to get elected as a snowball in demon land, he's always hidden it. My mom is also a witch, but her mother is human, and I'm at Midleton because that's what my parents wanted. Mom and Grandma were members of Tri-Delta, so that's why I joined a sorority. But the sorority would toss me out on my ass if they found out I'm a witch."

"That's why you feel like an imposter," Addie blurted out. Everyone turned to look at her, and she blushed. "I, I don't mean I think you're an imposter," she stammered, "I mean that's why you feel you are. Oh, crap, I'm sorry. I'll just shut up."

In a very quiet voice, Donna asked, "What are you? Why are you hanging around with supernaturals instead of humans?"

"She's a sensitive," Joanna answered for Addie. "Like the rest of us, she's an outsider who just wants people to accept her without thinking she's a freak."

"Is that what we all are? A bunch of freaks?" Lisa asked.

"Aren't we?" Joanna asked. "Addie, what is the common thread underlying each of us?"

"We're all afraid people will find out what we really are and won't like us." Addie almost whispered.

Lisa took a sip of her wine and seemed to hide behind her glass. Bev seemed to draw into herself. Donna's eyes narrowed, and she just stared at Addie.

Then Donna turned to Joanna. "Okay, I've opened up about me. How did you end up at Midleton? An elemental witch from Oregon just suddenly got an urge to move here to go to school?"

Joanna took a deep breath and told them her story. When she finished, and answered all the questions thrown at her, she asked Lisa, "And what are you doing here? There are definitely better schools for pre-med or pre-vet?"

"You know that large cats—werecats—are very different than werewolves, right?" Lisa chuckled. "Cats tend to be solitary, but people really are social creatures. So, a lot of female werecats partner with another female cat so they don't feel so alone. Kaylynn and I went to high school together. There was a male lynx who decided he wanted to mate with me. I was only seventeen, but he was almost forty, and he was very insistent. So, we got out of town. There are only six werecats at Midleton, all female, all paired. There aren't any living in the surrounding area. I think we're all here for the same reason."

"So, tell us about being a sensitive," Donna said to Addie with a challenging note in her voice. "Why do people treat you like a freak?"

Addie stared around, fright evident on her face, in her eyes.

"It's okay," Joanna said, laying her hand on her friend's thigh and giving Donna a hard look. "If people can't accept you for who you are, you don't want them for friends anyway."

"I see auras," Addie started. "And I feel other people's emotions. I can see Joanna's elementals, but I can't see your illusions. The other night in Cobbler's Lane, I didn't see the illusion you cast."

"You feel my emotions?" Lisa asked. "You're an empath?"

Addie nodded. "A lot of people are uncomfortable with that. They're afraid I'll tell people their secrets."

"Ya think?" Lisa snorted a laugh. "Isn't it hard to be bombarded with other people's garbage?"

"I've learned to block it out most of the time. And I don't always know how to interpret what I feel. But I don't go around gossiping about people's emotions. I have my own issues, so why would I want to spend my life caught up in other people's drama?"

The expression on Lisa's face seemed to say that she wanted to believe, hoped to believe Addie, and Joanna wondered what secret Lisa held that she wanted to keep buried.

"My freshman year my roommate asked to be moved when she found out I could read her feelings," Addie said. "I learned I can't tell guys, or they don't want even to come near me. I don't have many friends."

Joanna moved over beside her and pulled her into a hug.

Sometime later, Donna said, "I need to go home while I can still walk."

"You're not driving," Joanna said.

"Didn't plan on it. By the time I get home, I should be sober enough to put up with the party they're throwing at the sorority tonight."

"That's a good idea," Lisa said. "Let's walk back to the sorority house and hope the demon isn't out tonight."

"Forgot about that," Donna said.

"I'll take everyone home," Joanna said.

"I'm not sober enough to drive, but you're sober enough to fly?" Donna asked.

"I'm not the one doing the flying," Joanna laughed, "and elementals don't drink."

Chapter 14

AS THE MONTH PROGRESSED, Joanna began to feel some tension from Weatherspoon and Underwood, as well as Rupert Glockner.

Sunday evening dinner at the Glockners' had become a regular event. As Joanna prepared to go home, standing on the Glockners' front porch in the light of the full moon, Rupert said, "Be sure to set your wards extra well tonight."

"Do you think something is going to happen?" Joanna asked.

"Max is concerned about the page that was torn out of the spell book. If the demon manages to possess a conjurer, it could try to summon more of its kind."

"And since it was brought over on the full moon, you think that may be necessary for the summoning," Joanna finished. "That's why everyone has been so uptight this week."

Rupert nodded.

When Joanna got home, she checked her wards and reset them, did some studying, and took a bath, all to the sounds of werewolves howling in the distance. Usually she was asleep by eleven, but that night she sat in bed watching the clock as it neared midnight. When it finally showed twelve o'clock, she found she was holding her breath.

At one minute after twelve, just as she was starting to relax, the sound she had heard the month before ripped through the world. The sound she now knew came from reality being breached, but this time, it was louder and lasted longer.

An earthquake immediately followed it, and a strong wind buffeted the house.

After the first quake, Joanna had gone through the house and systematically laid strengthening spells on the walls, rafters, and roof. Now she was glad she had. The quake wasn't any stronger than the one the month before, but the initial jolt lasted at least five minutes.

Clambering out of bed, she rushed to the window. Fierce winds whipped the trees outside, bending them almost to the ground, and rain began to lash the sides of the cottage. Flipping a light switch, she discovered that the electricity was out, so she went to the living room where a fire elemental blazed four feet high in its ceramic bowl.

She wondered about the wolves in the forest, remembering that the last time this happened, one died and another was possessed. She hoped they were able to find shelter. The conditions outside were, as the expression went, fit for neither man nor beast.

Finding her phone, she attempted to call Rupert, but the line was busy. She disconnected and called Susan's number.

"Joanna?" Susan's voice came over the phone. "Are you all right?"

"Yes, I'm fine. How about you?"

"It feels as though the house is going to shake down around our ears. We're in the basement."

"I'll have to show you the spells to strengthen your house," Joanna said. "I don't guess you normally need that here, but we always did it in Oregon. Is Rupert available?"

A few moments of silence, and then Rupert came on. "Are you all right?" he asked.

"Yes. I wanted to tell you it was much closer this time. I think in the forest west of us. I don't know why I think that, but it just seemed that way to me."

"I was on the phone with Max when you called," Rupert said. "He thinks this was a larger breach, that more than one demon might have come across."

"Well, if the demon opened a portal, we can assume it knew the names of those it wanted to bring over, can't we?"

"That's what Max is afraid of."

"At least if it brought more fire demons over," Joanna tried to make her tone light, "they can't be happy with all this rain. Maybe we won't get any murders tonight."

Another quake hit, as strong as the first one.

"Rupert, if I can help, call me. I'm not going to get any sleep with all this going on."

"Thank you, Joanna. Be safe." He hung up.

Going into the kitchen, she filled the teapot but was afraid to try the stove. Instead, she went into the workshop, set up a tripod, placed a ceramic dish under it, and hung the teapot from it. Summoning a fire elemental, she put it to boiling the water.

A strange sound came from the living room, sort of a slow, rhythmic thumping. When she entered the room, it seemed to come from the front door. Drawing back the curtain on the door, she found herself face to face with a very wet lynx standing on its hind legs.

Joanna threw open the door. "Lisa! What are you doing here? Come in."

Instead of bolting into the house as Joanna expected, the lynx turned and bounded to the edge of the porch, then stopped and looked back.

"What is it?" Joanna cried.

The lynx jumped down from the porch and started toward the woods, then turned and came back.

"You want me to come with you?"

The lynx nodded and snarled.

"I need to get dressed. I can't go out there like this. Come in while I get some clothes on."

Lisa came up on the porch, but stopped halfway into the house, looked at Joanna, and snarled again.

"Okay. I'll hurry!" Joanna ran into the bedroom, grabbed a pair of jeans and a shirt, and put them on. Returning to the living room, she pulled on a pair of boots and a hooded raincoat. The lynx immediately turned and jumped off the porch, and Joanna followed her.

Lisa ran around the house and started down the path to the lake. Joanna had no hope of keeping up, so she called an air elemental and asked it to give her a ride.

She followed Lisa for about ten minutes, and then the lynx jumped off the path and approached a large fallen log. Joanna looked around and a flash of lightning showed that some of the area around the log appeared as if something had been dragged through the area.

Lisa went to one end of the log, where a bush and a low tree branch hid it from sight. Drawing near, Joanna saw that the log and the foliage created a small cave, protected from the rain. In the depression lay a cougar, its shoulder and side drenched in blood.

Joanna leaned closer and saw that its side was scored, as if by giant claws. A deep gash in its shoulder was the major wound. Its eyes were closed, but its ribs rose and fell to show it was still breathing. Lisa stood over it and made a distressed, mewing sound.

Calling additional air elementals, Joanna asked them to shelter the area from the rain. Then she bent down and cast the only healing spell she was able to work. Praying to the Goddess that it was effective enough at least to slow the bleeding, she turned to Lisa.

"I need you to shift," Joanna told Lisa. "I can't get her out of there by myself."

The lynx seemed to blur into a multi-colored pulsing blob, and then it coalesced into a naked girl with wet hair.

"Is she hurt anywhere else?" Joanna asked.

"No. It just got her once. Damn fool. She tried to protect me, but I was already out of the way." Lisa sounded angry, and Joanna could tell she was struggling not to cry.

"Help me lift her," Joanna ordered. "We have to get her off the ground so an air elemental can wrap itself around her."

Lisa knelt down by the cougar's head. "Slide your arms under her shoulder," Joanna directed, getting down on her knees and sliding her own arms under the cougar's hips and belly. "Are you in position?"

"Yes," Lisa called.

"Okay, one, two, three, lift!"

Most of the long cat came off the ground, and two air elementals wrapped around her. Joanna asked them to raise her a couple of inches, and felt the weight relieved from her arms.

"Okay," she called. "Lisa, you can let go of her now." Joanna stood, and the elementals slid Kaylynn out from under the log. Calling more elementals, Joanna had them wrap the cougar and Lisa, and then they all rose into the air, past the treetops, and sped toward the cottage.

As they flew, Joanna looked around. The storm was raging as hard as ever, heavy black clouds pouring rain down on the area. A bright light north of the lake attracted her attention. Even in the rain, it looked as though a small perfect circle of fire was burning in the forest. She continued to watch it, and it didn't spread.

Alighting by her back door, Joanna hurriedly opened it, and had the elementals lay Kaylynn on the large table in the workroom. Joanna pointed to the four cardinal points, and candles lit, their flames flaring two feet high and lighting the room. Lisa trailed in, wet, muddy, and nude.

Joanna went to the stovetop and checked to see if she could smell gas. When she couldn't, she lit a burner and retrieved a large copper pot from a shelf under the counter. Handing it to Lisa, she said, "Fill this with water and put it to boil. Then go into my bedroom. On the bottom shelf of the linen closet, there are two old sheets. Bring them. Then go dry yourself off and find something in my closet to put on."

While she was talking, Joanna was searching in a cabinet.

"Shouldn't we call a healer, or take her to the hospital?" Lisa asked.

"We'll do that as soon as we stop the bleeding. She's lost too much blood. Ah, here it is."

Whirling away from the cabinet, she approached the cougar's head. "Kaylynn, can you hear me?"

The big cat's eye fluttered, and it tried to lift its head.

"I'm going to give you a potion," Joanna said. "I need you to swallow it and not bite me. Okay?"

She lifted the cat's head and turned it. Using one hand, she pried the cougar's mouth open and poured the potion in. The cat sputtered and choked, then swallowed.

"Just one more," Joanna said, and poured another potion into Kaylynn's mouth. The second one went in easier. Out of the corner of her eye, Joanna saw Lisa lift the pot of water onto the stove, then run into the other part of the house.

When Lisa came back with the sheets, Joanna asked, "Did the demon bite her, or just scratch her?"

"Scratch her?" Lisa's voice rose almost to a shriek. "The damn thing almost tore her leg off!"

"But did it bite her?"

"No. Why does that matter?"

"Thank the Goddess," Joana breathed, placing one folded sheet on the cat's ribs and the other on the wound in her shoulder. "A demon's bodily fluids—saliva, blood, semen—are very acidic. At least we don't have to worry about acid eating into her flesh."

With the sheets in place, Joanna asked the two elementals that had carried Kaylynn to put pressure on the sheets. Then she directed a fire elemental to add heat to the pot full of water.

"Go get dry," she said to Lisa.

As soon as the water in the pot began to boil, Joanna started tossing herbs into it. She stirred it with a large wooden spoon and set a timer. "Lisa," she called, "get my phone from my nightstand."

Lisa came back, her hair wrapped in a towel, wearing a pair of cargo shorts and a t-shirt. She handed Joanna her phone. Still stirring the pot with one hand, Joanna dialed Susan's number.

"Susan? I have a werecat at my house who was wounded by a demon. Is there any way to get a healer here?"

"The river is flooding," Susan said. "There was a report about a demon in town. Rupert and the others have gone to try and find it."

"Can you get hold of Helen?" Joanna asked. "Susan, she's lost a lot of blood. I'm trying to stabilize her, I know that much, but I can't heal her. I got her here, but I'm afraid to transport her again until she's stable."

"I'll call Helen and see if she can bring a healer to your house," Susan said and broke the connection.

Looking into the pot, Joanna spoke an incantation and cast a spell. Nothing happened. She looked at the timer and realized that she hadn't waited long enough.

"Is she going to make it?" Lisa asked with a hitch in her voice.

Joanna looked toward her and saw she was holding and stroking the cougar's head, tears running down her face.

The timer dinged. Taking a deep breath to steady herself, Joanna spoke the incantation again and cast the spell. To her relief, the contents of the pot glowed, and with an audible pop, absorbed all the liquid. A thick, spongy mass lay in the bottom of the pot.

She lifted the pot off the stove and carried it to the table. Pulling the sheet away, Joanna started scooping the steaming mass out and spreading it on the cat's wounds.

"What's that?" Lisa asked.

"A poultice. It should seal the wound, have an antibiotic affect, and hopefully stop the bleeding. Susan said that she would try to contact Professor Weatherspoon. Maybe she can bring a healer. If not, we'll try to take her to a hospital."

"Is there anything I can do?" Lisa asked.

"Pray," Joanna said, packing the poultice into the gaping wound in the cougar's shoulder. "Here, help me with this sheet."

They took the bloody sheet and wrapped it around the cougar's shoulders, tying it tight to hold the poultice in place. Then they wrapped the other sheet around her ribs.

The phone rang, and Lisa leaped across the room to answer it.

"Hello?"

"Joanna?"

"No, it's Lisa."

"Oh. This is Susan Glockner. Tell Joanna that Helen Weatherspoon is taking a healer over there. She said it would be about twenty, maybe thirty minutes. How's your friend?"

"We, uh, Joanna gave her a potion, and we bound her wounds with a poultice. She doesn't seem any worse, but she's only semiconscious. It's been an hour since we were attacked, and she's lost a lot of blood."

"Was it the same demon that attacked you before?" Susan asked.

"No. This one was shorter and fatter. Built more like a human," Lisa said. "It was blue and *very* obviously male."

"Damn," Susan said. "That's different than the description of the one downtown. Gotta go. Call me if you need to."

"Let me talk to her," Joanna said.

"Wait!" Lisa said into the phone, then handed it to Joanna.

"Susan? Tell Rupert that the summoning took place about a mile north of the lake, between the lake and the river. I could still see the circle glowing when we transported Kaylynn back to my house."

"I'll tell him. Is the werecat going to make it?"

"I think so," Joanna said.

"Good," Susan said and hung up.

Chapter 15

KAYLYNN WAS SLEEPING PEACEFULLY when Helen flew in with a healer. They landed on Joanna's front porch, and she showed them to the workroom in the back of the house where the were-cougar lay.

Ruth, the healer, shooed Lisa and Helen out, and put Joanna to work boiling water and compounding another poultice.

"Nice job on this one," Ruth said. "I'm going to have to clear it all out and clean up the wounds, though, so I can sew her up,. Then we can apply the same thing again."

"I was afraid to give her anything for the pain," Joanna said. "I was mainly worried about stopping the bleeding."

"I can do that."

Forty minutes later, they walked out to the living room where Helen poured them some strong tea.

"She's going to have a few scars," Ruth told Lisa, "but I think she'll get her range of motion back. Once we have her on her feet again, I'll give her exercises to help with that. But you're going to have to limit her for several weeks. No hunting next full moon. Is she left-handed?"

Lisa shook her head. "Right."

"Okay, she won't have any excuse for not doing her homework," Ruth said, with a wink to Professor Weatherspoon. "And she shouldn't have any mobility problems once she shifts to human. But let's keep her in her cat form for about a week. She'll heal quicker."

"And what about the demons?" Joanna asked.

"I'm going to leave Ruth and your friends here," Helen said, "and you're coming with me. We need to drown that circle in conjunction with the spell Max and his conjurers are preparing. Thankfully, it's near the river."

THE AIR ELEMENTALS took Helen and Joanna toward the burning circle. As they drew closer, she saw that the entire circle wasn't on fire, just the rim and a pentagram inside. The areas that weren't on fire were scorched—the grass and bushes had caught fire and burned, but once the fires ran out of fuel, the fires went out. The place where the demon-conjurer had spread witches' salt was still burning.

The very middle of the pentagram was the deepest black imaginable. Looking into it, Joanna realized it was a hole that had no bottom.

Helen reached out and pulled Joanna close, shouting in her ear to be heard.

"The conjurers are marking a circle around that pit into hell. What we need to do is create a waterspout, bring it here, and drop it in. That will block the entrance to our world from the demons' world, and allow the conjurers to close the portal. Understand?"

Joanna surveyed the landscape below them. The portal burned in a small clearing in the forest. The river was perhaps half a mile away. In between was dense forest.

"We'll never get the waterspout through the trees intact," she told Helen. "We would have to jump it from the river to here, and that's too far. First, we need a tornado to clear a path from here to the river."

"We'll need a large tornado," Helen said.

Joanna nodded. "We have plenty of elementals. They're being drawn here by the demonic activity. And I have experience with tornados. We'll get the job done."

They set down on the ground, and Helen called on her phone. "Max? Helen. We're going to carve a path from the river to this portal. Yeah, a tornado. Clear everyone out of the area. When we've finished, you can re-establish your circle. Give us an hour or so?"

The question was directed at Joanna, who nodded. "That should be enough time."

Helen hung up and said, "We need to give them some time to clear the area. So, tell me about Bev Turner. She's a painting student of mine. Why do you think she needs special training in conjuring?"

Joanna told Helen about Bev reading Joanna's grimoire and the spell for calling a grand archdemon.

"That's a little frightening, considering she says she has almost no training," Helen said. "I'll definitely talk to Max about it. If she has that kind of power, we should have her out here tonight. I wonder how many other hidden gems we have wandering around campus."

When Max called and gave them the go-ahead, Joanna and Helen grabbed a couple of elementals and rode them to a spot on the river side of the burning circle. They landed on the edge of the natural clearing, close enough to the burning salt that they could feel the heat like that from a furnace.

They began pulling air elementals, setting them to chasing each other in a large circle, which drew more elementals to join the game. Soon, they had a small vortex spinning in front of them.

A large air elemental that followed the course of river was attracted and joined the vortex, tripling its size. Two high atmospheric elementals detected the disturbance on the ground and dipped down. Discerning the purpose and the need, they joined, and without any further intervention from Helen and Joanna, an F3 tornado roared toward the river.

The two women watched in awestruck silence. Trees, shrubs,

boulders, and anything else in its way was pulled into the swirling winds, leaving a flattened path the width of two football fields. It reached the river in less than ten minutes.

Once it reached the river, it stopped, bouncing up and down, pulling water into the vortex as the water elemental joined the party.

"I think we need to get out of the way," Joanna said.

They raced away from the circle into the forest as the enormous waterspout surged up from the riverbed and retraced the tornado's path. When it reached the burning circle, it extinguished the flames, and then dropped into the abyss in the middle.

An explosion rocked the ground, and an enormous plume of steam erupted into the air.

Joanna and Helen started laughing and high-fived each other, then Helen pulled out her phone and made a call.

"Show's over," she said to Max Brown when he answered. "Time to see if your part of this production works."

As soon as the world settled from the interaction between the elementals' waterspout and the demons' portal, Max Brown and his conjurers moved into position.

"The theory," Helen told Joanna, "is that we plugged the breach, and now they'll seal it. As far as we know, people have reported seven different demons. Max says we'll have to hunt them all down. But they don't need us right now. Do you have anything at your place for breakfast? I'm starving."

Chapter 16

A WEEK AFTER THE DEMONS' portal was sealed, Joanna answered a knock on her door to find Lisa and a tall blonde woman. The blonde's left arm was in a sling, and there was a heavy bandage on her upper arm and shoulder.

"Hi! Come in," Joanna said.

Lisa handed her a tote sack. "I know you eat meat. We brought you some venison. Better than the cow at the store."

"I'm Kaylynn and I wanted to come by and say thank you," the other woman said.

Joanna ushered them into her sitting room and brought them each a glass of lemonade after she put the meat in her freezer.

"Thanks for the meat," Joanna said, "but it really wasn't necessary."

"For saving my life?" Kaylynn chuckled. "I owe you a lot more than a couple of steaks, but just know that if you ever need a favor, I'll do whatever I can."

"Have you heard anything new about the demons?" Lisa asked.

"The last I heard, they tracked down the one you guys met," Joanna said. "They've either killed or banished five, and they're still looking for two. One of them was found in Pittsburgh." That city was more than one hundred miles away.

"Yeah, I'll be shocked if they find all of them," Lisa said. "I talked to Bev yesterday, and she said the Council was ordering mandatory training classes for all conjurers in the area."

"I think we're going to have to create some sort of formal training for all witches," Joanna said. "Too many costly mistakes from assuming parents and covens will take care of such things. My situation should have got more of the Council's attention. If we're not careful, we'll end up with another witch war."

Kaylynn shook her head. "Even with all the training and education in the world, you can't fix stupid. Some idiot is going to screw up because he thinks he's smarter than everyone else. The fool who caused this mess knew the law. That didn't stop him."

Joanna chuckled. "Dr. Underwood said that he did serve a useful purpose as a bad example."

"Yeah, but how many others died because of him?" Lisa asked.

~

*If you enjoyed **Elemental Witch**, get updates on new book releases, promotions, contests and giveaways!*

Sign up for my newsletter.

Dragon Tears

MARINA FINLAYSON

Chapter 1

Tony padded into the break room, dripping water everywhere and bringing the delightful aroma of wet fur with him. Werewolves are huge, and when a werewolf gets wet, so does everything in his vicinity. Rain dripped off his muzzle and pooled on the floor.

I leapt up from the table, holding my hands out. "Don't—"

But it was too late. He shook from nose to tail and water sprayed everywhere.

"Tony, you bastard! How many times have I told you—the break room is for two-legs. Now this place stinks of wet dog. And look at me. I'm soaked."

In the blink of an eye, the wolf became a short, powerful man, wearing the same navy-blue uniform with the High Moon Security logo on the breast pocket that I was. Only *his* was dry.

He grinned, unrepentant. "Lucky it's your turn to go outside, then. It's bucketing out there. You would have been wet in five seconds anyway."

"Don't hit me with your damn logic." I shrugged back into my jacket and prepared to face the storm.

"You know, the rain wouldn't bother you if you let your wolf out to play."

I wiggled my fingers at him. "Opposable thumbs, baby. Can't play Candy Crush without them."

He sat in the chair I'd just left and put his feet up on the table. "Can't play Candy Crush if your phone drowns either. But don't say I didn't warn you."

I paused at the door and gave him a stern look. "That sandwich better still be there when I get back." Werewolves are walking stomachs. They'll eat anything that isn't nailed down.

Tony curled his lip in the direction of my sandwich. "It's salad. It couldn't be safer if it was locked in a bank vault. How can you eat that crap?"

"You werewolves and your meat obsession," I said as I opened the door. "Just wait till you die of scurvy. Who'll be laughing then?"

"You keep eating that rabbit food and you'll be the first werewolf to die of a lack of protein," he called after me.

He hadn't been exaggerating—it really was bucketing outside. I zipped my jacket, turning the collar up and pulling my cap down firmly to keep the rain out of my eyes. What a night! Visibility was poor, and the rain drowned out any scents. There was no sign of Sam. She was probably patrolling around the front of the warehouse.

Warehouse was a bit of a misnomer—it made it sound like what was inside was for sale. This was simply a storage facility, sprawling on a vast industrial lot. Our tiny break room was just a shed tucked away at the back. Acres of concrete surrounded the main building, with not a blade of grass anywhere, the whole lot encircled by a high steel fence. The building was steel too, and was so massive it was probably visible from space. I'd never been inside it, but Tony said it was crammed full of treasure—and it wasn't the only such facility our employer owned in Sydney.

I'd found it hard to believe on my first day, when I discovered what my new job entailed. "How much treasure can one man own?"

Tony had shrugged. "Dunno. Ask Jeff Bezos. "

"Why, is he a dragon, too?"

Tony rolled his eyes. "No, but if a human can manage to scrape together billions of dollars in a single lifetime, why is it so hard to believe that a dragon could? Gabriel Arquette has been around a lot longer than Jeff Bezos, and he has magic on his side, too."

I trudged around the enormous building while the rain trickled down my neck and hammered onto the concrete. I found Sam on the south side of the complex, patrolling the fence along the street. With her colouring, she looked like a German shepherd. Well, a German shepherd on steroids. She would dwarf even the largest shepherd. I gave her a wave but she ignored me—not all of the pack were as friendly as Tony.

There were two massive roller doors on the side that faced the street, big enough to admit a semitrailer with room to spare. Or a dragon, I guessed. A smaller, person-sized door opened around the back on the north side, and that was it. No other doors, no windows.

As jobs went, it was a pretty easy one. High Moon Security was owned by Matt, the pack leader, and provided jobs for the whole pack. We were responsible for guarding the treasure stored here, but all we had to do was make sure no one came on site without permission from the boss. I'd only been here six weeks, and already I was bored out of my mind.

The others spent most of their shifts in werewolf form to alleviate the boredom, patrolling the grounds like overgrown guard dogs. I was as new to being a werewolf as I was to being a security guard, and much preferred remaining in human form. But the monotony of pacing around and around the vast building, while it was working wonders on my leg muscles, was just about doing my head in. I couldn't imagine a lifetime in this role, but apparently I didn't get a say in my own life anymore.

I huddled against the back wall of the warehouse by the small door, and stared out at the rain. Becoming a werewolf had *not* been my idea. Hell, six weeks ago, I hadn't even known werewolves existed outside the movies.

And then the attack happened. I shuddered and folded my wet arms more tightly across my chest. I didn't like to think about it. Bad enough that I still had nightmares about it.

But, bad as those moments of sheer terror and agony had been, what came after was infinitely worse. When Matt sat me down and explained why I'd recovered so fast from my injuries, and what my new life involved, I was revolted.

"You can't keep me here," I said. "I have my own life."

His face had softened into lines of sympathy. "Nat. Sweetheart. That life is over. No one's trying to trap you, we're trying to help you. And trust me, you're going to need help. The first time the change comes on you, you'll be grateful to have your pack around you."

"And I should just take your word for it? Who died and made you God?"

"He's our leader," Leon had growled.

I wouldn't have liked Leon, even if he hadn't been the one who bit me and turned my life upside down. He was a huge, muscled guy with a scar across one cheek, who never looked at you straight-on when he was talking to you. I couldn't see what Matt saw in him. They couldn't have been more opposite. Matt was a fit-looking guy in his late forties with a warm, paternal air, and he could have sold ice to polar bears. When *he* was talking to you, he made you feel as though you were the most interesting person in the room.

"*I* didn't vote for him," I said.

"Nobody votes," Leon said. "This is a pack, not a democracy."

"Then maybe you should ask people if they want to live in the Middle Ages before you turn them."

Thunder rumbled overhead, shaking me out of my gloomy thoughts. I looked up in time to see a bird flit across the dark sky and land on the roof above my head.

Strange. Why would a bird be out in this weather? It was three o'clock in the morning, and that was no owl. It had looked more like a sparrow.

Another one arrowed in and joined its friend. I stepped out of the shelter of the doorway to have a better look. For a moment I stared up and two sets of beady eyes stared down, then the birds hopped out of sight.

I high-tailed it back to the break room. Tony had his feet up on the table and was scrolling through his phone.

"So, tell me. On a scale of 'one to freaky magic shit', how suspicious is a pair of blue birds landing on the roof right now?" I'd seen a lot of freaky magic shit in the past six weeks, more than I'd ever imagined could possibly exist, and now I was suspicious of *everything.*

Tony's feet thudded to the floor. "Bright blue? Like a summer sky?"

"As far as I could tell in the dark, yeah."

"Shit. Sounds like goblin familiars."

"You can tell that because they're blue?"

"Same colour as goblins," he said. "Goblins are natural mages. Magic's a part of them and it colours their familiars."

"Right." There was so much to learn about this crazy new world I inhabited. I'd only just come to grips with the fact that there were human wizards, and now we had goblin mages as well? "Does that mean there's a goblin around?"

"Most likely." He switched to the mental speech of the pack. *Sam, you see anything out there? We've got a couple of goblin birds on the roof.*

I flinched. The mind speech felt like the biggest invasion of privacy, and made me want to scrub out the inside of my skull. I rarely used it myself, but I still heard broadcasts from the rest of the pack.

Nothing out front, she said. *Check the back.*

My eye fell on my half-eaten sandwich on the table. What were those birds doing up there? Spying? Maybe there was a way to get them down. I grabbed some bread and headed back out into the rain, which was finally easing.

Tony joined me a moment later, back in wolf form. I nudged him into the shelter of the doorway around the back.

"Stay there and be quiet. I'm going to see if I can tempt those birds down closer."

I tore the bread into little pieces and scattered the crumbs in a wide arc across the wet concrete. They looked pretty soggy and unappetising.

Still, I wasn't a goblin bird. How did I know what they found appetising? Maybe waterlogged free crumbs looked like a feast to them. I whistled a short trill, watching the roof from the corner of my eye.

A little blue head appeared, cocked to one side. I took an ostentatious bite of my sandwich, making appreciative noises, then scattered a few more crumbs as I walked away. In my peripheral vision, I saw another blue head join the first. Neither of them could see the wolf hidden under the overhang of the doorway.

Once I was far enough away to appear unthreatening, one of the birds plucked up its courage and winged its way down to the ground. It pecked greedily at my trail of crumbs. Nothing else moved. Good. Tony had the sense to wait for the jackpot.

I guess I shouldn't have been surprised. Werewolves were hunters, after all.

The second bird joined the first, hopping along behind it. Almost there. Just a little bit closer.

And wham! Right on cue, Tony surged out of hiding. His jaws closed on one blue ball of feathers as his paw slammed down on the other, pinning it to the ground. I ran back to inspect his catch.

They were both dead, not surprisingly. I felt a twinge of sadness as he spat out the one in his mouth. Poor thing. It was covered in spit and leaking blood from its wounds. We both stared at the forlorn little bundle a moment.

Yep. That's a goblin bird, all right, he said.

Then where's the goblin? Sam asked. *He won't be far.*

I tried the door handle, but it was locked, as it should have been. I set off at a jog, my boots splashing through puddles, checking the fences—checking for anything out of the ordinary. The world smelled fresh and clean, as it does after rain, but there was nothing unusual on the wind.

Not that I knew what a goblin smelled like.

When I'd completed my circuit of the warehouse, I stopped, frustrated. Tony was prowling the back fence and there was no trace left of the goblin birds. He'd probably eaten them. What else could I do? The place was well lit with floodlights, so I should have been able to see anyone trying to get in. Yet I couldn't help feeling I was missing something.

I eyed the overhang above the back door. Maybe there was another reason those birds had been on the roof, apart from the vantage point it gave them. My werewolf muscles tensed and I sprang, catching the overhang and pulling myself up. From there it was another big leap and pull to get onto the main roof.

The building looked even more enormous from this vantage point. You got the full picture of how vast it was, with acres of steel roofing stretching out into the darkness. Air conditioning units grouped at intervals looked like dice scattered from a giant's hand.

And the place where one of the roof panels had been removed stood out like a dog's balls.

I moved as quietly as I could across the roof until I stood at the edge of the hole. A rope was secured to an air conditioning unit and dangled down into the cavernous interior, disappearing into the dark.

We have a problem, I said, mind to mind. *The goblin's already inside.*

What? How did he get past us?

Magic, I guess. That seemed to be the answer to a lot of questions lately. And why was he asking me? I'd only just found out goblin mages existed. For all I knew, they could fly. *You'd better call for backup.*

We don't take orders from you, Sam said instantly.

Fine. You want to be the one to tell Gabriel Arquette you did nothing while a goblin tossed his warehouse? Be my guest. I'm going in to have a look.

Be careful, Tony said. *Goblins are slippery little bastards.*

I tested the rope before I committed, then shimmied silently down into the darkness. One good thing about being a werewolf was the superior night vision. I mean, not that I'd been running around in my former life going *Man, I wish I could see better in the dark.* And I certainly wouldn't have traded my humanity for it if I'd known. But it *was* kind of cool.

I'd actually made a list in that first week, when everything about my new life seemed negative. I was a glass-half-full kind of girl, but my positivity had taken a real hit when faced with the grim reality of losing control of my life. *Good things about being a werewolf*, I'd written at the top of the page. Then I'd stared at it, chewing my pencil. *See in the dark* had started the list, followed by *fast healing*. I'd hesitated over *good sense of smell*. Sometimes that was more a curse than a blessing.

But I used it now, sniffing at the climate-controlled air inside the warehouse as my feet sank into a thick Persian carpet. Strange perfumes floated on the air, mingling with the cold scent of metal and coins, and the slightly musty smell of the rain-dampened carpet I stood on.

I'd expected crates, neatly stacked, or some kind of shelving system, like a giant IKEA, but this place defied all logic. It was an Aladdin's cave. In some places, chests and boxes were piled high, almost to the ceiling, their haphazard arrangement spitting in the face of gravity. A mountain of coins and jewels glinted in the centre of the vast space. I half expected Smaug to rear his head over the top and blast me with fire.

How did Gabriel Arquette find anything in here? What was the point of owning all this *stuff*, if it was just jumbled together like so much trash? Bolts of silk in a rainbow of colours were stacked higher than my head, spilling onto the floor. Statues loomed out of the dark, some life-sized, some much larger. Suits of armour were lined up along the closest wall like soldiers standing guard, swords in jewelled scabbards dumped at their feet like sticks.

It was like the world's largest museum, if the curator had gone completely nuts. I stared around in awe.

There was no sign of the goblin. To be fair, there could have been a whole army of them—there were plenty of places to hide. You could spend days in here and still only see a fraction of the treasures the building contained.

Which made me wonder what the goblin knew that I didn't. If he'd just been going after valuables, I'd have expected to find him digging into that massive pile of money and jewels. The fact that he wasn't made me think he must be after something specific.

Good luck finding anything in this place.

I climbed a tower of sturdy cedar chests to get a better look over the mess. Maybe I could spot the goblin from up high.

How big are goblins? I asked, as it suddenly occurred to me to wonder exactly what I was looking for. Maybe they were only tiny. Maybe he'd flown in on one of those little blue birds.

They can pass as short people, Tony replied. *Don't let him see you. If he sees you he can cast a spell on you.*

Good to know. I crouched low and scanned the vast space, but nothing moved. Maybe I should just hang around near the rope, to catch him on his way out.

But what if he had another exit? I'd look pretty stupid then.

I caught the tiniest sound, as if something small had been bumped then rapidly set to rights. Should have added *excellent hearing* to that list of werewolf pluses. I stalked across the top of the stacked chests, moving silently as only a wolf can. Beyond the edge of my tower of chests was a gap between it and another stack, this one of wooden packing crates. The top of the crates was below my present height, but the gap was wide. Wider than I would have been able to jump as a human.

But that was before. Now I leapt across, landing with only a whisper of sound, my movements muffled by a mass of purple velvet that was heaped on top. Hopefully the patter of rain on the roof disguised the sound. Creeping across the crates, I peered down into a narrow corridor between them.

Below me, a small figure dressed in black was going through the drawers of an ornate cupboard. Jewels glittered inside, but he barely glanced into each one before closing it impatiently.

I retreated from the edge, considering my options. I could jump him from here pretty easily. He seemed absorbed in his search—but Tony had said not to let him see me. My eye fell on the mound of velvet. It was thick, heavy fabric in long lengths, like large curtains. Perfect.

I stole back to the edge with my arms full of velvet, just as he closed the last drawer and moved on down the tight corridor to an enormous grandfather clock. He opened the front and checked inside.

The rumble of a motor startled us both. The distant roller door at the front of the building was opening. The goblin slammed the front of the clock shut as I hurled the curtains and jumped down after them.

I smashed into the goblin and he collapsed under a smothering pile of heavy velvet. He squealed and kicked, but I grabbed at him, throwing myself across his struggling body. He scrabbled desperately at the thick drapes, trying to squirm out from under them, but I wasn't having that.

Several pairs of booted feet ran into the building. I found a lump under the velvet that felt like a head, and punched with all my werewolf strength.

"Move again and I'll kill you," I growled.

He abruptly went limp.

"Over here," I called.

When Matt and Tony and three other wolves arrived, I was sitting on my prisoner, who was still buried under an avalanche of purple velvet.

It was almost morning when Tony, Matt, and I got out of the limousine Gabriel Arquette had sent, in front of the most over-the-top house I'd ever seen. In fact, "house" didn't do it justice. "Small castle" would have been more accurate. This was a side of Sydney that was completely new to me.

It even had gargoyles on the roof. I gazed up in awe at the turrets and steeples towering over us. It had taken a full two minutes for the car to make its way up the long driveway. The grounds were massive, and patrolled by other members of the pack.

I jumped as the gargoyle I was staring at fluffed its stony wings and stared right back. "That gargoyle moved."

"Even gargoyles get tired of sitting still occasionally," Matt said, as if it were the most reasonable thing in the world.

Right. I added *gargoyles are real* to my mental list of Freaky Magic Shit. That list was getting awfully long.

A butler opened the enormous front door as we mounted the wide steps. An actual butler, as if we'd been transported back in time to Regency England. Admittedly, Regency butlers probably didn't sport a diamond stud in one ear and a neatly shaved head.

He had the snooty expression down pat, though.

"Mr Arquette will see you in the smaller parlour." I was kind of disappointed that he didn't have a posh English accent to go with that disapproving look.

He led us across the vast marble foyer to a door panelled in oak. The door handle was a perfect golden dragon.

Inside was a huge room papered in burgundy wallpaper, its floor covered in thick grey carpet. A fire crackled cheerfully in a fireplace so large that we could all have stood comfortably inside it, though I noticed discreet air-conditioning vents along the bottom of the walls, too.

If this was the smaller parlour, I couldn't wait to see the big one.

"I'll inform Jerome you're here," the butler said, before closing the door behind himself.

Matt dropped onto a comfy-looking couch in front of the fire and shut his eyes.

"Who's Jerome?" I asked.

"Arquette's chief bodyguard," Tony said, when Matt didn't answer. "He's a vampire."

"Why does a dragon need bodyguards? Aren't dragons more powerful than anyone else?"

Tony shrugged. "Prestige. It's all about appearances. Comparing dick sizes with the wizards and vampires. It makes you look shit hot if you've got combat wizards and vampires to do your dirty work—the more powerful the better."

I moved to one of the floor-to-ceiling windows and held aside the heavy velvet drapes. "Nice place he's got here. He must be pretty near the top of the heap."

"The absolute pinnacle," Matt said lazily, without opening his eyes. "No one has more money and influence than a dragon, and no dragon is more powerful than our esteemed boss."

"Why does he want to see us?" Tony had been fidgeting all the way here in the car, and now he started pacing back and forth in front of the fireplace. "Are we in trouble?"

"No, you're not in trouble, Mr Moretti," a new voice said. So much for werewolf hearing. A tall guy in an exquisitely cut suit had come in, and none of us had heard him enter. "You seem to have a fascination with velvet drapes, Miss Weaver. Fortunately, in this case, I suppose."

I let the curtain fall back into place and took a hasty step away from the window. I'd never met Gabriel Arquette before, but this had to be him. He was so powerfully muscled that he made Matt look weedy, and there was something so magnetic in his dark eyes that I couldn't look away. An aura of power clung to him but he wore it with ease, as if it were the most natural thing in the world for lesser mortals to bow down before him. A scent like woodsmoke on crisp winter nights curled around him. If he'd just woken up, it sure didn't show.

Matt leapt up from the couch and hurried over to join me. "Mr Arquette! Meet our new werewolf, Nat Weaver. She's the heroine of the hour."

"Indeed." That dark gaze studied me thoughtfully, and I quailed a little. It felt as though he could read all of my innermost secrets.

I lifted my chin. Stuff that. I didn't have any secrets. I might not be an immensely powerful dragon, but I had nothing to hide. I refused to be cowed by some rich guy in a fancy suit, even if he looked like my every fantasy come to life.

"Matt tells me you hunted down our intruder," Arquette said, a hint of laughter in his eyes, "and using quite a novel approach, too."

What was so funny? "I used whatever was at hand."

"Most werewolves don't bother with hands," he said. "Problems are usually met with teeth and claws. You're quite an interesting addition to the pack."

"That's me. Always interesting."

He gestured to the chairs in front of the fire. "Please, have a seat."

Matt put his hand on my back and guided me towards the couch where he'd been sitting. I shrugged him off and chose an armchair instead, while he and Tony perched uncomfortably on the edge of the couch. Arquette sat opposite me and crossed one designer-clad leg over the other. His shoe was so shiny I could see my face in it. I tucked my own feet under me, conscious that my boots were wet and quite possibly tracking mud over the dragon's plush carpet.

Arquette smiled at me. "Tell me what happened."

Matt had already given him a full report while we were on our way over here in the car.

"Like Matt said, a goblin broke in through the roof. Tony called for backup while I went after him and caught him." I shrugged, uncomfortable under the weight of his gaze. What did he want me to say? He already had all the details.

"So you took the lead, even though you're the newest wolf in the pack? Why was that?"

Damn. Had Samantha complained about me *giving orders*? I was glad she'd been left to hold the fort with Leon back at the warehouse. I hoped she got *drenched*.

"I guess because I was the only one on two legs at that point."

"And she noticed the birds on the roof," Tony added helpfully.

"Ah, the goblin's familiars. What happened to those?"

Tony flushed and looked down at the carpet. *I ate them* probably wasn't an acceptable response. But really, it had been quite efficient. We'd removed the threat and fed Tony's ever-hungry belly at the same time. Two birds with one wolf.

"We killed them," I said quickly, resisting the urge to mention Tony's love affair with protein, earning myself a grateful look from the walking stomach. "So the goblin wouldn't know we were onto him."

"I'm curious to know how you managed to catch two birds that were on the roof."

"I lured them down with bread crumbs."

"That was quick thinking," Arquette said. "That was your idea, too?"

"Yes." This felt like being in the principal's office. Any minute now I was getting a detention, though unlike my many visits to the principal's office, this time I wasn't quite sure why I was in trouble.

Although I had to admit, my high school principal had been

nowhere *near* this hot. I caught myself staring again at that handsome face and forced myself to look away.

"She's a real asset to the pack," Matt said with a proud smile.

Arquette glanced at Matt. "An asset that could be better utilised than guarding my treasure store." He flashed a quick smile at me. "Not that I'm not grateful you were there, of course. But how would you feel about a change of employment?"

Get out of boring warehouse duty? *Sign me up, baby.* I'd have scrubbed toilets if that was what it took. But I played it cool. "What kind of employment were you thinking of? I thought that the whole pack worked security for you."

"So they do. But there are different levels of security. I'm impressed by your quick thinking and ability to respond under pressure. How would you feel about becoming one of my personal bodyguards?"

I managed to stop my mouth falling open in surprise, but only just. That was *way* better than scrubbing toilets. Tony had had a lot to say about the lowly position of werewolves in Arquette's employment—how we were only considered good enough to patrol the warehouses and the grounds of this enormous estate. Matt was the only wolf the dragon dealt with. There were certainly no werewolf bodyguards.

"I thought you didn't use werewolves indoors?"

He glanced down at my boots, still tucked under the chair. "I daresay we can train you to wipe your feet."

Like a good dog. My temper flared, and I opened my mouth to tell him where to stick his job.

Then abruptly shut it again when common sense seized the reins. *No more warehouse duty.* This guy was offering me a ticket to freedom. I could put up with a little rudeness.

"Tonight has shown me the wisdom of diversifying," he said. "We've had a spate of attempted break-ins lately, so I'm reviewing my security arrangements."

"You dragons love your treasure, huh?" I was still annoyed, so changing the subject seemed safest.

"You could say that. But some things are too dangerous to let fall into the wrong hands."

"Yeah? Like what?" I'd seen a lot of expensive stuff in that warehouse, but nothing that I'd call *dangerous*. "Have you got Excalibur tucked away somewhere?"

Tony drew in a shocked breath.

What? I was just asking. Best to know upfront what my new job entailed. Besides, if Arquette wanted me to be his bodyguard, he might as well find out what he was letting himself in for. This dog wouldn't be rolling over for belly rubs.

"Jerome." He didn't raise his voice, but the door opened and a vampire walked in. For a moment I thought I'd offended him and was about to be kicked out, but the vampire smiled at me. "Jerome will show you around and explain your new duties. Assuming you want the job. Let's say a probationary period of six weeks so we can see if we suit. You'll be given a room here and expected to be on call six days out of seven."

A room *here*? This got better and better. Anything that got me out of the pack house, where seven different people had their noses in my business at all times, was a massive plus. For a bit of privacy, I could overlook the fact that my hot new boss was kind of a jerk.

"She's too new," Matt said. "She needs to live with her pack."

"She could hardly do the job if she lived somewhere else," Arquette said, dismissing Matt's concern with a wave of his hand. "Any questions?"

"Yeah." I was sick of meat, meat, meat. "Do you have any kale in this place?"

Surprise flickered in those dark eyes, and then he smiled. "Most people ask for a pay rise."

I wasn't most people, as he would soon learn. "Yeah, I'll take one of those, too."

∼

"So you're the new wolf," Jerome said as he led me up the immense staircase to the second floor. He had warm brown eyes and a friendly smile with no sign of fangs. I was immediately curious but figured it might be rude to ask about it before I'd even introduced myself.

I stuck my hand out. "Nat Weaver."

His hand was cool, but not unpleasantly so. "Jerome Bridges. I'm head of security here. Welcome to the team."

If he was upset at having a new recruit thrust on him without warning, he didn't show it. Maybe he was used to it. Gabriel Arquette didn't seem like the type to take other people's wishes into consideration.

"So, I'm a bodyguard now? Do I get a gun?"

"Can you shoot?"

"Nope."

"Then no, not right away." He led the way down a wide hallway with rooms opening off each side. "We'll give you weapons training, and training in unarmed fighting techniques, but really, giving a gun to a werewolf is like giving a gun to a T-Rex. Why would you, when their natural weapons are so much better?"

I glared at his back. "So I'm expected to go wolf and bite people for him?"

He stopped in front of a door made of some honey-coloured timber and studied me. His dark eyes stood out against his vampire-pale skin, and I was surprised to see a hint of sympathy in them. "Does that bother you?"

"I mean, I get it. He didn't hire me for my looks. But I'm more than just a bunch of fur with teeth."

Now there was no mistaking the sympathy. "I guess it's rough adjusting, huh? But from what I heard, Gabriel hired you for your brains. He likes problem-solvers." He opened the door with a flourish. "Ta-da. Your new home."

I stepped into a bedroom that was almost as big as the whole apartment I'd had before becoming a wolf. The queen-sized bed actually looked a bit lost in the middle of all that floor space. There was a desk and chair against one wall, a lounging area with a TV, and French doors that opened onto a balcony. The walls were painted a soft, restful green, and a white quilt embroidered with a delicate tracery of green branches covered the bed.

"Bathroom's through here," he said, crossing the carpet on silent feet. I caught a glimpse of a claw-footed bath and white-tiled walls before he threw open another door. "And this is your closet."

I couldn't help the grin that spread across my face as I took it in. "I've always wanted a walk-in closet."

"Hayman House," he said with an answering smile. "The place where dreams come true."

"Jerome," a voice called from the hallway. "You up here?"

"In here."

A pretty Chinese girl, her dark hair in an elegant bun, poked her head in the door and regarded me with interest.

"Stella," Jerome said, "meet Nat, our new recruit. Stella's our resident wizard," he said to me. "She's one of the best. Stella by name and stellar by nature."

Stella rolled her eyes. "Jerome has an unfulfilled dream to be a father, so he practises his dad jokes on us." I glanced at the vampire uncertainly, but he didn't seem offended. "Aditi's looking for you. Something about the ball and a string quartet."

"Damn." Jerome ran a hand through his hair. "I'll be glad when this stupid ball is over. I was going to give Nat the grand tour—take over for me?"

"Sure." Stella tucked her arm through mine and pulled me from the room. "What have you seen so far?"

"Not much. We came straight up here from the smaller parlour."

"Awesome. One grand tour coming up."

We spent the next hour wandering the house and grounds. The larger parlour—which was actually known as the morning room—fulfilled all my expectations. There were also three other lounge rooms, a games room, offices, two dining rooms of different sizes, a massive industrial kitchen, a fully equipped gym, so many bedrooms and bathrooms that I lost count ... and the list went on. Stella was an entertaining guide, though her chattiness was so disarming that she managed to find out as much about me as I learned about my new job.

"This is the monitor room ... so how'd you become a

werewolf?"

"Here's the kitchen … I heard Matt was a bit of a ladies' man before he hooked up with Tiffany …"

"This is the gym where you'll be doing your training … do you play any sports?"

"And this is Gabriel's study."

It looked like the library from a fantasy movie—book cases from floor to ceiling, with one of those attached ladders on wheels that let you climb up to the higher shelves. A row of tall, narrow windows marched down one side of the room. Between the windows were cabinets full of tiny treasures, or bronze busts on stands. There was even a suit of armour in one of the alcoves, fancier than the ones I'd seen at the warehouse. A massive chandelier dripping with crystals that might have been diamonds—and probably were, given the wealth on display throughout the house—hung from a golden ceiling rose.

A surprisingly modern desk in chrome and glass was covered with neat piles of papers and a closed laptop, suggesting that our boss actually used it for work and not just display.

"Oh, wow." My feet took me into the room without conscious thought on my part, drawn by all those books. "This is like a dream."

Stella looked around critically. "Well, it's a little cluttered for my taste, but that's dragons for you. They're the ultimate hoarders."

I drifted over to have a closer look at the suit of armour. It looked like it was made of solid gold, which wouldn't have been that practical. Maybe it was only for ceremonial purposes. I wondered if Arquette had ever worn it.

"He does have a lot of stuff in here. I thought he kept all his treasure in his storage facilities?"

"He likes to have the more valuable pieces close at hand. And some of these books are worth thousands of dollars. First editions, rare books. Many of them are signed by authors who have been dead for a century or two."

"Really?" I stared at the books with new appreciation.

A small glass cabinet near the suit of armour housed pieces of jewellery displayed on velvet cushions. Most of them were too ostentatious for my taste.

"Are those diamonds?" I asked, pointing to an ornate golden bowl of clear gems. "They must be worth a fortune."

They were each the size of my thumbnail, which was pretty big for diamonds. They were uncut, and reminded me of those glass blobs you put in vases to help your flower arrangements stand up.

Stella came to stand next to me. "Those are priceless. They're worth far more than diamonds. They're dragon tears."

I gave her the side-eye. Was she pulling my leg? "Dragon tears? Are they some new kind of gem?"

"No, they're literally dragon tears. When a dragon cries, their tears crystallise and form these." She sighed longingly. "With one of these, I could become the most powerful wizard in the country."

"Really? What do they do?"

"Just about anything your heart desires. They're pure magic. Each one contains part of the dragon's power. That's why Gabriel keeps these close—if someone took them, he'd lose some of his magical strength."

"So he just leaves them sitting in a cabinet? It's not even locked!" There was no keyhole in the glass door—it looked as though you could just pull it open.

"This estate is very well protected," she said. "We've got gargoyles on the roof twenty-four seven, werewolves roaming the grounds, plus cameras everywhere. And you might have noticed the height of the walls on the way in."

I couldn't help thinking of the goblin, breaking into the warehouse through the roof. High fences and werewolves hadn't kept him out.

"Still seems like a security nightmare."

She laughed. "No, that would be the ball. Poor Jerome is tearing his hair out. Come this way and I'll show you the ballroom."

She led me out of the study and back to the main corridor. At the end she threw open double doors, revealing a vast ballroom whose polished wooden floor stretched on forever.

My footsteps echoed as I crossed to a row of French doors. Outside, a wide stone terrace overlooked a rose garden with a central fountain.

"This is amazing," I said. "I feel like I'm inside a Jane Austen novel. Any moment Mr Darcy is going to ride up on his horse."

Actually, with his dark good looks and air of wealth, Gabriel Arquette would have made a fine Mr Darcy. Assuming Mr Darcy breathed fire.

"Wait until it's all decked out for the ball. There'll be thousands of flowers and the whole place will smell divine."

"So what is this ball you keep talking about?"

"Gabriel's hosting it next week. There'll be hundreds of people here. A banquet, a string quartet, rivers of champagne—it's madness. He does it every year."

"Who's coming?"

"Everyone who's anyone in the magical community, and not just the locals. People are flying in from all over the world. Poor Jerome takes the week off after it to recover. Half of them hate the other half, and just about all of them have an agenda. Now *that's* a security nightmare."

"It seems like asking for trouble to have the house full of strangers if he's already having break-ins at the warehouses." I thought of all the treasures in the library. Rare books. Golden armour. Dragon tears.

She laughed. "Oh, they're not strangers, sadly. Some of them are his worst enemies."

"Why would he invite his worst enemies?"

"You know what they say. Keep your friends close and your enemies closer." She laughed at the expression on my face. "Magical politics. You thought the human kind was bad. Xavier Mendes would rather dance on Gabriel's grave than in his ballroom, but he turns up every year just the same."

Even I had heard of Xavier Mendes. He was the leader of the Wizard Council of Australia, and not a man who was used to hearing the word *no*.

Kind of like Gabriel Arquette, actually.

The following Wednesday was my rostered day off. I'd spent the previous five days learning the ropes of my new position, getting lost a lot inside Hayman House, and collecting an impressive array of bruises during my training sessions. Werewolf healing got rid of them almost as quickly as I earned them, but they still hurt like hell.

I would have liked to spend my day off getting better acquainted with Arquette's spectacular library, but I was summoned to the pack house by Matt.

"It will be good for you to reconnect with the pack," he said. "We'll put on a barbecue for lunch."

I groaned inwardly at the thought of the meat mains with sides of meat and meat toppings that was the pack's idea of a balanced meal. But Matt made it clear that declining the invitation wasn't an option, so just before midday I pulled up outside the sprawling suburban house that had so recently been my home.

Matt and his partner Tiffany lived here full time, with a rotating cast of housemates. New pack members usually stayed here until they adjusted to life as a wolf and moved out to their own places. At the moment there was only one other new wolf, an elfin-looking blonde named Charity. Leon was also living here temporarily while he was building a new house, which had been a big part of why I'd been so thrilled to leave. I did *not* like Leon. I would forgive him for turning me approximately one second after hell froze over.

Most of the pack would be at work, but there were a couple of other cars out front, including Tony's, which cheered me up. Tony was the closest thing I had to a friend in the pack. He'd spent a lot of time sitting with me while I lay in bed recovering from the attack that turned me, reading to me from the newspaper or just chatting about nothing in particular. He had an encyclopaedic knowledge of obscure eighties bands and could finish a cryptic crossword in under ten minutes.

As far as I was concerned, that was more impressive than magic.

Charity met me at the door. She'd been a wolf for about six

months, but she was still expected to live here. It made me grateful for my new job all over again. Without it I'd be stuck here like her.

"It's so good to see you!" She pulled me into a hug, then whispered in my ear, "It's not as fun here without you."

"Is that jerk Leon bothering you?"

"No, nothing like that." She switched to mind speech. *Matt and Tiffany have been fighting. I spend a lot of time in my room.*

What a nightmare. Guess she hadn't broadcast *that* to the whole pack.

"Is that our guest of honour?" Tiffany called from the kitchen. "Bring her in."

I gave Charity a sympathetic squeeze before I released her and replied in the same focused mind speech so that no one else would hear. *That's rough. We'll have to get together on my next day off.*

"Here she is," Tiffany said as I walked in. She was making a salad, the knife flying through cucumbers and tomatoes in her large, capable hands. Tiffany was built on Amazonian lines, and she looked even taller and more imposing with her dark hair piled on top of her head as it was now. "The first wolf to get the run of Hayman House. How's the new job?"

"Busy," I said. The bifold doors at the rear of the house were folded back against the wall, opening the kitchen area to the covered patio outside. Matt and Leon were out there, barbecuing steaks. Even I had to admit they smelled good. My inner wolf started salivating. "We have salad today? I'm impressed."

"Gina insisted."

Gina turned from the stove and waved hello. She was Tony's mum and fully human, but she often cooked for the pack. This barbecue was really looking up if Gina's pasta was on the menu, too.

"What are they feeding you at that big house?" she asked, running a disapproving eye over me. "You look skinny."

"I'm eating plenty," I said. "More than ever, actually. But they've got me running every day and training for hours. I've never worked so hard before."

"And here we were imagining you lazing around in the lap of

luxury," Tony said as he came in from outside with an armful of bottles. "Want a beer?"

"Sure." I took a long swig from the bottle he offered and grinned at him. "There's plenty of luxury. You should see my walk-in wardrobe. It's going to take years of shopping to fill it."

"If you want a shopping buddy, I'm up for it," Charity said. "Tell us more about this luxury. It sounds wonderful."

I filled them in on my new role and described some of the people I'd met that week. They all knew Stella and Jerome, of course, since one of them was always with Arquette when he left the mansion, but Aditi and the rest of the staff were new to them and they enjoyed my stories.

"But seriously, how long have you guys been working for Arquette?" I asked as we sat down to lunch. "You really haven't been inside Hayman House before?"

"I have," Matt said. "But only as far as that room where we met Arquette last week."

"It's the rules," Leon growled. "No wolves inside. Like he thinks we're going to get muddy paw prints on his precious carpet. We're good enough to defend his front yard, but that's it."

The hostility in his gaze suggested he didn't see why those rules should have been relaxed for me.

"Have you seen all his treasure?" Tiffany asked. "I've heard stories, but I can't imagine what it must be like in there."

"Actually most of it's at the storage unit. But you should see his study. The books!" I put a hand to my heart and sighed dramatically.

"I heard he had some dragon tears," Matt said.

Tiffany frowned at him. "Don't all dragons?"

"Have you seen them?" Tony asked. "What do they look like?"

I shrugged. "Not that special, actually. They're just like little smooth chunks of glass. They don't have facets like gems. They could be those little marbles you use for flower arranging."

The men all looked at me blankly while the women nodded.

"Like little ice cubes," Tiffany said.

"How'd *you* get to see them?" Leon asked. It was clear from his tone that he didn't believe me. "Doesn't he have them in a safe?"

"No. They're on a shelf in his study."

"Just lying around?" he scoffed. "What kind of security is that?"

I glanced at Matt. "That does bother me a little, but no one else seems worried. I guess they think a thief wouldn't be able to get away with them."

"Yeah, because *we're* outside keeping him safe," Leon said, a sour look on his face. *Sour* was pretty much Leon's default position.

"It would be tough to get past us," Matt said, "but not impossible."

"There's the gargoyles, too," Tony pointed out.

"True." I'd learned a bit about gargoyles in the last few days. They were excellent guards, because they needed very little rest. When they finally slept, they went into a kind of hibernation state where they turned into actual stone, but with twelve gargoyles on the payroll at Hayman House, there were never more than one or two in hibernation at a time. "Poor Jerome is stressing out of his tree about having all these guests in the house for the ball, but I'm sure it will be fine."

"If any goblins land on *that* roof, the gargoyles will eat them," Tony said.

"No one's going to try that," Charity said. "Not when it's so much easier to walk in the front door as a guest."

I felt a twinge of anxiety. "So you think Jerome's right to be worried? But Arquette throws this ball every year, and there hasn't been a problem before."

"The attacks on the warehouses keep coming," Leon said, glancing at Matt. "It's like someone's looking for something."

Matt pushed his empty plate away and sat back in his chair, reaching for his beer with a sigh. "We think the same person is behind them. Any time we catch a thief, like this goblin of yours, they always turn out to be hired, and they don't know who hired them."

"And you think they'll try the house next?"

He looked stressed, which was unusual for him. Normally, he was the life of the party. This was obviously worrying him more than I'd realised. "Stands to reason, doesn't it? If they can't find what they're looking for at the warehouses, it's got to be at Hayman House. And I'd bet my left testicle it's those tears they're after."

Gina came out with a large tray of lasagne. I'd thought I was full, but it smelled so divine I realised I could make room. That was another one for the positive list: werewolf metabolism.

"Don't fuss about things you can't control." She served a generous slice onto my plate. "Jerome is paid to worry about these things. You're not."

Tony nodded. "The cream of the magic world aren't suddenly going to turn into house thieves."

I took my first bite, then closed my eyes in bliss. This was, without a doubt, the best lasagne I'd ever tasted. Then my eyes popped open at a sudden thought.

"They won't be the only strangers in the house, though. The place will be teeming with waiters and extra kitchen staff."

"All vetted by Jerome," Tony said reassuringly. "There won't be a burglar among them."

"Someone could pose as a waiter," I said, thinking out loud, "if they could sneak past the gargoyles somehow."

"And then what?" Matt asked. "The waiters won't be given the run of the house."

"But they'll have access to more of the ground floor than the guests. And it would only take a moment to duck into the study." Tiffany's earlier comment about ice cubes came back to me. The waiters would be carrying trays full of drinks. "They could swipe the tears and drop them into a drink, then whisk back to the kitchen with their tray and smuggle them out. No one would be any the wiser."

"Genius plan," Tony said, grinning. "Apart from the giant problem of sneaking past the gargoyles."

"*And* the wolves," Gina said, looking at him proudly. "Nobody gets past the pack."

Well, except for that goblin at the warehouse. But we *had* caught him. That made me feel better—and, as Gina said, it was Jerome's problem, not mine. I was just the new girl.

The new girl with a plate full of delicious lasagne.

"This is divine," I mumbled around a mouthful.

"Good." Gina added another generous helping to my plate. "Eat up."

"Your wolf needs feeding," Leon added. He took way too much interest in the wolf side of me, acting like it belonged to him just because he was the one who'd turned me—even though he didn't seem to like human me any more than I liked him.

I rolled my eyes. These people were always talking about *their wolves* as if they were totally separate. Like a furry best friend. Leon was particularly bad. To hear him talk, you'd think he had no control over what his alter ego did at all.

I wasn't buying it. I'd only experienced wolf form a couple of times so far, but I'd known exactly who I was and what I was doing. Blaming the wolf side for the bad decisions of the man was just passing the buck. Very convenient to have no accountability.

"Who wants the last piece?" Gina asked, holding up a big chunk of lasagne balanced on the server.

"Me," Leon said.

"Too late!" Tony grabbed his mother's wrist and tipped the lasagne onto his own plate. It landed upside down and more like a pile than a slice, but when it tasted that good presentation didn't matter. Tony smirked triumphantly across the table at the older man as he dug his fork into it.

Leon growled at him. Like, literally growled. Next minute, a huge grey wolf was standing on the table, gulping down Tony's lasagne.

Gina screamed, and Charity did, too. The suddenness of the change shocked us all.

"What the hell?" Tony was normally a pretty laidback guy, but his face darkened with rage. He leapt up and tried to shove the wolf away. A glass fell and shattered on the paving stones. Leon snarled at him.

"Get off my table!" Tiffany yelled as another glass tumbled down and smashed. Wine splashed across the tablecloth and dripped onto the ground.

Leon ignored her, and Tony lost it. His body shimmered into the change and a lighter grey wolf with a thick white ruff leapt at the first one.

It was too much for the table. It crashed to the ground in a confusion of broken crockery and shattered glasses. Both wolves sprang away, out onto the lawn, where they snarled and snapped at each other.

Leon was bigger than Tony, though Tony was faster. Tony darted in and took a bite out of one of Leon's front legs. Leon snarled and went for his throat, but Tony danced out of reach.

Matt was shouting for them to stop, but they both ignored him. Tony tried another lightning strike, but this time Leon caught him. Suddenly Tony was on the ground, trapped under the larger wolf's body. Leon's jaws closed on his throat and I smelled blood.

It smelled good, but I could taste Tony's fear, and suddenly I shared it. Leon meant to kill him.

My body reacted on instinct. A tingle swept through me, bringing the change shuddering in its wake. I dropped to all fours and launched myself onto Leon's back, my teeth seeking *his* throat. I found flesh and Leon yelped.

"I said *stop!*" Matt roared, and this time the bite of pack magic was in his voice.

I let go, unable to resist that power. I felt it in my bones, and they obeyed the leader's command instinctively, without any input from me at all. He strode out onto the lawn, his face thunderous, and all three of us cowered under the weight of his fury.

This was a side of Matt I'd never seen. He was always so friendly and charming, I'd sometimes wondered why he was the leader instead of one of the stronger guys. Like Leon, for instance, who looked as though he could lift a small truck with one hand tied behind his back. Now I saw the steel beneath that charming exterior.

"Change." He bit off the word, anger radiating from him.

We all shimmered back into human form. I had the taste of blood in my mouth, which hadn't bothered me in wolf form, but was frankly revolting to my human self—especially considering where it had come from. Blood trickled down the back of Leon's neck, but it was only a flesh wound. I wiped my mouth, hoping I wasn't smearing his blood across half my face.

Tony was in worse shape. Blood ran down both sides of his neck where Leon's teeth had punctured him. I shuddered and looked away. He was lucky he was still standing. That thick ruff of his had probably saved him, stopping Leon from getting a better grip. Tiffany tossed him a serviette, which he balled up and pressed to the worst of the wounds. It was soon soaked through.

Matt stalked over to stand in front of Leon. "What did you think you were doing?"

Leon stared down at his feet. "He disrespected me."

"So you attacked him over a piece of *lasagne*? That's not how we roll in this pack."

I couldn't help grinning. Leon looked like an overgrown kid getting told off by his dad. It was nice to see him getting taken down a peg or two.

"And *you*." Matt rounded on me. "You're so new you barely know which way is up, but you thought it would be a good idea to join in?"

I shrugged. "I thought Leon was going to kill him. I wasn't going to stand by and let that happen. Nobody else was doing anything."

"Because we know better," Tiffany said, giving me a cool glance. "Matt had it under control. As leader, it's his job to police the pack. Not yours."

"I hope you can control yourself better than this at your fancy new job." There was a world of disapproval in Matt's voice. Disappointment, too, which was worse. "Otherwise you'll be back guarding warehouses again before you've had a chance to finish unpacking."

On Saturday night, I stared at myself in the full-length mirror in my bathroom and smoothed the silky fabric draping my thighs. The guests would be arriving soon, and I was due in Arquette's study in five minutes for a last-minute briefing.

I'd never worn a dress like this before. It was midnight blue, a fitted sheath with a demure neckline but a dramatic slit up the side. Aditi had delivered it to my room this morning.

"What's this?" I'd asked as she bustled in with a long garment bag folded over her arm.

Aditi bustled everywhere. She was one of those people who seemed to have an inexhaustible supply of energy. Always on the move, always busy. She was Arquette's right-hand woman. The butler, Harten, was responsible for the day-to-day running of the household, but Aditi ran everything else in Arquette's life. She was way more than a personal assistant—she was practically vice-president of his little dragon empire, despite being human.

All that, and she still found time to achieve a level of personal grooming that was frankly scary. Her long nails were always perfect, her clothes beautifully styled, and her makeup impeccable. And I was straight-up jealous of her dark hair, which hung in a thick plait down to her butt. Indian women had the best hair.

She laid the bag on my bed. I'd just showered after my morning training session and I was still towelling my hair dry, so it was all over the place, hanging in wet tangles down my back and making my shirt damp. Not a single hair on Aditi's head was out of place, of course. None of them would dare.

"A dress for tonight."

"What do you mean? Aren't I wearing this?" I gestured at my work clothes of black trousers and plain white shirt.

"To a ball?" Aditi tossed her head in disdain. The diamond stud in her nose winked in the light. "Please."

"But I'm not a guest. I'm on duty."

"There's no law that says you can't look good while you're working." She headed for the door at her usual brisk pace, ready to move on to the next item on her agenda. "The hairdresser will be here at five."

"Hairdresser?" I squeaked, but she was already gone.

Now, as I stared at my reflection, I had to admit the hairdresser had been a good idea. I would probably only have pulled my auburn hair back into a quick bun to keep it out of my way, but she had piled it up in beautiful curls and loops, creating a style that looked effortlessly chic. I'd taken extra care with my makeup, too, and the dark blue shine of the dress brought out the blue of my eyes.

All in all, I was pretty hot stuff.

The dress's neckline showed my collarbones but nothing else. The slit up the side, on the other hand, just about exposed what I'd had for breakfast. I was all business on the top and party on the bottom. At least it would be easy to run in, if it came to that.

Though I guessed if running were required, I'd probably have to turn wolf. Hopefully, my beautiful hairstyle would survive the experience. Wouldn't want to waste all the hairdresser's hard work.

I hurried downstairs and knocked on the door of Arquette's study.

"Come in," he called.

I was surprised to find he was alone, working on something at his desk.

"Am I disturbing you, Mr Arquette?" It was the first time I'd seen him since he hired me. He'd been travelling with Stella as his security while I'd been training here at Hayman House.

"Not at all." He rose from the chair and came towards me. "And please call me Gabriel."

I peered around the enormous room, but Jerome and Stella were nowhere in sight. "I thought this was a meeting for the whole team?"

"Jerome and Stella have been to plenty of these balls before. I wanted a quick word with you." He stopped in front of me and I wondered why Jerome couldn't have briefed me. Surely that was his job? "Do you like the dress?"

"It's lovely. Thank you."

"Good." He ran his gaze up and down me in a quick appraisal. "I thought that colour would suit you. It brings out the fire in your hair."

"You—you picked it yourself?" I had assumed that was Aditi's doing. I blinked at him. When had he been paying so much attention that he knew what would suit me?

"Yes. It fits well?"

So well, in fact, that I wondered why that hadn't occurred to me before. It fit as though it had been tailored specifically for me, better than anything I'd ever bought off the rack. "Perfectly. How did you know what size to get?"

He smiled, and there was a hint of laughter in his eyes. "You could say I have some experience."

In what? Women's clothing? Dressing women? *Undressing* women? My cheeks warmed as my mind ran with the idea of getting naked with Gabriel Arquette. I mean, I had a pulse, didn't I? The guy was Hot with a capital H.

He tapped one finger against his full lips. *Don't think about his lips.* Good God, what was wrong with me?

It was the dress, I decided. It made me feel different. Special. Like there could conceivably be some reason for an ordinary girl like me to be alone with a gorgeous billionaire.

And he'd chosen it himself. Checked out my shape with what was clearly a *very* practised eye. The room was enormous and Arquette—*Gabriel*, dammit—was a perfectly respectable distance away, yet the moment felt oddly intimate.

"It needs something." It took me a minute to realise he was still talking about the dress. "Your neck is elegant, but too bare." He crossed to one of the glass cabinets between the long windows and pulled out something that sparkled in the light from the massive chandelier overhead. "Come here."

It was a necklace of enormous blue sapphires, with small, pale pink gems between them. I couldn't quite believe he meant for me to wear it, until he gestured for me to turn my back to him.

He reached around me from behind, settling the cool weight of the jewels around my throat. His breath tickled the back of my neck as he fastened the clasp. A thrill shivered through me as his fingers brushed my skin.

I swallowed, watching our reflection in the glass of the cabinet.

He was standing very close, though his attention was focused on his task. "This is … this is beautiful. What are the pink stones?"

"Argyle diamonds." His hands slid to my shoulders as his eyes met mine in the glass. "They're very rare."

My skin tingled, hyper-aware of his touch. *Pull yourself together, woman. He's rich and gorgeous and he may have just fastened a fortune around your neck, but he's still your boss.* Not to mention a dragon. And I was still just a lowly werewolf. This was not the time for Cinderella fantasies. He was just trying to make sure I didn't disgrace him tonight.

"Diamonds? Are you sure you want me to wear this? How much is it worth?"

He shrugged. "A couple of million."

"A couple of *million*?" My hand crept to the glittering stones around my neck. "What if I lose it?"

"You won't." He dropped his hands and stepped away. "Relax. Beautiful things are meant to be enjoyed."

His eyes lingered on my face. Hurriedly, I looked away and my glance fell on the bowl of dragon tears in the same cabinet he'd taken the necklace from. Just sitting there. So easy to access.

I cleared my throat. "You said you wanted a word?"

"Yes." He shoved his hands into his pockets, perfectly at ease. "I want you to stay close tonight. I'll introduce you to a few people. You need to know who's who in our world."

No wonder he wanted me to look good. "Aditi gave me a dossier with everyone's names and photos and a little bit about each one. I've been memorising them."

"Good. But you'll learn things from meeting them in person that you can't get from a quick summary. Xavier Mendes, for instance, looks pretty good on paper. In real life, he's something else."

"You don't like him?"

He laughed. "Does anyone? But he's head of the wizard council, so we all have to put up with him. A small-minded, vindictive little man. He has a particular vendetta against me. I've never been able to work out why."

"As your bodyguard, should I be worried?"

"You may be forced to laugh politely at his jokes, but that's about the extent of the danger. He wouldn't dare move against me. I'm more powerful than him and he knows it."

There was a knock on the door, and Aditi poked her head in. "You wanted to check the lighting before the guests arrived."

He smiled at her. "And I'm running late, aren't I? She runs my life like a drill sergeant," he said to me. "I'll see you in the ballroom."

I was left alone in the study. I stole another peek at the necklace in the glass of the cabinet. So sparkly! And so ridiculously expensive. How many years would it take me to earn two million dollars? Even at the generous salary Gabriel was paying me, it was more than I cared to think about.

The bowl of dragon tears drew my eye again. Was it because he was so obscenely rich that he left them lying there so casually? If he could lend a two million dollar necklace to one of his staff, maybe he really didn't care that priceless items were so vulnerable.

But Stella had said they contained part of his power. Surely losing them would be a threat to him? I chewed my lip in indecision. If he wasn't worried, I shouldn't be, either. But I was his bodyguard —shouldn't I be protecting him from *all* threats, not just the physical?

A moment later, I left the room, wiping my wet hand on my dress.

~

Xavier Mendes was every bit as obnoxious as Gabriel had promised. He was an older man of average height, losing his hair and obviously not happy about it. He'd grown the remaining strands long and combed them over his balding pate. His velvet robes were bright orange and seemed an odd choice for a ball. He looked like a lost parrot compared to most of the other men in the room, who were wearing black dinner suits.

And compared to Gabriel's quiet elegance, he just seemed

desperate for attention.

"A new conquest?" he asked, catching sight of me a discreet step behind Gabriel. We were positioned at the entrance to the ballroom so that Gabriel could greet his guests as they arrived. Mendes gave me a smile that was probably meant to look knowing and flirtatious, but came off as supremely creepy.

"My new bodyguard, Nat Weaver," Gabriel said. "Nat, this is Xavier Mendes, Prime Wizard."

Mendes dropped the smile and assessed me coolly. "You're not a wizard, or I'd know you, but you don't look like a vampire."

"I'm a wolf," I said, annoyed. It was none of his business, but I assumed Gabriel wouldn't want me to start the evening by being rude to his guests.

"Ah." He turned his attention back to Gabriel. Clearly a mere wolf wasn't worth the notice of the head of the wizard council. "Standards slipping a bit, eh?"

"Not at all," Gabriel said coolly. "Nat is a valued member of the team."

Mendes sneezed. "You've got the place full of damn flowers again, I see. Plays hell with my allergies."

The ballroom boasted more flowers than a florist shop. Huge arrangements were displayed around the room. Vines dripping roses twined above the French doors leading out onto the balcony, and along the backs of the chairs that lined the walls. Though Stella had promised a room full of flowers, I hadn't been prepared for the scale of the operation. The scent was divine, if a little overpowering to werewolf senses.

Hours later, my head was whirling. Gabriel had introduced me to a who's who of the magical world. I'd met the head of the oldest vampire family in the country, a woman dripping diamonds who'd admired the necklace I wore with the appreciation of a connoisseur. I'd met a whole parade of wizards, though thankfully none were as obnoxious as Mendes, and even a few dragons. Generally, dragons were even more territorial than wolves, but Gabriel welcomed them all like old friends and they seemed to have no issue with enjoying his hospitality.

He was dancing with one of them, a brunette in a shimmering gold dress, when Jerome found me standing by the open doors, casting longing glances out at the cool night.

"So what do you think of the movers and shakers of the magic world?" he asked. His eyes never stopped moving, roving over the glittering crowd, alert for threats.

"I'd be just as happy if they went and did their moving and shaking somewhere else," I said. Some of the guests had left, but the room was still packed. "Just as well this place is so big, or it would be like a game of sardines in here."

He quirked an eyebrow at me. "A game of what?"

"Sardines. Didn't you play that as a kid?" Suddenly realising that, though he looked like he was in his early thirties, he could actually be hundreds of years old, I hurried on before he could answer. "It's like a reverse hide and seek. One kid hides while everyone else counts. Then you go look for them, but when you find them, you squeeze into their hiding place too, until everyone's hiding and there's only one kid left looking."

"Sounds uncomfortable."

I grinned. "It can be. Depends on the hiding place. I don't recommend Maisie Jackson's mother's wardrobe. Too many hangers sticking into you, and it gets hard to breathe after a while among all the coats."

"I'll bear that in mind if I ever meet Maisie Jackson," he said gravely.

Music swirled around us. The string quartet was playing a waltz, and I watched Gabriel circle the floor while the brunette chatted animatedly.

"You must be glad this thing is almost over." A burst of laughter from the terrace made me glance outside again. The breeze on my face felt good. It was hot in here.

"It's always a relief to have it done and dusted for the year," he said. "There are too many moving parts. No matter how much I plan, I can't account for every possible scenario."

"At least the boss seems to be enjoying himself." We both watched the dancing dragons for a moment.

We weren't the only ones. Half the people in the enormous room were also watching, openly or not. There was something magnetic about the grace of Gabriel and his partner. For a moment I wished I were the one out there, whirling around the room in his arms. He'd gaze down at me with that same laughter in his eyes, his smoky scent enveloping me. The crowd would fade away, and it would just be the two of us, wrapped up in each other.

But I didn't know a waltz from a polka, and would probably stomp all over his feet.

Jerome snorted. "He puts on a good show. But actually he can't stand her."

"Really?" I studied them more carefully, but I couldn't pick it. "Well, he's in good company. Half the people here seem to be pretending. I've seen so many fake smiles tonight I've lost count."

As if my words had conjured him, Xavier Mendes appeared out of the crowd and made his way towards one of the doors to the terrace. He must have been an A-grade wizard, because no one would have elected him Prime on the strength of his personality.

Jerome grinned. "You sound fed up. Why don't you take a ten-minute break? I'll keep an eye on things here."

"Thanks." I threw him a grateful smile. "The flowers get a little overpowering after a while. My nose is starting to twitch."

I slipped out onto the terrace and drew a deep breath of fresh, unscented air. There were thirty or so people out here enjoying it, too, plus a couple of guys smoking. I hoped they'd all go home soon. It was after midnight. This girl was going to turn into a pumpkin soon if she didn't get some sleep.

Mendes emerged from the ballroom at the far end of the terrace and wandered over to lean on the stone balustrade, looking out over the dark gardens below. Surely he was sick of sneering at people by now? *Time to go home, Prime Whinger.*

He turned his head, surveying the other people on the terrace. I stepped to the side so that I was hidden from his view by someone between us. I'd had enough of his attention for one night.

When I peeked out again, he was sidling towards a grand set of stone stairs that swept down from the terrace into the garden. Hmmm. That didn't look suspicious *at all*. What was he up to?

Apparently satisfied that the others on the terrace were too engrossed in each other and their wine glasses, he slipped down the steps. The gardens were lit by soft, coloured lights, but compared to the terrace they were dark. I could see two wolves in the distance by the driveway, watching a parade of cars leaving, but none up close. That didn't mean they weren't there, of course. Someone could be watching Mendes right now.

He wasted no time in stepping off the path that led to a formal rose garden, hurrying across the grass instead, towards a small grove of trees. My curiosity grew. There was no reason he couldn't enjoy the gardens; they weren't off-limits to the guests. In fact, there was a couple seated on a bench in the rose garden right now, getting to know each other's tonsils up close and personal. But the way he'd looked around to see if he was being watched before he left the terrace made me suspicious.

I strolled down the steps and headed towards the trees where he'd disappeared. Maybe he had an assignation with a lover but, given his personality, that seemed unlikely. It was probably just some wizard business he didn't want anyone knowing about—but it didn't hurt to check. He could have done his wizard business anywhere, so why was he sneaking around at Hayman House?

It was surprisingly dark under the shadows of the trees. I moved as quietly as I could in human form, relying on my nose and ears to guide me. I heard the faintest murmur of voices and crept closer, straining to hear what was being said. I couldn't tell who he was talking to, other than that it was a man.

Blundering footsteps warned me that he was headed back my way. That had been quick! I melted into the shadows, keeping perfectly still. He passed so close I could have reached out and touched him, but he didn't notice me. He moved purposefully back towards the lights of the house, hands thrust into the pockets of his hideous orange robes, a self-satisfied smirk on his face.

I watched him stride back up the steps to the terrace, making no attempt to hide his movements this time, then I turned away.

Moving stealthily, I followed his scent back the way he'd come, hoping to find out who he'd met with in the darkness.

His trail ended in a secluded clearing amongst the trees. A stone bench stood beside a small, lily-covered pond. No one was there. I slipped into the clearing, breathing in its scents: water and pine sap, wet rocks and the slightly musty smell of the robe Mendes was wearing. There was wolf scent here, too. I recognised Matt's and Leon's scents, and an older one that might have been Samantha's, but that smelled days old. Matt's and Leon's were recent, which was hardly surprising, since most of the pack was out here patrolling tonight. There was only a skeleton crew covering the warehouses. But I couldn't pick up the faintest hint of any other scent.

While I was prepared to believe almost anything of Leon, it didn't seem likely that the Prime Wizard would have any business with a couple of werewolves. Given his clear contempt for me earlier, I doubted he even knew they existed. Was it possible that I'd misheard, and he'd actually been talking to someone on the phone?

Tony, where are you? I asked, directing the mind speech on a narrow band so that I didn't annoy the whole pack. If I was lucky, he might have seen someone approach the trees from a different direction.

Out back behind the swimming pool, he said. *Why?*

Never mind.

How's the ball? Must be more fun in there than out here. Have you managed to sneak a cheeky champagne or two?

I don't drink on the job, and the ball has way too many people.

Well, someone's *got their tail in a twist. Cheer up, it looks like most of them are leaving. You can put your feet up soon.*

Amen to that. I prowled slowly around the clearing, sniffing everything, looking for clues on the ground. But the darkness defeated even my werewolf eyes. I gave it up after about ten minutes of poking every clump of grass, and headed back towards the house. I was jumping at shadows. Mendes must have come out here for some privacy, to take a phone call where no one could overhear.

Light flooded the terrace from the row of open French doors. Inside, music still played. It was like a scene from a movie—

imposing house, lights blazing, music and laughter. On the roof, the gargoyles hulked against the night sky.

I had to smile, remembering how freaked out I'd been when I saw one of them move the day I arrived. How strange my life had become. If anyone had told me a couple of months ago that I'd be a werewolf, living in a dragon's mansion guarded by gargoyles, I'd have asked for a glass of whatever they were drinking, because it was obviously powerful stuff.

None of the gargoyles were moving now. Didn't they get bored? I wouldn't have been able to stand being up there with them, watching the world go by instead of participating in it. I stared at the closest one, who was perched on a corner just above the end of the terrace. What did he think about while the long hours passed?

His face was impassive, still as the stone he imitated. Wait … were his eyes *shut*? I squinted as I hurried across the lawn, shielding my eyes from the light of the house, trying to make out the details of his face.

I snatched a white pebble from the rose garden as I passed, then took the steps to the terrace two at a time. The gargoyle's eyes *were* shut. When I was close enough I lobbed the pebble at him.

Nothing. His eyes didn't open. No reaction at all. And the noise of the pebble striking him was unmistakeably stone against stone. What was he *thinking*? This was no time to go into hibernation! The property was full of potential threats.

I backed up, looking for another gargoyle. Maybe they could straighten him out. But the next one I found had his eyes closed, too. And the one after that.

The musicians were packing up as I burst into the ballroom. Aditi was up front, wishing everyone goodnight and thanking them for coming. Was the ball *finally* over? But where was Jerome? I scanned the room, my heart pounding, and found him by the massive double doors, watching guests file from the room.

"Where's Mendes?" I asked in an urgent undertone when I reached him.

"I think he left a few minutes ago, why?"

"The gargoyles have all been turned to stone. Someone's got

past the wolves."

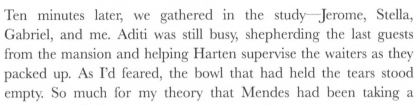

Ten minutes later, we gathered in the study—Jerome, Stella, Gabriel, and me. Aditi was still busy, shepherding the last guests from the mansion and helping Harten supervise the waiters as they packed up. As I'd feared, the bowl that had held the tears stood empty. So much for my theory that Mendes had been taking a phone call. He'd met someone in the garden, and whoever it was must have been handing them over.

And given the lack of other scents in that clearing, my money was firmly on Leon.

Gabriel's face was impassive, but Jerome and Stella looked grim. I busied myself sniffing discreetly around the area, but there were too many mingled scents. I recognised Gabriel himself, of course, and also Stella, Jerome, Aditi, Matt, and Harten, as well as Jean-Baptiste, the leader of the gargoyles. No Leon. Was he working with an accomplice? There were hints of a couple more I didn't know, but I doubted I'd be able to pick them out if I smelled them again—there was too much confusion for my nose. Maybe Matt would be able to tell more. We were waiting on him and Jean-Baptiste to return from doing an inspection of the property.

When they came in, I could tell from their grave faces that they had no good news. Gabriel didn't want the theft known, so none of the guests had been prevented from leaving, though Jerome had questioned the waiters discreetly. If I was right and Mendes was involved, it was too late anyway. He was gone, and it wasn't as though we could accost the Prime Wizard and strip-search him on a mere suspicion, even if we'd been in time to stop him leaving.

"Nobody got past us," Matt said. "The only people on the property were people who were supposed to be here."

"That's right," Jean-Baptiste said. He had a deep, husky voice like rocks grating together. "None of us saw an intruder."

"None of you apparently saw anything," Gabriel said mildly, "since you were asleep."

Jean-Baptiste's face flushed a mottled red. In human form, he was a big, solid man with greying hair, but at the moment he looked like a little kid caught with his hand in the cookie jar. "It must have been one of the guests."

"That doesn't narrow it down any," Jerome said.

"Mendes—" I began, but Jerome cut me off with an impatient wave.

"Yes, yes, you saw Mendes meeting someone in the garden. Do you smell Mendes in this room?"

"No."

"So he had help."

"Maybe someone on staff," Jean-Baptiste said.

Matt frowned and looked away. Did he suspect Leon, too? But why would Leon start stealing from Gabriel now? The pack had been working security for him for years.

Could it have been someone else on staff, like Jerome? Or Stella? She *had* said that a single tear could make her immensely powerful. The idea seemed ridiculous—but how well did I know any of these people, really? The only person whose innocence I was a hundred per cent certain of was myself.

"*I* would like to know who disabled my gargoyles," Gabriel interrupted, still in that mild voice. "Stella?"

"I found traces of magic on the roof," she said.

"Another goblin?" Gabriel asked.

"No. This was a wizard spell, and it could have been cast from the grounds or even inside the house. The caster would have to be close by, but not necessarily on the roof."

"Mendes didn't leave the ballroom all night," Jerome said. "Except for when he went out into the garden. I was keeping an eye on him."

"So he could have cast it before he left the terrace," Gabriel said.

"Yes." Stella frowned. "But why would he bother? He must have known the werewolves would be able to tell he'd been out there. Why would it matter if the gargoyles saw him?"

"That's true," Jean-Baptiste said in his gravelly voice. "Perhaps the spell was cast to prevent us seeing something that happened before that."

"But what?" I asked. "There's no sign of a break-in, and gargoyles can't see what goes on inside the house."

"Did you find out anything from the waiters?" Gabriel asked Jerome. The dragon was propped against his desk, arms folded casually across his broad chest, looking deceptively relaxed—until you saw the red embers burning in the depths of his dark eyes.

"One of them saw a waiter he didn't recognise towards the end of the night. The guy took a tray of drinks from the kitchen and headed off in the wrong direction. He called out to him to tell him he was going the wrong way, but the guy said it was a special order and kept going. He said it was odd, because he thought he knew everyone who worked for the catering firm, but he didn't see the guy again and he forgot about it until I showed up asking questions."

Mouth suddenly dry, I glanced at Matt, but he was still watching Jerome. A waiter with a tray of drinks. This was the plan I'd outlined that day at Matt's house, when we were talking about the tears.

Had Leon taken my worries and turned them into an actual plan? I wouldn't be surprised at anything that lowlife did, up to and including murder. But there'd been no trace of his scent around the cabinet where the tears were kept, and the other scents I didn't recognise were faint, as if they were from days ago. The only wolf scent that had been in here, apart from my own, was Matt's.

Wait.

Hadn't I picked up his scent even before he came in the first time? He'd arrived not long after me, but Gabriel had sent him and Jean-Baptiste out to sweep the grounds almost immediately. And he'd barely entered the room—his scent shouldn't have been as strong as it was.

The bottom dropped out of my stomach as a memory resurfaced. Matt's voice, at that same barbecue, saying he'd been inside Hayman House, *but only as far as that room where we met Arquette last week.*

So why was his scent all over this room?

Gabriel was speaking again, asking Matt if he could isolate the intruder's scent from the other smells in here, but I was only half-listening. My mind was spinning. Who had brought up the topic of the dragon tears at that barbecue? I couldn't remember. Had it been Matt?

"Too many smells in here to pick one out," Matt said.

"*I* picked one out," I said slowly, watching Matt's face. "I smelled Matt in here before he even came in."

His eyes narrowed. "As I said, there are too many mixed together in here to pick one out. I'm an experienced wolf and even I'm having trouble. It's no wonder you're confused."

"I'm not confused. I lived in your house for six weeks. I know your scent as well as I know my own."

The pack magic beat at me, pushing me to back down, to bow before the leader's superior knowledge.

Are you trying to get me into trouble? he demanded, mind to mind. *Shut* up.

Why are you sweating if you've done nothing wrong? I asked as the salt scent of fear reached me.

"Maybe she's not confused," he said to Gabriel. "Maybe she's trying to shift the blame."

"Blame for what?" Then I registered the hard look in his eyes. "Are you accusing *me* of stealing the tears?"

"She was at my house this week." He focused on Gabriel, ignoring my protest. "You can ask anyone who was there. We all heard her planning it, exactly the way it turned out."

"I wasn't planning anything! I was *speculating*."

"*Exactly* how it turned out," he continued inexorably. "Taking the gargoyles out of the picture, using a fake waiter with a tray of drinks to sneak in here and dump the tears into the drinks. She said they looked like ice cubes and no one would know the difference."

Jerome and Stella stared at me in horror.

"It wasn't me!" I turned to Gabriel, but his face had hardened until he looked more stony than Jean-Baptiste at his best. "That's not how it was."

"And then your waiter friend was supposed to take them back to the kitchen, weren't they, Nat?" Matt looked like he was enjoying himself now. "So you could *whisk them away and smuggle them out.* Those were your exact words, if I recall correctly."

"You're twisting it all around," I said. The look on Stella's face had gone from horror to disgust, and that look pierced me. "I would never steal. It doesn't matter what I said."

Gabriel stirred at last, and flames leapt in his eyes. "You're right. It doesn't matter what you said. It only matters what you did. Everyone, out. Nat and I need to have a little talk."

"I can explain," I said the instant the door closed on Jerome's heels. Gabriel's face was a mask, hard and unforgiving.

"Start talking."

A vase of flowers stood on a low table beside a comfortable armchair. The chair was positioned in one of the long windows, so that anyone reading there could take advantage of the light streaming in during the day. At the moment, the heavy brocade drapes were closed. I pulled out the flowers, scattering water across the carpet, and shoved my hand into the vase.

I brought it out full of small, clear shapes and held it out to him. "There! There's your precious tears."

"Those look remarkably like flower arranging marbles." His air of menace was gone, replaced by a quizzical look, as if I'd surprised him.

I breathed out as the tension in the room eased. "They're not. But that's what I thought, too, the first time I saw them. So I hid them in the vase, thinking no one would look twice."

"One wonders why you felt the need to hide them at all." His mouth twitched, as if he were fighting back a smile. He still hadn't taken the tears from me. I was starting to feel stupid holding them out, like a magician at the end of his trick when nobody claps. "What prompted this sudden urge to switch the tears out? Did you suspect Matt was planning something?"

My whole body unclenched as I realised he believed me.

"No. Not at all." Man, I'd been suckered *real* good. All this time, I'd been wary of Leon, seeing him as the dangerous one. But Matt hadn't hesitated to cut me loose and try to finger me for a crime *he'd* committed. Ruthless bastard. "I thought Matt was the real deal. Maybe a little bossy, but he seemed like a great guy. I can't believe he threw me under the bus like that."

"More than threw you under the bus. It sounded like a set-up that he'd put some thought into—probably as insurance. Notice that he didn't drop you in it until you started accusing him. He was probably hoping that with so many guests on site, suspicion would fall elsewhere and he'd get to keep his werewolf asset on my team. But explain to me this conversation where you supposedly planned the crime."

I got angry all over again thinking about it. "That jerk! *They* were the ones who asked about the tears, and I said they seemed so vulnerable. I was *worried* about them, and it felt like no one was taking their protection seriously. We had a whole conversation about why they were safe—because of the pack and the gargoyles." I cringed as I remembered suggesting that someone could force the gargoyles into hibernation to get past them. "But I said I was afraid one of the waiters could get access to them, and they'd be so easy to disguise as ice cubes in a drink. They set me up."

"How did they know where they were?"

I glanced down at the carpet, feeling a blush warm my cheeks. "Ah … well. I may have mentioned that they were on display in your study. I'm sorry. I can understand if you don't want me working for you anymore."

"We can work on your gullibility," he said. "Don't feel too bad. It's natural for a werewolf to trust their leader. Pack bonds are very strong."

"They don't feel too strong at the moment." Was it just Matt, or were they all in on it? Were they all laughing at the gullible new girl? Surely not Tony.

He plucked one of the tears from my hand, tossing it into the air and catching it again. It winked in the light from the chandelier.

"So, you knew nothing about any plan to steal the tears. You had no reason to suspect a crime was about to take place. So why did you hide these?"

I shrugged. "I was just worried they were so exposed. With all those people in the house for the ball, you know ... it didn't seem safe."

"But why do *you* care what happens to my tears? You're my bodyguard, not my bank manager."

I looked up and was caught in his gaze. He studied me as if he wanted to take me apart and see what made me tick. What was I to him? A problem to be solved? An asset to be exploited?

"Wouldn't it weaken you to lose them?" Or maybe I was just an employee who'd done something unexpected. I had a hunch Gabriel Arquette didn't like surprises. Dragons were at the top of the magical food chain, and they liked being in control. Only the fact that they generally didn't get along too well with each other had stopped them from taking over the world.

Well, that and the fact that they were kind of lazy. There was a reason they had a reputation for spending centuries napping on piles of treasure.

"Stella told me that they contained part of your magic," I continued. "So if someone took them, that would be a threat to your power. And you hired me to protect you from threats, so ..." I shrugged. It made perfect sense to me. "Can you please take them now?"

Finally, he held out his hand and I tipped the glittering stones into it, glad to be rid of them. No mysterious magic had emanated from them, and they were just as light as they looked, but the responsibility for them weighed heavily on me. I just wanted him to lock them away somewhere safe so I could be done with them.

He contemplated them for a long moment, rolling them around so they clinked against each other.

Then he tossed them in the wastepaper basket.

I jumped. "What are you *doing*?"

"They're worthless."

"But they're ... but you said ..." I was outraged. Part of me wanted to get down on the floor and rescue them, while the other part of me wanted to punch someone.

Preferably him. He was *laughing* at me.

"You know you look very cute when you're angry? Relax. They're not the real tears."

"*What*? You mean I went through all this angst for nothing?"

His smile faded. "Not for nothing. This exercise served a very useful purpose. I've known for some time that someone was after my tears, and I wanted to flush them out."

I glanced over at the empty bowl that had held the fakes, sitting there so accessible. "So leaving them out like that was *bait*?"

"Exactly. There has been a systematic pattern of attacks on my storage units over the past six months. I have a pretty good idea who is behind it—"

"Yeah, me too."

He smiled. "Mendes would like nothing better than to get his hands on a tear or two, but wizards don't like to get their hands dirty. I've suspected he had an accomplice in the pack for a while. That was part of the reason I took you on—to see if the culprit would seize the opportunity of the ultimate inside job. I wanted this done with."

I drew myself up, affronted. "You mean you suspected *me*?"

He laughed. "I see that offends you. Every wolf was a suspect, as far as I was concerned, though it stood to reason that Matt, as the leader, would be most likely. Not much happens in a werewolf pack without the leader knowing about it. But it could have been all of them—or none. There was a chance I was wrong." He held up his hands, palms out, in a placating gesture. "Obviously I was wrong about you. You've proven yourself more than trustworthy—you're prepared to go the extra mile to safeguard my interests." He grinned at me. "I have to say, that's a quality I admire in a bodyguard."

Lord, he was good looking when he smiled like that. That smile liquefied my insides, starting a fire deep in my core. And he thought I was cute. *Focus, Nat. You're not sixteen. This is no time to be mooning over your pretty boss.*

I cleared my throat. "So, Mendes went into the garden tonight to meet someone. I didn't see who it was, but it must have been Matt. His scent was all over the meeting place."

"Makes sense if his scent was in here, too. Mendes must have sent the gargoyles into hibernation so they wouldn't see Matt come in. But he would have wanted to keep his time inside to a minimum, so he slipped straight back out and met up with Mendes in the garden, where he was supposed to be."

Right. I'd wondered why Mendes had bothered taking the gargoyles out of the equation for a theft that happened where they couldn't see it anyway. And how he'd accomplished it if Jerome was right and he'd been in the ballroom all night. He must have enjoyed the ball immensely, knowing what was waiting for him at the end of the night. I remembered Stella's wistful look when she'd told me about the tears, and how she'd said a wizard would pay a fortune even for one. How much had Matt pocketed for his act of betrayal?

"What will you do with Matt?" I asked.

"I won't need to do anything, once Mendes realises he's been sold fake tears." This time, Gabriel's smile was savage. "I wouldn't be in Matt's shoes for all the treasure in the world."

"Speaking of treasure …" I took off the beautiful sapphire necklace and offered it to him. "Thanks for lending me this."

His warm hand enveloped mine and folded my fingers closed around the precious jewels. "Keep it."

"What?" I almost dropped it in surprise. "I can't do that!"

"Think of it as a bonus for tonight's work."

"That's way too generous!" Distracted by the feel of his hand around mine, I blurted out, "I thought dragons were supposed to be stingy with their money?"

Fortunately for my future employment prospects, he chose to be amused rather than offended. "I believe the term you're looking for is *hoarders*. Or perhaps collectors is a better way of putting it. We collect treasures and surround ourselves with beauty—beautiful gems and works of art, beautiful bits of magic, beautiful women." His gaze lingered on my lips.

I looked down, heart suddenly racing. *He's not talking about you, idiot. Pull yourself together.*

"But that means we know the true value of things." He gave our joined hands a little shake. "*This* is just money. True loyalty—now that's priceless."

I finally managed to extract my hand and stepped back, feeling a little breathless. I tried to put the necklace on the desk, but his eyes narrowed, and somehow I couldn't go through with it.

He pushed off the desk, coming to his full height. He only took one step but he made it look menacing.

"The other thing you should know about dragons," he purred, a dangerous gleam in his eyes, "is that we very much dislike having our gifts thrown back in our faces."

I cradled the necklace against my chest as if it were a newborn baby. Most of the time, it was easy to forget he was a powerful magical creature who could snap me like a twig. Right now, I was having *no* trouble remembering. "Right. Got it. No gift-throwing. Um ... where are the real tears?" *Good one, Nat. When in doubt, blurt the first thing that comes into your head.* Hastily, I added, "Never mind, you don't have to tell me."

That heart-stopping smile lit his face again. "What is there to fear? I said I trusted you and I meant it."

He pointed up.

Frowning, I looked up at the decorative ceiling with the giant ceiling rose in the centre—and the massive chandelier that hung from it.

The chandelier festooned with hundreds of tear-shaped crystals.

My mouth fell open. "*Those* are the real tears? But there's so many! There must be hundreds." And they were beautiful, faceted like diamonds. Nothing like the disappointing lumps of glass I'd thought were the tears.

"Thousands." He grinned, enjoying my astonishment.

"You must cry a lot." I tipped my head to one side, studying him. "You don't look the type."

He spread his hands wide. "What can I say? I like sad movies."

Sad *movies*? This man was full of surprises. "You should watch *Marley and Me* some time."

"I've seen it. My popcorn was nearly washed away. Now put that poor necklace back on before you break it."

Guiltily, I stopped twisting the necklace between my fingers and resettled it around my neck.

"That's better." He moved to the door, then paused with his hand on the doorknob. "About your probation …"

"Yes?" Had he changed his mind after all? Maybe he'd decided that werewolves simply weren't worth the trouble. I couldn't blame him. After tonight, I kind of felt the same.

"Forget about it. You're hired."

Hope you enjoyed reading this as much as I enjoyed writing it! To meet dragons, fae, gods, monsters, and magic-users of many kinds, check out more of my stories at www.marinafinlayson.com/books.

While you're there, why not sign up for my newsletter? You'll get book news, free stories, and special deals—plus glimpses into the writing life and the perils of owning the world's stupidest dog.

Lunaticking

DALE IVAN SMITH

Chapter 1

THE HOWL SHREDDED the silence of the Olympic Rainforest night, erupting from the canyon mouth, east of Tully and me. The hairs on the back of my neck stuck straight out. It sounded like something out of a horror movie.

"That's our wolf-dude," I told Tully. He loomed beside me in his leather duster, his dark face tight with concentration as he peered into his scry stone. He began chanting a Tag spell in Finnish.

I held my wand and peered into the darkness, brushing my bangs away from my eyes with my free hand. The waxing gibbous moon had sunk behind the wooded ridge west of us, plunging the canyon floor into darkness. Morning twilight hadn't begun yet.

"Got you," Tully said. A golden thread hung in the air, a glowing spell-line that connected him to the wolf-man manifestation.

"Let's go then," I said and started back down the trail at a half jog, my wand out, point down. I pulled a Link spell from memory. I'd cast it in German. Not much elegance, but plenty of sure strength, enough for this wolf-man manifestation, especially out here in the boondocks.

"Liz, wait up," Tully called behind me.

I looked over my shoulder at him. "Come on, old man, better keep up." Tully was thirty, four years older than me, and I never wanted to miss a chance to tease him about the age difference.

He broke into a run, and I ran faster to stay ahead of him, but Tully had longer legs, was former US Army, and a big-time gym rat. He passed me in seconds.

My breath burned as we ran. My boots felt like they weighed a ton each. Maybe I should have worn hiking ones instead of Doc Martens. We crested the rise in the middle of the canyon and then I could see the mouth, and the distant mountains, lit by the nearly full moon sinking in the west of us.

Tully stopped and I did likewise, bending over and gasping for air. He uttered a command word and purple mana pulsed along the golden thread of the spell.

The air shimmered, and a window of silver light appeared in front of Tully. He gestured and we finally glimpsed our target, after a night spent wandering through this forsaken forest.

The supernatural's gray fur was shaggy. Its jeans bulged and ripped, going down to just below the knees, with the tattered remains of a checkered shirt hanging from its broad shoulders. The eyes glowed red. It sniffed the air, mouth open, short fangs shining in the moonlight. The manifestation was right out of a Universal monster movie from the Nineteen Thirties. Manifestations modeled themselves on human ideas and self-conceptions. Everything from myth and folk lore to urban legends.

"Now that's a classic wolf-dude," I said. It looked like a stunt double for Lon Chaney Jr.'s wolf man.

Tully gestured with his hands and the golden spell-thread brightened. "Anthro-wolf, to use the correct designation." face narrowed in concentration. "It's a Level Three."

I blinked. That was a permanent on the Residency scale. "That was fast. We only picked it up yesterday." How could it solidify that quickly? Manifestations took time to coalesce.

"And why is it out here in the boondocks?" Tully asked.

"Good question," I said. This part of the Olympic Rainforest was deserted. There shouldn't be any here. "Maybe it wandered away from a populated area." I shook my head. To exist, manifestations needed people. Supernaturals flickered into existence from the interaction between mana and the human subconscious. Mana was the fuel for magic. It flowed through everything and everyone, invisible except for the few of us aware of its existence. There were very few humans out here, and supernaturals typically needed a large collective subconscious. Which meant there should only be the very rare fleeting manifestations, not a permanent prancing about.

I searched my memory for the ranged binding spell I needed. The Spinning Chain, I'd go with that. Ensnare him at range, and then attach the Link spell. Two spells in quick order. Despite the long night, I could do it.

I began slicing the air in front of me with my wand, warming up. The wolf-dude was a hundred yards distant. It turned and ran off, shoulders rolling, long arms nearly scraping the ground.

I chanted the Spinning Chain spell in Spanish. "I cast forth my hand and ensnare you from afar." My skin tingled as a spinning loop of golden light appeared before me. It turned to a muddy gray glow with steel glints, mimicking a real chain. "I bind thee!"

As I pulled back my arm for the windup, a chorus of howls echoed behind us. I couldn't stop the spell, but my aim went all skewed and the chain missed the lens and spun into the trees. My right tricep muscle suddenly cramped.

In the arcane lens, the image of the wolf-person disappeared into the trees, the lens dissipating a second later as Tully lost concentration.

We turned and peered back up the canyon. Moonlight washed the tops of the trees with light, but the forest beneath was dark. The chorus grew louder.

I massaged my arm. "More? How are they materializing out here in this deserted forest?"

Tully snapped his wand, flinging a quick spell in that direction. "Reveal!"

We waited. And waited.

Nothing.

"No mana. No magic." Tully said, after a minute.

"You're kidding." I flexed my arm. Still a bit cramped. "You're telling me those howls are not supernatural?"

"There's nothing magical there," he said.

"Maybe that supernatural can throw howls. You know, like a ventriloquist."

He gave me a side-eye.

"Okay, I admit, that's ridiculous. Maybe those howls were fleeting manifestations, Level Zeroes?" Level Zeroes were supernaturals that only lasted for minutes, sometimes just seconds. Most manifestations were phantasmal Zeroes, only a few solidified enough to become even a Level One, which might last an hour, or a day at most. Level Twos, perhaps a few weeks. Level Threes, like the wolf-man manifestation I'd failed to ensnare, were the lowest level of permanents.

"Multiple Level Zeroes?" Tully's tone told me he thought I was nuts.

"What else could it be?" I asked.

"How about actual wolves?"

I squinted at him. "There aren't any real wolves here in the Olympic peninsula."

"Actually, there is a wolf sanctuary here. Not close, but still here."

"You're suggesting that maybe an actual wolf left the sanctuary and happened to end up here, right when a manifestation outbreak occurred?" I asked.

Tully shrugged. "Okay, so it does seem pretty unlikely."

"There are no coincidences, just connections not yet found," I said, quoting our RU.N.E. field manual. The Regulating Union for Normalizing Enchantments loved to spell everything out, especially procedure.

His eyebrows rose. "You've actually read the field manual?"

"Hey, I've read it. I just don't read it for fun like you do." I put my wand away. Tully couldn't cast another scry until after dawn, and then it was going to be very difficult to locate any supernatural. Day magic was much more subtle than night magic, and manifestations usually went to ground once the sun was up.

"There's only one thing we can do," I said. "Go find breakfast."

Chapter 2

CHLOE STOOD at the edge of camp. Her skin tingled in the glow of the nearly full moon that hung low in the west, taking the edge off her anger at Russ. He and the others had been gone for hours, out on his latest "lope-about." Despite her annoyance at him, his expression made her smile. She shook her head. He seemed to do both to her on a regular basis.

Grass rustled behind her, and the familiar scent of a packmate filled her nostrils. It was Calvin. She turned to greet her friend. He smiled and adjusted his wire-rimmed glasses. She'd bonded with him on that ill-fated tour bus, when she was with her grandmother, and he with his grandparents. Before the terrible accident that changed the survivors forever.

Behind him the coming dawn had begun to smear the eastern sky.

"They still haven't returned?" Calvin pushed his glasses back up his nose. Despite everything, poor Calvin was still near-sighted and needed his glasses. It wasn't his fault.

"Not yet." She suppressed a grin.

"The moonlight gives your coppery hair a silver tinge," he said.

"You only now noticed?" She grinned. "Making a pass at me, Calvin?"

He blushed. "No, no, I'm not," he said hastily. "I wouldn't want to get between you and Russ."

"I don't belong to him," she said.

"Well, I didn't mean it like that, but you guys are a thing, right?"

They'd become a couple. Chloe and Russ hadn't committed to each other. Not yet. After the accident, they had been the first ones to shift and become wolves. Her human and wolf sides had both felt the attraction between them. It crackled like summer lightning.

For a time, they had been happy in the deep forest. The others learned to shift, and they bonded as pack. Then Russ began having dreams, dreams about another place, a better one. A month ago, they came to this place, near a fishing resort, not far from the highway, and not much farther from a town. They were able to get supplies, more clothes and shoes and other gear. But it also put them at risk of being discovered for what they had become.

Staying deeper in the forest was best. Chloe was sure of it. But Russ was certain being here was the best for the pack. He told Chloe he now dreamed of new members joining them. So, the pack had to wait here for the new members. She was still drawn to him, and she thought he was to her, but his dreams kept getting in the way.

She said they needed to move on. He said that they must wait.

Now the disagreement over what the pack should do next threatened what the two of them had together. She told him the entire pack needed to discuss staying or going. Russ agreed to it, reluctantly. He had agreed, saying it was only right, though she could sense the compulsion to just order them to stay. What was it about this place that made him so stubborn? When they'd been deep in the wilderness, he'd agreed that the pack needed to stay away from civilization and move as necessary. But these dreams now convinced him otherwise.

A chorus of howls echoed faintly to the east.

She shook her head again. "Russ and the others." The fishing resort lay west, but only a couple of miles. Too close to be howling.

"It sure sounds like it," agreed Calvin.

They stood there in silence, waiting for the pack to arrive.

Tyler returned first, still fastening his jeans as he walked out of the trees west of them. Barefoot as usual. His sleeveless flannel shirt was unbuttoned. His chest muscles flexed as he buttoned it, stopping two holes short of the top.

"Where's Russ?" Chloe asked him.

He brushed his long blonde hair away from his eyes. "He's still scouting."

Which meant he was still in wolf form. "Now?" She frowned. "He knows we have this meeting." She'd finally agreed to the discussion, and he stayed away?

Tyler shrugged. "He said he wanted to check out a possible intrusion."

Worry poked at her. "Intrusion? How many and where?"

"I don't know, that's all he said."

She frowned. Just like Russ to be the hero and investigate on his own.

Angel appeared next, pulling her black tank top down over her naked breasts. Her hair, which had been shoulder length when they'd all been on that tour bus three months ago, was now cropped close to her head.

Kat and Max walked behind her, both dressed in wool shirts and jeans, holding hands.

Chloe crossed her arms and stared up at the lightening sky. "Russ needs to be here."

"He's the Alpha," Tyler said. The rest of the pack gathered in a circle around Chloe, beneath a sequoia.

Calvin adjusted his glasses again, and smiled. "Pirate Code, Tyler, remember? We decide together. Russ decides in a crisis. This isn't a crisis."

Tyler bared his teeth, took half a step toward Calvin, who bravely stood his ground.

"You aren't the alpha," Tyler growled. "You're not one of the betas, either. Me and Chloe are. You're in the back of the pack, man, where you belong."

"Don't speak to him like that," Chloe said, putting a low growl into her own voice.

Tyler flinched, then lifted his chin up defiantly. "You aren't the alpha," he repeated, but there was less force in his words the second time.

Chloe uncrossed her arms "How about you shift and find our fearless pack leader and let him know we're waiting for him?" He shouldn't be chasing down intruders. The rules stated they must avoid outsiders.

Out of the corner of her eye, Angel smirked, but didn't say anything.

Tyler pulled his shirt off as he stalked into the trees. Angel headed to her tent.

Chloe plucked a long blade of grass from the earth, twirled the stem. A flood of scents filled her awareness—the sharp, sour tang of the grass itself, the dirt traces tangling from the roots, the moistness that sheltered earth worms, wriggling insects, the trace of a bee that had brushed against the grass blade, the almost metallic taste of a dragonfly that had perched on the blade not long ago.

She shook herself. Lately, the world had begun opening up to her in a flood of sensations while she was still in human form. Not like it had been for the first two months.

"Are you all right?" Calvin asked.

She blinked. She had forgotten he was still there. "I was distracted," she said. "So much to drink in here."

"You're more aware of everything now, aren't you?"

"I guess. Why?" she asked.

"Because I am, too. In all sorts of ways. I notice sounds far differently than I did a few weeks ago. Smells and tastes, too. But it's more than that." He fell silent.

"What do you mean?" she asked.

He tilted his head, looking at her. "Haven't you noticed tiny glints of gold and silver light, sometimes, when we transform? Have you seen how some rocks and hills have a really faint purple aura around them?"

She tugged idly at a strand of her hair, struggling to recall. "Maybe once or twice, but I thought it was just a trick of the light."

"I've seen it more than once or twice, but only because I've written it down in my journal. I have four entries. But the thing is, I can't actually *remember* any of them. I only know because I wrote down that I saw it."

Chloe shivered. "That's spooky. What do you think it means?"

"We're changing. I don't know why. Is it this place? Or just our wolf sides developing further?"

"I think it's this place. We need to move on," she said. "It's too risky to stay here."

"But this is something different," Calvin replied.

She nodded. "Another reason to leave."

"If only we knew why our senses are altering." He got to his feet. "Another reason to leave, I guess. I'm going to get something to eat. I'll keep an ear and an eye out for Russ and the others." He left and she leaned back on her arms.

The Moon had disappeared behind the wooded ridge. She could go and look for Russ, but they'd argued before he took the others out on the run.

It had been a bad fight. She clenched her fists at the memory. He left to lead the others. He should come back to her, not expect her to chase after him.

She exhaled slowly.

"We need to decide, together, as a pack," she said aloud.

Chapter 3

MY STOMACH RUMBLED. We walked side-by-side on a wide trail about a hundred yards from where Tully had parked the Crown Victoria. The sun was up now.

Tully grinned and I felt my face redden.

"You weren't kidding about wanting breakfast," he said.

I fake-glowered at him, which only made him laugh.

"Don't get on my case," he said. "Your stomach has spoken."

"Hilarious." But I was starving. "With our luck, the nearest greasy spoon must be a hundred miles away," I said.

"Gee, if only we had a way of locating said nearest greasy spoon," Tully said.

"You've been hanging around me too long," I said. "And it sounds weird when you say it that way."

"You're just jealous because I'm better at the banter."

I snorted. "Please."

He laughed and pulled out his arcane phone and called up the knowledge genii. I paced back and forth while he did.

That was when I spotted the huge wolf, upslope about fifty yards away, watching us from a stand of tall Hemlock trees.

It was dark brown, fur smooth, with a ruff of darker fur around a thick neck. Even from this distance, its golden eyes seemed to peer into my soul. I stared back, frozen, breath caught in my throat.

Tully muttered under his breath. His head was down, focused on the arcane phone, obviously oblivious.

I edged closer to Tully, while the wolf watched from the shadow of the trees, not moving. I'd only seen a wolf once before, at a nature preserve my mother took my sister and I to, when we were kids. This was like that, only deep blue sea and demons above, I swore I saw human awareness and intelligence in those deep golden eyes.

"Psst, Tully," I hissed.

He stopped in mid-mutter. "Still trying to locate a greasy spoon. There isn't internet here, and you know how the knowledge genii is in daylight, in a remote area He glanced up, annoyance flickering across his face. I nudged my head in the direction of golden wolf. He looked in that direction, and his eyes widened.

He stood stock still for a moment. "Reveal," he whispered under his breath, in Swahili. The air around the creature shimmered.

The wolf turned without a sound and disappeared into the trees.

We were silent for a moment, then I let out the air I'd been holding with a sharp exhale.

"Did you see that? Icy depths, that was something," I swore. I swore magically, of course, since cursing with ordinary swears produced ordinary results, as one of my mentors used to say.

"Wolf," Tully said. A single word.

"No kidding. But that was no ordinary wolf."

"My reveal doesn't show anything supernatural."

"Well, it is daylight," I replied.

"No, I mean *nothing*, nothing at all."

It had been a long night. "Nothing? Nada? Zilch?" That couldn't be. Tully was a seer. Unless…

"The wolf's not supernatural," Tully said.

"But it looked so intelligent."

"Wolves *are* intelligent, Liz."

"I mean, in a human sense. Besides, I haven't heard of any wolves hanging out in the Olympic rainforest," I pointed out.

He gazed at where the wolf had been. "You're right, but there was no trace of magic, none whatsoever."

"That's weird." I yawned suddenly. I covered my mouth just before I yawned again. "I'm getting too old for old-nighters," I said.

Tully chuckled. "You're twenty-six."

I rubbed my eyes. "I feel fifty." My arms and legs suddenly weighed a ton. I couldn't remember the last time I'd gone a night without sleep. "Gods, I wished we'd nabbed that Level Three, then we could have gotten a good day's rest."

"Burning the candle at both ends is part of the job," he replied.

I yawned again. "We need some rejuvenation." I reached into my jacket and pulled out a stoppered glass vial. The sparkling silver liquid inside moved like mercury. R.U.N.E.'s alchemists had created a potion that could give you the equivalent of eight hours of uninterrupted, near perfect sleep. There was only one catch. We'd crash tomorrow morning.

Tully raised a hand. "Hold on, Liz. We should talk about this. Maybe we could nap this morning, keep the potion in reserve."

"Trust me. You're going to need fresh-as-daisy-status." I uncorked the vial, sipped. The liquid tasted like the freshest spring water ever. Instantly, my body felt lighter, and my mind suddenly sharper. I stretched, flashed Tully my most brilliant smile. "See, good as new."

He frowned. "I'm not a fan of that stuff. Coffee's one thing, magical sleep substitutes are another. Besides, maybe we'll need it more in a day, or a week."

I tugged at his coat sleeve. "We still need to find the manifestation. This gives us until tomorrow morning. Daytime or no daytime, we're going to have to keep looking for it. Besides, it's also weaker in daytime."

"Finding it's going to be the hard part." Tully reached inside his duster and pulled out his own rejuvenation and drank it down. "I'm going to regret this."

"That's what morning afters are for." I giggled. Rejuves tended to make me a little silly.

Tully sighed. "It's going to be a long day."

He found a diner, a few miles away. *Lakeside Eats* turned out to be a log building with a high shake roof. A wooden statue of a brown bear holding a salmon stood beside the double-door entrance. The gravel parking lot had a couple of pickup trucks parked alongside the building, and an ancient Volkswagen van.

"I think I'm going to have pancakes with an extra side of bacon and about a gallon of their blackest coffee," I said as we walked up to the entrance. "How about you?"

A red-faced, balding guy in a rumpled suit sat on a wooden bench behind the brown bear statue and glowered at me. "You're late." My heart sank. I knew him.

I forced a smile. "Field Supervisor Simkins, great to see you again, *sir*."

"No, it's not," he said. "For either of us." An ancient-looking, battered brown leather briefcase lay on the bench beside him. "Agents, I'm here because this outbreak is spiraling out of control."

"Come on, we just started yesterday evening," I said.

He scowled. "That's plenty of time to have gotten the job done."

Easy for him to say. "It might take more time than that."

"The quicker, the better, and already done is best," Simkins replied. Straight out the R.U.N.E. field manual. Time was of the essence.

He didn't try to hide his disdain. "Just because your mother is a Senior-Director Wizard doesn't mean you get out of doing the work."

"She tell you to say that, sir?"

"As a matter of fact, yes."

Typical of my mother. Bear down on me twice as hard because I was her daughter.

"We've got this," I said.

"No, you clearly don't," Simkins retorted. "Now, let's go into this dive, and get what they think passes for food here into you both, and

I'll go over what happens next." He got to his feet and headed toward the door. Tully started to follow him, then stopped when he saw I hadn't budged. Simkins noticed a moment later and tramped back to me, still frowning.

"What is it, Marquez?"

I fingered the amulet hanging around my neck. "How did you get here, sir?"

Tully gave me a worried glance. "Liz, what are you doing?"

"He could be a chameleon," I hissed behind my free hand.

"The teleportal network reaches even here," Simkins said acidly.

"Not that I'd heard." The Olympic rainforest was way too out of the way to be worth dragons forging a teleportal. There's no way they put one out here.

Simkins shrugged and looked at Tully. "It must be rough to working with her."

Tully shrugged in reply. "I manage."

"Very funny!" I said. They turned and entered the restaurant. For a moment, I thought I smelled ozone trailing from Simkins, but didn't see where it might be coming from. I shook my head, and followed them inside.

Chapter 4

WHEN TYLER RETURNED, Chloe and the others ate a breakfast of pan-fried trout, potatoes from the garden, and wild blackberries. Kat had put aside portions for Russ and Tyler both. But Tyler returned alone.

"Where is he?" Chloe demanded.

Tyler wouldn't meet Chloe's gaze. "He said to tell you he'll be here soon. To go ahead and finish breakfast. He needs to *think*. He saw two people on a trail a mile from the narrow canyon."

Ming scowled at Tyler. "So, he sent you while he thinks things over?"

"I'd better go talk to Achilles," Chloe said. Tyler gave her a confused look. "Right, you don't know *The Iliad*. Bad example. This is more like *The Odyssey*."

"No one's turning me into a pig," Ming said.

"They don't need to," Angel snapped. A moment later they were nose to nose, fists balled, and nostrils flared.

"Stand back!" Chloe said. The moon had disappeared from the morning sky, but they still felt it. It was always like this after the first quarter moon had grown, until the waning last quarter moon. They all had short fuses. "We're still human," she said, keeping her voice calm. "We're in this together."

Ming exhaled, took a step back, and lowered her fists. "You're right."

Angel still glared at Ming.

Chloe could sense the wolf inside Angel, longing to lunge at Ming's throat. She held up her hand. "Stop with the dominance game. Did you hear Tyler? Russ said he saw two people, looking for us."

Angel shook herself, then turned away. "She backed down first, you all saw it."

Chloe bit back what she wanted to say. *Because you let your blood get up.* "We need to be ready to move," she said. "I think we should secure our stuff.

Max and Kat groaned. "I hate take-downs," Kat said in that rich British accent of hers. But they did as she suggested.

An hour later their belongings were stowed in their backpacks. The tents had come down and were rolled up. Russ might get angry with her, but if there wasn't anyone looking for them, and the pack voted to say here, then it was just practice, and Russ always said, it never hurt to practice.

But Russ still hadn't appeared.

She tightened the draw strings on her tent bag, then went to find Tyler. Kat and Max sat beside their belongings, holding hands, heads bowed together. She hated to interrupt but they needed to know.

"I'm going to the big tent," she told them. That's what they'd dubbed the one that Russ used. It was also where they held meetings, dinners, and slept together in the winter. It had extra supplies. They were going to have to hide those, or figure out a way to take them.

She found Tyler sitting on a log near his tent. "You haven't taken your tent down."

He looked up, his eyes worried. "Sorry, I've been thinking about Russ."

She felt a twinge in her chest. Tyler was younger than he

appeared, perhaps twenty. He'd been with an older man on the bus, who resembled him. She hadn't known their relationship, and after the crash, Tyler never spoke of him, even when the rest of them talked after their first full moon as a pack, in the big tent. She guessed it might have been his father, or an uncle. She remembered Tyler seeming cold toward the older man. Perhaps the tour had been a reconciliation attempt by the older man.

"I'm going to check on Russ," she said, keeping her voice gentle.

Something flickered in his eyes, then he stood up. "I'm coming with you."

"Good," she said, and smiled.

She let Ming know, and asked her to tell Angel.

The big tent was a half mile deeper in the forest, in a narrow clearing surrounded by tall cedars. The idea was to give the pack a safe place to hole up if people found the camp.

The front flap was open. She went to the entrance. "Russ?" No answer. She'd last been in this tent yesterday, morning, before the fight.

The air stank of drying blood. Chloe hesitated. The inside was dark, just a sliver of light from the open flap illuminated an over-turned cot. A shadowy figure sprawled on the floor. Chloe's jaw tightened. She pulled the flap all the way open.

The figure on the floor was the corpse of a deer. A doe. Chloe tasted bile. The doe's throat had been slashed open. She covered her own mouth, fighting to avoid throwing up.

Blood splattered the cot, ceiling, and walls. Chloe took a few steps inside, her legs shaking. In the next room another doe lay sprawled beside an overturned cot, her head back. Behind her Tyler quietly retched.

There was no sign of Russ. The air had an odd smell, like burnt herbs and old bone, mixed with the drying deer blood.

She stepped around the animal's corpse. There were burn marks on the deer's flank. Chloe knelt beside it. The throat had been sliced open, just like the other doe. A wolf's jaws would have ripped the flesh, not sliced it. It had to have been a blade of some sort.

She went to Russ's mountaineering backpack, rifled through it, looking for the knife. She found it in a side pocket.

Russ's knife, a big one, the kind a mountain man might use to skin a bear, or pick his teeth with. The blade was spotless.

Tyler waited outside. His eyes were huge. "The deer, did Russ slaughter them?"

It seemed impossible. Russ could be a bad boy, but beneath the macho exterior was a kind heart. He might kill an animal for food, but he wouldn't murder one.

Then she noticed the black burn marks on the tent floor. The burn marks formed a triangle. Surrounding the triangle was a circle of dull black dust. She leaned down, touched the dust with her fingertip.

Iron.

It was iron. Iron shavings.

Chapter 5

SIMKINS, Tully and I sat in a booth in the back of the *Lakeside* restaurant with Simkins with his back against the rear wall. The place was maybe a quarter full, no one near us. The busing station was on the opposite side of the back wall from us, behind the booth there, and probably noisy enough to mask us from eavesdroppers.

But Simkins wasn't taking any chances. He leaned what looked like a walking stick against the wall behind him. If I peered closely, I could see feathers carved in the wood, like an owl's. The Muffler was an artifact, so it was magically alive even if it was inanimate.

It muffled our voices unless you were within just a couple of feet, and also hid us from magical prying eyes. Simkins didn't want any rival agencies listening in.

Lakeside was exactly the sort of greasy spoon diner I craved this morning. I ordered a stack of apple pancakes with a side of bacon, strong black coffee, while Tully had a veggie omelet and fruit. Simkins had toast and sliced cantaloupe. He drank chamomile tea.

"Didn't think you were the herbal type, sir," I said.

"It's good for the stomach, Marquez. Calms it, which I especially need right now."

"What is it you wanted to see us about, sir?" I asked, sweetly.

Probably too sweetly, since Simkins scowled. He finished his toast. "First off, what exactly happened last night?"

I glanced at Tully. He took the hint.

"We spent the night tracking manifestations, class zeroes and ones," he said. "All were anthro-wolf types."

Simkins squinted at Tully "All of them?"

Tully nodded.

Simkins turned his stony gaze on me. "How many?"

"Too many to count," I replied.

"That's not an answer. How many?" he asked Tully.

"Sir, I lost count after thirteen."

"*Thirteen.* Out here?" Simkins was incredulous.

"We kept zapping them, but more kept showing up," I said. "We walked up that canyon to a ridge. Tully finally got a fix on a level three wolf-man, which might have spawned a single level zero, but nowhere near as many as we encountered."

"Doesn't make sense," Simkins said.

"No sir," Tully agreed. "What's more, I had difficulty tracking the Level Three."

Simkin's scowl changed to a puzzled look. "Interference?"

"Yes, sir," Tully said. "I couldn't identify from what. We finally acquired the supernatural at the mouth of the canyon, during pre-dawn twilight." He looked at me.

"I tried a ranged binding, a Spinning Chain spell." I felt like an idiot. I'd muffed that binding.

Simkin rolled his eyes. "I take it by your sudden silence you failed."

I squirmed on the bench. "I was distracted."

"I'm surprised that doesn't happen more often."

I kept calm. "Sir, howling broke out behind us and threw off my aim and the level three got away. Later, we saw a wolf."

"Looked like a timber wolf, sir," Tully added.

Simkins's eyes narrowed. "Out here? Very odd."

He stared at me, obviously turning this over in his mind. He pulled out his arcane phone, tapped something out. He laid the phone down, sipped at his tea. Then motioned at a waitress. "Could I have some coffee, ma'am?"

He sipped his coffee in silence while Tully and I looked at each other and waited. The minutes ticked by. I began drumming my fingers on the tabletop. Simkins flashed me an annoyed look. I stopped, then what felt like an hour later but was probably like five more minutes, began tapping them again. I didn't do well sitting still and waiting. I wanted to be moving.

"You have a lot of energy for someone who was up all night," he said finally.

"We took our rejuvenations."

"Good. At least you recognize that we need to get this wrapped up quickly."

I blinked. I figured he would have been annoyed.

"Always, sir," I said. The longer a manifestation was allowed to be permanent without being sworn to follow the laws of the Compact, the more chances it had to cause problems. Swearing to the laws of the Compact bound it to those laws and made things much easier for we sorcerer-agents. The lowest penalty for breaking any of those laws was imprisonment in the Silos, at least. The highest was magical erasure. "I'm ready to get back at it," I added.

"I guess I've made you wait long enough," Simkins replied.

"I've wondered why we're sitting here burning daylight. *Sir*."

"You won't have to wait much longer," Simkins said. "Agent Hassan should be here shortly."

I pursed my lips. That name sounded familiar. "Fakira Hassan?" I'd never met her, but I knew her by reputation, about my age, very competent. "But she's a Clair, not a field agent." Clair is short for Clairvoyant, the magical kind. Clairs could suss out details in the arcane. Cousins to Seers like Tully, but more connected to manifestations. Typically they were stationed in watch houses, in the bigger cities, tracking disturbances in the arcane.

"She's a field agent now. We need her out here. She's been pushing an idea about what's behind this. She didn't get any traction until the office confirmed multiple manifestations out here."

"What's this idea, sir?" I asked.

Simkins smiled at me coldly. "I'll let Hassan explain it. It's her baby."

Which made it pretty clear he didn't necessarily agree whatever her theory was.

Tully's eyes were lit with a look I hadn't seen before.

I leaned over and looked up at him. "You know her, Tully?"

"Yeah, we-we've met before."

Tully sounded a little rattled. *That* made things more interesting.

I turned back to Simkins. "Well, you're the boss."

He leaned forward. "Nice of you to finally acknowledge that."

"What else were you going to brief us on?"

"Just to emphasize that the number one priority here is locating and collaring the source of the outbreaks."

A soft chime sounded. He picked up the phone, thumbed the screen. Smiled. It was creepy when Simkins gave a full-on smile, it distorted his face into something almost likeable, but didn't quite get there. I'd seen goblins that looked more human than he did when he smiled.

He put his phone away, stood. "Agent Hassan is here."

I turned around but Tully blocked my view, so I had to watch Tully's face to see if she'd entered. The wooden *everything* of the restaurant glinted darkly in the low lighting.

"Don't see her," he said.

"Must be wearing an obscuration charm," I said, trying to be helpful.

"I'm not sensing the mana such an artifact would attract, Liz," Tully replied.

Simkins's smile vanished. He shook his head. "Like I said, half-assed rookies. She's *outside*."

"Hey, you try being on your game after pulling an all-nighter."

"You did drink your Rejuvenation."

Touché. Tully and I followed him outside, trooping through the deserted lounge and out a side door. I squeezed my eyes shut, trying to adapt to the bright sunlight.

I'd never met Fakira Hassan. I had only read her name in

various R.U.N.E. reports. She'd been transferred a half dozen times. Clairs normally put down roots, but not her.

A slender woman with elegant features waited outside. Her light brown skin glowed in the morning sun. She wore a gray hijab, a mountain jacket, corduroy trousers, and hiking boots. She gazed at the distant mountains, her eyes half-closed.

She turned and lowered her outraised hand, which held an ebony charm on a silver chain. She smiled.

Tully was dark-skinned, but I swear he blushed at that smile.

"John," she said. "It's wonderful to see you again."

"You, too, Fakira."

She looked at me. "You must be Elizabeth Marquez."

"My reputation precedes me," I said.

"Not the way you think," Simkins said.

"Reputations can be good and bad," Hassan said, "just like all of us. From what I've heard, yours is exceptional."

I glowed at the compliment. She was silver-tongued, that was for sure.

"I didn't expect to see you in the field," I said, words tumbling out.

"We Claires should get out into the field more often. The great task of maintaining the balance with magic and mana is out here, not back at a watch station."

"That's a lofty way of putting it," I said.

Her eyes twinkled. "You could say that I just like a little excitement. Besides, I'm cross-trained as a field agent."

"You're a girl after this girl's own heart," I replied.

"Enough banter," Simkins said acidly. "We need to nail the source point of the outbreak before dark."

Hassan walked over to a navy-blue SUV with tinted windows.

"How'd you rate an urban assault vehicle?" I asked her.

She smiled. "It's who you know."

I glanced at Simkins.

"You drive this vehicle," he told me. "That will let Hassan scan. I'll ride with Agent Tully."

That surprised me, but maybe Simkins wanted to grill Tully

about me. Or, maybe he just wanted to let me take point. Or, unthinkable as it seemed, he just didn't want to ride with me.

I pulled out onto the highway and headed south.

"How did you rate a new vehicle?" I asked her, keeping my eyes on the road.

"Here I imagined you would ask me where we were headed."

I shrugged. "You'll tell me in a moment. We girls share."

"I was issued the SUV from the Seattle office and told to drive here at once to meet you." Straight forward. "To answer the unspoken question, I'm following an arcane thread that began in British Columbia. Subtle but it runs through each apparition of a wolf-person and has the signature of the Iron Circle."

My eyes widened. "Deep blue sea," I swore. "You think the Iron Circle is behind this?"

She nodded fractionally. "I sensed their hand in the arcane emanations."

I shot her a glance. "I didn't think that was possible." The Iron Circle were masters at hiding, which made them very difficult to track down.

She shrugged. "It certainly isn't easy. But I'm convinced it's them."

That was a very unpleasant thought. What was the Iron Circle doing creating wolf-dudes? Especially out here in the back of beyond?

The Crown Vic followed two car-lengths behind me, close enough I could see Simkins talking non-stop to Tully, who nodded and kept his eyes on the road. That looked a lot like a lecture. Even from this distance, I could tell Tully didn't look happy about it at all.

Well, better Tully than me.

Chapter 6

"SOMETHING'S WATCHING US," Chloe whispered to Ming. They stood in the evening shadow beneath a huge maple tree. A lake shimmered a hundred yards away. High above the water, a bird wheeled in the sky. Too far away for Chloe to see what it was.

It had been hours since Russ had gone missing.

"I don't see it," Ming said. "Where?"

"No, it's a feeling crawling up the back of my neck." Chloe slowly turned, peered into the shadows. Something flickered purple in the half-light beside a fallen maple. She squinted. A black dragonfly outlined in a faint purple glow hovered above mushrooms growing from the trunk. She blinked and the purple glow vanished. It must have been a trick of the light. The dragonfly sped away.

Motion off to the right made her and Ming both twist around.

A moment later, a white wolf slipped between the trees, padded over to Ming and sat.

Chloe relaxed. It was Calvin in wolf form.

Ming sighed and stroked the wolf's fur. "You scared us!" The wolf licked her hand.

There was a time when that would have bothered Chloe, but

now, after a few months of this existence, it felt normal, right, part of who they all were. Another side of themselves.

Pack life forever.

But Russ was missing. He could be cocky, overly macho, determined, and annoying as hell. He was also loving, kind, and cared about her and the pack. He went the extra mile, and put others first. She ached at the thought that he might be gone forever.

Ming pulled her hand back. The wolf disappeared into the shadows. A minute later, Calvin appeared, dressed in outdoor clothes—washable forest green trousers and khaki shirt.

"Your shoes are untied," Chloe pointed out.

He glanced down. "Geeze. Thanks." He bent and tied the laces. He patted his face. "My glasses, where are they?" He fumbled at the zippered chest pocket, pulled out a pair of black framed glasses, put them on, glanced around. His spare pair.

"My eyes always take a minute to go back to being myopic after I shift to human."

Shift to human, Chloe noted. He used to say, *go back to being human*. But that was the way things were now.

"Too bad you can't keep your wolf vision when you're human," Ming said.

Calvin shrugged. "Well, my corrected human vision has some advantages over wolf vision, so I'm glad to have it. Good thing I've gotten a few pairs of these, though."

"Did you find anything out there?" Chloe asked.

Calvin adjusted his glasses. "It's odd. I didn't find any trail that was recently used. I caught human scents from far off. There was something else though, something, not quite a smell, not quite a sound, sorta of a taste of the night."

Ming snorted. "Is that the technical term?"

Calvin looked at Chloe pleadingly. Ming always seemed to throw him off balance.

"Does the night leave a taste?" She asked him.

He swallowed. "Not that I'd noticed until recently. More like an echo." He frowned. "Sorry, I know I'm not making sense." He kept his gaze on Chloe. "An essence? A resonance?

You guys know how when you're outside sometimes, in the middle of the night, with the stars twinkling overhead and darkness all around like a cloak, that you feel the night's presence?"

"Didn't know you had poetry in you," Ming said, without sarcasm.

"Hey, I love poetry," he said. "I've read tons. All the classics, both in English and Mandarin. My Grandmother Hui would give me poetry books all the time I was growing up, for birthdays, Christmas, Chinese New Year."

"My grandparents are all third generation," Ming said.

"Glad you are sharing a cultural moment, but can you stay on track, please?" Chloe asked, trying to keep the tension out of her voice. She shuffled her feet. She wanted to find Russ. Now.

"Sorry," Calvin said. "There's a weird vibe out here. Night might be the wrong word, but it's that feeling you get when the world suddenly seems spooky."

I think I get at what you're saying," Chloe said. "But we're still in daylight."

"I know, but," he nodded in the direction of a rampart of tall firs that lined the mountainside on the far end of the lake, "but under those trees, it felt like night was there with me."

"What about Russ's scent?" Chloe couldn't keep the worry out of her voice.

"Sorry, I lost it once I rounded the lake. It was strong, then it just stopped."

"Just stopped?" Chloe asked. Calvin should have been able to keep following Russ's scent. Scent trails usually lasted for a while, especially a fresh one.

"That doesn't make any sense," Ming said.

Calvin nodded. "No, it doesn't. I can't figure it out." He pushed his glasses back up his nose. "There's one more thing. That spooky scent of night is really strong there. It might be obscuring Russ's smell."

Ming shook her head. "You're really not making sense, you know that, right?"

"Sorry. I can't explain it any better than that. But, you know how our wolf senses are stronger at night?"

Chloe and Ming both nodded.

"So, we all need to go there once night has fallen," she said. "Or, at least begin following the trail again after dark."

Calvin sat. "I need to go over something with you. Might as well sit for a bit, since we have to wait for nightfall."

The three of them sat together.

"I've been thinking about the slain deer you found in the big tent," Calvin began.

That was the last thing Chloe wanted to think about right then, but she forced herself to listen. "Go on."

"It looked like a ritual sacrifice," he said.

Ming snorted. "Damn messy one."

"It was, and I think that was part of the ritual." Chloe and Ming both stared at him. "I got interested in ancient religious practices when I was in college, as part of my archeology studies. Anyway, the markings on the deer bodies and the weird triangle burned into the floor surrounded by a circle of iron dust seem ritualistic."

Ming bit her lip. "You've got a point." She shuddered. "But who would do that, and why?"

"Satanists, maybe," Chloe said.

"Modern ones wouldn't break into someone's tent and then ritually kill a deer," Calvin said.

"Then, who?" She asked. The other two didn't answer. They sat beneath the sprawling branches of the huge maple tree, lost in their own thoughts for a time.

A searing boom echoed behind them, in the direction of camp. Another boom, followed by a crackling, like the Devil's own fireworks.

She jumped to her feet, began undressing. "Something's happened back at camp." They all shed their clothes, shifted into wolf form and ran between the trees, back toward camp.

Chapter 7

IT WAS a slow crawl through the rainforest. We had to keep stopping so that Fakira, aided by Tully, could magically search for our Level Three. Driving made locating the supernatural difficult, especially with so few arcane signposts. Simkins got increasingly annoyed that we hadn't been able to get a fix on Wolf-dude. He called five times in two hours, the last two times magical hologram-style.

His annoyance boiled over when we drove down a very unimproved gravel road with potholes so huge you could lose a dragon in them. I navigated the SUV around the worst of the holes. Behind us, Tully wasn't so lucky. The Crown Vic bounced up and down like an ancient battleship in heavy seas. After a mile of this, the Vic's headlights flashed.

My arcane phone chimed. A 3-D image of Simkins appeared above the screen, sweat streaming down his flushed face. "Pull over, Marquez. Now."

I parked the SUV in a dirt turnout beneath young pines, and Tully pulled the Crown Vic in behind us. Fakira and I got out and walked to the back of the SUV. Simkins threw open the Vic's passenger door and staggered out. For a moment, I thought he was going be sick.

He loosened his tie. "This is going nowhere. We're just getting bruised and banged up."

Tully walked over with his usual panther-like grace. "It shouldn't be this hard to find a Level Three out here in daylight." He rubbed the back of his neck.

"I concur," Fakira said.

"Interference. Something's making it very hard to track manifestations out here," I said. "Or someone."

"Iron Circle," Fakira replied.

Simkins massaged his closed eyes with his thumbs. "As much as I hate the idea, it's looking more and more like a real possibility."

Coming from Simkins, that was practically a full-on apology.

Fakira was graceful about it. "We need to do a ritual casting."

Simkins glanced at his watch, an honest-to-heaven old Timex, complete with silver wristband. "We've got maybe six more hours of daylight. Can you do it in two?"

"Three would be better," she said. "But two will do."

That was the problem with ritual magic, it took freaking forever.

"Good," Simkins said.

"The catch is we'll need to drive again," she said.

Just like that, Simkins's scowl was back. "Why?"

"I found a vibrational node."

It was my turn to massage my eyes. That was Thaumaturgy, which was the arcane equivalent to advanced calculus. Really advanced calculus.

"You only just discovered this out now?" Simkins groused.

"I'd been correlating the inclines and differentials while Liz drove," Fakira replied, her voice calm. She must have had plenty of practice handling irate R.U.N.E. managerial-types, one of my least favorite activities. "We could do it here, but the vibrational node is a much better location," she explained. "If my suspicions are correct, we'll need the spell topology there to help pierce the obfuscation network that the Iron Circle has set up here."

I was a veteran sorcerer-agent, and I only understood half of what she just said. Clairs had the thirty-thousand foot view of magic. We sorcerers worked on the ground floor. Memorizing spells was hard enough. Figuring out the geometry of the arcane—no thanks.

Simkins scratched the back of his head. "Okay. Let's go there."

We piled back in the vehicles. Fakira directed me, her eyes closed, hands resting on her knees, palms facing up, with fingers and thumbs touching in a classic meditative pose. It took an hour, but eventually, we stopped at the top of an overgrown dirt road above a bramble-filled hollow.

I parked the SUV, got out and crossed the road. My eyes widened. A gabled rooftop, shrouded in moss poked up from a stand of tall hemlock. One turret had caved in. The rest of the house was hidden behind trees.

Tully stepped beside me. "Weird place for a house."

Fakira tapped her arcane phone. "Apparently a millionaire arranged to have it built in the 1920s." She looked at Simkins and smoothly answered his unspoken question. "This is from my phone's own knowledge genii. I certainly wouldn't attempt to contact the greater ones back home."

Simkins nodded. "Is that abandoned house the basis for the vibrational node?"

She peered intently at the ruins. "It seems likely, especially given that their magic draws strength from the derelict and the discarded, and the effect such places have on all of us."

"Should we investigate the house?" I asked.

"That might be unwise," she replied. "It might set off an alarm."

"Or cause a disturbance in the magical force," Tully said.

I grinned and pointed at Tully. Hey, I was a fan. Sorcerers had lives, too, though working for R.U.N.E. made me wonder, given the hours we kept.

Fakira laughed quietly. "Something like that."

Simkins just shook his head.

She turned to Tully. "I'll need your help, John."

"Whatever you need," he said. Was there a slight hitch in my partner's normally unfazeable voice? Methinks Tully might have been smitten.

Fakira turned to Simkins and me. "Our summoning will likely trigger apparitions."

Simkins nodded. "Marquez, you've got sentry duty. I'll play bodyguard."

"Will do," I said. No more time for jokes, things were about to get real serious real fast. Summoning a manifestation was always risky. Fakira and Tully would need protection because they both had to concentrate. If the summoning went wrong, there would be an angry supernatural to deal with. Plus, there was always the possibility, however unlikely, out here in the sticks, that the summoning would draw other manifestations. I'd been on the lookout for those.

Fakira took out an old-style steamer trunk from the SUV. We placed it in a clearing hidden from the house behind a rampart of sword ferns. She and Tully sat cross-legged, facing each other on a black woolen blanket. A silver pentagram medallion the size of a hubcap between them on the blanket. Silver pentagrams were embroidered on the blanket's edges. Incense burned from a bronze brazier beside Fakira. She and Tully's arms were spread wide, around the circle of the pentagram, clasping halfway. Their eyes were closed, and they chanted in Latin.

The air hummed softly, and the space between them wavered, like air over asphalt on a hot day.

The sun had gone down, and twilight had begun.

I paced slowly outside the circle, wand out, scanning for anything that might show up on us. Simkins leaned against a pine trunk and watched the calling without expression.

I'd just finished my latest circuit when the air rustled between Fakira and Tully. A dark, bat-winged form hovered there. It looked like a fruit bat to me, but after a moment I could see it was a foxlike creature with bat wings. A seekie. Its eyes were huge, bulbous, and the blood-red tongue flicked out like a whip.

I wetted my suddenly dry mouth.

A memory from the Academy surfaced. Me, freaking out when my lab partner summoned a seekie, as part of a final year exercise in locating hard to find manifestations.

I clenched my hand, trying to keep myself from running. What was it about seekies that got to me? My fear must have been obvious because I glimpsed Simkins frowning at me. I took a breath, nodded at him and tried to look calm.

The seekie chittered and Fakira chittered back. It chittered a second time, then flew in widening spirals around us, trailing faint silver light. Fakira and Tully continued chanting. The golden glow around them grew increasingly tinged with purple as they pulled more mana in to fuel their spell.

Now was when things were likely to get supernaturally hairy.

I marched myself into the trees, wand out, and began muttering a detect spell in Portuguese. Nothing like what Tully was capable of, just a first alert for manifestations. The tip of my wand glowed faintly silver.

Nothing. I began my circuit again. Minutes ticked by. I stole glances at Fakira and Tully as I patrolled.

A howl split the air and I stumbled backwards, smacking into a tree. So much for the detect spell. Another howl erupted to my left. I scrambled back up on my feet, grabbed my R.U.N.E. issued amulet.

A silver gray furball on two legs, hair standing straight up, looking like he'd just gotten fifty thousand volts, stalked toward me, snarling.

"Banish!" I said in English and snapped my wand. The tip changed from silver to bright gold, and a spell flew at the manifestation. It vanished it in a shower of purple mana particles.

I turned in the direction I'd thought the second howl had come from. Flung off another spell.

Something turned purple in the darkness.

I let out my breath. *Hammer and tongs*, I swore, *that had come on fast.*

I turned back toward the others, but a wolf-man stood between me and the clearing.

I pointed my wand at it, fighting the trembling in my hand. "Banish!" I said in Slovakian. It came out as a croak. The third banish of the day, and my last. Any spell could only be cast three times from dawn until the next dawn. That was one of the laws of magic.

The sphere of golden light smacked into Wolf-dude most scary and shattered into a million golden pieces, not one particle of purple among them. No mana.

Its muscles flexed.

I was going to have to bind it. And fast.

The manifestation's muscles all compacted, like a coiled spring.

Everything seemed to slow down. My brain raced, trying to get the binding spell together. I began chanting in German, my left hand stroking my silver motorcycle boot chain on my left shoulder.

The wolf-dude uncoiled with a thunderous series of snaps, its howl shredding the air. The monster of Filmland wolf man had become a rage-filled primal beast, with muscles stacked on top of muscles. His gray fur had become a deep red.

Cursed abyss, I swore silently. "Bind to me!" I shouted in German, but my words were muffled by the explosion of sound. A wall of fur and teeth hurled at me.

The spell shot from my wand, chains of silver engulfing the creature. It slammed into me. I hit the ground hard. Its mouth yawned wide and red. This was no temporary manifestation.

I willed mana from the air around me and into my spell so fast my temples began throbbing fiercely. "Cease!" I spat in German. The creature froze. "Up," I managed to croak out. Get off me."

It rose, shaking visibly, fighting against my binding. I balled my fist, sending more mana into it, strengthening my spell.

I brushed sweat from my eyes with the back of my left hand, my right kept the wand centered on the beast.

"What to do with you?" I muttered at the manifestation.

It glared at me, its eyes full of fury. There was no question what it would do with me if I set it free. It was too solid for me to banish. It was easily a level four on the permanency scale. But where had it come from, and how it had transformed so quickly into this primal form?

"Who turned you into rage wolf?" I asked. It certainly wasn't me or the rest of my team. We were trained to control our subconscious. That was the first thing they taught us in the Academy.

Altered beast didn't answer.

I marched us back to the clearing. Fakira and Tully still sat facing each other, eyes closed in concentration.

"Glad to see you have *that* secured," Simkins said, pushing himself off the tree trunk he'd been leaning against. His wand pointed in my general direction, but wasn't yet aimed at the manifestation.

"May I present altered beast," I said, tugging at the spell leash. The manifestation's low growl made my teeth vibrate.

"One moment," Fakira said. "There. I've anchored my connection to the arcane web." She and Tully both stood. She turned around, gaze taking in the thing. "Fascinating. A primal wolf-creature manifestation. So much rage inside it."

"Altered beast has a lot of unresolved anger," I agreed.

Tully groaned. "Funny, Liz."

"Can we please stay on task," Simkins said.

Party pooper.

Fakira considered the manifestation. "It's definitely connected to the Iron Circle's arcane web."

Her face took on a faraway look. "Wait." She closed her eyes, whispered to herself. "There's another disturbance," she said at last.

"Where?" Simkins demanded.

"Just outside of Aberdeen."

Demons dance, I swore silently. Aberdeen was a good sized town in the Olympic Peninsula. A supernatural outbreak there would be disastrous. Wolf-men, altered beasts, out and out wolves, and maybe even a bigfoot or two for good measure.

Simkins wasted no time. "Okay, people, let's move. We've got to stop that before it crashes the everyday." R.U.N.E.'s first dictate was to protect the everyday, the reality that the vast majority of people existed in, and not let the arcane intrude.

Fakira had not moved. She stood with her eyes closed, obviously still tracing the arcane contours of the Iron Circle's web.

The rest of us waited. Simkins opened his mouth, closed it again. The altered beast thrashed against my leash.

"Contain that thing!" Simkins hissed.

I whispered a hold spell in Old English, and the creature froze. I wiped sweat off my forehead. "That's a good, altered beast," I muttered under my breath.

Simkins began pacing. Even Tully looked worried. Time was wasting.

Fakira opened her eyes. "Sorry, that took longer than I wanted." She turned to face Simkins. "We have a second problem."

"Why do problems always come in pairs?" I asked.

He ignored me. "I'm guessing it's also ugly?"

She nodded. "I'm afraid so. The Iron Circle is in the middle of a very powerful ritual spell, not far from here. I wish I could be more specific."

Simkins rubbed his face. "That would be helpful." He stared off into space for a moment. "Okay, Tully, you and I will go to Aberdeen. I'm going to put in a call to the office and have a burner team meet us there." Burners destroyed the arcane. There wasn't a teleportal in Aberdeen, so the team would need to fly there from Seattle. "Marquez and Hassan, you'll need to find out what's up with that ritual and keep me posted. The problem is, the regional office is stretched thin at the moment. The two of you will need to deal with this one on your own."

"Are you taking the Crown Vic?" I asked, hoping he didn't stick us with it. I much preferred the new model SUV.

"No, we're not. It will remain here, locked. You'll have the SUV."

I squinted at him. "But how will you two get to Aberdeen?"

He ignored my question. "Wait here," he told Tully. He strode to the Crown Vic and returned with the battered brown leather brief-case he had that morning. "You are not to mention what you're about to see to anyone," he said. He laid the brief case on the ground, squatted beside it, and reached for the latches. A sudden breeze ruffled his striped tie.

I couldn't resist. "Very cryptic of you, sir, given that we don't know what we're agreeing to not talk to anyone else about."

He refrained from unlatching the briefcase. "I'm serious. This is that important."

"I swear I will never mention this to anyone," Tully intoned.

"I swear it, too, will never mention this to anyone," Fakira said.

"Likewise," I said. Simkins scowled at me. "I swear never to mention what I am about to see to a living soul," I said, making my voice as emotionless as possible.

Simkins rolled his eyes, then unlatched the briefcase. Inside was a scroll tube, the old-fashioned kind, in brown leather with brass stopper, lying in a molded gun-style case in a deep red color. Silver R.U.N.E. pentagrams embossed each corner of the case. He pulled the scroll tube from its molded holder, closed the briefcase and got up.

My nose twitched. I smelled ozone. From their expressions, so did Fakira and Tully.

"What you're about to see is ultimate secret level," Simkins told us. "Remember the oaths you just swore and be bound by them."

My mouth was suddenly dry. "Yes, sir," Fakira, Tully and I said at the same time.

He unsealed the stopper, which swung open. Hinged. Very fancy. He drew out what looked like an ivory-yellow vellum scroll. My eyes widened. That wasn't vellum.

It was dragonskin. The shed skin of a dragon that had molted was extremely valuable and rarely given to any human, especially since dragons were said to molt only once a century. R.U.N.E. must have paid through the nose to get that dragonskin.

"Unseal," he said in Latin. The dragonskin scroll unrolled and as it did, it reshaped itself into a metallic bronze door, set inside a bronze frame. The air around the door wavered, like heat waves above asphalt on a scorching afternoon in the Mojave.

"A portable teleportal," Tully said. "I didn't think that was possible."

"Officially it still isn't," Simkins replied.

I snapped my fingers. "Ozone! You used the portable teleportal to meet us at the *Lakeside*. I knew the teleportal network didn't reach there. But how did you bring it with you?"

"It's a diminishing-use artifact," he said.

I gave him a blank look.

Fakira apparently understood. "First use lets you bring it with you."

"Yes. The second leaves it behind."

"The third must destroy it," she finished.

"That's right," Simkins said. "Which is why under no circumstances whatsoever are you to use this. It's a unique device."

"Understood, sir," Fakira said.

He nodded at Tully. "Let's go."

Standard teleportals were part of a network forged by the dragons, with each end anchored on a specific location. This apparently could be used to go anywhere, which made it very powerful. And very dangerous.

Simkins opened the door, revealing the familiar looking midnight black corridor that stretched toward a glowing golden doorway.

"Good luck," I said.

"May fate favor your endeavors," Fakira said.

"Thanks," Tully replied. "Good luck with yours." He stepped into the corridor and vanished. Simkins followed. A moment later the door closed, and the scroll rolled up. Fakira picked it up from the ground and put it back into the scroll tube, stoppering it. She put that back in the briefcase and latched it.

I sighed. "Just you and me. What's our next move?"

"Help me roll up this rug. Then, let's check out that ruined house."

"You mean the one down there that might be alarmed and dangerous?" I asked.

She smiled grimly. "There's no might be about it."

Chapter 8

CHLOE-AS-WOLF PANTED as she raced through the woods, her two companions charging right behind her. A thousand scents filled the forest, calling out, but she ignored them. She had to reach the rest of the pack. Something threatened. The pack must be protected. They were close now. A blue dragonfly flitted past her, reappeared, swooped ahead of her, moving impossibly fast, then and streaked upward and out of sight.

The human part of her protested at the pace. *Wolves trot for extended distances,* it reminded her, *they don't run for miles.* She pushed that thought aside and kept running.

She plowed through undergrowth, vines whipping at her, and then burst out on the far side. The camp was nearby now. She finally slowed to a trot. Her human side recognized the stench of brimstone mingled with hot iron. She stopped, still panting hard. She had to shift. Her human side would make sense of this.

She willed the shift. Her fur disappeared and her bones shifted until, naked, Chloe shivered in the twilight air. With the transformation her lungs had stopped burning. She rubbed her skin to warm it. A moment later Calvin and Ming appeared, naked and shivering as well.

Chloe led them to their clothing stashes. The combined brimstone and hot iron stink still filled her nostrils. The silence terrified her. What had happened to the rest of the group?

She reached the giant sword fern that sprouted from an old tree trunk, and found the spare backpack she'd hidden there. She dressed quickly and rejoined Ming and Calvin, who were also now clothed. She led them around the huge maple and into the clearing.

She gasped. Where one of the tents had been, there was a fallen, scorched wreck.

The body of a man sprawled beside it, the coppery tang of blood thick in the air. He wore a long, black woolen coat and a heavy wool shirt and trousers, also black. Tattoos covered his shaved head, runic symbols Chloe didn't recognize. Beside him lay a splintered wooden staff, both ends capped in iron. The man's throat was slashed. Blood spattered his coat and shirt.

Chloe bit back bile. Today had become blood-soaked. Ming covered her own mouth and glanced away.

Calvin knelt beside the man. "Dead, obviously," he said, his voice sounding flat, emotionless. *A year of medical school*, he'd said. "Cause of death likely exsanguination from the throat wound."

"He looks like someone cosplaying a video game wizard," Ming said. She turned away again, gagging.

"He does," Calvin agreed.

"Where are the others?" Chloe asked. She trudged away from the tent. Then she spotted

Max, propped against a tree, pressing a big padded bandage against his left side. Blood covered his chest and face.

Kat rushed from her tent, holding a first aid kit. She spotted Chloe. "You're here!" Tears welled up in her eyes, but she continued running over to Max to kneel beside him.

Angel emerged from another tent, carrying a bottle of water which she brought to Max.

"Where's Tyler?" Chloe asked, a lump in her throat.

Angel's expression went cold. "Dead." She pointed at the ruins of the tent. She uncapped the water bottle, helped Max sip. He coughed, spewing water on her, but she ignored it.

"What happened?" Chloe asked.

Angel jerked her head in the direction of the corpse. "I heard him ordering Tyler, trying to get him to obey, like you would a dog." She spit in the dead man's direction. "Tyler wouldn't. "That bastard then roared something in a language I didn't understand. Tyler yelled that he couldn't move. Max, Kat, and I ran to help him. The bastard turned and tried to command us with his voice. He stopped us for a moment. Tyler broke free and transformed. But that wizard or whatever he was pointed his staff at Tyler." She swallowed. "Flame geysered from the staff and engulfed Tyler. He ran into the tent, but it was also on fire and collapsed on him. He howled. I hope to never hear that again." She knuckled her right eye, and moisture wetted her cheek. "I broke free and threw a knife at the bastard, hitting his arm. He whirled around, and Max charged him with an axe, slashed his throat. That's when his staff or whatever it is splintered. Max got hit in the side by a big splinter and maybe a bunch of small ones."

Calvin squatted beside Max and examined the wound. "It's deep," he said. Internal organ damage." Kat stifled a sob.

Chloe and the others clustered around him. He was pale, drenched in sweat.

"Transform already," Angel spat. "Don't die."

Chloe knelt beside him next to a quietly sobbing Kat.

His breath was a series of shallow gasps. Going into shock.

"Do it," Chloe told him.

He coughed weakly. "I'm not sure I'm strong enough to shift. You all are sounding distant now."

If he didn't transform now, he'd die.

"It might not be possible," Ming whispered in Chloe's ear. None of them had been this injured when they'd shifted before. And, it did take vitality to shift. Vitality that was quickly ebbing away from him.

She unbuttoned his shirt, while Angel pulled off his shoes and socks. Together, they removed his pants and briefs.

"Transform," Kat said.

Max ignored her. His eyes had a faraway look.

"Max," Chloe said, trying to get him to focus, but he kept staring off into the distance. "A lot of men would kill to have three women get him undressed."

A faint smile crossed his face, then faded.

"Please," she whispered in his ear.

"Okay," he mumbled, but his eyes closed.

No. No, he couldn't die. Not like this. Not ever. No one else in the pack could die.

"I can save him," an unfamiliar voice said from behind Chloe.

About Chloe's age, with long black hair, and gray eyes that seemed to stare into her soul, he leaned against a pine. His brown flannel shirt was open, revealing a thick carpet of chest hair, which didn't hide the fact that his chest and abdominal muscles were very well developed. His blue jeans were clean and new, as were his hiking boots.

She sniffed the air. He smelled of musk and earth. He smiled, his white teeth dazzling. Her skin tingled.

She could smell the wolf in him. It drew her, but she pushed the feeling away. She crossed her arms. "I don't know you."

"I'm of the wolf, like you."

"Since when?" Angel demanded.

"That's hard to say."

"Try."

Strangers were dangerous. He was a stranger, Chloe told herself. Her body replied that he was familiar, one like them. She could see it in the way he moved when he stopped leaning and ambled across the clearing. The musk smell became stronger.

The stranger gazed down at Max. Max's eyes were closed, and his breathing was shallow. "He doesn't have long. Let me help save him."

Angel shot Chloe a warning look. "We don't know this guy. He just shows up now, and we're supposed to let him "help" Max. How?"

"We have to do something," Ming said.

Angel was right. This was crazy. Trust a stranger? Max would die if he didn't shift, but he was too weak.

"Help him," Chloe said. "Please."

The stranger nodded, crouched beside Max, and placed his palm against Max's chest. For an instant Chloe thought she saw a barely visible purple aura flash around the stranger, and a subtle gleam of silver light from where he touched the skin.

Max inhaled loudly and his body shimmered, golden light infusing his flesh. He blurred and then a brown-black wolf lay there. There was no wound in his side. Max-as-wolf stood up and trotted off into the trees, returned, and darted around Kat, making little playful yips.

The stranger watched Max's wolf antics. "You see? All it took was sharing some of my own vitality."

"How did you do that?" Calvin asked him.

"Does it matter, in the end?" His voice had deepened, become more resonant.

Calvin stared off into space. "No. What matters is that you helped Max heal. Thank you."

"Hey Cal, you okay?" Ming asked him.

He smiled. "I am." Max trotted up to me and Calvin ruffled his fur. "Max is healed. That's what counts."

Max darted back to Kat and circled her. She laughed, tears of joy streaming down her face.

Ming smiled back at Calvin. "You're right." She laughed softly. "This is wonderful."

Angel sidled up to Chloe. "This is weird, right?"

"Yeah, it is," Chloe replied.

"What should we do about it?" Angel whispered the question

"Get some answers to start with." She turned to the stranger.

"Who are you?" Chloe asked him.

"August." The name rumbled up from deep in his chest. It sent electric fire down her spine. She hungered for him, wanted him so badly it hurt. It was so sudden it knocked the breath out of her.

"You two need a room?" Ming asked lightly. "Or maybe the rest of us should just clear out?"

August turned his primal gaze to the other woman, and Chloe felt the fire leave her body. She blinked. What had just happened?

Ming laughed. "That's not going to work with me. I like girls."

Chloe shook herself. "What did you do?" she asked, her voice rising. Her blood pounded in her temples. It was like waking up from a night of binge drinking, which she'd done exactly twice in her life.

August's expression turned apologetic. He held up his hands. "I'm sorry, ladies. Sometimes, the heat is too much for me."

"How did you do that?" She asked. Her chest tightened. That had been scary.

He spread his arms wide. "Honestly, I don't know. It's just who I am. I felt a connection to you, and I could tell you did as well to me."

"But I don't know you."

"Yet. But, more important, I can help you. I heard you earlier, talking about your missing pack member. Together, we can rescue him."

Chloe narrowed her eyes. "Who has him?"

"The same people who have my own pack."

"You're kidding me," Ming said. "You mean, there's more of you?" Chloe expected Calvin to have a thousand questions, but he simply listened, as did Kat.

"Yes. You're not alone," August told them.

"How come we haven't seen you before now?" Angel demanded.

"I had a dream about this area," he replied. "I brought my pack here. There are four of us."

Chloe exchanged a glance with Ming. He said he'd had dreams that told him to come here. Just like Russ.

The idea that her pack wasn't the only pack, that the eight of them weren't unique, started a storm of conflicting feelings inside her. It had been the eight of them for three months. Now Russ had been kidnapped, Tyler was dead and August arrived to help them.

"What happened to them?" she asked August.

"I was out scouting yesterday, and when I returned to our little camp, my other two packmates were missing. I followed their trail that led to a wooden lodge. There were people there, people dressed like the mage." He pointed at the corpse. "They had staves and were casting spells on my packmates, and one other." He described Russ.

"What were they doing to them?" Ming asked.

"Making them change to wolves, commanding them, making them change back. One of the mages was writing in a big book."

A shudder ran through Chloe.

"Together, we can rescue our brethren." August sounded so confident. She felt that confidence fill her. How did he do that? Her blood began pounding in her ears. Her wolf side urged her to shift. She yearned to shift, to run free, but she hesitated. They needed to use their human intelligence to solve this.

Chloe looked at the others.

Kat's hand ruffled Max's fur. "Let's transform. We need our wolf side."

Ming smiled. "Yes!"

Angel scowled. "This is all pretty damn sudden," she said. "We don't know you."

"Look inside yourself," August sang, "and you will find me there." His voice rang out. The music reverberated in Chloe's mind. She felt her wolf's urging to shift again.

Angel's expression turned inward. She closed her eyes and hummed. "We are one."

Calvin nodded, folded his glasses, put them in his shirt pocket, and began undressing. Angel and Kat followed, then Ming.

"Don't fear our connection," August sang. "It makes us power-ful. Let us shift and free your friend and mine. Let us greet the rising Moon." He blurred into a huge black wolf with glittering eyes. The others followed, leaving Chloe alone in human form. Max and Kat darted around her.

Chloe sensed them urging her to shift. She hesitated. The others watched her expectantly, wolf eyes glowing. *But eyes don't really* glow, she thought. A dragonfly flew out the gathering night and landed on her hand. It was outlined in faint silver light.

Chloe's wolf side spoke in her mind. *Let me come out*, it said, *and together with the others we will save our packmate. Night is my time.*

I must stay human, she thought. August had somehow bewitched the others. She needed to convince the others to rejoin her, break free of whatever this was. She shook herself. "Listen, change back," she urged the others. The pack watched her, not moving.

The dragonfly fluttered across her field of view and hovered in front of her.

The silver light outlining it spread out until it was all Chloe could see. She tried to shield her eyes, but the light came through anyway.

She shook herself, and her fur ruffled. The night air was filled with a myriad of smells. Moss, sour and slightly acidic. Pine needles with their sharp tang. The smell of decaying plants and ancient bark and a thousand other scents. The world was truly alive now to her wolf, revealing so many aspects hidden from her human side.

One of the others chased its tail, while the rest continued watching her expectantly. Especially the newest member, glorious in his midnight black fur.

She trotted beside him, yipped. He returned a yip and then took off at an easy lope.

She trotted after him, her muscles loosening into the easy stride. Beside her, the others followed in single file.

Chapter 9

FAKIRA WALKED AHEAD OF ME, chanting. A nearly invisible dome of magical energy surrounded us, just the faintest gleams of silver indicating magic. It was an arcane stealth spell, which made us invisible to magical detection. It had taken Fakira two hours to create, because the ritual spell was far more potent than the one she and Tully had cast earlier. That was after the hour she'd spent probing the arcane contours of the ruined mansion and vicinity. The Iron Circle had conjured three layers of magical detection. All were inanimate, but of course, like all manifestations, alive in the supernatural sense of the word.

It was the second part of twilight, the nautical phase, and Arcturus twinkled orange in the west while Vega shone blue-white nearly overhead. We slow-walked the quarter mile of the pot-holed drive and stopped at the wrought-iron gates topped with spikes. A ten-foot-high stone wall, also topped with spikes, ran around the mansion

Altered beast yanked at the leash spell. The edges of the leash turned purple as I pushed more mana into the spell.

"Naughty, naughty," I said, wagging a finger at the manifestation. I twirled my wand. *"Dominatio,"* I said in Italian. "I thrust my will upon thee."

Altered beast's eyes widened, then went slack.

"I liked you better when you were wolf-dude," I told it.

Fakira came to a stop and peered intently at the gate.

"It's gotta be trapped," I whispered. "Right?"

She didn't answer. Seconds ticked by until it had been a minute, then another. I fought not to fidget, and instead kept my focus on altered beast. So far, he obeyed the leash.

Fakira broke the silence at last. "There are iron dragonfly sculptures flanking the front door to that mansion. I sense more on each of the building's far corners, hidden from this perspective."

"Are they alarms, traps, or both?" I whispered.

"Both. I'm trying to get a lock on all five."

"Five?" I asked.

"The fifth tops a lightning rod on the roof." She pointed up at the roofline. Yup, there it was, looking like a freakish metal sculpture, iron dragonfly perched on top. "We couldn't see it from the hillside because of the trees between the hill and the house."

"The iron dragonflies must be artifacts," I said. I relaxed a little. At least they wouldn't be able to move.

"Not exactly," Fakira said softly. "They are forged manifestations."

I groaned. "Stupid me. I should have realized." Forged manifestations were a specialty of the Iron Circle mages. Not artifacts nor truly animate manifestations. Instead, they were artificial supernatural creatures that could be made inert and activated as needed. It took a lot of blood sacrifice to fuel such nightmares.

"I can't bind them," I said. "There's too many, I've never tried to bind a forged before, and besides, I've still got altered beast in tow."

"It's a problem," she replied. "Let me think on it."

I shut up and waited. More time passed. This was a highly unfun situation we'd landed in. I glanced at altered beast. It waited, motionless. I looked closer. It wasn't exactly motionless. Its fur rippled, the hairs tinged copper. *Copper.* That wasn't good.

Fakira still studied the house, hands on her hips.

"Psst," I hissed. "Take a look at altered beast." Tully would have at least shot me a look of annoyance, but Fakira calmly focused on the manifestation, whispered something too quiet for me to make out. Her eyes widened.

"Your 'altered beast' is connected to sacrifice magic. Copper being the color of that. The Iron Circle shaped its creation."

"You mean, a forged?" I asked.

"No. It's a full animate manifestation, but it's creation was shaped, augmented might be a better way of putting it, by sacrifice magic.

I frowned, thinking. "Why didn't I see that before?"

"It's very subtle. Our proximity to the Iron Circle's arcane web makes the connection more vivid. I suggest having a shackle ready, in case your enhanced anthro-wolf suddenly reacts to being physically close to the web."

I pulled up a shackle spell from memory. It would take a lot of mana, especially if altered beast suddenly went berserk, but better than having our throats ripped out.

"Can we get inside the mansion?" I asked Fakira.

"I just harmonized my stealth conjuration with the iron dragonflies."

"Just like that?"

She smiled. "Just like that."

"That rocks," I said, which produced a wan smile from Fakira.

"We still have the gate as an obstacle," she said.

I rubbed my chin. The gate was at least nine feet tall. The lock on the gate itself was grapefruit sized. The key for that had to be huge.

"The lock's not magical," Fakira said.

"No, just gigantic." We'd need a ram to get through the gate. Then the light bulb went off. I turned to altered beast, flicked my wand, pulling on the magical leash. I pointed at the gate.

"Charge!" I ordered it.

Fakira waved a warning "Elizabeth, wait!"

But it was too late. Altered beast slammed into the gate like a half-ton linebacker. Metal screeched and the gate flew open.

"Voila!" I crowed. The supernatural pounded toward the mansion's front entrance. "Stop!" I shouted, but the creature's focus on carrying out my first command must have deafened it to my second.

"Marquez!" Fakira yelled.

"I know!" I pulled back my wand arm to snap out a shackle spell. "I chain thee to me!" The spell traveled the length of the leash in two shakes, reaching the rampaging anthro-wolf just as it thundered up the steps. Unfortunately, momentum applied to supernaturals, and it crashed into the double-doored front entrance. There was a distant sound of splintering wood. The doors flew inward, the right-hand one coming off its hinges and disappearing inside.

I winced. "Oops."

"Now they will know there are intruders," Fakira said. "Unless they don't have a modern security system." She laughed, the tension leaving her voice. "Given how dark the interior is, the place probably has no power. Especially since the Iron Circle dislikes modern technology."

We reached the steps and stopped. The mansion's interior was dark.

Fakira pulled a flashlight from one of her coat pockets and shone around the inside.

I gasped. The interior had been hollowed out into a huge three storied amphitheater-like space. Fakira turned her flashlight on the floor, revealing an iron equilateral triangle thirty feet to a side, embedded in the marble floor.

"That's a lot of iron," I said. An iron circle surrounded the triangle. The circle's outer rim glowed with a copper light. "This place practically vibrates with sacrificial magic. I wonder where all the mages went?"

"The answer lies within," she said.

"I was afraid you'd say that."

Chapter 10

THE DARK FOREST flowed past as the pack trotted forward. August's midnight black wolf beside Chloe as together they led the others. They crossed a stream, went up a slope and then down again toward a clearing. August knew where to go, and she happily trotted alongside him. Whatever her human side had worried about had vanished with the shift, leaving her content. She could taste the night. It was like a cool mountain lake filled with mysteries.

There were new wonders to notice. Spectral birds and flying serpents in the night sky, and ghostly creatures like tiny humans with gossamer wings that fluttered around the pack, then vanished, only to return and vanish once more. There was a great reddish glow ahead of them, like nothing she'd ever seen before.

He suddenly broke into a run and streaked ahead of them to the clearing.

She ran, too, but when she reached him, he had transformed, the night breeze sending his long raven black hair streaming behind him. He smelled musky and welcoming. She slowed her easy lope to a trot, then the change came over her without her willing it.

Chloe shivered in the night air, naked. The ground was rough against her bare feet.

August stood before her and smiled. He wore a sweater, jeans and hiking boots. His hair was pulled back in a ponytail. She tried to recall if that's how he was dressed before. It seemed important to know even though she wasn't sure why it was important.

The rest of the pack blurred back into being human, and naked. Ming rubbed herself. "It's freezing here."

"No shit," Angel groused.

Chloe whirled back to face August. Anger cleared away the cobwebs in her mind. "We should have taken our time. We've left all our gear and our clothes and boots behind."

A dragonfly hovered nearby, this one bottle green, its multifaceted eyes shining silver. The air warmed, became hot. Chloe looked away, throwing up her arm. The air boomed, and then there was a flash of brilliant golden light. She bent over, covered her ears, eyes squeezed shut.

The golden light faded, and darkness returned behind her shut eyelids. Someone said something. She strained to hear, her ears aching from the boom.

She opened her eyes, blinked to clear them.

"You didn't leave your belongings behind," August said. He pointed at their backpacks lined up near where the dragonfly had hovered. Their clothes lay neatly folded in piles on each of their backpacks, atop their shoes.

"How the hell did these get here?" Angel demanded

"Don't look askance at a gift, isn't that the saying?" August replied.

"Don't look a gift horse in the mouth, you mean," Ming said. She went over to her backpack, began to dress.

Chloe shivered. "Ming's got the right idea." She strode to her own backpack, and began pulling on her clothes. The others followed suit.

"That's a neat trick," Calvin said, buttoning his jeans. "How did you manage it?" He asked August.

"I didn't," August said.

They all stared at him, mouths agape.

"That's a whacko thing to say," Angel grumbled.

"Gift horses, right? They are here, isn't that what matters?"

"But things don't work that way," Calvin pointed out. "Physics doesn't allow for quantum tunneling or whatever this might have been, not with everyday objects. An electron, maybe, but not something on the scale of a backpack.

August's expression showed no hint of comprehension of what Calvin had just said.

"Those are the rules," Angel said, annoyed. "Even a dropout like me knows backpacks, clothes and shoes don't just magically reappear from miles away from where you left them."

"They didn't, August said. "My friends brought them."

"What friends?" Chloe asked. She pulled down her sweatshirt, looked around warily. "I thought you said mages had taken Russ and your friends. "So, who are these friends?"

A blank expression came over August. He cocked his head, as though he were listening.

"Old friends who are here to help us rescue packmates," he said, his tone flat.

"That's creepy," Ming said, taking a step backwards.

"Definitely freaking me out," Angel agreed.

Calvin adjusted his glasses. "Your story has changed." He turned to Chloe. "This is all wrong."

Chloe glared at August. "Why are you lying to us?"

Behind him, a few hundred yards away, moonlight illuminated a high-roofed wooden building on a low hill. The building looked like an old-style Alpine lodge. A broad wooden porch ran along the side facing them.

"Where did that come from?" Calvin asked.

"It was hidden by my friends," August replied.

Chloe's muscles tensed. This was all wrong, all lies. People stood on that porch, their figures indistinct in the shadows beneath the roof.

"Are those your friends?" Chloe asked.

He nodded. "They'll be yours, too."

She balled her fists. "No." She turned to the others. "This is wrong. We need to find Russ."

"My friends and I can help you find him." August's tone was insistent.

A dragonfly outlined in silver light landed on August's shoulder.

Its body was jet black. Its wings were veined with black, and its multifaceted eyes were an iron color. It was like looking at a sharp-edged lump of coal. The air had a sudden whiff of something hot and metallic, with a tinge of sulfur.

"What's that smell?" Angel demanded.

August ignored her question. "Come with me, packmates, and meet my friends." His words rolled like quiet thunder over them. He waved at them. "Come with me." He turned and began walking across the meadow toward the lodge. Kat and Max followed him. Ming twitched, and strode after them. Calvin did likewise.

The power of those words pulled at Chloe. Her legs wanted to follow the others.

"No! Don't listen to him," she shouted. She punched the air.

She ran after them, grabbed Calvin's arm. "Calvin, snap out of it!" He continued to walk toward the lodge, his face expressionless. She dashed to Ming. "Ming, it's some sort of mind control."

"Screw this!" Angel shouted behind her, turned and sprinted back the way they had come.

"There's no reason to worry," a voice said.

Chloe looked around, frantic, but there was no one there.

"We will help you," the voice said. Moonlight illuminated a bony-faced woman striding toward her, holding an iron-shod staff like the man who had died at their camp had used. Another mage? Before this day, the only magic she'd known was shifting. This was something else. Something mysterious and dangerous.

"You have more power in you then you realize," the woman said. She wore a long black coat, just like the dead man had worn back in camp. As the woman passed August and the others, she held up her staff and said something in a language Chloe didn't recognize. The air glowed copper around her and then Ming and the rest were wolves once more.

"The light of the full moon increases your power ten-fold," the woman said, her voice like a curtain ripping. "I can help you harness it."

"Haul ass!" Angel shouted behind her. "You can't save them if you get captured."

Chloe turned and sprinted uphill toward a stand of Hemlock where Angel had gone.

She reached the tree line, gasping for air and forced herself to get inside the wood, so that the trees would hide her. If anything could hide her from mages that used dragonflies to cast magic spells. She bent over, breathed in lungfuls, while her heart pounded in her ears.

Angel joined her and stood silently nearby while she regained her breath.

The full moon's glow seeped around the hemlocks, touching ferns and underbrush here and there with silver light.

She touched Angel's arm. "Thanks for yelling at me."

"Sure. But, Chloe, what're we going to do?"

"I don't know. Let's head deeper into this wood. We need time to think about what just happened."

They were alone out here. Even if they hiked all the way into the little rustic fishing resort, who would believe them? More than that, who could help them free their shifter packmates from magic?

Chapter 11

"I DON'T LIKE THIS," I said. Fakira and I stood back-to-back in the middle of the circle-and-triangle, the amphitheater-like space dark around us. "Dead center in a sacrificial thaumaturgy is the last place I ever wanted to be."

"Not an appealing place for me, either." Her back was warm against mine. I had my wand out, while she held a scry crystal. "Uncover," she said in English. Soft golden light illuminated the vast room. The place was completely bare. Mold covered the walls and tendrils of moss hung from the distant ceiling.

I made a face. "Disgusting. But that's the Iron Circle for you." They were all about creating nasty reactions in the subconscious.

I felt Fakira shift slightly against me. "Now comes the hard part," she said.

"Retroactive," she chanted in English. The floor began to shimmer with a copper light that warred with the soft golden glow of the Uncover spell.

"Retroactive," she repeated, this time in French. Indistinct images began to swirl around us. I felt her shift slightly once more, as she readied the third casting of the spell.

"Retroactive," she said, the third time in Mongolian. At least, I think it was Mongolian. That was her final uncover. We could use a spell three times in one day. Each time needed to be in a different language. Each language put a slightly different emphasis on how a spell worked.

Fakira inhaled sharply, and I felt her wobble. Three spells repeated so quickly, in order to pull forth the memory of what had happened here, must have been utterly exhausting.

The images steadied and resolved into a scene.

"Three months ago, tonight," Fakira intoned.

A huge iron bowl stood in the center of the triangle, filled with blood. Mages stood at each of the iron triangle's three points, while more watched from beyond. Torches blazed in a great arc around the vast space. Deer corpses sprawled in a far corner of the vast room.

Fakira's Retroactive spell brought to life a rush of sensations and emotions. Smoke made my throat itch, and the scent of freshly spilled blood roiled my stomach.

Moonlight shone down through a skylight directly above the blood-filled iron bowl. An image appeared above the bowl. A tour van, late at night, bounced over a rough gravel road. Fir trees rose in a wall on either side. The logo on the vehicle's side proclaimed, "Olympic Generations: Young and old seeing the rainforest together." Then the imaged shifted to inside the vehicle. Sixteen people filled the passenger seats, a mixture of young and old, just like the logo said.

The driver apologized over the intercom. "Sorry again folks, we should be in Forks soon for the night, and then off to the coast in the morning now that our unexplained mechanical problem has been fixed."

A smattering of tired laughter at the driver's announcement. Someone groused about being stuck for hours and still being out at midnight. The driver apologized again.

The headlights suddenly shone on a colossal phantasmal dragon blocking the road.

The driver swore and braked. A tire suddenly exploded, and the van careened sideways and rolled over, tumbling into the phantasm.

Moonlight flooded down on the wreck, mirroring the moonlight flooding down on the huge iron bowl. Smoke seeped from the van's sides. The driver and half of the passengers were dead. The survivors pulled themselves out as the light brightened in intensity until it hurt to watch, and I was forced to look away. When I looked back, the Retroactive had ended and the vision was gone.

"Abyss be cursed," I swore.

Fakira was silent. I took a step away from the center of the circle and turned around. She still held her scry stone, which glowed gold, but now also had veins of copper light shining within it. I wet my suddenly dry mouth and swallowed.

The scry stone abruptly went dark and Fakira swayed. I grabbed her to help her stay standing.

"Hey, are you okay?" I asked. I was an idiot. Of course she wasn't okay. "You look dead on your feet."

She took a deep breath. "You could say that. But that's not important. What we saw was a ritual from three months ago. It's definitely the source of your "wolf-dude" manifestations, and what I had sensed before coming to the rainforest."

"Hey, good work."

"There's more," she said wearily. "This ritual is temporally paired with the ritual happening right now, the one the seekie uncovered. And now I know more about that one: it's a ritual of ensnarement."

I didn't like the sound of that at all. "Do you know where it's occurring?"

She closed her eyes, concentrating again. "Perhaps twenty miles through the forested hills, but far longer by car."

"Not good. We might be too late. Do you know how many are being ensnared?"

"I can't give you any more details than that," she said. "Sorry."

"We'd better get there pronto," I said. "And I know how we can do it."

"Supervisor Simkins expressly forbid us from using the temporary teleportal."

I shrugged. "Sure he did. But he didn't know about this. We need to use our initiative."

"We should call him," she said, but I could tell she wasn't enthusiastic about the idea.

"I'm fine with asking for forgiveness after the fact," I replied.

She laughed weakly. "You must do that a lot." She swayed again.

I grabbed her a second time to keep her upright. "Do you have a rejuv potion?" I asked.

"Yes, but I'd rather not drink it. I'd be unconscious after dawn."

"I think you'd better." As a clair, she probably didn't redline herself often.

She didn't protest. She drank the potion down. The color came back into her cheeks, and the twinkle returned to her eyes.

"Instant recovery," I quipped.

She nodded. "However, if this adventure lasts long enough, you may have to carry me back here."

I kept quiet about having already drank mine. We were all in now. "Let's set up that teleportal."

A few minutes later the dragonskin door was open, revealing the familiar black tunnel. The rising Moon shone beyond the far side of the portal.

"I'll go first," she said. "You have to manage your manifestation."

She stepped through.

My captive had stood stock still during all of this. "Come on, chuckles," I told it, and tugged the spell leash. It followed, glassy-eyed.

I stepped into a moonlit meadow and altered beast followed. Behind us the teleportal folded in on itself with an audible popping sound. The air crackled. There was a black spot blacker than black which faded away seconds later.

The full moon hung low in the east, above the rampart of trees in front of us. The meadow we stood in sloped down to the right. Maybe a half mile away stood an alpine lodge on a low rise. Two groups of people stood in the meadow down there near the lodge.

Fakira joined me and looked at the scene below. "Definitely the mages. Do you see the spell lines?"

I squinted. "Just barely." A glowing triangle surrounded by a circle encompassed both groups. The second group blurred and became wolves.

"*Demons dance*, did you see that?" I swore.

Fakira's voice was grim. "The mages are manipulating those people."

"Those are humans? Not manifestations?"

"Yes." She sounded very certain.

She was the Clair and could see the arcane to a degree I could only dream of. "How is that possible?" I asked.

Fakira looked up at the full Moon. The Sturgeon Moon it was called. "Somehow the Iron Circle set up a sacrifice ritual that harnessed the Moon and the mana that flows from it."

The Moon was huge in human culture, mythology, biology, you name it, and thus a powerful element in the collective human subconscious. Which explained wolf-dudes. But that was different from being able to directly affect humans.

"Just like that, a law of magic is broken," I said.

"Perhaps bent is more accurate," she replied.

I took a deep breath. I didn't like what I was about to say, but we both had a duty to protect the balance between the Hidden supernatural and the greater world. "We need to stop that ritual. Now." The problem was, we were heavily outgunned. "I count six mages, and their ensnarement looks to be already well underway."

"It's worse than that, now that I can see it close up," Fakira said. "The shifters, for want of a better term, have been in the process of being magically ensnared for weeks. This is the culmination of that process." She thought for a moment. "I noticed an arcane incline from the ritual site to another vibrational node of supernatural power in those wooded hills above us. The node appears to be fueling the ensnarement. Severing the connection at the node would interrupt the spell, and give the ensnared a chance to escape."

"But how do we sever that connection?"

She closed her eyes, concentrated. "Free whatever is in the node."

"The node originates from a manifestation?"

"I'm not sure what it is, only that it's alive."

"Then we'd better get searching," I said. "Come on, altered beast." I tugged on the leash. He still might come in handy and if not, he needed to take the Oath of the Compact, or accept the consequences, as the Second Law of Magic stated.

"You don't have to pull so hard, beautiful," said a deep male voice, like melted chocolate. I whipped around.

Primal altered beast was no more. The manifestation was now a super-hunk, in flannel shirt, jeans and hiking boots. His black hair swept back from a killer handsome face with high cheekbones and wide set eyes. I couldn't decide if he were native American or Latino. His dark-eyed gaze smoldered at me. An electric tingle ran down my spine.

"Gah!" I took a half-step backward, nearly dropping my wand. "What happened to you?"

His smile turned mischievous. "I sexy-fied myself, beautiful." He looked at Fakira. "Lucky me, to be in the presence of two such visions." He blurred and shifted into a golden-brown timber wolf. The wolf radiated sensuality.

"All right, buster, time to cool it." I turned up the compulsion in my binding. I was going to pay for that later with a headache, but then again, later I would be unconscious, thanks to the rejuvenation potion I had drunk earlier.

Sexy wolf stiffened and blurred back to super-hunk incarnate. "Okay, okay, I'll dial it back," he said. "Ease off."

I pulled back on the compulsion. Anything to get out of earning a headache for pushing that spell too far.

"Let's get to those trees," I said. We strode toward the wood. "Why did you transform?" I asked the manifestation.

"I had to let the wolf out, babe."

I rolled my eyes. "No, I meant, why did you change from a primal mountain of lupine fury to this?"

He put a hand on his chiseled chest. "The world shapes me."

I looked past him at Fakira.

"The manifestation is responding to something in the collective subconscious here," she explained.

That made a crazy kind of sense. First he was wolf man right out of an old movie, then altered beast, a primal lupine thing out of a video game, and now he was sexy wolf, like the popular conception of hot werewolf shifters.

We reached the wood, ducked into the shadows there. I stopped under the eaves of the Hemlock trees, letting my eyes adjust to the darkness there.

Moonlight dappled branches, grass, and fallen tree limbs, but I still couldn't see well.

"I can take the lead, beautiful," the manifestation suggested. "No trouble for me to see in the dark."

"Not exactly keen on that idea," I said. "How are you going to know where to go?"

"You can trust me, babe," his tone was like velvet. "I can smell magic after all."

"You're a comedy legend in your mind, too," I shot back.

He gave me a hurt look. "But I *can* smell magic. In my wolf form."

"Actually, he has a point," Fakira said.

Super-hunk brightened. "Trust a beautiful lady such as yourself to recognize an open heart."

"Ick," she said, and looked at me. "Let him lead, and I'll put a hand on you to see through your Binding to him. I can give him instructions on where to move."

I smiled. "That's an excellent idea. Super-hunk becomes super-natural hound." I gestured ahead of me with my wand. "You heard the lady, transform and lead on. Just keep it at a walking pace."

He blurred back into sexy wolf, sniffed the air. He started forward, deeper into the woods, heading north. Fakira put her hand on my shoulder and walked behind me.

About fifty yards in, there was a clearing where a hemlock had fallen years ago, and I glimpsed a massive cliff to the north, in the direction we headed.

"Are you still tracing the connection?" I asked her.

"Yes. It's headed toward that cliff."

"I hope it doesn't lead to above the cliff," I said. "I'm really not up for scaling that."

We went on for a few more minutes. We reached another fallen tree clearing. Sexy wolf suddenly stopped and sniffed the air.

"Something's there," Fakira said. "Something supernatural."

Chapter 12

CHLOE AND ANGEL walked deep into the wood, finally reaching a dark glade where they stopped.

"We can't just leave the others," Angel said.

Chloe leaned against a tree trunk, crossed her arms. "I know. We have to do something."

"Those mages are creepy as hell. Like that dude back at the camp, only these are very alive."

Angel was right. How could the two of them take on six of those?

They talked about options. Going for help. Changing and attacking. Sneaking up and trying to persuade the others. None of it was good.

The Moon crested the tree ops and the glade brightened. The moonlight called to Chloe. *Change*, it urged. *Become your true self*. She could change and free the others from whatever those people were. Find Russ. Restore the pack.

She felt the shift begin. The urge was even stronger than the past two full moons. She started to reflexively unbutton her flannel shirt. The button was cool and smooth in her fingers. She ran a tip over the flannel. Glanced down at her hiking boots.

"No," she said. "I need to *think.*"

Angel trembled beside her, a shaft of moonlight spearing her. Her trembling grew. "Screw it," she muttered," and blurred, her clothes ripping. The boots slipped off her hind legs. Angel thrashed and was free. She faced Chloe. Her wolf lips pulled back in a snarl, which started deep in her thick throat.

The moonlight turned Angel's yellow eyes bright gold. The snarl grew louder.

"We have to think, *Angel*," Chloe said, fighting to keep her voice level. "We can't just give into this side of ourselves. The pack is both wolf and human. What did Russ always say? Use both sides of ourselves."

Angel's snarl faded. The wolf form shimmered and sparkled in the moonlight, and then Angel rose up on two legs, her naked human figure white against the shadows.

"Damn, it's cold out here at night," she said. "Why did I give into that freaking Moon? Now my clothes are ruined."

"But you listened to me," Chloe said.

"First time for everything, huh?" Angel shivered. "It's August. It should be warmer than this."

"Nighttime in the mountains," Chloe said.

Angel started to say something, but something crashed through the ferns. A branch snapped.

They both crouched in tall grass and peered into the darkness. A golden-brown wolf padded into the clearing. Chloe's eyes widened. Was it a packmate, escaped from the mages? She didn't recognize it. Angel tensed like she was going to stand up.

Chloe put a hand on her arm. "Wait," she whispered.

A woman in a black motorcycle jacket, jeans and Doc Martens stomped into the glade, followed by a second woman wearing some sort of head covering and a much more sensible outdoor jacket, along with hiking boots.

The first woman took a few more steps further into the moonlit glade, and Chloe could see her features. She had tousled raven black hair, bangs covering most of her forehead, and wideset eyes. A boot chain glinted silver on one shoulder pad. She held a thin wooden something in her right hand. Chloe's eyes narrowed.

A wand?

The second woman's headscarf was illuminated by the moonlight now. A hijab. She held a fist-sized gemstone in her left hand. It glowed softly gold. After a moment, she noticed coppery gleams in the glow.

Chloe stiffened. The two women must be mages.

The wolf sniffed the air, then trotted into the underbrush on the far side of the glade. The two mages followed, and the group disappeared.

"Mages," Chloe whispered.

"You think?" Angel said. Nice she hadn't lost any of her sarcasm.

"I do think," Chloe said.

The corner of Angel's mouth crinkled in a fleeting smile. "Who was that wolf? You don't think it was just a wolf, do you?"

"Not by the way it acted," Chloe replied.

Angel rubbed her arms. "So, it's a shifter like us."

"Maybe. Maybe it's one of August's packmates. Assuming he wasn't lying." She didn't know what to think about August.

Angel frowned. "He was full of it. I could smell his bullshit from a mile away."

"But what if he's bewitched by those mages, just like our pack?"

"What do we do if he is?" Angel asked.

"Break the spell. And find Russ and rescue him. Do you think he's actually in that lodge?"

"Hell no."

Chloe sighed. "Me, neither. Which leaves us back to where we started."

"We could trail those two mages and hit them from behind," Angel said. "We'd transform first, so we'd be attacking them in wolf form. We could free the captive wolf, too."

"Risky," Chloe said. "But I don't know what else we could do.

Just then, the undergrowth rustled again and the golden-brown timber wolf reappeared, followed by the two women.

The dark-haired one in the motorcycle jacket stopped in the glade, wand out. Her gaze found Chloe.

"Hello there," she said. "Don't worry, we're not here to harm you."

Chloe and Angel both stood up.

"How can we trust a mage?" Chloe asked.

The woman in the motorcycle jacket exchanged glances with her companion.

"Under the circumstances, being forthright is the best course," the other woman said.

"You're right." The first woman reached into her pocket, pulled out a thick wallet, opened it, revealing what looked somewhat like an old-fashioned sheriff's star-and-circle.

Chloe's eyes widened. "Why do you have a pentagram in your wallet?"

"Because we're sorcerers," the other woman said. "I'm Fakira Hassan, and this is Agent Elizabeth Marquez."

"Magic is our bailiwick," Elizabeth said.

"Are you connected to the people out in the meadow?" Chloe asked, tensing. Her heart raced. Beside her, Angel looked like she was about to shift back to wolf form.

"No. We're actually trying to arrest them."

Angel snorted. "You're magical cops?"

"Yeah, sorta," Elizabeth said.

"We've been lied to by others today. Why should we trust you? Maybe this is another trick."

Annoyance flashed across Elizabeth's face.

"Your wariness is understandable," Fakira said smoothly. "You don't know us. We've told you our names. What are yours?"

"I'm not telling you," Angel said, a menacing edge to her voice.

"You'd look more dangerous if you had a stitch of clothes on you," Elizabeth said.

Angel gave her a nasty look. "My other side really wants to say hello."

"Can't keep it under control?" Elizabeth taunted her.

"I'm in control," Angel retorted. "When I shift, you'll know I mean it."

"Angel, back off, okay," Chloe said. She ignored Angel's answering glare. "I'm Chloe, and you already know she's Angel."

"First names only?" Elizabeth asked.

Angel jabbed a finger at her. "We don't need your permission!"

"No, you don't," Fakira said, and smiled sympathetically.

"It's what we go by," Chloe said, omitting, *in our pack.*

"We can help you," Fakira said.

"August claimed he could help us, too," Chloe said. "How do we really know that you aren't with those mages, and just trying to ensnare us?"

"We're not mages," Elizabeth said. "We're sorcerers. There's a difference."

"We don't know that," Angel retorted. "August said he was like us."

Fakira's eyebrow went up. "August?"

"The shifter that came to us this morning and offered to help us."

Angel spat. "He put some kind of spell on us."

The two sorcerers exchanged glances. "Sounds like a manifestation," Elizabeth.

"A what?" Chloe asked.

"It's complicated."

The moonlight seemed suddenly brighter. The two magical cops shielded their eyes. *Change,* the Moon urged Chloe. *Change.*

"Nobody tells me to change," she heard Angel mutter.

The air crackled, showering faint purple sparks everywhere. Elizabeth stumbled backwards and fell.

The golden-brown timber wolf, which had been silently watching the whole time, blurred, shifted.

A devastatingly handsome man with long flowing black hair, dressed in a muscle shirt and tight jeans and black leather boots, smiled at Chloe. "Don't listen to them, ladies," he said.

"You remind me of another liar," Chloe said, hands on hips. "Who are you?"

He grinned. "An admirer. Change with me and let's ditch these two-legs."

"Not so fast, buster." Elizabeth rose up and pointed her wand at the stranger.

Chapter 13

MY TAILBONE ACHED like Hades from landing on it. I pointed my wand at the rebellious manifestation. "Not so fast, buster."

The little sneak gestured at Chloe. "Come beautiful, help me against these mages."

Chloe gave him a disbelieving look.

"Lash!" I shouted in Portuguese. Silver tendrils shot from my wand and encircled the manifestation. He arched his back like I'd just run fifty thousand volts through him, which, magically speaking, I had. That headache waiting for me was going to be nasty.

Super-hunk's too-sexy-for-his face smile contorted into a hideous rictus as pain shot through him. Supernaturals felt pain.

"Mercy!" He screamed.

I snapped my free hand's fingers. "Rebind," I said in Lakota.

His expression went slack. I wiped sweat from my forehead with the back of my hand.

The two women stared at me in horror.

"If they don't listen, there's not much else I can do if I want to keep them around."

"You mean there's worse?" Angel said, her voice incredulous.

"Destroying them. It's a last resort, but they have to behave."

I turned back to formerly-known-as-sexy wolf. "Do you swear to obey the laws of the Compact, not harm humans, and to coexist with stability and balance?"

His gaze focused on me.

"Take the oath and coexist," I told it.

"Please," Fakira added.

"Since you beautiful ladies request it, how could I not?"

I rolled my eyes. "Then get on with it. Say you swear."

He opened his mouth to speak. He howled. I winced and covered my ears.

Chloe and Angel blurred and altered right before our eyes. Chloe's shirt and jeans ripped into shredded as a red wolf with amber eyes came into focus. I took a half-step back. Fakira did likewise. Angel had shifted into a gray wolf.

"The manifestation, it's linked!" Fakira aimed her wand at the still-howling supernatural. "Illuminate!" An arcane link suddenly became visible, a coppery blood color, shaped like a chain which stretched off into the night in the direction of the Iron Circle. "He's linked to the mages. I hadn't perceived it before, it must have been triggered by an implanted spell."

Dual bound. No wonder he acted so erratically.

"Their binding is too strong now to be severed," Fakira said.

The two wolves watched me. "I wish I could tell you there was another way," I said.

The bound shifter manifestation convulsed, caught between the compulsion of the oath he had been about to swear and the mages.

"I'm sorry," I whispered. He may have been obnoxious, but permanent manifestations were alive. My stomach tightened. I wasn't a burner, but all binders knew the command spell to destroy a bound manifestation. There were consequences. Anyone the manifestation was connected to would experience a sharp pain.

"Dissolve," I said in Russian.

The supernatural reared up again, the howl turning into an ear gouging shriek. Skin blackened and its clothes burst into flames. The link turned to spectral fire.

The mage at the other end just got hit with agony so intense it would make them shriek like the dying manifestation. It hit me between the eyes, and I stumbled. Fakira managed to stay upright.

My shoulders slumped. Eldritch horrors, that hurt.

"I had no choice," I told the wolves.

Chapter 14

"HOW ABOUT YOU FOLLOW US?" the woman named Elizabeth told Chloe-in-wolf-form. Chloe sniffed the air. Elizabeth was not afraid. She held out her hand. "We need to leave now," Elizabeth added.

Everything was so sharp and clear in the light of the full moon. Before, her wolf could not understand language this clearly. Something had shifted. Shifted. She opened her jaws in a smile. The two humans called sorcerers both backed up. She wanted to tell them that it was all right, that she was merely laughing. Their worry filled her nose. She nudged her clothes, and Fakira nodded, scooped up Chloe's clothes and boots and they went into the woods.

They went downhill after a while, eventually leaving the trees. Below them a stream burbled in the moonlight.

"Okay, so how do we defeat the bad guys?" Elizabeth asked. She must have been asking Fakira, because she looked at the other sorcerer.

Sorcerer. Chloe rolled the world around in her wolf mind, and marveled that it held such interest to her in this form. But it did. Something had shifted inside her. The world glowed softly white. The mother moon.

A ghostly silver wolf appeared before her. Russ! She darted to him and passed through the specter. There was no scent, no brush of fur against her nose. Sadness filled her. They had argued, but he was pack. He'd been taken. He was her mate. In wolf form, it was all so clear. *Where are you?* She asked the specter, barking softly.

Elizabeth and Fakira stared at her, as though she'd gone crazy. Loco Lobo, like Russ used to say.

She circled around the ghostly version of Russ-as-wolf. *Where are you?* She repeated. And again, Russ's spectral wolf did not answer. Was the wolf only in her mind? Then she noticed her packmate Angel staring at the spectral wolf.

Is that packmate Russ? Angel growled the question.

It is his ghost self.

The two sorcerers watched their conversation, puzzlement obvious on their faces.

"We have to go," Elizabeth said to her. "The bad guys are coming."

Chloe bobbed her head.

"You see that!" A look of triumph filled Elizabeth's face.

Let me come to you, Chloe told the wolf-phantom. *Show me how to find you. Please. We are a pack.*

That was it. They were a pack. Tracks in snow. The musk oil smell of fur and skin. The keening howl. Those were all markers of wolf kind. But there was also the indescribable, the something that made the wolves stop and watch, and be, waiting.

It was that that gave them a trail to Russ, she knew it. She must trust it, even as she needed to trust Russ for being who he was. It was the scent trail her packmate Calvin had lost, and it was more. It had a hint of…magic her human side called it.

She and Angel circled around the two sorcerers. Then started off again, deeper into the forest.

"They're headed toward the vibrational node," Fakira said. Chloe did not understand what that meant, but she saw that Elizabeth wore an even greater look of triumph than before.

"Lead on," Elizabeth told Chloe and Angel.

The trail ended at a sheer cliff face, moonlight turning the exposed face white. Twenty wolf paces away a cave mouth yawned, the inside black. Russ's phantasmal wolf appeared at the entrance, went inside. Angel sat on her haunches. Liz and Fakira appeared from the tree line, breathing hard.

"Curse the abyss," Elizabeth gasped. "Keeping up with two wolves is real work."

Fakira approached the cliff. "The vibrational node is within," she said.

"Now we just need to find the entrance," Elizabeth said.

It was time to change. Her body didn't want to, but now she needed to speak with the sorcerers, using their shared language. Last time the change had been triggered by being near the... the shifter manifestation. This time, she decided to shift, and felt suddenly free once more to do it. As though back there, her wolf side had taken over, unbidden by her, commanded perhaps by the mages.

Her skin rippled and after what felt like forever she stood, naked and sweating, on two legs once again. She stepped into the moonlight.

The sorcerers handed Chloe her clothes. She hesitated for a moment, then pulled them on, but put her boots in backpack, slung over one shoulder.

"Feels weird to be two legs again," Angel said. Angel no longer had clothes but didn't complain.

"Just remember, that this is as much us as the other form."

Elizabeth grinned at them. "I'm glad you shifted."

"Easier to talk that way," Chloe said. "This may sound crazy, but we saw a ghostly version of Russ, our missing pack leader. The phantom led us here."

"Magic is usually crazy," Elizabeth said. "But tonight is a whole new level of crazy."

Chapter 15

HOWLS ERUPTED below us in the wood.

Fakira peered into the trees. "The Iron Circle is coming, with the shifters."

"They are bringing the pack here?" Chloe asked. "Why?"

Fakira held up a hand as she continued gazing into the trees below us.

I motioned to Chloe and Angel to follow me so that we wouldn't disturb Fakira's concentration.

Angel crossed her arms and glared at me. People often glared at me, so I did what I always did when someone glared—ignored it. "What's going on?" She demanded, her voice loud and sharp.

I put a finger to my lips. "We need to keep it down," I whispered. "Fakira's concentrating."

"Fine," Angel hissed. She jerked her head at Fakira. "What's she doing?"

"Trying to put things together by reading the magical lines, so to speak."

"I don't know what that means," Chloe said. "You mentioned earlier that you're sorcerers, and somehow that's different than those mages."

I sighed. "I wish we had more time. But this has been a lunatic night." They both gave me blank looks. So much for my wit. "Okay, I'll cut to the chase. I'm breaking regulations right and left telling you what I'm about to tell you." But they needed to know, so that they understand who Fakira and I were. "Fakira and I are agents for a secret international agency, R.U.N.E., which stands for Regulating Union for Normalizing Enchantments."

"That's a mouthful," Angel said.

"Which is why we run with an acronym. Our job is to protect the ordinary world and the Hidden one from each other. Supernatural creatures manifest from the interactions between the human subconscious and mana."

They both blinked.

"Sounds insane," Angel muttered.

"It is. Sorcery is the conscious manipulation of mana. Fakira is a clair, short for clairvoyant. She can see the magical geometry of the hidden arcane world."

"What about you?" Chloe asked.

"I'm a Binder, a sorcerer who can connect to, and control, manifestations."

"Supernatural creatures if I understand you," Chloe said.

"Got it in one. The mages are bad guys who use blood magic. Basically, they use sacrifice in ritual spell castings. They've got a big ritual going here. We're trying to figure out why, but your pack is at the heart of it. You're unique. Humans can control magic, be influenced by magic, even controlled by it, but can't *be* magic. And yet, you are inherently magical."

"I don't understand," Chloe murmured.

"Neither do we. We do know that the Iron Circle was involved in the accident that created you."

Angel's face hardened. "How do you know about the accident?"

"Fakira and I saw an after-image from the Iron Circle ritual the caused the accident. We saw your tour bus hit a spectral dragon."

"I only glimpsed it for a second," Chloe said. "It was huge, like a ghost or a hologram."

"Some sort of phantasmal projection."

"Why don't you know more?" Angel demanded.

"That's Fakira's department."

"Why are they called the Iron Circle?" Chloe asked.

"Because iron is part of their rituals," I said. "They're blood mages, and iron is in blood. It's that simple."

Out of the corner of my eye I glimpsed Fakira turn and stride in our direction.

Chloe looked nauseous. "There was deer blood splattered all over the tent Russ had been in, from two slaughtered deer. We found a triangle of blood surrounded by a circle of iron dust."

"That's a sure sign of an Iron Circle ritual," Fakira said. "The mages abducted him for a ritual spell of great potency."

"They're using him to power some sort of magic?" Angel asked.

Fakira nodded. "Yes. The group below is maybe a half mile away. I diverted a dragonfly that was scouting with a lure, so that should delay them a little longer.

Chloe's eyes lit at the word. "Dragonflies! I've seen so many. Outlined in silver. Very strange. One was there when our clothes and gear teleported from our campsite to near that lodge."

"The mages are sure throwing the magic around." I eye-rolled at Fakira. "That had to be forged for sure," I said, and quickly explained what it was. "If we can get to your friend Russ, and free him, that will break that ritual spell the Iron Circle is casting. Rituals take a Hades long time."

"Why do you swear funny?" Angel asked.

Everyone was always a critic. "It's a sorcerer thing. Really," I added when she gave me a that-sounded-like-utter-nonsense look.

Fakira nodded. "I can *see* magic. The problem is, the Iron Circle sealed this place against my arcane sight."

I looked at Chloe. "But you can see your friend's ghost wolf or whatever it is."

"Yes, and he just reappeared," she said.

"Show us, please," Fakira requested.

Chloe walked along the cliff, stopped at a mass of tangled bushes.

"He wants us to go behind the bushes."

"Great," I groused. Still, we had to do what we had to do.

The bushes had prickly thorns that snagged my jacket. I stumbled into a dark cave mouth.

I held up my arcane phone. "Illuminate," I said, and the cave illuminated.

"Magic phone?" Angel asked.

"Of course."

"I should lead," Chloe said. "I can't explain why, I just should."

"That's the supernatural for you," I said. I hated to have her lead. It went against everything I'd been trained as a R.U.N.E agent. We protected ordinaries at all costs. The two wolf women weren't ordinaries, but that didn't make me feel any better. Fakira walked behind me and Angel brought up the rear.

I held my arcane phone in my left hand, and my wand in my right as we walked through a twisting maze of tunnels.

"There's mana residue here," Fakira said in my ear. "It's fading —probably a month old."

That meant a lot of mana, and probably a few kobolds were used to dig.

"Kobolds," I said.

"What are you talking about?" Angel asked.

"Supernaturals that are really good at digging. They made these tunnels." I pointed at the groves in the intersection, running around each tunnel mouth. "They do that with their claws."

After what seemed like hundred miles but was probably more like a half mile of twisting tunnels, we reached a low-ceilinged cave. The others had to stoop, but I was short enough that I could still stand upright.

Chloe stared at the far wall.

"Chloe?"

"It doesn't make any sense," she said. She glanced down. "But that's where you are looking," she said to her invisible ghost-wolf pal. She nodded and gazed up at the cave ceiling. "He says that's where we must go."

I fiddled with my shoulder chain, craned my neck to look up. "Last time I checked wolves can't tunnel through solid rock." A faint silver glow reflected from the rock. "Fakira?" I glanced back over my shoulder.

She peered into her scrying stone, silver light highlighting her skin, and whispered a reveal spell in Somali. As I watched the light turned from silver to gold. Filaments of gold spell light spread up and out, etching the rock wall with light. Patches of rock remained in shadow. Fakira's face tightened. The shadows indicated active opposition to her spell.

I drew my wand with my right hand and held my amulet in my left. How do you hide a true werewolf? I asked myself. That was what Fakira was trying to uncover. It would take a lot of power. Especially since, as tonight had demonstrated, true shifters played by a different set of magical rules than we sorcerers and the manifestations we dealt with did.

I glanced at Fakira. Sweat beaded on her cheeks. She was pushing the spell. I looked back at the far rock wall.

Misdirection. The Iron Circle was all about that. Wolves didn't misdirect, but they did glide between trees, moving silently, disappearing into the shadows beneath trees.

Fakira repeated her spell, this time in French. The golden filaments were brighter, but still didn't reveal anything more than the rock, and even then, only where the black patches weren't. Where that darkness was, not even the rock was visible.

I caught the faintest whiff of sulfur and hot metal. I looked around frantically. That smelled like dragon. I shuddered. The colossal scaled ones exuded magic through every part of their majestic, terrifying selves.

I squatted down. The smell was thicker near the rock floor. I brushed my fingers against the earth.

The stones there were warm.

Dragon magic was one way that the Iron Circle could have hidden Russ. But the Iron Circle weren't dragons, they were human.

Which meant that there was a dragon under our feet. I took a step back, then caught myself. I was being an idiot. If there was an actual dragon beneath this, it wasn't like taking a step back would make me safer. And how in Hades's name would the mages have imprisoned one without R.U.N.E., the Lodge, the Aquarian Circle and all the rest not knowing about it?

"What is it?" Chloe asked me. Her voice quivered. Her hand hovered above my arm. She'd wanted to get my attention but was afraid. Of me.

I swallowed. "The bad guys have harnessed forbidden magic to trap your friend." I glanced at Fakira. She'd finished her spell. "It's below us, Fakira. That rock wall you've been probing is some sort of super elaborate Divert." My mouth was suddenly dry. The magic seems draconic."

"Dragons aren't wolves," Angel said. "Even I know that."

I bit back a retort. No, they weren't. But I vaguely remember a connection.

Fakira knelt and examined the floor, then peered into her scry stone.

"The primal roar is the sound of all beasts," Fakira intoned. "Dragon, monster, and human all roar. So do wolves."

But, if it wasn't an actual dragon, then what? Answer: had to be a draconic artifact. *That* was something the mages could create. Not easily, that was for sure. What a nasty thought.

Fakira stood up, put away her scry stone and drew a wand from her jacket. Mahogany with brass tip. She drew a figure eight in the air above she'd examined. "Uncover," she said in English.

There was a silver ripple in the air, then low hiss. Beneath our feet a huge, scaled figure of a dragon with a wolf's head appeared, huge wolf paws and snake-like tail.

Angel jumped back, while Chloe stifled an exclamation.

"What is that thing?" She asked.

"An artifact, similar but still different than the dragonflies you saw. It doesn't move. Much."

"Is it alive or not?" Angel demanded.

"Yes," I said.

"That's not an answer."

"It's a supernatural. It's just an inanimate one. Mostly."

"The qualifier makes me nervous," Chloe said.

"It's door," Fakira said. "Or maybe hatch would be more

accurate."

"We need to get this to open. Binding plus linking," I said to Fakira. The floor was hot to the touch now. I could feel it in the soles of my boots. The others were shifting their feet. The artifact must be reacting to Fakira and me, being sorcerers.

"I'm not sure that's a good idea," Fakira replied.

"What other choice do we have?" If I could bind and link to it, I could control it.

I rattled off the spell combination, using Latin.

My muscles burned, and exhaustion filled me.

I poured mana into my spell. *Bones of the earth, you'll open for me,* I told the artifact.

Fakira put her hands on my shoulders. More mana flooded into me, overriding the sudden fatigue I felt. My muscles no longer ached.

Steam rose, and the artifact glowed red.

It wasn't going to make this easy.

I put more mana into the spell.

Gotcha, I told the artifact, as I reached deep into it, and made the connection between myself and it. *My blood is in you,* I said. *I move through you. I command you.* The wolf-headed dragon form shuddered.

Open, I commanded, and the *floor* uncoiled, and became a ramp leading down.

I started forward, but Fakira put out a restraining hand.

"One moment," she said. "Let me reactivate the stealth spell."

"There isn't time!" I whispered. "Wait, you can reactivate a spell?"

She smiled. "Clair specialty. Only works with a ritual.

She began chanting in Malay.

"Stealth spell?" Chloe whispered.

"The mages won't be able to magically detect us," I said.

Angel frowned. "What about just seeing us?"

"We'll need to hide in the shadows."

She raised an eyebrow.

"Obviously you're not a role-player," I said. Another quip fallen flat with her. She was a tough room. "They'll be busy maintaining their ritual spell. This will give us an opportunity to see what's going on. Then, Fakira needs to figure out the geometry of the ritual."

Chloe and Angel both looked puzzled. I shrugged. "It's a clair thing."

"That's your answer for everything," Angel groused.

"Tonight it is," I agreed.

Fakira finished her chanting. "We're good to go," she said. "Let me take the lead."

"Be careful on the stairway to Hades," I said.

Her eyes twinkled, and I grinned.

The ramp was narrow enough we had to walk single file. It curved down in a spiral until we reached a marble smooth floor. Fakira went first, then me, followed by Chloe, and Angel last.

"Weird thing to find underground," Angel said behind me.

"Kobolds again. They're good at polishing rocks." The walls and ceiling were as smooth as the floor. The tunnel stretched off into the distance.

Fakira started to creep forward.

It was my turn to put a hand on her arm. "Hang on. I just had a thought."

I was still bound to the dragon artifact. I put mana into the spell, and ordered it closed. The ramp coiled upwards and closed.

Angel jumped.

"I meant to do that," I whispered.

She gave me a dirty look.

"I did. Honest." I chanted a Lock spell in Italian and put it on the dragon artifact. "There, that should cover our rear for a bit," I said.

"Can't the bad guys open it with a spell or something?" Chloe asked.

"They'll have to unlock my spell first." I continued maintaining my Binding. It was going to really knock me for a loop when the time came, which hopefully wasn't before dawn, when I paid the price for drinking that rejuvenation potion this morning. Hopefully by then, we would have won, and it wouldn't matter.

Of course, I was an optimist.

Chapter 16

THE TUNNEL SEEMED to go on forever. Finally, light appeared in the distance. I turned off the illumination from my arcane phone. We crept forward. Eventually the tunnel opened into a huge hemispherical chamber, lit by pale light, like moonlight coming from the ceiling above. We stopped just short of entering the chamber and crouched down.

The light sources were three gigantic crystal orbs imbedded in the rocky ceiling, for all the world like miniature versions of the Moon. They were laid out in a triangle pattern, one orb above the center of each triangle.

"Those orbs are shining the Moon's actual light into the chamber," Fakira said.

The walls were covered in triangles etched in the rock, like a demonic version of an old biodome. The floor was black rock. There were three giant iron triangles embedded in the floor, each surrounded by a circle of iron. The three circles were inside an even larger iron triangle, also embedded, the points of which touched the surrounding rock wall. The base of the wall was iron.

The layout of this place was giving me a headache. Then I saw that there was a pit in the center of each triangle, maybe four feet across. I couldn't tell how deep. A larger pit, ten feet across was in the exact center of the chamber

"I can sense what's within each pit," Fakira said in a low voice. "The pits at the center of each triangle have a mage within them. The one to the left also has a wolf. The one to the right, also a dragonling."

My eyes widened. A dragonling? The Iron Circle were playing with fire. "That explains the dragon artifact-as-portal." Dragonlings were small dragons who could appear as human. They were diplomats and provided a bridge between dragonkind and humanity. If one died here, it would go down very badly for we sorcerers. The dragons would require one of us to die to maintain the balance between us. Wouldn't matter that the Iron Circle had kidnapped the dragonling. They would decide who would die.

"The dragonling is part of the larger ritual," she said. "I don't know how yet. I need time."

"What about the pit in the triangle farthest from us?" I asked her.

"I can only detect a mage."

Chloe and Angel had crept up alongside us. "Russ is in that far pit," Chloe said. "I sense him."

"So do I," Angel said.

No surprise, given how closely the pack was linked.

"We need to rescue him," Chloe said.

"Now," Angel added.

I glanced back at them. Their nostrils flared. They were almost shaking. It had to be related to their shifting ability.

"We'll save him," I said. "But we have to think."

"Let's kill the mages and free Russ," Angel said in a low voice.

"It is not that simple," Fakira said. "If we interrupt the ritual now, Russ, the wolf and the dragonling all perish."

I met Chloe's gaze. "We'll free your friend, and the others. But we have to be smart."

She nodded. "Angel, let's do what they say."

Angel's eyes had narrowed, and she clenched her jaw. "We got to save them."

"We will, I promise," Chloe said, and she laid a hand gently on her packmate's arm. "Together, we'll save them."

Angel exhaled slowly. Her jaw unclenched. She looked at Chloe. "I trust you, but I don't trust these sorcerers. They'll want our power when this is done."

"We don't have time for distrust," I said.

Angel glared at me. "This is *exactly* the time for that. Sorcery is dangerous, we can't trust it. Which means we can't trust you or the mages."

Before I could reply, I felt arcane pressure on my Lock spell. "Looks like the rest of the mages are here." I winced. Multiple mages were testing the Lock. "Can you hurry up getting the lay of the magical land?" I asked Fakira.

She nodded.

I gritted my teeth, aimed my wand in the direction of the dragon artifact above and willed more mana into the spell. It cursed hard to maintain the spell and talk at the same time.

"That's a good idea," Fakira said. She sounded like she was pushing a boulder up a hill. "The thaumaturgical architecture here is quite complex. It took me a lot to trace it, but I think I've got it. The ritual spell they are casting involves the death of the pack, the wolf, and the dragonling. But only if the other mages and the rest of your pack reach this chamber. But if we can hold this chamber until dawn, the Iron Circle's spell will dissipate." She paused. "Dawn is an hour away."

"Night went by fast," Angel said. "What happened?"

"Magically induced time dilation," Fakira said. "I wasn't sure until now."

"The faerie effect," I said. "Figures."

"The arcane architecture of this place distorts time. I should have guessed, but it was so well concealed. We spent hours getting through these tunnels, and it took Marquez at least two hours to get through that lock."

"This is like Fairyland," I said. "Time goes by slower in here."

A hurricane of magic force battered at my lock. "I won't be able to hold this until dawn."

"But dawn's only an hour away, and you said time passes faster outside," Angel said.

"Yup, but I'll be lucky to hold this for another three minutes of time *in here*. Trust me."

"We're screwed, then," she said, sounding defeated.

"Can't you make a shield or something inside this room?" Chloe asked.

"Neither of us are that kind of sorcerer," I said. I struggled to think while still maintaining the spell against what felt like an avalanche of magic smashing it. It came to me. "The dragonling. I can link to it through my Binding." I had bound the dragon artifact, which was connected to the dragonling. "I'll have to push mana into that link and that will take let them unlock the portal."

"I'll help," Fakira said. She put a hand on my shoulder. "Now that I have this place mapped, I can help with a shield."

"What can I and Angel do?" Chloe asked. "There must be something."

"You and Angel should shift into your wolf forms. Call to your friends. Your connection is even more powerful than you realize. That may break through the control the Iron Circle's blood magic has given them over your packmates."

"Fakira and I will be unconscious once dawn breaks," I said. "Potion redlining. You don't want to know." I glanced at Fakira, sweat running down my face in rivulets now, thanks to the avalanche pressing against my spell. "Anyway, your pack will have time to make a break for it. If that's what you want."

"What other choice do we have?" Chloe asked.

"Join the Hidden." I struggled to keep my head up. I needed to stop fueling my Lock if I was going to have any energy left to link to the dragonling. "Be part of the Compact, the supernatural order."

"Sounds like B.S.," Angel said.

"It's your choice," Fakira replied.

I reached through my binding to find the dragonling. It was easy, since the dragonling was indeed still connected to the portal. An instant later, I felt that alien, overpowering sensation that never failed to turn my skin cold and make my stomach clench.

The dragonling was in agony, but it was still draconic. The connection was faster than language. The portal went down, and the mages and their captives headed our way.

Chloe and Angel shifted and streaked past me, pelting back down the tunnel. *I hope they make it*, I thought hazily.

I have you, the dragonling said in my head. *Together we will hold them off.*

We cast a new spell, just as, incredibly, Chloe and Angel came loping back into the chamber with their packmates. If I survived, I'd have to ask them how they did it.

The spell went up. I swayed. Not long now.

Chapter 17

I WOKE up with a splitting headache. I smelled Hemlock trees. That wasn't right. I'd been underground. The light was so blasted bright, my eyes teared up.

"I can't be in heaven," I groaned. "There aren't any headaches in Heaven."

Rich laughter around me. I sat up, rubbing my eyes.

"Are you that sure you're going to get to Heaven, Elizabeth?" Fakira asked. She sat cross-legged beside me. Her eyes twinkled.

We were the Hemlock wood, and the welcoming sight of a clear, warm summer morning greeted me.

A group of people stood in a circle around us.

"Hello, Elizabeth," Chloe said. Next to her was a bearded, brown-haired man, handsome, with green eyes.

"Russ?"

"That's me. Thanks for saving me." His hand ruffled a fur of a wolf. Russ saw my glance. "He's an actual wolf. Call him our cousin if you will." His laugh was gentle.

The others smiled.

"You decided to stay," I said. My gaze found Angel.

She shrugged, and nodded at a silver-haired, blunt-featured man with sky blue eyes, dressed in a golden suit, of all things.

He nodded. "Adrian, at your service," he said.

"Lord Dragonling," I began, but he shook his head. "Please, just Adrian. After what we've all been through, I think first names are in order."

"Call me Liz."

I got to my feet. I looked at the wolf shifters. "Welcome to the Hidden," I said.

THANK YOU FOR READING "LUNATICKING," I hope you enjoyed it! I certainly had fun spending time with Liz again, as well as getting to know Chloe and her pack.

I've written a novel, Gremlin Night, featuring Liz and her partner, Tully, which you can find here at my website. I've also written a prequel story about Liz's time guarding the Silos, where R.U.N.E. keeps prisoners, and it can be found in the anthology Street Spells, linked here at my website. Happy reading!

Prowl

N. R. HAIRSTON

Chapter 1

THE WOLF SWIPED at my throat. I jumped back and held up my hands. I was a skunk. Well, I was human, I just had skunk DNA.

That meant I fought with my thiols. Thiols was that god-awful smell those with skunk DNA released when trying to get away from an attacker, but it had multiple uses.

I directed my thiols at the wolf's neck. It shot from my hands, wrapping around his throat. The thiols was purple, a clear sign I was pissed off. My thiols could be used as a spray, but I could also turn it hard, thready, like rope.

I used my thiols to lift him up, cutting off his air supply. His feet dangled, eyes wide. Those with wolf DNA had superstrength and telekinesis, but I wore a pure silver ring. It bit into a tiny portion of his neck, eating into his skin and muscles.

"What do you want?" I asked the wolf. "Because you can't have my skunk oil." To get it, he'd have to remove it from the lateral glands in my back. A painful process.

He didn't answer. I gave him the once over. He was tall and slim of frame with dark hair. His face looked rough, haggard. Most of the time when a skunk was attacked, it was for our oil. Was this guy a dealer? Did he want my oil to get high with? Skunk oil could heal anything from broken bones to gaping wounds. Vampires rubbed it on their skin and could come out in the sun.

Many used it to conceive. Some rubbed it on their sexual organs and were able to climax for hours. When heated to a certain temperature, skunk oil got you so high, you didn't come down for days. Put all those things together and you had one of the most expensive and sought-after drugs on the market.

I looked at the wolf in front of me. He was gagging now, struggling for breath. I had a target on my back because of people like him. Both drug dealers and drug users hunted skunks like me. The only way to get skunk oil was from a person with skunk DNA like myself.

Drug dealers never asked, they often snatched us off the street, holding us hostage and bleeding us dry. Skunks learned to fight at an early age.

We never made it easy. If you were going against a skunk, you'd better bring ten of your friends. Everyone knew that, so why had this guy come alone?

I heard movement from my right, but I steeled myself. I wouldn't look. I couldn't become distracted. If I lost my hold on him, he'd no doubt use superspeed to knock me out, then drain me. He *could* take my oil without draining me completely.

When you drained a skunk, you left us unable to move for months, sometimes years. It broke our bodies down, sometimes it even killed us.

Most who trapped people with skunk DNA wanted an unlimited supply of skunk oil, so they wouldn't kill us unless they didn't know what they were doing.

The footsteps on my right grew closer. I sniffed the air, dread filling my stomach. This guy wasn't alone. His whole pack had joined us.

I planted my feet on the ground, ready to fight them all if I had to.

The footsteps were right on me now. "Anise, why don't you put Greg down."

My heart plummeted to the ground. I'd know that voice

anywhere. Alec was head Alpha of the Cain River Pack. He was known for hunting down skunks and draining them of their oil.

Skunk oil was a highly addictive drug. Those who used it for prolonged periods would suffer horrifying withdrawals if they didn't get it every day.

Was Alec a user, or a dealer? I didn't know. I guess it didn't matter. He wanted to take something that didn't belong to him. He wanted my skunk oil, and I didn't see him asking nicely.

The wolves in Alec's pack formed a circle around me, closing me in. I could feel the sweat on my palms, but I told myself not to panic. I'd gotten out of situations like this before.

I still held Greg in my grip, my pure silver ring steadily breaking his body down. I took a deep breath and let him down, hoping for a quick escape. "Sorry, Alec," I said, deciding to go the humble route. "Greg and I had a small misunderstanding. It's cleared up now."

I heard low growls coming from the other wolves, could see them getting closer. My heart played hopscotch in my chest. My fingers curled at my sides. They could no doubt smell my fear. I hated that, hated being weak in front of them.

"Didn't know you guys were having a pack meeting," I said, my eyes frantically searching for an escape route. "I'll take my leave now."

"You're invited," Alec said, walking closer.

He probably heard the gulp in my throat, but I kept my head high. "I'm late for yoga. I'll catch up with you next time." Thiols swirled around my hand, waiting for one of them to attack.

Alec kept coming toward me, claws extended. His broad shoulders looked hard, threatening. His tan skin glistened under the unforgiven sun. Alec stood over six feet tall. I was only five-six, which meant I had to look up to him. His face was square, eyes a glowing orange.

He had strength and power, but Alec was also vicious. He played by his own rules and ripped out the throat of any who opposed him.

His cruelty was most brutal when directed towards those of us with skunk DNA. I took a deep breath. The odds were not in my favor, but I wasn't out for the count yet.

Angry black thiols whipped around me. If Alec got too close, it'd slice into him. He'd quickly self-heal, but it might buy me enough time to get away.

I took a step forward, not willing to show him my fear. "I said I was leaving, Alec. You got a problem with that?"

He leaned his head to the side, looking like he thought I should know better. "Anise, come on. You know how this works." He tsked at me. "You just can't mind your own business. Always sticking your nose where it doesn't belong."

I worked as a private detective. Anytime I got a lead that someone was collecting skunks, I hunted them down. A few other skunks worked at the agency with me. They always helped when asked. We'd freed many skunks from Alec and others like him. That made me an even bigger target.

Alec motioned to Tode, one of the enforcers in his pack.

Tode smiled at me. I could feel fireflies under my skin. Tode was bigger than a bear and his bite was much more vicious than his bark.

My thiols swirled around me as a warning. I looked at Alec and gritted my teeth. "If he touches me, I'll kill him." I didn't give him time to respond. These guys had superspeed. They could attack in an instant and I wouldn't see it coming.

Lethal red thiols filled the air and spread to each one of them. If they moved an inch, it'd slit their necks open. I put up a shield, pink thiols floating around me. I'd pay for this later.

Using my powers at this level exhausted me. A thiols shield was a skunk's best weapon, but we rarely used it because it depleted our energy so severely.

"I don't want to fight," I said, looking at Alec and his pack. "Just let me go." I took a few steps back. I was so focused on the pack in front of me, I didn't sense the lone wolf coming from my left.

A blur caught my eye. I turned too late. The wolf barreled into my shield. I went tumbling back, the smell of blood filling the air. My thiols shield had sliced off the wolf's arms up to his elbows.

He let out a monstrous roar and stumbled back. I hit the ground hard. The fall broke my concentration, causing my shield to vanish.

I had to act before they realized how much of an upper hand they had. Thiols shot from my mouth in the form of a silver mist. An awful, horrendous smell filled the air. It did its job. All the wolves dropped to their knees, gagging. The smell would enter their nostrils, invading their senses. Wolves had super smell. It made them even more sensitive to the horrible scent we skunks released.

I rose shakily to my feet and held out a palm. My thiols lifted Alec and his pack in the air, tossing them away from me. I swallowed hard, fear eating into my gut.

I had to get out of there. I turned to run but saw another blur. Shit. I was in trouble. Alec was head alpha for a reason. While the rest of his pack were still struggling with my thiols hold, Alec had already broken free.

Before I could get away, he grabbed me by the neck, lifting me in the air. Sweat covered my skin, my pulse banging loudly in my ears. I couldn't let him drain me. I wouldn't.

"You know what happens next, Anise," Alec said. He was smug, so sure he'd already won. His voice went low, seductive. "Why fight it?"

Blood trickled down my arm where I'd fallen earlier, and I could feel my energy waning. Still, I wouldn't give up. I wouldn't give a predator like Alec the satisfaction.

"If you want my skunk oil," I said through gritted teeth, "Then you'll have to kill me."

"Not a problem." Alec squeezed my neck tighter, and I could sense his pack closing in, surrounding me.

I was weak. The shield had taken a lot out of me, and my thiols was nearly depleted. It'd take anywhere from a few hours to a few days to build back up. I gagged from the pressure on my throat. The only asset I had left was my mind and my fists.

I went slack in Alec's grip, hoping he'd think I passed out. He grunted, then shook me a few times, before loosening his hold and throwing me over his shoulder. I was dizzy now, disoriented, but knew I had to stay in control.

I figured he wanted to take me home and drain my oil, but I wasn't down for the count yet. A skunk's claws were half the size of a wolf's. It was a laughable comparison, but a skunk's claws did have one thing a wolf's didn't.

From my position over his shoulder, I dug my claws into his back, injecting the last of my thiols into his bloodstream. The thiols was red and angry, it cut into his heart, liver, and lungs, making him gasp and fall to his knees.

The pure silver ring I wore had a tiny blade on it. I jabbed it into the back of his neck. Just long enough for him to fall over from the pain.

I took that opportunity to run. I'd only made it two feet when another wolf appeared. This new wolf was tall and broad-shouldered. He had tan skin and dark hair. His face was so chiseled, you could probably chip a tooth on it.

My mouth went dry. He was... beautiful. I could sense this new wolf was more alpha than Alec. Heck, he was the most powerful wolf I'd ever come across.

He walked with a confidence and power that had all of Alec's pack dropping to their knees and baring their throats. I needed to get away. I needed to run while they were distracted, but I couldn't.

My body wouldn't budge. It wanted to move closer, to get near this new wolf. It wanted...

This new wolf looked at Alec. "Am I late to the party?" His voice rolled over me, a deep baritone I felt all the way to my bones.

I swore under my breath. What was wrong with me? I needed to go.

"Alec?" this new wolf said. "Just what are you doing?"

Alec was on his knees, panting. His heart and liver were probably still stitching themselves back together. "Stay out of this, Brick," Alec said.

My head snapped up. Brick? As in head Alpha of the Black Wood pack? Black Wood was the biggest pack around. Its leader Brick was said to be ferocious in a fight. I'd heard a lot about Brick. We lived in the same town. I'd just never seen him up close.

Brick's eyes went to mine. His pupils dilated. I saw confusion cross his face, though he quickly covered it. "This ends now," Brick said, voice reverberating through the air.

Alec grunted, still on the ground. He must have sent out a signal to his fellow pack members because they all lunged toward Brick at the same time. Brick growled and most of them cowered back.

I saw a blur. When it cleared, Alec and a few of his pack members were on the ground. They had open wounds and gashes.

Before I had time to process the strength and power it took to injure so many wolves at once, Brick had gathered me in his arms and supersped me away.

Chapter 2

ONCE WE'D GONE FAR ENOUGH, Brick stopped moving in superspeed. He put me down but kept a strong arm around my waist.

I was thankful for that because I would've fallen over had he not been holding me up. I felt like I'd gone a hundred rounds in the spin cycle of a washing machine.

"Tha... thank you," I said after I'd taken a moment to catch my breath. Since my head no longer felt ready to explode, I took a good look around, trying to figure out where we were.

Tall trees, with long rectangular-shaped green leaves, loomed over us. The soil underneath my feet was loose and wet. Off in the distance, I saw a house big enough to hold over a hundred people. Was this where he lived? Had he brought me home to his pack?

I started to ask, but a wave of dizziness came over me and I swayed. Dammit! I'd used up too much energy, fending off Alec and his pack and now I was paying for it. I needed rest. But first, I needed to find my way home.

I swallowed hard, still looking around. Could I even make it home in my condition without getting caught by a skunk hunter?

Brick sniffed the air. His eyes went to me. "You can stay here until you're better." His features softened, but just for a second. "You'll be safe here."

I nodded, my body feeling like I'd been running a marathon for the last few years. "Thank you," I said, though I didn't plan on staying long. I didn't know this man, didn't know his pack.

One thing I'd learned was, nowhere was safe. Not for those of us with skunk DNA. If one of his pack members had a skunk oil addiction, then Brick most definitely couldn't assure my safety.

I'd stay because I didn't think I could make it anywhere safe without getting caught. I'd stay, but I wouldn't let my guard down.

Those with Wolf DNA could sniff out any feeling, any emotion. Brick must have smelled my fear. He gave me a frank look but didn't say anything.

We walked in silence until we came to the clearing that would lead to the house. For some reason, my heart beat out an offbeat, funky tune whenever I looked at Brick. I flexed my hands. It was unnerving. I didn't understand the effect he had on me and that made him dangerous. If I didn't understand it, I couldn't control it.

When we got to the front door, Brick opened it and allowed me to walk in first. He stayed close behind, probably in case I fell over. I was still very weak.

The house was immaculate. The ceilings were so high, it'd take someone with the ability to levitate to clean them. Floor-to-ceiling pictures lined the walls, and I wondered if these were his pack members.

The floors were made of mecen. I whistled low in my throat. Only those of extreme wealth could afford to build with mecen. I assumed the entire house was made of that material. Mecen could withstand, fire, wind, flooding, and a host of other things.

Most wolf packs lived a wealthy life. Wolves were immortal, so they accumulated a lot of cash over the years. They also pooled their money, so everyone in the pack always pitched in their fair share.

We walked until we came to a living room big enough to fit a few football teams in. It was spacious, lavish. Four wolves sat in the room. I swallowed hard, fingering my pure silver ring. Wolves and I had never been on friendly terms. I got along with wolves better than I did the vampires, but I was cautious around both.

Brick may have been fine, but I didn't know his pack. They looked up when we entered, though I suspected they'd smelt us the moment we'd hit the clearing, maybe even before that.

My fingers curled. I knew they could smell my fear, and it pissed me off. I hated showing vulnerability in front of anyone. I grew up on the streets. My family had been killed for their skunk oil when I'd been a small child.

My earliest memory was digging through a trash can, looking for food. I'd found out from a young age what it meant to be an unprotected skunk. I'd had to fight, every single day growing up.

I'd taken some hard hits, but I'd learned from them. Packs, especially wolf packs, meant family. I shook my head. I'd never known the meaning of the word family. I was envious of those who did.

The only reason I knew when my birthday was, was because I'd run across a few psychics and telepaths growing up. I knew I was twenty-eight years old. I knew what'd happened to my family, because no matter psychic or telepath, the story never changed.

They'd been slaughtered by a group of vampires. Killed for their skunk oil. A three-milliliter dose of skunk oil gave vampires the ability to walk in the sun for a full eight hours.

It made no sense for vampires to kill skunks. Not if they wanted an endless supply of skunk oil, but maybe these vampires already had enough skunks and didn't want more. I didn't know why my family had been killed, but I'd vowed long ago to find out one day.

I ran a hand down my face, shooing those thoughts away. It was over now. No need to keep thinking about the past.

"Hi! I'm Lati," a perky voice said, bringing me out of my reverie. I looked up to see a tall girl with purple and green hair. She was probably in her mid-twenties. She was slim with big curious eyes and a smile on her face.

My shoulders relaxed just looking at her. She appeared open, friendly. Now, that could all be an act, so I knew to still be on the lookout for any unforeseen attacks. "Well, my name's Latitude," she went on to tell me. "They just call me Lati for short. Makes it easier for them, I guess. Latitude can be a mouthful."

I gave her a tight smile but didn't say anything.

She grinned. "Yeah. I can find anyone, at any time. I'm psychic! You might not know this, but all wolves have a special power. It's decided by the bloodline. I come from a family of psychic wolves!" She sounded so proud.

I let out a slow breath. For now, I was leaning against the archway, Brick's hand on my back to keep me steady. I hated that I required his help, but I was all out of energy.

I needed food and I needed rest, but I couldn't be rude. So far, none of the wolves in this room had attacked me. I'd continue to show them the utmost respect until they gave me a reason not to.

Lati pointed to a tall dude, with thick muscles, and a scowl on his face. He was tapping away at a keyboard, not looking at anyone else in the room. He didn't seem very sociable, which was fine. I certainly understood that. "This is Corn," Lati announced. "He doesn't play well with others."

Corn let out a grunt, but he never looked up. He kept tapping on his keyboard, a furrow between his brows.

"He's harmless," Lati mouthed to me, then pointed to the guy sitting beside Corn. "This is Drift. He never stays in one place long. He likes to leave, a lot."

She shook her head, eyes now sad. "Poor Corn. What will he do when Drift finally leaves?"

I looked back at Corn. His eyes stayed on the keyboard. I raised a brow. Would Corn even notice when Drift left? It didn't seem likely by what I'd seen so far.

"You're a skunk," the last person in the room said. She made it sound like an accusation.

The air tensed in a way that said something more was going on here than I'd realized. I stood up straighter, ready to bolt if need be. As skunks, we could never hide who we were.

Even if wolves hadn't been able to sniff us out, our appearance often gave us away. All skunks had bushy black hair with white streaks. Our hair could be cut, but it could never be dyed. I'd tried multiple times and it never held.

Right now, my hair was short and spiked with the whites on the end.

"She's a skunk," the other lady said again. She was of average height and weight, same as me. Tattoos covered her body, and she had piercings on her nose and lips. She seemed angry, disgusted even.

"Spin," Brick said her name around a growl. "That's enough."

"What if Mata had been here?" Spin asked. I noticed she took special care not to look Brick in the eyes. Those with wolf DNA often took that as a challenge.

Brick said something else, but I couldn't hear him. Spin's words had put me on edge. It shouldn't matter if another member of the pack was here or not unless that member was addicted to skunk oil. From the way Spin behaved, I guess this Mata was a skunk oil addict.

I started to back away, my pure silver ring ready. It wasn't safe for me to stay here.

"No one will hurt you." Brick turned until he was staring directly at me until the only thing I could see was the yellow of his eyes.

I swallowed hard. Something about his eyes made fireflies come alive in my heart. They pulled me in, making me want to drown, to stay here forever.

No, a voice in my head said. *Danger.* "I… I have to—"

"I'll stand guard outside your room if you don't feel safe. You need to eat, and you need to rest. If you go out there now—"

"I can take care of myself," I said before he went any further with this. "I don't need you outside my door. I've survived this long without your help. Don't infantilize me." I'd love to sleep a full night, knowing I was protected, but it wasn't something I should depend on or get used to.

"Okay." He threw his hands up and backed away. "You'll be safe here. I promise."

I started to say something more, but my knees buckled, and I had to grab ahold of the wall to keep from falling over. I needed sustenance to help get my energy levels up. If I went out there now, I wouldn't be able to protect myself. I was stubborn but not stupid.

I'd eat, I'd rest, I'd regain my thiols, and I'd leave. Later, if all went well here, I'd find a way to repay Brick and his pack for their kindness.

I swallowed hard, hoping this Mata didn't come home anytime soon. Pack wolves stuck together. If he attacked, and I tried to defend myself, I could easily find myself missing a jugular.

Chapter 3

THE DINNER TABLE was packed with every meat known to man. Those with wolf DNA loved their meats. It was a myth they didn't like vegetables. The table was also filled with carrots, greens, potatoes, corn, thinly sliced tomatoes, asparagus, broccoli, cabbage, and radishes.

Everything looked delicious. I'd always been a meat and potatoes kind of girl. I couldn't wait to dive in.

I ate my food in silence, observing the packs interactions with each other.

"You know, it's usually a lot rowdier in here at dinner time," Lati said, waving a chicken bone around. "Black Wood is the biggest pack in Barebic. We have over thirty members. They'd be here today, but they're off taking care of pack business a few states over."

Drift laughed and snatched a piece of corn-on-the-cob from Lati's hand, taking a big bite of it. "Why don't you tell her which state they're in, Lati?"

She started to speak, then her eyes widened. She put a hand over her mouth. When she spoke, it was muffled. "It's pack business. You know that."

Brick's brows were drawn tightly together, but he didn't say anything.

Corn ate with a knife. He stabbed his meat with the knife, and he picked up his asparagus and threw it into his mouth with the blade. He didn't say much, only grunted now and then.

Lati smiled. I got the feeling she wanted to ease the tension in the room. "You have on sneakers," she said to me, looking down at my footwear. "Corn collects shoestrings. Do you mind leaving yours for him?"

I blinked. Was she serious? Corn stabbed a piece of beef. Drift shot Lati an annoyed look but didn't say anything.

I gulped down some water, not sure what else to do. I liked the family atmosphere they had. It was nice, how easy they were with each other. I'd never had that type of relationship before, and it was heartwarming to see.

Spin looked at me like she wanted to skin me alive. "Be out of here by morning."

Before I could answer, Brick growled, turning yellow eyes her way. "She stays as long as she wants. I won't hear another word about it, Spin."

I put down my cup and frowned. I didn't need him defending me. I wasn't used to it, and I didn't like it.

My eyes flashed silver. I looked at Spin. "Don't ever speak to me like that again. I'm not your dog and I don't take orders." I stood. "You'd do good to remember that."

Her jaw tightened. It was clear she wanted to respond, but when her eyes landed on Brick, she gripped her fork and looked down at her plate.

"Show me to my room please," I said to Brick. "I'd like to rest now."

He leaned back in his chair, staring at me in awe. He looked at me like I was something unique and different, something he'd never encountered before.

His eyes penetrated mine, all the way down to my soul, my bones. I cleared my throat, unnerved because I didn't understand the torrent of emotions that'd been steadily rising in me since our eyes had first connected.

"Follow me," he said, leading me down a long hallway.

We stopped in front of a closed door. Brick gently pushed it open. "Yours, for as long as you want it."

I nodded my thanks and walked inside. It was neat, orderly. The room was huge, about the size of some living rooms. It held a bed big enough to fit four comfortably, and more dressers than anyone would ever need.

The carpet was black, as were the walls. It was nice, cozy. I felt a sense of relief just being in there.

"This is one of our guest rooms," Brick said. "Everything's newly washed. There's a bathroom just through here." He pointed to the left side of the room. "I'll have Lati rustle you up something to wear."

"Thanks," I said, not sure how else to respond to such generosity. I wasn't used to it.

I expected him to leave after that, but he just stood in the middle of the floor, staring at me. "I've heard of you," he finally said. "You free skunks, whether they're taken by the vampires or the wolves. You're a pain in a lot of drug dealers' sides. They want you gone. For good."

I nodded along as he talked. He was telling me information I already knew. A lot of calls about missing skunks came into the detective agency where I worked. My boss didn't always take the cases.

I ran a hand through my short hair. Whether my boss took the cases or not, I always did my best to track down the missing skunks.

I'd gather other skunks and we'd go on the hunt. Sometimes I went alone. If a skunk was being held captive, I felt it was my job to find them and bring them home safely to their family.

If that made me a target for people like Alec and the vampires then so be it. I didn't regret anything. I would always do what I thought was right.

"Alec will be a problem," Brick said. "How will you deal with him?"

I shrugged. "I'll figure it out. I'm not scared of Alec."

"I know," he said, voice low. "You were pretty fierce out there, but you can't—"

"Don't do that," I said before he could finish his sentence. "I've been taking care of myself this long, so just don't."

He leaned back against the wall, arms folded. "So, shall I just keep walking the next time I see you surrounded by a dozen wolves?"

I stood in the middle of the floor, not wanting to sit on the bed until after I'd had a long bath. "If you want. Look, Brick, I'm not asking you to save me. I won't hold it against you if you don't. I appreciate that you did, but I can take it from here."

He smiled. "You have a hard head. I kind of want to knock on it."

"What?" I asked.

He held up his hands. "Not... Like in a playful way. You know, 'knock, knock.' Like that."

"You want to play with my head?"

"No. I mean..."

I watched him carefully. "You don't find that strange?"

He cleared his throat. "What I meant was..."

I leaned my head to the side. "What an odd thing to want. Do you often fantasize about playing with people's heads?"

His eyes flashed orange. "It's... Not... Fun... I mean.... It's..."

"If it's not fun, then why do you do it?" I was teasing him, though I wasn't sure he knew that.

"I don't," he said, finally coming back to the strong and powerful alpha I'd first met. He stood tall, eyes now confident. "I like you," he said. "I don't know why. I feel a strong sense of protectiveness over you. Not because I think you're weak. You've survived this long on your own."

I bit my bottom lip, trying to stay in control. I could feel my body gravitating toward him, wanting to be near him. Something in his aura called out to me. It made me want to attach myself to him and call him mine.

Bits of blue thiols swirled around my hand. I quickly hid my hand behind my back. Blue was sweet thiols. Blue thiols could make a person do whatever I wanted, but it drained me too quickly. I was nearly depleted, eating had helped, but I needed rest.

I'd had romantic partners before. Heck, I'd been with a few wolves, but nothing special. This feeling, these emotions were new, and I wasn't sure I liked them.

I looked toward the bathroom. "We'll talk tomorrow," I said.

He nodded but didn't leave the room.

"I'm taking a bath now," I said.

His eyes watched me with an intensity that left my mouth dry and made other parts of me ache. I wanted him.

He took a step forward, voice low, gravelly. "You have a good night, Anise. I'll see you tomorrow."

He left the room, taking every bit of air with him. I flopped down hard on the couch. He made fireworks explode in my heart. I'd never felt like that before. I was in trouble. I thought about his words. *Tomorrow.*

I stood, heading for the bathroom. Tomorrow wasn't a given. Tomorrow I planned on hunting down every member of Alec's pack one by one.

I'd survived this long by going on the offensive. If you came for me, I was coming for you. Alec was a powerful alpha, but I wasn't the type to bare my throat for anyone.

Chapter 4

I LEFT before dawn the next morning. I placed a note on the kitchen table before my departure, thanking Brick and his pack for their kindness. I didn't want them involved in this. Alec and his pack were vicious.

I'd hate for them to catch Lati, or a different pack member alone and exact their revenge. The fewer people hurt, the better.

Though I never left the city I was raised in, I never stayed in one house long. I'd never really had a home and I didn't have one now. As someone with skunk DNA, I was constantly on my guard.

Drug dealers and drug users hunted my kind, but they weren't the only ones. Vampires were notorious for holding those of us with skunk DNA hostage.

They hunted us because they felt they had the right to. They hunted us because they saw us as prey, prey that was vital to their existence, so why shouldn't they take us over? They never saw the person underneath.

Vampires ruled this city. All local packs had to pay dues to them, to keep the vampires from attacking. Anyone wanting to open a new business in Barebic had to get the vampires' approval first.

The whole thing left a sour taste in my mouth, but it'd been that way for as long as I could remember.

The day was cold, rainy, like the weather had reached into my heart, detected my mood, and acted accordingly. Since it was still early, not many people were out.

Barebic was a flashy place, with nice cars and sturdily built homes and businesses. Usually, only the wealthiest lived here. The cost of living was through the roof. The average yearly wage for Barebic was more than I'd ever seen in my lifetime.

I grabbed my bags from the abandoned house I'd been hiding them in and threw them over my shoulder. I'd been born in Barebic. It was my home. I didn't want to leave it. I knew this city like the back of my hand. Which made it safer for me to stay.

I'd be hunted no matter where I went, but at least in Barebic, I knew which areas to avoid. I knew which holes and crannies I could dip into if things got too hectic.

A cricket sounded off in the distance, making my ears perk up. I sniffed the air, loving the smell of morning dew.

Early morning was my favorite time of day. Everything was still, quiet, not yet disturbed by the honking of horns, or the shuffle of feet on their way to work or school.

I sat by the river and thought of my next move. Alec. He'd never stop chasing me if I didn't fight back.

I was a threat to the wolves and the vampires, because I not only freed skunks when they were captured, I often called on other skunks to help me do it.

We needed organization. Skunk hunters were dangerous to all skunks. Not many skunks would refuse a request to take out a few skunk hunters because it made it safer for them and their families with the hunters off the streets.

But we never stayed in touch after we'd freed whatever skunks were being held captive. We never tried to form a pack of our own. We were too busy trying to stay alive.

Angry, black thiols swirled around me. Alec thought he had me in a corner.

I picked up a wet piece of grass. One thing about me was, you back me into a corner and I'd tear down the whole house, town, city, or state to get out of it.

Alec probably thought I was running scared. I let out a bitter chuckle. He'd learn soon enough who he was dealing with.

I put my things in a different abandoned house, one that I used sometimes. It was private, off the road. It was through a forest, so not many people knew it was there. You couldn't see it from the highway.

I kept my money in a different spot. I'd been saving for a while now. I thought about work.

For the last two years, I'd served under a man named Jones. We took cases from all over. Jones' workload was huge, so he employed over ten detectives under him. Jones had fox DNA. Foxes were known to carry poison in their claws and saliva. Their hair color changed, depending on what time of year it was.

Jones was a direct guy. He wasn't nice, but he didn't need to be. He treated us fairly and always paid on time. I didn't have close ties with anyone at work, but we were all on friendly terms.

I stretched my arms wide, then wiped down my clothes. I'd opted for blue jeans, a white tank top, and sneakers today. I had to be able to run. Most of the time I liked to keep it simple.

I thought back to Jones. My first stop would be work. Jones employed three other skunks besides me. Because of this, our work-place was sometimes attacked.

I never left home without a weapon, but I kept some at work too. I kept pure silver for the wolves. Most wolves could shake off the effects of regular silver in a day or two. Pure silver was different. I could take a piece of pure silver, no bigger than a penny, and kill a wolf with it.

The pure silver ate into a wolf's skin. Once it got a taste, it was hungry for more and wouldn't stop until it'd burrowed through blood, tissue, and bones. Once the pure silver was done, nothing but dust would be left.

The only thing that'd saved Alec and Greg was that I hadn't left my pure silver ring on them. Had I laid it on their skin and left, they'd both be ashes right now. I didn't want to kill Alec if I could help it. I just wanted peace.

A wound from pure silver took months, sometimes years to recover from. Pure silver was only harmful to those with wolf DNA. I kept pure silver knuckles in my desk.

For vampires, I had teko. Teko supposedly carried the UV light from the sun, only magnified by a thousand. It was designed to hurt vampires. It'd been made in a lab, specifically formulated with ingredients that protected anyone who wasn't a vampire from its harmful rays.

Vampires used skunk oil to walk in the sun, but teko had been formulated with that in mind. The downside was, once the teko was removed, the skunk oil would help them start the healing process. It took a load of skunk oil to heal wounds from teko, which made skunks an even bigger target.

I also collected link chains of all kinds. I kept them throughout various places in the city, never knowing when I'd need one.

I kept a few at work. I had a link chain made of teko and I had one made of pure silver. I also had a knife made of both materials and a few other items that came in handy.

A lot of my weapons were in jewelry form. They looked innocent until you got closer. I kept a pure silver and teko ring with me at all times, but I needed more if I wanted to fight Alec and his pack.

I walked the short distance to work. It was still early, so the office was empty. We worked out of a large building in the industrial part of Barebic.

Our office, "Leather Creek Detective Agency" was sandwiched between two factories. The office itself was only as big as two living rooms, but it was enough space that we weren't constantly tripping over each other.

I walked inside, going straight to my desk. I unlocked it and looked over my weapons. I threw on a pure silver necklace and a teko one. I tucked them under my shirt. No need showing them off and attracting more attention.

I also grabbed my teko shades, sticking them in my pocket. I still had on my pure silver and teko rings, but I put on a few more.

Since Alec seemed to be on the hunt, I figured I'd arm myself before facing him and his pack again.

I grabbed a few more things from my desk, then slipped out the back, anxious to leave before any of my co-workers arrived.

I didn't want to explain why I was carrying around link chains this early in the morning. The other skunks here would probably help if I asked, but I didn't want anyone getting hurt or killed on my account.

It was different when we were chasing down hunters, freeing other skunks. I didn't mind asking for help then, but this was different. Alec was after *me*. It was up to *me* to deal with him.

Once I had my supplies, I started to plot. I'd been on Alec's radar for a while now. Because of that, I'd learned everything I could about him so that I could better protect myself.

Alec usually went for a morning run with his pack. The key was finding out where. The location was never set in stone. Probably because predictability would make his pack an easy target.

I decided to put my nose to use. It was nowhere near as elite as a wolf's, but I could follow a basic scent. Since I already knew where Alec lived, I went to his house first. Perhaps I could follow his scent from there. He lived down a long winding road, deep in the country.

His estate wasn't as big as Brick's, but it was still impressive. Alec had a pack of twenty. His house probably took up a whole acre of land.

Like Brick, Alec's house was made of Mecen. It was a dull brown, but the yard carried vibrant colors like orange, yellow, and purple. Heck, he had blooming flowers all the way up to the front porch.

I clicked my tongue. If I didn't know better, I'd think this house belonged to a wealthy, influential family, set on doing good in the community.

Luckily, I knew it belonged to a group of bloodthirsty wolves, intent on collecting skunk oil, no matter the cost. I sniffed around a bit, trying to find the general direction they'd gone.

At least ten vehicles sat in the front yard, and the scent from them kept throwing me off. I couldn't pinpoint a particular scent with any accuracy, and after twenty minutes of trying, I decided to lie in wait.

It'd probably be easier to get Alec alone, but I decided I didn't want that. Alec needed to fear me. His pack needed to understand that I wasn't an easy target. Me maiming them all in one go, would show them I wasn't the defenseless skunk they thought I was and maybe they'd leave me alone after that.

I sniffed the air. This was Alec's home. He'd be back sooner or later. When he came, this time, I'd be waiting for him, and I didn't plan on backing down for any reason.

Chapter 5

IT WAS another half hour before Alec and his pack finally arrived back from their run. I was high up in the trees, all the way on the tip-top branches.

I had shuriken daggers in my hands. They were small and round, with eight different points, made completely of pure silver.

My heart beat out a sad, downtrodden, tune. I didn't like taking things this far, but Alec needed to know I wasn't one to be messed with.

He needed to understand that if he came for me, there was a chance he'd lose a good chunk of his pack. A wolf's pack was its lifeblood. Wolves were fierce when it came to their packs.

Apparently, when they lost a pack member, the pain was worse than a thousand deaths by pure silver. I watched Alec and ten of his pack members arrive in the front yard. They started to sniff. They could tell something was off. Soon, their noses would lead them to me, but I'd be ready.

I looked at Alec and wondered if it was worth it. Would he weigh my life against the members of his pack? Were their lives worth the skunk oil in my back?

Alec's eyes went to the tree I was hiding in. Welp. I guessed I'd find out soon enough. Before he could react, I flew from the trees slinging the daggers. I used my thiols to help direct them.

The first two hit two of the wolves, knocking them back. Alec and the other eight charged, but I used my thiols to send them tumbling.

I threw the next two. That was two more down. I had to put up my shield. They were coming at me fast. I threw out two more daggers, then two more after that.

Eight wolves were on the ground now. Alec let out a roar. The air blinked. I braced myself, but Alec stopped right in front of me. I had my shield up and Alec and the two remaining wolves were smart enough not to run up against it.

I threw out the last two daggers, then, I landed on the ground in front of him. His fellow pack members made gurgling sounds, the pure silver eating into their bones and tissue.

I slung a rope chain of pure silver out. Alec dodged to the side, but I used my thiols to wrap it around his neck, anyway. It bit into his skin, lapping up blood and bone like they were candy. He fell to his knees, a look of rage and shock on his face.

"I'm just one person, Alec," I said. "You have ten pack members with you, but all of you are on your knees."

By now, the pure silver had eaten the skin around his neck and was going for the blood and tissue. "I only want to be left alone," I told him. "You're not entitled to my skunk oil just because you want it."

He gagged, blood coming from his eyes and mouth. Unless he got help, the pure silver wouldn't stop until it'd eaten every inch of him. I heard the leaves rustling. The rest of his pack was arriving. I had to get out of there.

I removed the chain from his neck and used my thiols to call my daggers back to me. Alec and his pack would be alright. They kept piles of skunk oil on them. Skunk oil was the only thing that could heal the wounds from pure silver. Without it, they'd be out of commission for months, maybe even years.

I jumped back into the trees, but before I left, I had one final warning to give. "What if I gathered my own pack, Alec? What if I found a few skunk friends and we decided to hunt? If one skunk can take out half your pack, think would twenty could do."

My pulse quickened. An idea formed in my mind. That wasn't a bad idea. Before the rest of Alec's pack could give chase, I shot through the trees.

I knew some pack members would be busy helping Alec and the others who'd been affected by the pure silver, but I didn't doubt some would try to find me.

I ran, hopping tree branches until I knew I was clear. I landed in a park full of small kids, running and playing. I let out a breath of relief, wiping sweat from my forehead. I wasn't likely to be attacked out here in the open.

We did have laws in Barebic. Anyone found kidnapping skunks, or harvesting skunk oil, without the approval of the skunk it came from would face life in prison. Barebic supposedly had zero tolerance when it came to skunk chasers, but it was all an act.

Vampires controlled this entire city. They hunted those of us with skunk DNA relentlessly. They made the laws, but only enforced the ones that benefited them.

Vampires wouldn't protect us. They wanted our oil more than anyone. The only reason they didn't round us all up was because agencies like Sypo would crush them if they got that severe.

Sypo was a national organization. They had the resources to send skunk hunters running scared, and they weren't infiltrated by the vampires.

Barebic's population was only three million. Sypo only dealt with cities with five million people or more. Sypo mostly turned a blind eye to cities like mine, only stepping in when things grew too out of control to maintain.

I wiped sweat from my brow and looked around. I didn't like being in one place too long. Besides, if Alec and his pack had drunk skunk oil, or rubbed it on their wounds, they'd be in the process of healing now.

I needed to move. I walked for a while, before deciding to go to work. I couldn't be sure Alec and his pack wouldn't still come for me, but I knew it would take them a few hours to recuperate. There were still members in his pack I hadn't hit with pure silver, though…

I made it two blocks from work before my stomach let out a hungry growl. I'd done a lot of running and fighting recently. It'd awoken my appetite. I stopped at a food truck selling fried fish. The name of the truck was, *High Moon.* My nose tingled, the smell making me dizzy.

I loved deep-fried fish, with a side of homemade chips. This truck wasn't far from work, so I often ate here. The guys who owned the food truck were amazing. Ant and Gray took special care with their food.

I placed my order then went the next block over to the nearest public restroom. There'd been three customers ahead of me at the food truck.

Ant and Gary would probably cook their food first before getting to mine. I figured by the time I got back, my fish would just be coming out of the deep fryer. I licked my lips, ready for lunch.

I never made it. I stepped cautiously out of the bathroom, alert for any signs of danger. The air blinked. When it cleared, four vampires stood before me. Tone, Qyne, Pitch, and Dre.

Before I could move, Dre had me by the neck. I gasped, my heart sinking to the pavement below.

TONE WAS A VAMPIRE PRINCE. His father was the head vampire Elder in Barebic. Tone had come with three more vampires. They walked in sunlight today, which meant they'd taken skunk oil. Apparently, they wanted more.

Tone stood six-three. He was a muscular man, with short curly black hair. He kept his nails razor long and his teeth sharp as knives.

Tone and his clan were sadistic, making Alec and his pack look like a bunch of preschoolers. Fear made my bones shake. I had to think fast if I wanted to make it out of this alive.

Dre's hand around my neck tightened, cutting off my air supply, my ability to think. Dre was one of Tone's top enforcers.

Dre was thick all over, with a big, shaved head, and tiny ears.

Most vampires killed for food. Dre killed for the fun of it. Disposing of me right now would be considered an afternoon delight for him.

Qyne was Tone's sister. She was a vampire princess. She was slim but just as vicious as her brother. She had red hair. It flowed in waves down her back. Qyne ran a long tongue across her sharp teeth.

She dressed like a schoolteacher but fought like a fiend. Qyne was a force to be reckoned with.

Last was Pinch. Tone's father was head Elder, but Pinch's father was right under him. The two were brothers.

"Anise," Tone said, smiling at me. "Seems like you're in a hurry. Off to free more skunks?"

Dre loosened his hold on my throat so I could answer. That was all the opening I needed.

Red thiols shot from my mouth into Dre's eyes, face, and neck. He screamed and let me go, the thiols cutting into his skin, splitting it open.

Qyne grabbed me by the hair, pushing me to my knees. I hit the ground hard, just in time to receive two quick kicks to my face by Tone.

My head bounced backward, the pain excruciating. It felt like someone had taken a meat cleaver, dipped it in fire, then went to hacking on my face. Blood shot from my nose and mouth.

Tone kicked me again. This time in my ribs. I curled over on my side, as best I could. His kicks were relentless. It felt like tiny blades, ripping into my skin, tearing me apart.

I gasped, trying to catch my breath. I needed an exit strategy. I fumbled in my pocket, trying to find my teko shades. The UV light from them would blast Tone and the others, allowing me to get away.

"Flip her over," Tone said. "Let's get this over with."

A shudder went through me, and real fear danced in my veins. They were going for my skunk oil, right here on the street. If they drained me, they could kill me, or at least make it so I couldn't move for months. I had to do something.

I tore the teko chain from my neck, clicking a button on the side of the charm. UV rays shot out, and the smell of burnt skin filled the air.

I didn't wait around. My body was sore. It hurt to breathe, to move. I shot thiols under my feet.

It lifted me in the air, propelling me six feet forward. With the UV light gone, Tone and the other vampires would heal, but it'd take a while unless they got ahold of more skunk oil. Either way, they were hurt for now, so I needed to run while I could.

Using my thiols like this, while I was hurt, quickly drained my energy. I needed skunk oil to heal. Normally, I could use my thiols to remove it, but my hands shook too badly. I was scared I'd make a mistake and hurt myself even more if I tried.

I needed someone to pull it from my back and give it to me. I could go to work, but Jones and the others weren't prepared to take on a team of vampires. Brick's face flashed before my eyes. He had a whole pack standing strong beside him.

I took a deep breath, my ribs feeling like they were on fire. I didn't know if I could trust Brick's pack. One of his wolves was addicted to skunk oil, but for now, it was the best option.

In my condition, it took me an hour longer than it should've to get there. I'd stopped multiple times to rest, plus I had to be sure Tone and the others hadn't followed me.

I made it to Brick's doorstep bloodied and bruised. Lati opened the front door. Her eyes widened when she took in my condition. I grunted, took a step forward, then promptly fell over.

Chapter 6

WHEN I OPENED my eyes again, I was lying on the couch in the living room with Brick, Lati, Corn, and Drift around me.

Corn had a shoestring wrapped around his hand. Why did he…? That's right, Corn collected shoestrings.

"Five minutes," he said, winding the string around each finger. "You've been out for five minutes."

I groaned and tried to sit up, but my body ached in protest. I felt like I'd been put through a woodchipper. The pain was blinding. "Back," I said, looking at Brick. "Oil."

Brick sat on the couch with me, rubbing wet hair out of my face. "You want me to take the skunk oil out of your back and give it to you?" he asked.

I nodded, not able to do more.

Brick growled low in his throat, almost like a warning. Lati, Corn, and Drift all took a step back.

"Anise," Brick said softly. "I'm going to lift you in my arms, okay?"

I nodded again to show my approval. Brick was very careful. He gathered me to him, making sure my arms were wrapped securely around his neck before he rose. He carried me down the hall, to the bedroom I'd slept in the night before.

Once in there, he laid me gently on the bed. "This will hurt," he said, voice soft against my ear.

"Been there, done that," I grunted out.

"I'll grab something to hold the oil." He left the room and came back with a red pitcher.

Brick leaned over. His face was right up against mine. Our breaths mingled together. "I can use a knife, or I can use my claws. Which one shall I open you with?"

"Just get it done," I said, not caring if he used a long sword at this point.

He placed a warm hand on my back, then his nails went up my spine, scraping, cutting. I hissed in pain and put both my hands between my thighs.

Sometimes when the oil was removed from our backs, untamed thiols shot out. That's why skunk hunters usually tied us down when they took our oil, binding our hands.

It hurt. It really hurt when they removed the oil from our backs. We often lost control of our thiols. Since I didn't see any equipment, I assumed Brick would use telekinesis to remove the oil.

"Be ready," Brick said next to my ear. "I'm ready to rem—"

He started removing my oil before he finished that sentence. Which caught me off guard, but it was okay. I clenched my teeth and held my breath until it was over.

"Here." He brushed hair out of my face, then guided the pitcher to my mouth. I drank, lapping up as much of it as I could. It was my oil. I could do what I liked with it, but that didn't give others the right to use my oil without my permission.

"I'm going to rub some on your wounds. Is that okay?" he asked.

I nodded. I could already feel the effects of the skunk oil. It burned through my system, healing my organs, my wounds. I tried not to gag. Skunk oil tasted like dried-up leaves.

"Here," I handed him a black chain from around my neck. It

had a small vial attached to it. I usually kept skunk oil in it. I'd been out since the first fight with Alec yesterday.

Brick took the chain from me and looked at the vial. "You want me to fill this with skunk oil?"

"Please," I said, and he nodded. He filled it to the top and handed it back.

"Thank you," I said, putting it around my neck again.

Brick dipped a cloth in the pitcher and rubbed some on my face, my cuts. It tingled, then stung. He dipped the rag again. He looked at me like he wanted my approval, before lifting my shirt and rubbing oil on my chest and stomach.

It probably took thirty minutes from start to finish, but by the time we were done, I felt a hundred percent better.

Brick stood on the other side of the room, shoulders wide, cloth crumpled in his hand. "I smelled vampire on you." His eyes flashed silver. "Tone. He touched you. Dre, Qyne, and Pitch. I smell them on you too."

I sat up. He was upset, I realized. His eyes held anger tipping into rage. The word *mine* repeated itself in my head, but I pushed it away.

I stood, stretching, working out the kinks. I felt so much better. "Yeah, Tone and the others caught me coming out of the bathroom. I'd just fought Alec and his pack."

Brick gazed at me with cool eyes. "You went up against Alec alone?"

"I'm not weak," I said, a little pissed we had to have this conversation again. "I went up against Alec and ten of his pack members. I left them on the ground bleeding. I didn't have one wound when I left there."

Brick nodded. An appraising look flashed through his eyes. Did he approve?

I took a breath and relented. "Things didn't work out so well against Tone and his crew."

Brick watched me like he was reading my soul. My heart sped up. I felt myself being drawn to him, like a magnetic pull. It was a force bigger than him, bigger than me. Something was pushing us together. It made my knees weak, my breath short.

I swallowed hard, not sure of my next move. Brick's gaze stayed on me, eyes blazing. He could feel it too. I wasn't sure how I knew that. I just did.

I took a few steps forward. So did he. When he spoke, his voice was low, husky. "They're probably tracking your scent as we speak. Tone is head Elder, Egre's son. They won't let this go. They'll want to make an example of you. You can't just attack the prince of vampires and get away with it."

"So, what do we do?" I asked because I wasn't stupid. No, I didn't appreciate Brick acting like I couldn't take care of myself, but I also understood that going up against the head vampires in the city was a lot different than going against Alec and his wolf pack.

I'd fought with the vampires before, but it'd always been one of their enforcers. I'd never directly fought one of the head families, only those under them.

Egre ruled this city. He was the unofficial mayor, president, and king. He had clan members on the city council, in law enforcement, and other high-up agencies. His clan was a proud one. He wouldn't let this attack against his son go unanswered.

No, I wasn't weak, but I couldn't take on the vampires by myself. I wasn't suicidal. If Brick and his pack wanted to help, I was more than happy to let them. I imagined no one liked being controlled by the vampires so this would be a benefit to them as well.

Brick opened the door to the bedroom. "Let's talk with the others,' he said.

Most of Brick's pack was still on business in another state. Lati, Corn, Drift, and Spin gathered in the living room. Brick waited until everyone was seated before he started to speak. He summed up my altercation with Tone and the other vampires in less than three sentences.

I gave him an appreciative glance, impressed with his ability to get straight to the point. The only words he used were the necessary ones.

Lati tapped away on her keyboard. "We need to call our other pack members home. If we're going to war with the vampires, we need them here, don't we?"

Brick nodded. "Call them, but war is not what we want. The loss on both sides would be heavy. I'll talk to Tone and Egre. Maybe we can resolve this without violence."

Spin glanced between me and Brick. When she spoke, I saw she had three piercings on her tongue. I'd been so shaken last night, I hadn't noticed them then. "Anise is in better health now. That means she used skunk oil to heal."

She looked at Brick when she spoke her next words. "If you have any leftover oil, maybe we can save some for Mata. Help him with his withdrawal symptoms."

Anger rose in me, causing thiols to build up and explode through my eyes and fingertips. The disrespect. The disregard. I came slowly to my feet.

Red thiols flashed through my eyes. "Why would you ask Brick if you can have my skunk oil?" My voice was low, deadly. "If he gives it to Mata without my permission, I'll kill them both. Then I'll kill you and every member of your pack. When you talk about me, about my oil, you look at me. Don't ever address someone else about me when I'm right here in the room."

Spin's eyes flashed silver. She stood, claws out. "Mata needs that oil. He's trying to quit but it's painful."

"He's not entitled to my oil," I said, red thiols swirling around me. "How many of my kind has he killed or hunted to get our oil. He's not entitled to shit."

Now, I did help those addicted to skunk oil when I could. If they were trying to do better, trying to stop using, then I didn't mind giving them a little oil to offset the pain from withdrawal.

I probably wouldn't mind helping this Mata, but Spin had gone about it all wrong. I wasn't opposed to the idea of helping him come off skunk oil, I just wouldn't be bullied into it.

Spin took a step toward me. Brick sprung up, standing between her and myself. He growled, claws so long they curled. A wolf's claws often grew long when they were angry. The madder they were, the longer and more deadly their claws became.

Brick growled again, eyes now completely silver. He released a scent in the air. My head jerked up. I recognized that smell. *Mine. Mate. Mine.* I looked at him, not sure how I felt about him claiming me.

Spin paled, eyes wide. She fell to her knees, baring her throat. The others in the room did the same.

My eyes were bigger than basketballs. Brick looked like he was on the verge of mate rage. His eyes were wild, his teeth longer than normal. His claws scraped the ground. Mate rage was when somebody threatened your mate. A wolf protected their mate above all else.

Approach a wolf's mate while that wolf was in the middle of mate rage, and you'd find yourself missing a jugular. No matter who you were to said wolf.

It took a while for Brick to calm down. Once he did, he took a seat and looked at me. "We'll go to Alec and his crew for help."

Chapter 7

WE WAITED until the rest of Brick's pack came home before we went to Alec's. Brick figured it was best to go to Alec's once we'd gathered enough people. Probably to make sure Alec listened instead of trying to attack.

In the meantime, I called the other skunks I worked with. I told them we were making a move on the vampires. They, in turn, promised to talk to other skunks, their families, friends. I didn't know many who hadn't been hurt by the vampires or at least had family members who'd fallen victim to them.

I figured I'd have enough money saved to open my own agency soon. The vampires would have to approve of me opening my own business, but hopefully that unofficial rule changed today.

I loved being a private detective, but I also planned on making a safe haven for skunks like myself. If the Sypo wouldn't protect us, we'd protect ourselves.

I reached out to other skunks I knew. The one's who'd helped me free skunks before. I figured it wouldn't be a stretch for them to help out now.

Little by little, Brick's house became filled with wolves of all shapes and sizes. I was surprised to even see a few foxes and other species among his pack.

The room was full of people now. Brick had a huge living room, more than capable of holding everybody comfortably. I fingered my pure silver ring, my throat doing its best to close up on me.

How many of these people had skunk oil addictions? How many would see me as a quick way to get high? I knew at least one would, Mata. Had he arrived yet?

I didn't like thinking like this, but experience had taught me I needed to be on my guard at all times, especially when a lot of people were around.

I keep my hand on my ring, ready in case anyone lost control, and came after me. "No one here will hurt you." Brick stepped up beside me. "I promise you that, Anise." His brows were drawn tightly together. His eyes held affection, concern.

Well, he couldn't really make that promise, but I still let out a breath and nodded. "Okay," I said. "Let's do this."

∾

BRICK HAD CALLED AHEAD to let Alec know we were coming. That way, when the entire pack arrived at his house, Alec wouldn't see it as an ambush and attack us.

Alec was on one side of the yard, his pack behind him. Brick was on the other side, his pack and the others who'd gathered at his house behind him.

I stood with Brick and his pack, but fifteen skunks had joined us. They stayed beside me. I'd hoped for more but hadn't even dreamed this many would appear.

Alec watched us with calculating eyes. His gaze went to me. "There's a reward out for your capture. Did you really think you could attack the freaking prince of vampires and get away with it?"

I shrugged. I already knew about the reward. Word tended to travel fast in Barebic. I took a few steps forward. "Did Tone think he could attack me and get away with it? Did you?"

I looked Alec and his pack over, but my words were to every

non-skunk out there. "If skunks want to sell their oil, that's their business, but we don't owe you shit. How silly, thinking you can take our oil without consequences."

A few of the other skunks moved closer to me. They stared Alec and his pack down, red thiols swirling around their hands. Warmth fluttered through my chest. I was touched. It always filled me with pride when skunks joined forces and worked together.

Alec spit on the ground, eyes cold, hard. "Why should we help you take on the vampires?"

I noticed more and more wolf packs had started to arrive. I hoped that meant they'd be joining us too. I knew Brick wanted to end this thing peacefully, but I feared we were past that point.

I looked at Alec, deciding to play it straight. I wouldn't cuddle him, and I wouldn't beg. "You can do what you want, but the vampires rule this city. Do you really like paying allegiance to them?

"Do you enjoy handing over twenty percent of your pack's income to them? Does it give you pleasure, letting them make all the rules for this city? Wouldn't you want to be on a few ruling boards? Why must everything be the way Elder Egre wants?"

I looked at the other packs out there. "This city is theirs unless we take it from them now. Why are they entitled to such a large portion of your income? Why must every decision be made by them? How many of you have wanted to open a new business, only to have them deny your permit? Why do they make all the decisions? I'm tired of them running shit, aren't you?"

I could hear the crowd mumbling in agreement. I even heard a few growls. I looked at Alec. "Don't act like you're doing me a favor. How many more millions will you have if we end the vampires' reign over us?"

I got his skepticism. Other wolf packs had banded together before and tried to take out the vampires. They'd lost, and their bodies had been put on display for days, their rotting and stinking corpses spread throughout the city for all to see what happens when you ran afoul the vampires.

Those with fox DNA had once banded together. They'd lost. Same for those with bear DNA and tiger DNA. No one could defeat the vampires on their own, but none of the different groups had trusted each other enough to work together.

Until now. Maybe all it took was giving up a small bit of trust for an outcome we all wanted. I looked up to see even more skunks arriving. I saw bears and other species too. My heart sped up triple time. We were doing this. We were really... No!

My eyes got huge. I turned around and looked at Brick. If all of these people knew we were staging a coup, the vampires would too. They had ears everywhere. Nobody could keep something this big a secret from them.

Brick sniffed the air. He turned to the right, then the left. Alec began to sniff too. Vampires could mask their scent, but if a wolf knew to look for it, they couldn't hide it for long.

Brick turned back around. He released a warning scent in the air. So did Alec. They were here. The vampires had come. The vampires had superspeed that was on a higher level than the wolves.

The vampires could kill us all in the time it took to strike a match. "Put up your shields!" I yelled as loudly as I could. "They're here!"

As soon as I said it, I felt something lift me in the air and throw me hard across the yard.

Chapter 8

I JUMPED up in time to see Alec's front yard become swarmed with vampires. It was broad daylight, so they must have been covered in skunk oil. They came in hard and fast, ripping apart anyone that didn't already have a shield up.

Two came at me from the right. My shield was firmly in place, but it was a temporary fix. It'd only hold for so long before it drained me completely.

One vampire was tall with blond hair. His claws were so long, they looked like blades attached to his hands. He swiped at me, but my shield cut his fingers off.

I immediately went on the attack. Like wolves, vampires self-healed. He wouldn't be hurt for long. I shot red thiols out of my mouth and into his face. It sliced through his eyes and nose. If I kept the attack up, he'd be dead before he had time to heal.

The other vampire with him bared his teeth. I put on my teko shades, clicking a button on the side. They blasted sunlight into his face, too much for the skunk oil in his system to protect him. He screamed, the UV rays burning into his skin. Then I shot red thiols into his stomach, cutting it open.

I turned back to the other guy. The rays from the glasses hit him in the face too, burning it off.

I moved on from them. I was looking for Tone. He'd attacked me and started all of this. I planned on finishing it. Bodies continued to drop around me. The vampires were fierce in battle, but with so many of us there, they were in for a true fight.

Somebody bumped up against me and my teko shades fell to the ground. I bent to pick them up, but someone else knocked against me, then someone else.

I turned in a circle, knowing I couldn't keep looking. If I became too distracted, I'd make an easy target. I kept walking.

I saw Lati with her claws out, teeth bared. A vampire ran up on her. She used her claws to split him open, his insides emptying out onto the ground.

Corn lifted a vampire in the air, then brought him close to his face. Without warning, he bit into the vampire's neck, ripping his jugular out. Then he pulled out teko knuckles. He beat the vampire with them until the only thing left was ashes.

Drift walked with a teko blade. A vampire was bringing his teeth down on a fox's neck. Drift swung the teko blade, slicing the man open. Smoke filled the air, the vampire's body burning. Drift swung the blade again, taking the vampire's head off.

I had my teko link chains in my hand, but I also had a teko dagger. Three more vampires ran up on me. My shield was still in place, but it was weak and wouldn't hold for much longer.

Once it dropped, they could use superspeed to rip me apart. I took a deep breath, sweat making my palms wet.

The three vampires ran up on me fast. I'd dropped my shades and they'd gotten lost in the shuffle. For the moment, I only had my blade and my link chain. I raised them both, ready for battle.

I never saw the vampire behind me. Something swiped at my legs, dropping me to the ground. The thiols from my shield cut into the vampire's hand, causing him to scream.

Still, he'd been able to touch me, which meant my shield was weaker than I'd thought. The three vampires in front of me

attacked. Because my shield was so weak, they were able to penetrate my skin.

Their claws ripped into my face and throat. It felt like a hundred
sharp blades, slicing into me, ripping me apart. I panted, my breath
coming short. If I died, those three were coming with me. I slung
my link chain, catching one around the neck.

The UV rays burned into her skin, making her scream. Her
fellow vampires didn't try to pull the chain from her neck, because
then they'd be burned too.

The vampire behind me yanked my hair back, so I was looking
him in the eye. I shot thiols from my mouth right into his face. It
went down his throat. His eyes turned huge, and he went to his
knees. He gasped for breath, reaching out.

The vampire I'd wrapped my chain around lay on the ground,
unmoving. The teko had burned through her neck, severing her
head from her body.

The other two vampires were still on me, clawing and biting.
Then I saw one being lifted in the air. I was surprised to see Spin
standing in front of me. She bit into the first vampire's neck, ripping
his jugular out.

The second one grabbed at her. She tossed the first one aside,
then used her long claws to rip the second one's insides out. I
jumped to my feet and nodded at her before she hopped back into
the fight. I was thankful, despite our differences, she'd still come to
my rescue.

I grabbed the small vial of skunk oil around my neck. I drank a
little of it down, letting it start the process of healing my wounds.

Alec was in hand-to-hand combat with a vampire. Alec had a
teko brick in his hand. He swung it, hitting the vampire until the
man's face was burned away. Another one grabbed him from
behind. Alec roared, then ripped the vampire's jugular out.

Four vampires jumped on Brick. I heard a whoosh. Brick was
using superspeed, but so were the vampires. When the air cleared,
all four vampires were on the ground. Their heads were no longer
attached to their bodies.

Two more ran at Brick. He grabbed one by the throat. The man struggled to get free. Brick used his superspeed to rip the man's heart from his chest.

The second vampire swiped at his throat, opening it up. Brick used his claws to part the man in two. One half of him went to the left, the other to the right.

Tone and three other vampires had a skunk on the ground, ready to rip his back open. I made sure my teko knuckles were securely in place. By now, my shield was completely gone, but I had enough teko on me to fend off an attack.

I went in hard and fast. I swung my teko link chain. It hit two of them in the face. I followed up my attack, hitting the vampires again and again until they were too badly burned to move, much less fight.

Tone and the other vampire let the skunk on the ground go and focused on me. They both ran toward me. I hit the first one in the face. My teko knuckles burned into his skin. He hissed, but I kept hitting him again and again.

Tone grabbed me by the throat, lifting me in the air. I shot thiols out of my mouth into his face. It cut into his right cheek, opening it up. I felt a whoosh of air. He must have used superspeed, because the next thing I knew, I was on the ground, his long claws opening up my chest.

My breath caught, but I wouldn't panic. I brought up my hands and hit him on both sides of his face, my teko knuckles burning into his skin. Then, I shot thiols out of my mouth, slicing his right hand off.

He grunted and fell back. I took that small moment to drink down a little more skunk oil then hopped up, hitting him with more thiols. He was powerful. He fought through it. Swiping at my neck and face, opening both up.

My veins filled with rage. I opened my mouth and thiols shot out, ripping into his body, leaving wounds and holes everywhere.

"You've made your point!" a loud, commanding voice said. The voice echoed through the crowd, causing most there to fall to their knees. I stopped my attack and turned.

My eyes widened. I gasped, fear making my hands shake. Elder Egre now stood before me.

Chapter 9

EGRE STOOD with ten of his Elders. I gulped. These were the most powerful vampires in the city. They wouldn't easily fall. With Egre here, the fighting paused, all eyes on him. Brick stood on one side of me, Alec on the other.

Egre was tall with black hair that hung down to his shoulders. He looked like a man in his late forties, but vampires were immortal. Egre himself was a few thousand years old.

He was slim of frame, but his body, his aura, commanded respect. He looked like a man who was always in charge. He was charismatic. It was no wonder all around him did his bidding without question.

His claws were out, long and curved. His eyes bored into mine like they were judging every decision I'd ever made. "What you want is impossible," he said. "Why would we hand control of this city over to you?"

Sweat and blood dripped into my eyes. I wiped them away. The skunk oil hadn't healed every wound yet. I was weak, barely able to stand. I looked at Egre, then at the numerous vampires on the ground.

My heart shook, but I wouldn't show fear. Being in the presence of someone so powerful would make anyone take a step back. "We don't want complete control," I said, panting. "We want to share control. Number one, no one should have to pay you over half their income. You do nothing for us. Why should we show you our allegiance? Skunks are hunted daily. You don't protect us. You attack us. We owe you nothing."

Egre raised a brow. "And where are skunks on the food chain? Why would I negotiate with you? If we round you all up and keep you as our personal drinking fountains, not one person would do a thing about it."

He looked at Brick, Alec, and the other non-skunks. "Wouldn't it be convenient?" he asked. "To have all the skunks in one place. I'm willing to share them with you. We can use their oil anytime we like, and no one will stop us. Not even Sypo if we handle it correctly." That was a promise he couldn't keep, and everyone here had to know it.

But that wouldn't stop him from trying. I licked my lips, determined to keep my cool, but it wasn't easy. I felt my thiols building, raging, turning deadly. Brick growled. His claws extended, scraping the ground. He bared his teeth, eyes completely silver.

When Brick spoke, his voice was low, guttural. "Anyone touches her, I'll kill you and your entire family." The other members of his pack came to stand beside and behind him, putting on a united front.

Alec sniffed the air. "No. Calm your mate rage," he said to Brick. He sniffed the air again. "No one's willing to face Sypo for this vampire."

The air whooshed. When it cleared, Elder Egre held a woman and a man in his hands. He had both by the throat. Each had black hair with white sprinkled in.

My hands shook. What was he planning? My thiols continued to rage. Soon it'd be out of control, and I wouldn't be able to guarantee anyone's safety.

Black thiols flashed through my eyes. I was ready to lose it. It wasn't something we skunks did often, but anyone who'd ever seen a skunk lose control of their thiols knew to get the heck out of dodge.

I stepped to Egre, black and red thiols swirling around me. "Put them down, now," I said.

He looked at me like one would a bug on a shoe. His eyes went from the man to the woman. Then he extended his claws, using them to rip both their heads off before slinging them to the side.

My rage reached its breaking point. Black and red thiols lifted me in the air. I threw my head back and screamed, thiols shooting from every part of my body.

Egre, and the ten elders with him, ran toward me, using super-speed to attack. My thiols knocked them back.

I tried to stay in control, aiming my thiols as best I could at Egre and his crew. It tore into them, ripping through bone and muscles. Then I was falling. Everything was cloudy now, carrying a red hue.

I landed in Brick's arms. Alec and the others continued the fight with the vampires. I was done for. I'd used up too much energy, but I wouldn't end this battle on my back.

I stood, Brick right beside me. Once he knew I was okay, he jumped back into the fight. It wasn't long before Egre and the other vampires were brought under our heels. Now it was time to negotiate.

I stayed on my guard, not sure another group of vampires wouldn't attack just when we thought this thing was over.

Chapter 10

NO HELP CAME for Egre and the other vampires. They'd given us their best and lost. In the end, they'd had no choice but to negotiate. I sat on a couch in my private rooms, legs tucked under me. For now, I was staying with Brick and his pack. We'd see how that went.

I'd decided to help Mata come off his skunk oil addiction. I hadn't moved into Brick's until Mata had been six months clean without slipping. It was an ongoing process, but for now it was working out well.

I held my mug of hot chocolate to my lips, taking a small sip. We'd worked out a new way to run this city. I'd made sure those with skunk DNA were placed on every board. Others wouldn't look out for us. We had to do that for ourselves.

Both Brick and Alec now held top positions, as did many members of their packs. No one had to pay the vampire's outrageous fees anymore.

I set my mug of hot chocolate down. Things weren't perfect. Skunks were still hunted, but the laws were swifter now. I did end up opening my own agency. My office was also a place skunks could come if they were in trouble.

It was slow in the making, but it was a start. I heard a noise and looked up to see Brick standing in the doorway. He had on black jeans with a black sleeveless top. He walked into the room. I whistled under my breath. No one should be that sexy. It really was illegal.

Brick sat beside me, then leaned over and gave me a kiss. His lips were hard, chapped. I smiled. That's just how I liked them.

I squeezed Brick's hand. Was he my mate? My heart told me that he was. I didn't doubt it, but we were still getting to know each other. We'd decided to take things slowly and see how they progressed.

I had my own private quarters in his house. We weren't at the stage where we could share a room yet.

Brick threw an arm around me, and I snuggled closer. "How's your day been so far?" I asked.

He started to answer but stopped when my phone rang. I picked it up.

"Anise," a smooth, silky female voice said on the other end.

"Speaking," I said.

"This is Faut," the lady answered. "I work for Sypo."

I sat up in my chair, gripping the phone. Why would Sypo be calling me?

"I'd like to set up a meeting," Faut said. "We heard about your recent fight with the vampires. We've decided we do need a presence in Barebic. We're setting up an agency there. We'd like you to join us as one of the team leaders."

The lady paused like she was waiting for me to say something. When I stayed silent, she continued to talk. "What do you say? Will you take the meeting?"

I turned to Brick. Wolves had super hearing. His ears had no doubt picked up every word she'd said. I saw shock in his eyes, but also excitement. He seemed happy for me.

It would be a lot, juggling this and my agency, but I knew I could do it.

I smiled, finally feeling like things were falling into place. "Yes," I finally said into the phone. "I'll take the meeting."

I HOPE YOU ENJOYED *PROWL. Anise and Brick are the stars of an upcoming series. If you'd like to know about the series, please join my mailing list for updates. You can join my mailing list here: https://www. subscribepage.com/anisebrick*

IF YOU'D LIKE *to read more of my books that feature wereskunks, please check out my Magic and Mischief series. You can find all of my books here: https:// linktr.ee/N.R.Hairston*

Full Moon's Curse

JENN WINDROW

Chapter 1

MY MOMMA always warned me not to piss off a witch. And judging by my current incarceration behind silver-lined bars, it was clearly another bit of parental advice I ignored, only this time, I might not live long enough to regret it.

It had been three days since I fell into the witch's trap. Three days of starvation and torture. Three days of being forced to live in my wolf form without shifting.

I wanted nothing more than to scratch the witch's eyes out with my claws, to tear her throat out with my teeth, but I was trapped, and paws made any escape attempt rather difficult. So, my revenge would have to wait. Instead, I sat, fuzzy, furious, and filled with a kind of rage only a werewolf possessed.

I paced back and forth, careful not to brush against the silver bars of my prison. Trying to avoid another singeing silver burn to my body. At least I had learned that lesson.

My hell away from home had a bowl of water, something that might pass as food but smelled like the inside of a dead rodent, and a blanket to curl up on, like I was a stray dog she had found on the street. I had news for the witch who had stuffed me in this cage: werewolves don't make good pets.

It felt like an eternity passed before the door to the basement creaked open. A sliver of light slithered down the stairs like the tip of an arrow pointing right at me. The toe of a sensible black flat hit the first step. At the fifth step, I finally saw the face of my captor.

I expected an old woman with grey hair and warts, but what came down the stairs was the exact opposite. She was only a few years older than me, mid-thirties if I had to guess. She had red hair that women paid a fortune for in the high-end salons, green eyes that almost glowed, and lips that tilted down in a perma-pout.

She stopped on the last step and stared at me.

Had I been human, I would have asked her what she wanted, but I was a wolf and wolves didn't talk. We did bite, however, so I bared my teeth and gave her my most feral snarl.

"You're angry." Her voice had an almost sing-song lilt to it. "Understandable. But I promise you, Julia Monroe, you will be set free tonight. Right after we have a little talk."

My answering growl rattled the cage.

"Now, now. Calm down." She walked to my cage and knelt in front of me and the smell of wolfsbane stung my nose. "I will restore you to your human form for our conversation, but in case you have any ideas of escaping, know that I have spelled the house so you can't leave until I allow you."

She bowed her head and chanted in a language I guessed was Latin. Sparks of green magic dripped from her fingertips and sizzled on the floor.

Her magic seemed to reach inside of me and pluck at the thin thread of control I had over my wolf.

The change from wolf to human came on fast. My skin started to tingle, then burn, like someone had lit my fur on fire. My bones popped and cracked and shattered, rearranging themselves into my human shape. The change always stole my breath but being forced to shift left me panting on the floor and gasping for air.

Skin replaced fur, a ski slope nose replaced my muzzle, and red nails replaced my claws. It took a few minutes for the human part of my brain to click back on, but when it did, I screamed from the pain.

Fear sent my heart racing. Fear that this witch was in control of the most primal part of me—my wolf—and that fear triggered my mouth. "What do you want, bitch?"

With a twinkle of her fingers, she opened the cage door but blocked the entrance so I couldn't step out. "You are going to do something for me."

"What makes you think I would do anything for you?"

Her smile was one thousand percent Wicked Witch of the West. "Because if you don't, I'll make sure you spend the rest of your life as a wolf."

A shiver shimmied up my spine, and just like that, she had my undivided attention.

Chapter 2

THE WITCH'S threat hung in the space between us like a silent-but-deadly fart. If I had any chance of continuing to walk on two legs and not four, I had to listen to her demented list of demands.

Needing to regain a bit of control and dignity, I snatched the blanket, wrapped it around my naked body, and shoved my way past the dangerous metal bars and the witch guarding them. "What do you want me to do for you?"

"I want someone dead and you're going to do the killing." She practically purred the words.

My legs were still wobbly from the forced shift so I leaned against a worktable covered with all kinds of plants and herbs and bottles, the only other piece of furniture in the room besides the cage. "I don't kill."

"You're a werewolf. It's your nature to kill."

That was true of most werewolves, but after my parents were butchered by their own pack, and my twin brother Julian and I had to hide for years to keep from meeting the same fate, I lost my urge to hunt and kill even the smallest creatures.

She didn't deserve an explanation, so I repeated myself. "I don't kill." Then to really hammer my point home I added, "Anyone."

Her smile withered. "Then I suggest you get over your morals. Quickly."

It wasn't morals that kept me from killing Thumper, it was my aversion to blood and guts and the texture of slimy things sliding down my throat, unless, of course, I was tearing out the throat of the witch-bitch in front of me. Then I would choke it all down for a chance to watch her die.

"And if I don't?"

"Then like I said, you'll stay a wolf forever. Only allowed to change back to your human form on the full moon."

She was talking about reversing the werewolf curse. Was that even possible?

Maybe, maybe not. But she already proved she could force my shift with a flick of a finger. I wasn't a gambling kind of girl. "You seem to be a capable witch, do it yourself."

"My magic is formidable, but this requires a different kind of power. A primal, furious rage only werewolves can wield"

In other words, I was her werewolf weapon. "There are literally hundreds of werewolves that are down with killing. Why pick me?"

"You have a connection to the one who wronged my family. A connection I plan to exploit."

I had no idea who she was talking about, but after a near-death experience with an ex-psycho, my connections with the supernatural community were limited to my brother Julian. And lately even that relationship was strained.

She tapped her jade-colored nails on the table. "I hear the price for a werewolf on the black market is upwards of six figures these days. Your claws and teeth alone would fetch a fair price in the dark arts should you be captured and fall into the wrong hands."

My already wobbly legs went weak, and I grabbed the edge of the table to keep from falling over.

If there was any hope of getting out of here, I had to play the ever-faithful wolf-for-hire. "Who needs to die?"

"I knew you would eventually come around." She picked up a potted plant and plucked a few brittle brown leaves, dropping them into a mortar on the table.

I shrugged a shoulder "It seems I am out of options."

She ground the leaves into a fine powder with the pestle. "My request is simple. Locate the leader of the Chicago coven and kill her. Just one, tiny witch who needs to be removed so I can take her place."

"This is all about power? You want to be the leader, so you're killing the competition?"

She slammed the pestle on the table. "The position of high priestess was never hers to begin with. It was my mother's, then mine. It is my birthright. But my mother never got the chance to lead. She was shunned by the witch community, then murdered for one tiny infraction." She added some gooey liquid from a dirty jar to the powder. "But now that I have you, I'll be coven leader and those who stood against my family will be punished."

More than most, I understood wanting to right the wrong when your parents were murdered, to punish the people who hurt you. But she had picked the wrong wolf to wage her war. "And if I help you, you'll reverse the curse?"

"If, in twenty-four hours, she is dead, I will reverse my curse. If not, *woof-woof.*"

That gave me one day to find an escape clause. "So, I'll ask you again, who needs to die?"

"Her name is Kyoko Uno."

An off-the-Richter-charts tremor shook my core and stole my breath.

The witch she wanted me to kill wasn't any old witch, she was a friend and ally of Julian. She was the witch who had fought by his side. Who saved his life. Who helped stop Delano Melazi, the afore-mentioned ex-psycho, from enslaving every human in Chicago.

I had never met Kyoko, but if the rumors were true, killing her would be a suicide mission. And I wasn't suicidal.

However, I wasn't going to tell her that. So, I nodded my head like a good little henchman and pasted a smile on my face. "When do I start?"

"Right now." She dipped her finger into the mixture in the mortar and touched my forehead.

A bolt of lightning zipped through me burning me from the inside out. I fell to my knees, hands clenching my head to keep it from exploding. A wave of nausea rolled through me, filling my mouth with bile. I threw up on her floor.

Fucking witch.

She handed me a bundle of clothes and my missing phone. "When you wake up, I suggest you move quickly." She yelled an indistinguishable word and my world went dark.

I came to in the middle of some random woods. My head hurt, my stomach hurt, and my mouth was coated in sick. But all of that was nothing compared to the ache of betrayal encompassing my heart. An ache so deep, I wasn't sure it would ever heal.

The witch had laid down her ultimatum. Find Kyoko and kill her or be stuck as a wolf forever. Only allowed to change back to my human form on the full moon.

There were two small problems with her plan. One, I had never killed anyone in my life and didn't plan on starting today. Two, killing without cause would get me excommunicated from the pack. I may not be an active member, but they were still my family.

Both of those things were insurmountable problems I wasn't sure I could climb.

Before I could worry about anything else, I had to get out of the damn woods. I listened to the sounds all around me. Crickets and nocturnal creatures sang a soothing song, but those weren't the noises I was hoping to hear. Using my enhanced wolf hearing, I searched for sounds of civilization. There in the background, I heard what I was looking for. Cars zooming past at eighty miles per hour.

I replaced the blanket with the faded jeans and flannel shirt I had been wearing when the witch abducted me and looked at my phone. Twenty-three hours and ten minutes.

The curse clock was ticking.

Like every other problem I had encountered in my life, I needed help to find my way out of the witch's tangled web.

There was one person I could rely on. The only person who had always been there for me, no matter how much trouble I was in. The only person I could count on. My twin brother Julian.

I just hoped he still cared enough to open the door.

Chapter 3

I FOUND my way out of the woods and hopped a bus to the brown-
stone where my brother lived. Until a few months ago, I had lived
there too, but the need for my own space, my own life, and the urge
to escape the ghosts of my parents, drove me out on my own.

Gathering my courage, I walked up the steps to the front door. I
reached out my hand to knock, then my anxiety spiked and I pulled
back. Julian and I had been close growing up. After our parents'
murder we only had each other. He had protected me for years
when we were on the run. Kept me safe from anyone who hunted us
because of our family lineage. I owed him my life.

Then a vampire named Terrance had swept me off my paws,
becoming more important to me than my own blood. It turned out
Terrance wasn't some low-level vampire, but an ancient vampire
named Delano Melazi, hell-bent on revenge. Our relationship had
twisted me up inside. At the time I had been too weak to see he was
using me. After Julian rescued me, shame and betrayal had driven a
wedge between the two of us. A wedge we still hadn't found a way
to remove.

"This is crazy. He's my twin." I held my breath and knocked.

I hadn't even counted to three little pigs when the door opened.

Julian greeted me, his smile making it all the way to his blue eyes, and a fresh load of guilt tightened my chest.

"Julia, this is unexpected." He even sounded happy to see me. "What's wrong?"

I wanted to pretend for just a moment that I was here for a sisterly visit with no ulterior motives or the need to have him come to my rescue yet again. "What makes you think something is wrong?"

"Your clothes are filthy and ripped. Your hair is a tangled mess. No makeup. And as your Alpha, I can feel the worry shaking your bones." He opened the door wider and I followed him to the living room, our mother's favorite room.

This room was another reason I needed to move out of the house. Not one thing had been changed since the day they were murdered. It was a permanent reminder of what we had lost. From the art on the walls to the candy dish on the coffee table, it was as if time had taken hold and refused to let go.

Julian hadn't kept it as a mausoleum on purpose, but being around the constant memories of what we lost didn't hurt his heart like it did mine.

I sat on the couch and picked at the tattered remains of my flannel shirt. "No Alexis tonight?"

Alexis was his kick-ass vampire girlfriend with her own set of complications. She had helped save me from Delano, but our relationship started out rocky and hadn't really improved over time. She's not who I would have picked for him, but she made my brother happy. If anyone could take down a witch and her curse it was her, but I was grateful she wasn't here.

"No, not tonight." His words were laced with loneliness. "Now, what is going on?"

I took a deep breath to calm my threadbare nerves, then dove in. "Three nights ago, a witch abducted me—"

"Do you need a doctor?" He rushed over and examined me for serious injuries.

I waved him and his worries away. "Just surface damage. It's nothing. I'll heal." And that was true. Werewolves healed fast. The cuts and bruises were nothing compared to the gaping wounds that festered internally. "I need your help breaking the curse she placed on me."

The word "curse" sucked all the air from the room.

"You were cursed by a witch?" When Julian said it, it sounded kind of ridiculous.

"Yes. And the cost to remove it is too high."

I told him every last detail. The who, what, and why. Plus the consequences if I failed my mission. When I finished, he stood and paced the room. Brother code for "let me work through the pile of shit you laid at my feet."

"Well, that's a complicated mess. I am not sure how to clean it up." He scrubbed his hands over his face and through his hair. "There is only one thing we can do."

I knew I wasn't going to like his suggestion even if it was the smartest option to solve my problem.

He pinched the bridge of his nose. "We need to talk to Kyoko."

When I tried to interrupt, he held up his hand in the universal sign of "I've heard enough."

"She deserves to know that her life is in danger. And breaking this curse isn't something we can do alone. If anyone knows how to reverse a curse it's her."

And just like that, I went from being tortured and cursed by one witch to certainly being killed by another.

Chapter 4

JULIAN MADE SOME PHONE CALLS, then we got in his car and navigated through the city streets. We pulled up in front of an old warehouse the city should have torn down years ago. Two cars filled the mini-driveway, a red two-seater Mercedes convertible and a midnight blue Chevelle.

The sight of the Chevelle made my insides quake and quiver. Bringing me back to the night I had spent locked in the back seat under werewolf guard.

Julian parked next to the Mercedes and got out of the car, but I hesitated before opening my door.

Showing up at Julian's had been hard enough but knocking on Alexis Black's door was another level of terrifying I didn't even know existed.

Alexis killed supernaturals for a living to satisfy a holy contract with an angel. She was known around Chicago as Evil's Assassin and every sane other-worldly creature avoided her. I knew being Julian's sister offered me some level of protection, but there was still a pack of wolves playing slice-and-dice with my internal organs.

Julian opened the passenger side door. "You can't hide in the car all night."

"This is a mistake. It was bad enough that I came to you with my problems. You love me, you'll help me out of a familial bond. But no one in that house has any reason to like me, let alone help me."

He knelt between me and the open car door. "You're right, I will always help you because you are my sister." His lips turned down in a small frown. "But you're wrong about them. Each person in that house will help you because that's what they do. They help those who need it."

I trusted Julian with my life so I got out of the car and followed him to the front door.

He pulled out a key and opened the heavy, dented metal door to the warehouse. If I thought the outside was grim, the inside was one health code violation away from demolition. Paint-chipped walls, worn-away linoleum, and blood splatters were the opposite of a welcome mat.

Julian pulled back the gold cage door of an old service elevator and waited for me to get on. He shut the door behind us and slapped a red button. The gears rattled and we lurched upward.

The elevator stopped at the top floor. The gold bars kept me separated from the people in the room who I really would rather avoid, but it was the second time today I had been caged, and I was growing sick of feeling trapped.

Julian reached down and squeezed my hand. "It's okay, they don't bite."

"It's not their teeth I'm worried about."

He pushed back the grate of the elevator and stepped into the room. I followed, trying to stay hidden behind him as much as possible. I peered around his shoulder, a quick peek at the group waiting for us in the living room.

Four people gathered on a cream-colored leather sofa. Alexis was the only one I recognized, but I had heard enough rumors about the others to guess who they were. Alexis was just as I remembered from our first not-so-pleasant encounter. Dark hair, blue eyes, and a fuck-with-me-and-die attitude. A tough guy sporting a crew cut and wearing camos and combat boots sat next to her. He had to be Reaper, the only human in their group. And even though I knew how many supernaturals the two of them had killed, they were nowhere close to the scariest people in the room.

The man at the end of the couch had to be Alexis's brother André. Same dark hair and blue eyes, but there was a lethal glint in his eyes that made him seem even more dangerous and deadly than his sister. André's arm was wrapped around a beautiful Asian woman with short black hair and eyes to match, like an anime character come to life. But there was something about her, a spark, a power that seemed to flow through her veins, almost making her glow. If I had to guess, I would say it was her magic. Strong magic. Magic I didn't want to mess with.

That power belonged to Kyoko. The witch I was supposed to kill.

"Julia, welcome to our home." Alexis sounded like she meant it, but I knew deep inside she blamed me for all the trouble I caused Julian. I remembered all the hate-filled words I had hurled at her the last time we met and my cheeks heated.

I stepped around Julian, realizing how useless it was to hide from a group of supernaturals. "Thank you. I'm sorry to bother you with my problem, but it concerns you too."

André removed his arm from Kyoko's shoulder and leaned forward. "Julian said it had something to do with Kyoko and the coven?"

I knew enough about his kill-first-ask-questions-never reputation to tread lightly. "It does, and if I could solve the issue on my own, I would, but I can't think of any way out other than coming to you for help."

Alexis pointed to an overstuffed chair across from the couch. "Please have a seat."

Julian placed his hand on my back and encouraged me with a small shove to sit. I was grateful for the coffee table barrier separating me and the deadly crew across from me.

Julian took a seat next to Alexis on the couch his hand finding hers.

Alexis gave him a quick kiss on the cheek. "Tell us what happened and how we can help."

I told them everything. All the dirty details the witch had shared with me. It wasn't until I was done telling the story for the second time that I realized I didn't know the witch's name. In fact, there were no details that could help us identify her besides the way she looked, and I had learned the hard way that looks could be altered with a tiny bit of magic.

André stood with a feline grace. "What would stop me from killing you right here, right now. With you dead the curse is broken, and Kyoko is safe, right?" His voice held the kind of menace I expected from someone who was comfortable with killing.

I swallowed back the fear that clawed up my throat.

Julian jumped up from the couch and was at my side before I could blink. "No one deserves to die. Not Julia and certainly not Kyoko."

I appreciated the sentiment. My whole life I had depended on my big brother security blanket to save me from myself, but it was time to wolf-up and grow some lady balls.

"No one is preventing you from killing me, but once I am dead, what would stop her from cursing someone else to kill Kyoko? The way I look at it, it's the enemy you know and all that."

The space next to Alexis shimmied and purple and blue sparks shot in the air right before a bleach-blonde goth ghost appeared. "The chickie has a point."

Alexis patted the ghostly hand. "This is Nathan. He's a ghost. You get used to him."

Nathan gave me an over-exaggerated wink. "I'm the randy bloke and the humor of our little group."

André cleared his throat. "Yes, Nathan is fun and all, but let's get back to what matters. Explain to me why I shouldn't stab you through the heart to protect Kyoko?"

"Because Julia is right, it's better to work with her." Reaper scratched at the scruff on his chin. "We need to find the witch, kill her, and then everyone is safe."

Kyoko who had been quiet during the conversation, ran her

hand over a multi-colored tattoo of a fox just above her heart. "I know the witch you speak of." Her words carried a hint of a Japanese accent. "The Eastey's can trace their line to Salem. They sat on the Coven Council for centuries until Blair sided with Lysette and Delano. After we killed Lysette, the coven removed the Eastey bloodline from the registry and killed Blair for her betrayal."

"She said that was her mother." I added.

"Then her name is Roweena."

André narrowed his eyes and screwed up his mouth. "You said they removed their name from the registry, what does that mean?"

Kyoko chewed at her bottom lip "Once you are removed from the coven you are also removed from the collective. That makes her a lone witch, weaker than a coven witch. Roweena still has power, but only the power she was born with."

"But she was strong enough to curse Julia." Alexis sounded a bit skeptical.

Kyoko frowned. "The only way to cast a curse after you've been shunned is through blood magic. Dark magic."

"But we can remove the curse and save Julia, right?" Julian's anxious tone matched how I was feeling inside.

Kyoko pulled her hair into a bun and stuck two fox head hair sticks in to hold it up.

"A blood curse is tricky to reverse without killing the person it is tied to. In the end, someone will have to pay the blood sacrifice."

My heart sank into my stomach.

She had left out one tiny detail: if we couldn't kill the witch, I had a choice to make. Kill Kyoko or be stuck as a wolf forever.

Both options sucked.

Chapter 5

WHEN I HAD WOKEN up in the middle of the woods, I knew that the next twenty-four hours would decide my fate. I just didn't think my future would be so bleak.

"So, it's either you or me?" I didn't mean it as a threat, however I was in a room full of people who didn't trust easily and my words were quickly taken the wrong way.

André pulled a dagger from his boot, jumped over the coffee table, and pressed it against my throat in the flash of a bat's wing. But before he could end my life, he was tossed across the room and a five-foot-tall magical glowing orange fox stood before me. Eyes the color of flames, fangs dripping magical drool, and claws sharper than André's blade.

At that moment I was positive I was going to die.

Every survival instinct told me running would only get me killed, so I raised my hand in an I-come-in-peace gesture. "I have no intention of killing anyone. But I don't want to be stuck as a wolf for the rest of my life either."

The fox loomed over me, and I had no doubt that even in my wolf form the fox would tear me apart.

Kyoko placed her hand on the fox's head and said something in

Japanese. The fox took one last look at me, snorted, then with a magical orange poof returned to the spot on her chest where the tattoo lived.

"What did you say to him?" I asked, still not sure I wasn't going to die.

"That you are not an enemy, just someone in a no-win situation that needs our help." Her voice was soft and sweet, just like her words.

"Thank you. I appreciate it." I slumped deeper into the chair. "I don't want to hurt you."

Alexis stood next to Kyoko. "Can you tell if she is actually cursed? I mean maybe the witch was lying to scare her into doing her dirty work."

Kyoko looked at me, her eyes sparking with orange magic. "I can use my magic to search for her spell." She stepped closer and I couldn't help but grab the arm of the chair. "It shouldn't hurt, but if Roweena's magic is strong, it won't tickle either."

One witch had already screwed with my brain today, and I wasn't so sure about adding another to the tally, but my choices were very limited. So, I pushed past the urge to flee and sat straight. "Do what you have to do."

Kyoko reached out to touch me but stopped before she made contact. "Will my magic trigger your wolf?"

That explained the hesitation. The fear that I might go all big bad wolf and eat her while she tried to help me. "I have complete control over my wolf, but I don't know if my will is stronger than the curse."

Julian grabbed my hand and held it tight. "As Alpha of the pack I can control her wolf if she can't."

His answer must have satisfied Kyoko—or she trusted him way more than me—because she placed her hand over my heart. "You were asleep when she cursed you?"

"I was passed out. I'm pretty sure she drugged me because I don't remember most of the three days she held me."

"You're going to feel my magic call to hers. If her magic fights back, I will stop before it can hurt you."

She began chanting in Japanese. Orange sparks traveled from the tips of her fingers, raced up her arms, and encompassed her whole body until she was surrounded by her own magic. The tickle she mentioned started out as a minor annoyance but quickly morphed into an all-encompassing pain that almost knocked me off the chair.

My wolf awoke and pushed at the mental barrier I had put up to control her. The barrier weakened and my control slipped.

"You will not shift." The command came from the Alpha wolf and not my brother.

My wolf backed down.

Kyoko removed her hand and the burning vanished. Relief washed through me.

"I'm sorry," Kyoko said softly.

"It's not your fault."

She sat on the floor in front of me, her eyes still glowing orange. "She didn't lie. You are cursed." Something in her tone told me the rest of the news wouldn't be any better. "It's deep and nasty and tangled around all your internal organs."

"Magic is some ugly shite." Nathan bobbed up and down behind her.

"Not all magic is ugly, but this is. Even removed from the collective she is strong, powerful."

"Is there any way to reverse it without hurting her?" Julian gave my shoulder a squeeze.

Kyoko lowered her chin. "There are only two ways to remove this curse. Either I die or Roweena does." Her voice trailed off on the last word. "Unless…" She paused and that tiny pause of hope had me holding my breath. "Unless I can get some of Roweena's blood. I might be able to counteract the curse using her blood. But there's no guarantee it will work. It would be a risk you'd have to be willing to take."

My options were limited, but I would do whatever I could to keep Kyoko alive and my body fur free. "I'm willing."

André smacked the coffee table and I jumped. "Looks like we have a witch to hunt, bleed out, and kill."

"Julia doesn't know where she lives. How are we supposed to find her in such a short time? "Alexis asked.

Kyoko looked up again and smiled. "Because she left a signature on her magic. Something so tiny I doubt she even realized she was doing it."

"And you can locate her from the signature?" Reaper asked.

"I can. And when I do, I look forward to killing her and removing her line from the world. For good." The anger that had slipped into her words turned Kyoko into something far scarier than any other creature I had ever encountered.

Chapter 6

THE GOOD NEWS was we could locate the witch who cursed me. The bad news was someone had to die to free me from her nasty little hex. Neither option sat well in my tangled mess of nerves.

I had faith that Kyoko was a more bad-ass witch, but there were still so many unknowns. Those unknowns made me seriously consider letting the curse have its dirty way with me, making me furry forever. But to keep Kyoko safe from any more assassination attempts, this had to end today. No matter the outcome.

Reaper unrolled a map of the city across the kitchen table, holding down the corners with some snarky coffee mugs. "Kyoko, are you able to use magic to pinpoint her location on the map? At least it would give us an idea of where to start searching."

"I'll need a drop of Julia's blood."

I held out my arm. "Take what you need."

She pulled one of the hair sticks from her bun and removed the fox head, revealing a thin blade. "This won't hurt, I promise." She pricked my finger.

I was tempted to suck at the blood that bubbled, but instead I looked at Kyoko. "Where do you want it?"

"Place a drop on the map over Alexis's house."

Reaper pointed to the spot, and I did as I was told.

Kyoko leaned over the table, her magic already flaring. She touched the tip of her glowing finger to my blood and said a few words in Latin. The drop of blood wiggled and jiggled like blood-flavored gelatin, then it started traveling along some invisible line on the map. Every so often it would stop, spark, then start moving again.

Moments later the mixture of blood and magic stopped in the center of the map miles away from the city center.

"What's in that part of town?" André asked.

Reaper pulled out a laptop and placed it on the table. He pounded away on the keyboard, then turned it around so we could all see the screen. "This is an aerial view of the area." He pointed to the screen. "And right here in the center is an off-the-beaten-path cabin surrounded by a fortress of trees."

"Isolated. Quiet. Out of the way." Alexis leaned against the edge of the table. "If I was an evil witch looking for revenge, that would be my ideal location."

Nathan popped up beside her. "A perfect place to get her wicked witch on in private."

André took the computer from Reaper and zoomed in. "And so far away from the rest of the world she would never be found unless you were searching for her."

Kyoko pulled her hair back in a bun and stuck the stick back in. "But we were searching and we did find her. With her magic coursing through Julia, her days of hiding are over. She threatened my life for a position I never wanted, for a wrong I didn't commit. Under witch law her life is forfeit."

My eyes widened and my mouth popped open. And I thought werewolves were vicious.

Nathan sat on the table, swinging his legs back and forth like a little kid. "Don't any of you wankers read? How many horror stories start with a bunch of blokes wandering into the woods and never being seen again?"

André cocked a brow. "I wouldn't call two vampires, two were-wolves, one-gun happy human, and a pissed off witch your typical group of wankers."

"You forgot the ghost." Nathan gave him a saucy wink.

"Yes, the ghost. Heaven knows we wouldn't be able to save the world without your dirty limericks and witty banter." André rolled his eyes so far back I thought he might be able to see his own brain.

The ghost bounced up and down over the table. "That reminds me, Julia, have you heard this one—"

Alexis quickly slammed her hand over his mouth. "Let's save her life first, then you can blister her ears with some filthy limerick."

He rubbed his hands together. "I have just the one."

Julian put his arm around my shoulders and pulled me close, but he looked at Kyoko. "Now that we know where to find her, what else do we need to kill her?"

With a small smile, she said, "Me. I'm all we need to kill that bitch."

Chapter 7

OFF TO HUNT DOWN A WITCH, we left the comfort of the house and piled into two separate cars. Julian took my hand and led me over to the Mercedes, and I had to admit I was relieved to have some time away from the constant conversation over my mega-ton fuck up.

We followed the Chevelle, winding through the streets of Chicago. The landscape slowly changed from bustling skyscrapers and busy streets to trees, trees, and more trees.

Silence stretched between Julian and me. Not the silence of two people who had grown up together, but the uncomfortable silence of two people who hadn't found common ground in a long time.

It was about time to try and heal the wounds I inflicted. "Julian, I owe you an apology."

He glanced at me. "For what?"

"For betraying you. For walking away the way I did after you saved me once again." I swallowed back the tears that threatened to topple. "Delano messed me up more than I realized. I spent months listening to him tell me you were the enemy, the reason I was unhappy. I know now that none of it was true, but it took a long time for me to stop blaming you for all my problems. I'm sorry. I know that's not enough, but it's all I have right now."

He reached over and grabbed my hand. "You don't owe me anything. None of what happened was your fault. You were brainwashed by a psycho. Just one of the many reasons he deserves to die."

Not wanting to think about the murderous asshole who was still terrorizing the city, I changed the subject. "Do you think we will be able to kill Roweena?"

"I think if anyone can it's the people in the car in front of us."

"You trust them that much?"

"I wouldn't want anyone else by my side when shit goes sideways."

I knew he was one million percent sincere, because, like me, Julian didn't trust easily.

The remainder of the ride was quiet, but this time the silence was comfortable. Twenty-seven minutes later the Chevelle turned into a frontage road that led into some very deep woods, at least by Illinois standards, and everyone piled out.

"We're on foot from here." André put his arm around Kyoko and pulled her close. "You ready for this?"

She bobbed her head and snuggled under his arm.

"Who needs a weapon?" Reaper opened the trunk and pushed a button on the side. A door slid back revealing a hidden compartment full of guns, ammo, and stakes.

Everyone but Nathan and I armed themselves with whatever they could carry.

Alexis reached into her boot and pulled out a dagger. "Maybe this will send a message to the witch community to leave us and ours alone."

A tear slid down my cheek, and I had to say something to express the emotions that were welling up inside of me. "I just wanted to say thank you for helping me. I know you don't have to, and I wouldn't blame you—" I stopped and looked at Alexis— "if you just let me die."

Her lips lifted in a half-smile. "You're Julian's sister. No matter what happened in the past, if you need help, we will help you."

Her kind words ignited a bomb of regret over my bad decisions and even worse behavior.

"Let's get going." Reaper and André led the way through the thick foliage.

It felt like an eternity of tripping over pinecones and tree limbs until we found a small cabin tucked away in the woods. Smoke billowed from the chimney, and a layer of green glowing magic clung to the cabin's exterior like moss on a tree.

"Her house is spelled against intruders," Kyoko said.

"How do we draw her out?" Reaper cocked a small-caliber pistol.

"You don't." The voice came out of the darkness, but I would know it anywhere. It was Roweena. "I knew cursing the alpha wolf's sister would get me my desired results. Everyone who did my family wrong in one place. At one time. Under my control."

She lifted her hands like a composer readying his orchestra for a concert. The wind around us picked up. Clouds covered the stars. And a green bubble of witch magic snapped up around us.

We were trapped.

Chapter 8

ROWEENA HAD TURNED me into her Trojan horse.

As if my guilt wasn't bad enough, I could now add leading my brother and all his friends into a trap. A trap they might not escape. The wall of witch magic surrounding us snapped, crackled, and popped. Little sparks flew from the surface and fell to the ground around our feet.

Alexis stepped so close to the magic, I was afraid the tip of her nose would singe off. "I would suggest you free us before we dismember you and bury you in several unmarked graves."

Roweena ran her finger down her magical wall and the magic leaned into her touch like a pet responded to its master's touch. "You could try to escape, but I wouldn't recommend it. Stepping through my barrier will have some very unpleasant side effects ending in your death."

"I don't understand." I gulped back my sob. "You asked me to kill Kyoko."

"And I still expect you to kill Kyoko. But you see she isn't the only one in that circle guilty of murder. I was raised to believe in an eye for an eye. All I needed was one lost soul to help me gather the guilty for their sentencing"

She knew all along that I would run to Julian for help.

Somehow not knowing how deeply I had betrayed them all made it worse.

"I knew we couldn't trust her." Reaper's growl would have been at home in the toughest werewolf.

Alexis wiped a tear from my cheek. "Julia didn't know the witch wanted to trap all of us. She is a victim too."

The kindness and trust she was showing me sent another tear tumbling.

"I didn't know, I swear."

The witch smacked the side of her magical wall sending a burst of green sparks into the air. "The she-wolf is correct. She was just an unwilling pawn in a game she didn't know we were playing."

Delano had used me. Roweena had used me. I was sick and tired of being a tool to hurt the people who would lay down their lives for me.

"Well, now that you've got us, what do you plan on doing with us?" Alexis asked.

Roweena pulled a crystal pendant from her pocket, held it up by the chain, and watched it sway. "This was my mother's. It's spelled to warn the wearer of danger, like an alarm. But in the end, it didn't save her." She closed her hand around the crystal. "After she was murdered, I started researching those responsible for her death. And then I learned all the best ways to torture each of you."

"Why do the bad guys always drone on and on?" Nathan poked at the magical wall. "Bloody bore if you ask me."

"It's not any fun if you don't know how you're going to die." Her lips ticked up into a cold smile. "First, I'll kill the human. Next, I'll remove that platinum trinket on Evil's Assassins finger and watch the ghost fade away into nothing. I figure after those two deaths, Alexis will do something stupid, and she'll die trying to avenge her friends."

She really had done her research.

"Then I'll make Kyoko watch as I kill André, but not until after André removes your brother's head." She pointed at Julian and my stomach clenched. "Then you'll kill Kyoko like I originally planned." Her smile was brighter than a million-watt bulb. "And after that your curse will be lifted. You'll be free to live the rest of your life with the memory of watching all of them die."

"You bitch." André lunged at the wall of magic, but Kyoko grabbed him by the back of the coat and stopped him before he became a crispy critter.

Kyoko placed her hand on his chest to settle him, then she looked at Roweena. "It's me you want, not them. I took your place on the council. Set them free and take your anger out on the witch who deserves it."

"Tempting." She popped a hand on her hip "But it is more fun to torture you with their deaths, before you die."

"All I hear is that you are too afraid to fight me one on one. If that's the case, then that means you're not as powerful as you pretend to be."

The witch's smile faded, her eyes glowed with green magic. "You want to fight? Prove who is the bigger, badder witch? Fine, I'm flexible. You'll be the first to die."

She waved her hand toward the wall surrounding us and the magic fizzled and faded until we were free.

"But it's just you and me. Magic against magic. Witch against witch. And only one of us leaves this clearing alive."

Kyoko showed her teeth in a feral grin. "Prepare to die a slow and painful death."

Chapter 9

I ALWAYS CONSIDERED myself a lover not a fighter, and tonight wasn't any different. But when fate sticks you in the center of a supernatural battle, you adapt. The fact that their lives were in danger fell squarely on my small shoulders, and I would do anything to make sure that Roweena was eating worms at the end of the night.

Even if that meant I was in the grave next to her.

André drew his sword and rushed forward, but Roweena lobbed a green ball of magic at him forcing him to dodge and roll.

Roweena snarled. "I said, witch against witch. Once she is dead, the vampires will get their turn." She had another ball in her hand ready to send it flying at anyone who didn't follow her rules.

When no one else moved, she focused on Kyoko. "You have something that is mine, and I plan on taking it back."

"Even if you kill me, the witch council will never hand the coven over to you." Kyoko's tone was matter of fact.

"Then I will kill everyone who votes against me until they understand who is in charge."

"I was there the day your mother was executed. She was crazy to the end and you're a chip off the crazy block." Kyoko rubbed her hand over the fox tattoo. "Kitso mamorimaso."

The tattoo glowed, then her magic shimmered around her. A moment later five feet of glowing fox stood between her and Roweena.

Roweena chuckled. "Do you really think your familiar can save you?"

"I think two against one is better odds." Kyoko ran her hand over the fox's glowing fur.

"Silly witch. Weren't you listening? I spent weeks researching everything about you. Did you really think I would come unprepared?"

Roweena waved her hand in my direction. Green sparks fell from her fingers, but instead of falling to the ground they floated like wicked lightning bugs. The particles of magic danced around us, coming together until they formed a slow-moving tornado. A tornado of magic that was twisting and turning in my direction.

"You may have a kitsune by your side, but how will you and your familiar stand against two werewolves?"

Fear rattled my bones.

Julian grabbed my hand and pulled me back to the safety of the group, but the tornado kept coming, twirling and swirling on its path of destruction. I stepped behind Julian. The tornado hovered in the air in front of us for less than a second before lurching forward and encompassing us in a funnel of magic.

The magic choked me, suffocated me. My hand slipped from Julian's, and I fell to my knees. Roweena's magic triggered the primal part of me. Breaking through the barriers that kept my wolf docile. My bones broke. My skin split. My blood heated. Canines ripped through my gums, and claws tore through my flesh.

When the change was over, I opened my eyes. Julian lay on the ground next to me. His black fur was still wet from the shift, his lips pulled back in a ground-rumbling growl.

Roweena snapped her fingers. "Wolves, to me."

Her command flipped a switch deep inside me, compelling me to obey. To guard her. To fight for her. To kill for her.

I fought against the compulsion. Fought to stay in control, but her magic was too strong and I lost the battle.

"Wolves. Now."

With Julian beside me, I crawled on my belly to my master.

Chapter 10

ROWEENA WAS USING us as her wolf-shaped shield. And right now, with her magic coursing through us, we were powerless to stop her.

The bitch of a witch may have forced us to change. Compelled us to follow her orders. But I refused to kill on command, even if it meant I wouldn't live to see the next full moon.

"They are mine to command." Roweena ran her fingers through my furry coat, and I shivered under her touch. "And here's a warning you don't deserve. If I die, they die. Our lives are bound together."

"How is that possible?" Kyoko asked. "You would need their blood to tie a spell to your life force."

The witch knelt next to me and grabbed my muzzle. "When this one was passed out, I siphoned her blood. It's how I was able to force her to change. And since they're twins, their blood is similar enough that my spell worked on both."

My heart sank hearing that my betrayal of Julian went blood deep. Hell, it went bone deep. Now, because of me, he was stuck as a wolf and being used as a weapon against the people he cared about. And there was no way to free either of us without our heads and hearts going boom.

Alexis pulled a dagger from her boot and stepped in front of Kyoko, taking her place as the leader. "We will find a way to break your bond, and when we do, you'll die."

"But can you break the bond before I kill you?"

Roweena's hands sparked with magic. It crawled up her arms, wrapped around her body, and surrounded her until she was nothing more than a walking, talking, magic cocoon. She mumbled some words, and a bolt of lightning shot out of the sky and hit the ground at Kyoko's feet, almost taking off a toe or two.

"It's hard to perform magic when you're on the defense." More lightning bolts randomly hit, keeping everyone on the run.

Kyoko sparked up her own magic, orange instead of the green I was familiar with. Kitso left his place by her side and positioned himself between his master and Julian and me.

"I fought against much tougher opponents than you and I'm still standing." The confidence in Kyoko's words could not be missed.

Roweena had said that our lives were tied to hers, which meant that if Kyoko was successful in killing her, Julian and I would die too. As much as I didn't want today to be my last, I would welcome death as long as Roweena no longer walked the earth.

Kyoko held out her hands, orange flames rising from her palms. She blew at the flames, and they shot from her hands like a missile.

A missile aimed at her enemy.

Roweena dodged the flying flame, but an ember of magic landed on the edge of her long skirt, sparking a small fire. The magical flame grew. She stamped frantically at the flames trying to engulf her.

"Kitso, now." Kyoko yelled, more flames dancing in her palm.

Kitso rushed forward in a blur of orange fur. When he was inches away from Roweena, he raised his paw, razon-sharp claws extended, and struck her face.

Rowena screamed. Four bloody furrows ran from her forehead to her chin. She rushed to cover them, but her blood dripped from the deep cuts. Kitso swiped some before bounding back to his master.

Kyoko held out her hand and Kitso ran his paw over it, smearing blood on her palm. She closed her other hand over the bloody one and lowered her head. Another flame shot from her hands, but this time, she sent it in our direction. It hit the ground, surrounding us in the center of her magical fire.

"Kizuna o tachikiru" she yelled.

The flames around us grew, trapping us in yet another cage.

Kyoko's flames didn't touch either of us, but I felt something while standing in that small circle. An invisible hand reaching into my chest. Power rolled through me until it found the part of me that controlled my wolf. The power circled around, grabbed hold, and squeezed. If I had been human, the pain would have drawn an unholy scream from my throat. As a wolf, all I could do was let out a howl.

Julian howled next to me.

As quickly as the pain started, it stopped. When it did, Roweena's magic disappeared too. The hold she had on my ability to shift, the connection I felt since I woke up in that cage, was gone.

Had Kyoko's Hail Mary worked?

"You're free from her control," Kyoko yelled.

It was time for Roweena to die. And I would do the killing. Even if it meant I would be cut out of the pack forever.

My whole life I had been afraid. Afraid that what had happened to my parents would happen to me. I allowed everyone else in my life to protect me, save me from my own mistakes, and stand up for me when I should have been standing up for myself.

No more. It was time for me to fight my own battles. To protect those I loved. And the people who stood by my side when they didn't have to.

Kyoko might have been Roweena's target, but she used me to try to hurt her. To hurt Julian and Alexis and Reaper and André and Nathan. Alexis had helped Julian save me once, it was time for me to repay the favor.

Instead of shifting back to my human form, I took advantage of the strength and speed I had as a werewolf. I licked Julian's muzzle, silently telling him that I loved him, appreciated him. He would do whatever he could to save me from Roweena, but this wasn't his fight. It was mine. And I was going to do what I had wanted to since the moment I woke up in her cage.

I was going to tear her throat out with my teeth.

With one last look at my brother, I ran through Kyoko's magic.

Roweena and Kyoko were facing off in the center of the clearing, so focused on each other and the magic balls they were lobbing at each other, they didn't notice the wolf sneaking up behind them.

Without a second thought about whether I would live or die, I attacked.

I hit Roweena in the center of her back with my paws, knocking her to the ground. She rolled over, a look of terror pinching her face into something unpleasant.

I bared my teeth and a drop of drool fell to her cheek, sliding down.

She struggled under me, pushing at my chest to throw me off, but I extended my claws and pricked her flesh. She screamed. I dug deeper, forcing them into her skin as far as they would go. Her scream faded into a whimper.

"If I die, you die," she pushed out with a labored breath.

Kyoko had said otherwise, but that was a risk I was going to have to take.

With one last growl and as much wolfie smile as I could muster, I wrapped my jaws around her throat and sank my teeth into her soft flesh. I squeezed and squeezed and squeezed.

Blood filled my mouth, coating it with a metallic taste. I gagged but didn't let go. Instead, I bit down harder until her heartbeat slowed, sputtered, then stopped.

I released my hold, and Roweena's limp corpse fell to the ground. I waited for a magical dagger to pierce my heart, but nothing happened.

At least not to me.

Green magic enveloped the witch, the wind picked up all around us, and then everything stilled.

Eerily quiet. Eerily silent. Just fucking eerie.

"That can't be good." André grabbed Kyoko and pulled her away from Roweena's body. The rest of us followed.

Silence was soon replaced with a high-pitched buzz. The buzz grew louder, closer. Roweena's body lifted off the ground as if raised up by invisible hands. It spun once, then it exploded with an ear-destroying bang.

The impact knocked me back and I collided with a tree, falling to the ground. I looked around the clearing. Everyone else had been laid flat from the bomb Roweena's death had triggered.

I forced myself to shift back to my human form. When I was walking on two legs again, I rushed over to Julian, both of us no longer wolves and as naked as the day we were born. Being a wolf, we learned long ago to be comfortable around dangling bits, but I still averted my eyes from my brother's. I checked him over for injuries, but besides a few bloody cuts on his face and arms, he seemed to be fine.

"Julia, are you okay?" He gently patted me down looking for wounds, but careful to avoid my own lady parts.

"I'm fine. I killed her." The words felt foreign on my tongue and an inappropriate giggle escaped. However, I sobered up quickly, tears forming in the corner of my eyes. I had taken a life. That meant my days in the pack were over because death equaled excommunication.

Reaper tossed a go-bag at our feet. "Get dressed. I've seen enough naked Monroe's for one lifetime."

Julian and I quickly dressed.

"What is it with witches and destructive death bombs?" Nathan asked, floating just over Alexis's shoulder.

"They like to deliver one last F-you to the world before they go out." Reaper stuffed his weapons back in all the hidden places on his body.

"You saved us." Alexis rubbed my arms affectionately.

I tried to smile at her words, but my mouth quivered with a frown instead. I turned toward the woods. As much as I didn't want to leave, it was better for everyone if I went peacefully, especially after the chaos I had caused.

"Julia, where are you going?" Julian grabbed my arm, stopping me in my tracks.

"I won't force you to excommunicate your own sister." I started sobbing. "I'll go quietly."

"You're not being excommunicated. You killed out of self-defense. No wolf would ever be ousted for that."

"A death is a death." We both knew the rules.

He placed his hands on my shoulders, forcing me to meet his eyes. "Yes, a death is a death, but sometimes it's unavoidable. Today was one of those times. I'm the Alpha, my word is law."

I wrapped my arms around him, hugging him tight. "Thank you for everything."

"We're family, it's what we do."

"Julia, do you know what you need now that you've saved everyone's knickers?" Nathan's lips spread into a lopsided grin.

I wrinkled my nose at him. "No. What?"

"A poem to mark the momentous occasion." He winked, and everyone else groaned. "There was an old whore pulling tricks. Who at one time could handle five pricks. One day she did cry. As she pulled out her glass eye. Tell the boys I can now handle six."

Alexis slapped a hand over his mouth. "Nathan, that was filthy." Then she turned to me. "Well, you've now been christened by one of Nathan's limericks, so you're officially part of the team."

My heart swelled. They had accepted me. Even with all the horrible things I had done in the past. Even though I led them into a trap. It wasn't until Alexis had said the words, that I realized how much I needed that acceptance.

Before tonight, I had been content being a lone wolf. I thought keeping my distance from the supernatural community would keep me safe. Protected. Out of the supernatural war that had been brewing in Chicago for months.

But the war had found me anyway.

Every wolf needs a pack at their back. Maybe I had finally found mine.

*Want more from the world of Alexis Black? Start with **Evil's Unlikely Assassin**, book one in the award-winning Alexis Black Novels. For more information, exclusive content, and spur of the moment contests, please feel free to join my **newsletter**! Just for joining, you'll get **Premium Evil**, an Alexis Black short story collection for free.*

A Myth in Moonlight

BECCA ANDRE

Chapter 1

THE MOON BROKE through the clouds, illuminating the prehistoric effigy mound in its cool blue light. I took a step closer to the low rail of the observation platform, mesmerized by the sight before me. This was my first trip to Serpent Mound, and though an Ohioan from birth, I had always been more apt to visit historical sites far from home rather than those in my own back yard.

Against my better judgment, I had climbed the rickety lookout tower, but was now glad I had taken the risk. The view of the winding, three-foot-high mound in the tranquil wash of moonlight was amazing. I could clearly see the nearby coiled tail and even get an impression of the distant head swallowing an earthen egg.

"Nice view," a male voice said from right beside me.

Thinking I was alone, I jumped in surprise, then grabbed the handrail when I found myself much too close to the edge.

"Sorry." Conor gripped my upper arm as if afraid I was about to tumble over the side. "I didn't mean to startle you."

"I'm fine."

He immediately released me, and I realized I must have snapped the words.

"I wasn't paying attention," I hurried to add. "I figured I was the only one foolish enough to climb this thing."

He pressed his lips into a fine line as he studied me through narrowed eyes. "I think you just called me a fool."

"I didn't mean to imply—"

"I'm kidding, Leena." He broke into a laugh, the moonlight glinting in his fair eyes. "Come on, you'd have to be a little foolish to climb this thing in daylight, let alone total darkness."

I smiled at his good humor, trying to hide the anxiety worming through my stomach. It hadn't occurred to me until this moment that the other students in my folklore class would have difficulty navigating the tower steps at night. Had Conor noticed that my night vision wasn't natural?

"This trip would have been much more informative if we'd come during the day," Conor continued, casting an annoyed look in the direction of the serpent's head where Professor Giles had gone with the bulk of our classmates.

"This class is part of his Magic in Myth curriculum," I reminded him. "You've got to expect a little magic—and Serpent Mound at night is certainly magical." I added the last in a rush, then watched his face closely. I didn't know Conor well. In truth, I'd only known him for about five weeks, having met in this very class. I knew he was a history major and that he appeared to view anything magical with distain. I hoped I was wrong about that.

Conor studied the scene before us. The moon was full and without the clouds, I figured he must be able to make out a fair amount of detail.

"I guess you have a point," he conceded. "But I was hoping for a little more *fact* from this class. It was described as a history of local folklore in the catalog—which sounded like a fun elective for me. I enjoy local history, but all the professor has lectured on is fairies and werewolves."

"If you can set aside your expectations, you might find it entertaining."

A hint of his smile returned. "Perhaps." He focused on me. "You've never said why you took this class. You're a science major, right? That hardly seems the type of person who'd be interested in unicorns."

My attempt to hold in a laugh became a snort. "Unicorns? Professor Giles has never lectured on unicorns."

Conor shrugged. "I'm sure I saw it on the syllabus."

"Right." I smiled as I shook my head. "In answer to your question, I've always had a fascination with myths and such. When I saw the class listing, I though it sounded like fun, and I needed an elective." I wasn't about to tell him that I'd been hoping that a better understanding of the old myths would help me puzzle out my own gift. "Come on. Everyone could use a little magic in their lives."

"Hmm." He pursed his lips and I watched him closely, hoping for some indication as to how he felt about—

A sound, eerily like a high-pitched female scream, carried across the moonlit grounds. For a moment, I thought it might be some kind of night bird we didn't have in Cincinnati, but when a couple more screams joined the first, I realized they were human.

Conor whirled and started down the stairs, taking the narrow steps far too quickly. Maybe his inability to see well in the low light hid the danger or maybe heights didn't make him as uneasy as they made me. Whatever the case, he was long gone by the time I reached the ground.

The screams had come from the direction of the serpent's head, and since our classmates were the only people out here—I assumed —it had to be them. Had someone fallen over the cliff that bordered that end of the mound? Maybe Conor was right. A nighttime visit wasn't such a good idea.

A paved trail bordered the mound on both sides, forming a loop around the thirteen-hundred-foot-long earthworks. My legs were burning by the time I approached the head of the serpent.

Conor easily outdistanced me, disappearing around the end of the mound, though the screams had quieted before we were halfway there.

Slowing my pace, both out of a need to catch my breath and uncertainty, I rounded the egg-shaped earthworks beyond the mouth of the serpent. Where was everyone?

On the other side of the oval mound, a trail led down the bank. From the pictures on the internet, I knew the path led to a railed deck built on the edge of a cliff that overlooked the stream far below, but the encroaching forest blocked my view. I hadn't gone far when I spied two women sitting on the edge of the leaf-covered trail. I recognized both from class.

"What happened?" I asked.

"We were attacked," one girl answered—I couldn't remember her name. "This big dog ran out of the woods and bit Kristie." She nodded at her companion.

"It might have been a coyote," Kristie added, gripping her calf where I assumed she'd been bitten.

"Where are the others?" I asked.

"They walked down to the overlook with Professor Giles. I stopped to get a rock out of my shoe."

"When I heard her scream, I came back," the other girl said, then turned to Kristie. "Wasn't Pete with you?"

Kristie forehead wrinkled. "I never saw him. Do you think the coyote grabbed him before me?"

The other girl gripped her dark braid and looked over her shoulder, her brown eyes wide as she studied the forest that surrounded us. How well could she see into that shadowed darkness? Could she define the individual trunks of the tall, closely spaced trees, or was she just watching for movement?

"Leena?"

I jumped at the sound of Conor's voice as it carried to me from farther down the trail.

Promising to get help, I left the girls and hurried to Conor. He knelt beside a young man—was this Pete?—who was sitting up, holding his shoulder. The zippered hoodie he wore had been pulled down, exposing his white T-shirt and the spreading stain on his sleeve that looked black in the moonlight, but I knew would appear bright red in sunlight.

"What happened?" I whispered, squatting beside them.

"It was this big dog," the young man answered. "It ran out of the woods and jumped me."

"Where are the others?" Conor asked. "Professor Giles?"

"He led them down the trail to the overlook. I was waiting on Kristie. She stopped to tie her shoe or something." He looked up at me. "I heard her scream. Is she okay?"

"It bit her in the calf," I answered.

His brow wrinkled with evident concern. "Is it bad?"

"I don't know."

With Conor's help, he got to his feet. "I'll go check on her." Still holding his shoulder, he hurried back toward the girls.

"We need to find the others," Conor said. "Come on." He didn't wait for my response before heading on down the trail.

Glancing at the shadowed forest all around us, I hurried after him. Had the animal run off? If it was a wild animal, did it have young nearby? Maybe that was why it had attacked. Or was it rabid?

"I knew I should have brought a flashlight," Conor grumbled. Professor Giles had insisted that we leave them behind. He wanted us to view the mound in the light of the full moon, insisting there were lunar as well as solar alignments built into the mound by its creators.

As for myself, the lack of a flashlight wasn't normally a problem, but I didn't like the shadows beneath the trees where the moonlight didn't reach. Even my excellent night vision couldn't completely penetrate that darkness. I was so tempted to do something about it, but I—

A snarl was the only warning I got before a huge canid bounded out those very shadows I had been longing to illuminate. For just an instant, I was frozen in place, watching in fascinated horror as it ran right at me. Nope, not a dog, or even a coyote. That was a wolf. A gigantic two-hundred-pound representative of a breed only seen in northern climes. Had it escaped a zoo?

These thoughts flashed across my mind in the space of seconds, then my survival instincts kicked in. Running wasn't an option. I could never outrun a wolf, but maybe I could scare it away. Did I dare—

"Leena!" Suddenly, Conor was there. He shouldered me aside, stepping into the path of the closing wolf.

I pressed both hands to my mouth as the animal sprang. It hit Conor square in the chest and took him to the ground.

Conor grunted on impact but managed to get his hands up in an attempt to keep the wolf from his throat. The deep snarls and snapping jaws made it clear that animal wasn't ready to concede defeat.

I spun in a circle as I studied the ground, looking for a weapon—maybe a large stick or a rock. But I saw nothing suitable.

Conor cried out, and I looked back. The wolf had clamped down on his forearm.

Out of options, I opened myself to the moonlight, drawing in that soft blue glow. Joy filled me as our immediate surroundings plunged into darkness an instant before a bright silver-white light exploded around us. I knew that light was coming from me.

"Hey!" I shouted.

The wolf lifted its head. I expected the golden eyes of a typical wolf, but this animal had blue eyes, like a husky. However, its coat was the usual gray with whiter fur along the belly, inner legs, and jaw—which made the blood on its muzzle stand out.

I held those blue eyes with my own, the intense silver light I controlled twinkling back at me. His raised hackles smoothed, and he covered his exposed teeth as the serene tranquility of the moon calmed him. Interesting. I had never tried this on an animal.

Conor turned his head, and like the wolf, stared at me with the same wide-eyed shock. Crap. The last thing I wanted was to dazzle him with my power. I needed to hurry.

"Go!" I shouted at the wolf, then pulled in more moonlight, creating a brilliant flash.

To my utter amazement, the wolf tucked his tail and, with a whimper, turned and sprinted for the trees. Once he was beyond the glow of my moonlight, he vanished into the shadows. Was he gone, or would he return and—

"Leena?" Conor whispered.

With a gasp, I looked down to see him staring up at me. I let go of the moonlight, and we were suddenly plunged into darkness.

Maybe it was my relief that I'd driven off the wolf, or just the absence of the magic, but my legs turned to jelly. I reached out, hoping to brace myself, but there was nothing to grab. Instead, I just wind milled my arms for a moment, then fell on my butt. Hopefully, Conor was still flash-blinded and hadn't seen that.

"Are you okay?" I asked, trying to direct his attention away from, well, everything about me. "Your arm?"

"Is bleeding," he muttered. "A lot."

Oh damn. I pushed myself up onto my hands and knees and crawled toward him across the dewy grass. As moonlight returned to fill the lightless void I had created, my night vision rapidly returned.

Conor was sitting up, cradling his arm against him. Even from a distance, I could see the bloodstains saturating the sleeve of his jacket. He stared in my direction, though it was clear that his unfocused gaze wasn't on me. But that wasn't anything to be concerned about. I'd read that mundane humans could take up to half an hour to regain their night vision.

"Hey," I said, letting him hear my voice so he knew where I was. "Let me see."

He pulled away when I touched his shoulder. "I need to keep pressure on it," he said, the words coming out in a rush. "Maybe you should call for help."

Did he really need to keep pressure on it, or was he afraid to let me touch him?

Heart in my throat, I pulled out my phone and dialed 911.

Chapter 2

THE UNIVERSITY SENT someone to drive the school van home, but only four other students and I needed the ride back to Cincinnati. Conor, Kristie, and two other young man had been sent to a local hospital for treatment, along with Professor Giles. He hadn't been bitten, but when he'd tried to run back up the trail to help those who had, he'd brained himself on a low-hanging tree branch. The head wound had bleed heavily, but the EMT felt confident he'd just get a few stitches to go with his concussion.

The ride home had been accompanied by excited conversation about the evening's events, but I hadn't joined in. I was just glad that none of the other students had seen what I had done. It was bad enough that Conor had.

Being magical wasn't that big a deal in Cincinnati. Magic had become much more accepted since it had returned to the world twenty-five years ago. Or perhaps I should say it was tolerated. But I preferred to keep my ability to myself. Not that manipulating moonbeams would gain me much renown, but knowledge of my talent could lead to knowledge of my past.

It was a relief to finally get home. I had never been so glad to return to my little apartment just off campus. I was also grateful that I didn't have an early class the following morning and could sleep in.

Before I turned out the lights, I composed a text to Conor, asking how he was. After a bit of back and forth with myself, I finally hit send. He didn't answer before I dozed off.

With a math class at eleven, I didn't get to sleep the whole morning, but my grumpiness faded when I checked my phone. Conor had answered my text around 3 am. His response seemed a bit stilted and formal, but I knew I shouldn't try to read too much into a text—especially one sent after a long night in the emergency room.

According to Conor's terse report, the punctures in his arm hadn't required stitches, just a lot of disinfecting. Then he'd received the rabies shots. I'd always heard bad things about that, but apparently, it now required a shot at the wound site—which was some kind of preventive—and a shot of the vaccine in the upper arm. Although, it sounded like he'd need up to three more shots of the vaccine over the next couple of weeks.

Glad to hear you'll make a full recovery, I typed, then hesitated. *Do you still want me to come over this afternoon? I'll bring lunch.* We'd been planning to work on the essay Professor Giles assigned before the trip.

I hit send, then waited...and waited. Was he asleep, or was he trying to find a polite way to say that he didn't want to see me anymore? Not that we were anything more than friends, and new ones at that, but I'd be lying if I didn't admit that I had been hoping for more.

Pulling up my legs, I wrapped my arms around my shins and rested my chin on my knees. Was Conor upset about my display of power and the unusual way I could manipulate moonlight? It seemed that most mundanes either regarded the magical with fanatical awe or they distrusted us. Perhaps Conor fell into the second category—not that I wanted him to worship me either.

"Wallowing won't fix anything." I pushed back the covers and got to my feet. "Besides, you might not have a reason to wallow." After all, Conor really might be sleeping and would answer me when he woke.

Trying to push aside my worries, I headed for the shower. If I didn't hear from him by the time class was over, I'd give him a call.

MATH CLASS CAME AND WENT, but Conor maintained his silence. It was nearly one in the afternoon. Surely, he wasn't still asleep. Was he ghosting me?

The more I thought about it, the angrier I got. If he didn't like the magical, he should at least have the cojones to tell me so.

My anger carried me across campus but began to fade as I walked the two blocks to Conor's neighborhood. What if he'd simply forgotten to charge his phone, or he'd had a class and failed to take it with him? From what I'd learned of him in our short acquaintance, he was punctual and polite, but also forthright and outspoken. If he had a problem with me, he wouldn't run away. He would tell me how he felt.

My hesitant steps came to a stop outside his door. Despite my effort to convince myself that he wasn't ignoring me, I couldn't eliminate my fear.

"You're not going to run," I whispered to myself. "Let's have this out and be done with it." I reached up and firmly rapped my knuckles against the door.

To my surprise, the door popped open a crack. It hadn't been latched. My fears surged again, but this time, for a different reason. I'd failed to consider another possible cause for Conor's silence. He might be unwell.

"Conor?" I called though the opening.

He didn't answer.

Pushing the door fully open, I stepped inside. Something crunched underfoot, and I noticed that a clear glass bowl lay in pieces against the entryway tile. Had it been sitting on the small table by the door, perhaps to hold keys?

"Conor?" I called out again.

A soft noise carried out of the hall on the other side of the living room, but no voice answered me. It was possible that he might be wearing earbuds or something, but the open door and broken bowl suggested a bigger problem.

Closing the front door, I crossed the living room and started down the hall. This was my first visit to Conor's place, but I didn't need to be given a tour to figure out where everything was. Down the short hall were two partially open doors. The tile trim and towel rack visible through the one on the right suggested a bathroom, so I moved toward the door on the left.

"Conor?" I took another step closer and knocked on the half-open door.

Like the outer door, my knock caused it to swing inward, but it only moved a few inches before clunking against something on the other side.

Conor still hadn't answered me, so I peeked around the door to see what was preventing it from opening.

To my horror, I saw Conor lying face down on the carpet. Aside from the clean white bandage encircling his forearm, he wasn't wearing a stitch of clothing.

I tried to ignore the heat in my cheeks as I dropped to my knees beside him. I gripped his bare shoulder, noting how cool his skin felt.

"Conor." I gave him a gentle shake. "Hey, wake up."

As if my command had done the trick, he gasped and opened his eyes.

"Conor?"

He pulled in another breath and twisted around to stare at me. "Leena?"

"Yeah. Sorry to just barge in, but when you didn't answer my text, I came to check on you."

"I don't…" He sat up with ease, then glanced down. "Oh, shit."

"Sorry," I repeated, my cheeks now on fire. I snatched up a

towel that lay on the floor a short distance away and handed it to him.

"I think I should be the one to apologize." He draped the towel over his lap, a blush coloring his pale skin.

For some reason, the blush was oddly endearing in a guy who had always struck me as so confident and carefree. "No, you don't need to apologize," I answered. "I invaded your privacy."

"For the record, I don't make it a habit to sleep naked on my bedroom floor."

I smiled at his attempt at humor. "I wasn't judging."

He tried to return the smile, but a worried look replaced his amusement almost immediately. Glancing around, he raked a hand through his auburn hair, the movement doing interesting things to the muscles of his arm and chest.

"I have no idea how I got here," he said, the words little more than a whisper.

I returned my wandering eyes to his face. "What happened?"

An uncertain frown creased his brow. "I remember feeling a little off on my way home, like I was coming down with a cold or a fever. I thought a shower might help, but I don't remember much after I opened my front door."

That explained the unlocked door, discarded towel, and his current state of dress—or undress.

"Maybe you should visit a doctor or something."

"Maybe." He got to his feet, snugging the towel around his waist as he did so.

I quickly stood beside him, afraid he might fall, but he seemed steady. He didn't sway or brace himself on the wall. "Do you still feel sick?" I asked.

"Actually, I feel fine." He shrugged, seeming a bit embarrassed about the whole thing. The blush had faded, and he did look less pale than he had. "I should get dressed."

Now that he seemed all right, my earlier insecurities returned. Did I really need to confront him about my magical nature? "I'll go."

"Go?"

"Home. I just wanted to make certain you were okay. I'll—" A knock at his apartment door made me jump. "Expecting someone?" I asked softly, then felt a bit foolish about whispering.

Conor frowned. "No."

"Shall I answer it while you dress?"

"I would appreciate that."

With a nod, I turned to go.

"Leena?"

I stopped and looked back.

"Don't leave. We need to talk." His green eyes met mine.

I took a deep breath and released it. "All right."

Pulling his bedroom door closed behind me, I walked back to his living room. Anxiety coursed through me, but it had nothing to do with the visitor at his door. The only thing Conor could want to talk about was what he had seen last night. It looked like we'd be discussing my magic after all.

Releasing a shaky breath, I rolled up on my toes and peered through the peep hole. A man I didn't know stood on Conor's front stoop.

"Can I help you?" I called through the door, keeping my eye to the peep hole.

"My name is Detective Brody." The man lifted a wallet containing a shiny gold badge to the peep hole.

For an instant, my stomach dropped, and I was consumed by the need to run. Then I reminded myself that the past was passed. This cop wasn't here for me.

"I'm investigating what happened last night at Serpent Mound," the detective added as if he sensed my desire to flee. "Is Conor Middleton in?"

Had the university given him Conor's name? But why call the police department—the Cincinnati Police Department—for an animal attack two counties over? But those questions didn't make me doubt this man's credentials. I opened the door to Detective Brody.

He smiled in greeting, then pulled open his sports coat to tuck away his badge, giving me a brief glimpse of the holstered gun under his left arm.

I swallowed. "Conor will be out in a moment."

"Might you be Selena Terrell?"

"I am," I answered, my tone hesitant. How did he—

"I stopped by your apartment earlier," He answered the question I hadn't voiced.

"Oh. May I ask why?"

"I was hoping you could tell me about the events of last night."

"Oh. Yeah, sure. No problem. I can do that." I realized I was rambling and made myself stop. "Come in." I stepped back and gestured for him to enter. "And most folks call me Leena."

"Nice to meet you, Leena."

We didn't get to continue our conversation as Conor emerged from the hall, dressed in a pair of jeans and a T-shirt. I introduced the two men, watching Conor's expression as they shook hands. He didn't appear overly bothered by the detective's arrival, but then, Conor didn't have a past like mine—I assumed.

Accepting Conor's invitation to join us in the living room, Detective Brody took a seat on the recliner, leaving the couch for Conor and me. I sat on the edge of my cushion, watching as the detective pulled a small voice recorder from the pocket of his sports coat. He set it on the coffee table before us but didn't press the record button.

"Is the university investigating what happened?" I gripped my suddenly shaking hands, silently chiding myself for this display of nerves.

"Not exactly," Detective Brody answered. "I am."

"Oh?"

"This isn't the first animal attack we've had."

"In Cincinnati?" Conor asked.

"But we were at Serpent Mound last night," I cut in. "How could it be the same animal?"

Detective Brody's eyes met mine. There was something knowing in his look, but it was more than just him having knowledge I lacked. Whatever it was, it gave me a chill.

"I don't believe it's an animal," Detective Brody answered. "Well, not in the traditional sense. There's an intelligence behind it."

"I don't understand."

Detective Brody dropped his gaze and shifted in his seat, looking uncomfortable. "It's just a hunch." He reached for his recorder. "Tell me about last night?" Not waiting for our response, he pushed the record button.

I glanced over at Conor, and he shrugged. Whatever it was about the detective that made me uneasy, it didn't seem to affect Conor. He rested his bandaged forearm on the cushion beside him and began to recount the events of last night. He described how we'd been atop the lookout tower, admiring the moonlit mound, when we heard screams.

"Screams?" Detective Brody asked.

"From the far end of the serpent," I spoke up, then took over. "Conor and I ran toward the sound and found a couple of class-mates who had been bitten. Then the wolf had run out of the woods, coming right for me."

Detective Brody stopped me there, asking me to describe the big canid. I did as he asked, wondering if he had other eyewitness accounts that described the same animal, but I didn't question him on it since the recorder was running.

"Go on," he prompted when I finished.

"I stepped forward, hoping to scare it away." Conor took up the tale once more. "But it came after me instead and took me to the ground."

"It bit you?" Detective Brody asked.

"It was going for my throat, but I got my arm up." Conor rubbed the opposite hand over his bandaged forearm. "If not for Leena, I'm sure it would have killed me."

"Leena?" The detective's gaze shifted to me.

My heart was pounding so loudly, I barely heard my name, but I didn't hesitate. The lie rolled off my tongue with an ease born of experience. "I grabbed a thick stick and chased the wolf away."

Detective Brody looked up, then glanced at Conor, seeming to look to him for confirmation.

It wasn't until that moment that I realized what I had done. I had asked Conor to lie for me—to the police.

Chapter 3

"LEENA CHASED THE WOLF AWAY?" Detective Brody asked Conor.

A momentary pause followed, and I felt certain they would hear my pounding heart.

"Yes, she chased it away," Conor answered, keeping his focus on the detective.

Gratitude filled me as I struggled not to slump, or sigh in relief. Conor hadn't lied. He just failed to mention that I hadn't used a stick.

"It ran off into the woods," I said before the detective could ask anything else. "Then I called 911."

Detective Brody studied us with those knowing eyes, then leaned forward and shut off the recorder.

I released a quiet breath, but didn't glance at Conor. I addressed the detective instead. "Do you think it's the same animal?" I was curious, but also needed to fill the silence.

"You're the first to get so detailed a look," Detective Brody answered. "Especially with regard to the eye color."

His answer did nothing for my pounding heart. Did he know how well I could see in the dark? Was he baiting me? What if—

"It's also very helpful," he continued, stopping me from conjuring more elaborate scenarios. "I can rule out the nagual."

"The na-what?" I must have misheard him. I needed to pay attention.

"Nagual. Mesoamerican shapeshifters. They're a kind of Old Magic more common to the desert Southwest."

In the magical world, you were either Old Magic or New. The monikers had come into use back when magic had reappeared. A small percentage of the populace had developed an ability to wield this New Magic. People born since that time, people like me, often came into their magical ability at puberty. But we weren't the only magic users in the world.

With the acceptance of New Magic, those who had always possessed magic came out of hiding. It turned out that the old myths and legends hadn't been total fabrications. Magic had always existed in one form or another. Necromancers were the dominate Old Magic users in Cincinnati. I had never heard of the nagual.

"Do these nagual live in Cincinnati?" Conor asked, a frown on his face. Was he annoyed to learn there were more magic users in the city than he realized?

"Only a few," Detective Brody answered. "The key point is that their animals—and they're not limited to wolves—have golden eyes."

I sat up straighter, suddenly understanding his earlier comment about our canid attacker not being a traditional animal. "You think this wolf is a shapeshifter?"

Detective Brody's unsettling gaze held mine. "I do. Let me show you something." Without waiting for my response, he reached inside his sports coat and pulled out a cell phone. "This footage was shot from a security camera. It's not the best quality, but it reveals enough."

A few taps on his phone screen, then he passed it to Conor, who sat closer. I leaned over to get a better view of the screen. The detective was right. The image was washed out and grainy, but it was clear enough that I could make out the wall of a building. A line of small, square windows positioned one atop of the other traveled up the side of the building above a single door with no handle.

"I know that building," Conor said. "It's here on campus."

"That's right," Detective Brody answered.

Before they could commit further, the door in the video burst open with a suddenness that startled me. The video had no sound, so I didn't hear the door crash off the wall as a man in gym shorts and a T-shirt rushed through the opening.

He glanced back at the door, then hurried over behind a nearby tree—though our angle allowed us to see him. He hesitated a moment, then glanced up at the sky. I was about to ask what was happening when he began to quickly remove his clothes.

Even though the man's back was to the camera, I felt my cheeks warm—for the second time today. "Um, what…"

"Sorry, I should have warned you," Detective Brody answered. "But just watch."

I took a breath, about to ask if he knew who the man was, when a flash of light engulfed him. The glare was so bright it made me squint, then it was gone and so was the man. Though the spot where he stood wasn't empty. A huge dog—no, a wolf stood in his place.

"Dear God," Conor whispered.

The large canid lifted its head and glanced around, then took off at a trot that carried him out of frame. The video ended.

"Was that the same wolf?" Detective Brody asked.

Conor tapped the phone screen, rewinding the footage and pausing it at the moment the wolf lifted its head. The image quality was poor and in black and white, making it difficult to tell if it was the animal that had attacked us last night.

"I don't know," Conor said. "It was on me so quick that I didn't get a good look."

"He's certainly big enough to be the same wolf," I answered. "I remember thinking that it looked like one of those arctic wolves and wondered if it had escaped from a zoo."

"Sorry." Conor handed the phone back to Detective Brody.

"Between the speed of the attack and the low light, I can't say for certain that it was the same animal."

Detective Brody sighed. "I guess that would have made it too easy." He slipped his phone back in his coat pocket.

"Do you know who that was?" I asked, nodding toward his chest where he'd tucked away his phone.

"Unfortunately, no. With the low light and poor image quality, the facial recognition software couldn't get a match. And there's a gym in the building which was probably the reason he was there. Since it's open to all students, no records are kept on who comes and goes."

"Seems odd that some shifter is running around attacking people," Conor said, anger underlying his tone. "Let alone driving all the way to Serpent Mound to do it."

"True, but it has to be the same person," Detective Brody insisted. "New Magic shifters are extremely rare and often come from a lineage of powerful magic users—a couple in direct line to an Element."

The Elements were not just the most powerful magically, they were also the leaders of the New Magic Community. They came in families of four, each possessing a matter-specific form of telekinesis that gave them power over a state of matter: solid, liquid, gas, or plasma. Though for some reason, they had been named for the original elements of the ancient world: earth, water, air, and fire.

"As far as I could learn, there are no New Magic wolf shifters," Detective Brody added.

"You seem very knowledgeable," I said. "I thought you worked for the CPD, not the PIA." The Paranormal Investigation Agency policed the magical world, not the Cincinnati Police Department.

"There was a recent incident that forced me to learn more about shifters. As for my responsibilities, I'm liaison to Magical Affairs for the CPD."

"Ah." Things were starting to make more sense, but that did nothing for my anxiety. If Detective Brody had a connection to magical crimes, he may not be as ignorant of my past as he appeared.

"You said there were other attacks," Conor prompted.

"Three in the past two weeks. One took place shortly after that video was captured."

"Were they all on campus?" I asked.

"Two were, one was just off. That's what led me to request security footage from nearby cameras." Detective Brody got to his feet, and we did the same.

"Thank you for your help, both of you." He pulled out a couple of business cards and handed one to each of us. "If you think of anything else, call me?"

"Of course." Conor followed him to the door.

Was it just my imagination, or did the detective suddenly want to get out of here? Maybe he had an appointment.

With a final word of thanks, Detective Brody let himself out, and Conor closed the door behind him. I was about to comment on the detective's rushed exit when Conor faced me, an angry scowl on his face.

"So the animal that attacked me was a man?" Conor demanded.

"I guess?" I could see why Conor was angry. That was much more troubling than if it were simply a rabid animal.

"Shouldn't you have noticed what he was?"

Because I was magical. I looked down, studying my clasped hands. "Only an Element has the ability to recognize another magic user simply by being near him or her." At least, that's what I'd heard. I'd never met an Element.

"Well, I guess there's that," Conor muttered.

I looked up. "Are you suggesting that I knew what he was? You thought I was protecting him?" That went right through me.

Conor huffed. "No, but…"

"But what?" I demanded, now as angry as he appeared to be.

"You lied to me."

"When have I ever lied to you?"

"Okay, not a direct lie, but all this time, I've been bad-mouthing magic and you just sat there and took it." He was clearly still angry, but I now sensed an element of chagrin in his tone. That surprised me—and cooled my own irritation. Was he more upset over his own magic bashing than he was about me being magical?

I decided to let him off the hook. "Your comments were usually within the context of the class and some old myth that wasn't even true."

"Apparently, werewolves are real."

"The man in the video appeared to be a New Magic shifter. As Detective Brody said, they're very rare and from what I understand, quite different from the werewolves of myth."

"They seem pretty similar to me." Conor's frown remained in place. "They both become wolves."

"And that's where the similarities end. A New Magic shifter inherits his ability and is in complete control of his magic. Even when he's the wolf, he's mentally very much himself. According to legend, mythical werewolves acquire their magic through a curse or the bite of another. They can't control anything about their magic and often don't even remember what happened when they were the wolf."

"So you're saying I won't go wolf at the next full moon."

I smiled at what might be an attempt at humor. "Of course not."

"Huh." Conor looked away, frowning at nothing in particular. "That leaves me to wonder what the hell happened last night. It seems some crazy magical dude bit me."

"That, or he was there for someone else, and we got in the way."

Conor's gaze returned to me. "He went after you."

"And he'd already attacked two others. I have no beef with a New Magic shifter. I don't even know any. I think I was closer. You shouldn't have stepped between us."

"Because you knew you could use your magic stop him?"

I hesitated. "At the time, I thought it was just an animal. It had already knocked you down, so it seemed like my only option."

Conor considered me a moment. "But if you had known he was a shifter, it wouldn't have been a last resort? Can you do more than glow?"

There was no way I could tell him about *that*. I turned and paced across the room. For a moment, I considered walking out the door. But the idea lasted only an instant. I wasn't going to run.

Crossing to the window instead, I stared out over the wooded park next door. "I can channel moonlight," I answered, keeping my back to the room.

"Channel moonlight?" Conor hadn't moved.

"Draw it into myself."

"Glow."

Close enough. "Yes," I answered.

"What else?"

He had to realize that I didn't want to talk about this. His disregard for my discomfort was starting to make my anger return. I faced him. "What do you mean?"

"You implied that had you known the wolf was human, you wouldn't have considered your actions a last resort. Or was it more at him being magical and not just human?"

"I believe you're the one who implied that," I reminded him. "I just said it was the last resort on an animal."

"You're splitting hairs to avoid answering."

"Because it's none of your damn business." Maybe he did have a problem with me being magical. This wasn't going to work. "I should go." I turned and headed for the door.

"Leena, wait."

I stopped, my hand on the doorknob.

"Look, I'm sorry." Conor moved closer as he spoke. "It was wrong of me to pry. You clearly don't want to talk about it."

I took a breath and released it. I would love to tell him everything, but he would never look at me the same.

"I appreciate that you revealed yourself to save me," he added.

I hadn't expected that. Maybe he did understand. "You're the one who threw yourself in front of a monstrous wolf."

Conor released a breath, appearing annoyed. "And the thing took me down in an instant. It was more suicidal than heroic."

I faced him. "Well, I thought it was heroic."

He shrugged, a faint blush coloring his cheeks. Once again, that glimpse of humility surprised me. He had always come across as so bold and opinionated. It was becoming clear that I didn't know Conor half as well as I thought I did.

"I'm sorry I never told you," I said. "But people look at you differently when they know you're magical."

"It probably didn't help that I was always bashing your kind."

I tried not to flinch at his phrasing. "I don't consider myself as having a *kind*."

"Because you're unique?" A hint of humor twinkled in his green eyes.

"That is the nature of New Magic." No two talents were exactly the same.

"I'll take your word for that."

We lapsed into a silence that grew more and more awkward with each second that passed.

"So, what are we going to do?" Conor asked, though his question didn't remove the awkwardness.

"Um, go on pretending I'm normal?"

"I never meant to suggest you were *ab*normal, but that wasn't what I was asking. What are we going to do about this werewolf?"

"I believe the proper term is wolf shifter."

"He *bit* me. Werewolf is mild for what I really want to call him."

I couldn't help but smile at that. Though I sobered as I thought about what he said. "What *do* you want to do about him?"

"Find out who he is before he attacks someone else. Maybe I'm overreacting, but I swear he was going for my throat. What if the next time he attacks, he kills someone? Clearly, he must be unhinged."

I hadn't stopped to think about any of that—much to my chagrin. I'd been more concerned about protecting my own secrets.

"If this guy is from Cincinnati," Conor continued, not noticing my silence, "then he either followed his intended target to Serpent Mound, or he was part of our class."

Goosebumps rose on my arms. "You're right."

Conor's smile looked a little smug. "You up for a wolf hunt?"

"Man hunt, and yes, we need to find out who he is. But how?"

"We start with Professor Giles. He can get us the names and contact information for each person in class."

That much was true. "Then what? I'm not certain that confronting this guy is such a good idea."

"Let's get the names first, then we'll go from there. I'll grab my jacket." Conor turned and hurried off to his room.

I let him go without further protest. Working together would give me a chance to judge how Conor truly felt about my magical nature. Okay, maybe that was the wrong reason to agree to this, but there it was.

THOUGH I STILL WASN'T SURE how I felt about this venture—the last thing I wanted to do was get close to the magical—I had to agree that Conor's suggestion to speak to the professor first was a good one. Professor Giles was a bit eccentric, but most of the students in our class were part of his Magic in Myth curriculum, and he knew them well.

Since he'd suffered a concussion from that run-in with the tree branch, I was a bit concerned that we wouldn't find him in, but when I saw a guy from our class leave the professor's office, I suspected he must be in.

"Pete, hey," Conor greeted our classmate. "How's the leg?"

This was Kristie's Pete? He wasn't the guy with the injured shoulder that Conor and I had found along the trail at Serpent Mound.

"A little sore," Pete answered. "You?"

"The same." Conor hesitated. "So, um, any weird side effects?"

Pete smiled, a twinkle in his blue eyes. "Like what? Howling at the moon?"

Conor chuckled. "No nothing like that. I just felt a little off last night. I might have run a fever."

"No." Pete frowned. "It was probably those damn shots."

"Yeah, probably." Conor looked a bit disappointed. He no doubt wanted someone to share his symptoms. It would seem less troubling if he wasn't the only one to experience such a reaction. "The professor in?" He hooked a thumb toward Professor Giles's door.

"He's in." Pete shook his head. "I can't believe he knocked himself unconscious at such a critical moment. Here's his class fending off some rabid beast and he misses it." He smiled, the gesture a cross between affectionate amusement and annoyance. Everyone seemed to love the professor. Well, everyone except Conor.

We thanked Pete and, wishing him well, continued down the hall to stop before the professor's door.

Conor glanced over, meeting my eyes. "This should be interesting. I doubt the blow to the head helped." He shook his head, but unlike Pete, he wasn't smiling in bemusement. "You know, the professor once told me he knows that fairies are real."

"For the record," I whispered, "He's a mundane. So, one of yours."

Conor twitched an eyebrow. "Touché." He rapped his knuckles against the door.

"Come in," a muffled voice called from inside.

Still smiling over the exchange with Conor, I turned the knob and pushed open the door. I had never been in Professor Giles's office, but I knew it would be a unique experience. He didn't disappoint.

The walls that weren't paneled in glossy dark wood were painted to look as if they were made of rough-hewn stone blocks—like a castle wall. Sconces reminiscent of oil lamps provided the illumination, and the bookshelves that didn't hold an assortment of worn hardback books held a collection of interesting objects and figurines. The wall behind his desk displayed a pair of crossed swords, and pictures of mythical landscapes adorned the other walls. Yes, the professor really got into his subject matter.

"Miss Terrell, Mr. Middleton," Professor Giles greeted us from behind his large, elaborately carved desk. The piece of furniture looked like something from a medieval manor. "It's nice to see you both."

"Thank you, Professor," I answered. "It's good to see that your injury was indeed minor."

He reached up to touch the small bandage near his hairline. "I feel a bit foolish to be honest. Waylaid by a tree while my students faced a much more dire threat." His words didn't match his actions as he leaned back in his chair and smiled, a twinkle in his pale eyes.

"You don't look like you view it as so dire," Conor commented, his tone cool.

"Oh, I do, but it always amuses me when a non-believer is forced to face the error of his ways."

"Excuse me?"

"You were set upon by a werewolf, Mr. Middleton."

"Why would you assume it was a werewolf?" I asked before Conor could say anything. Conor had never been a fan of the professor's, and the muscle ticking in his jaw made it clear that this conversation wasn't going to win him over. "Were you visited by the Cincinnati Police?"

Professor Giles looked a bit puzzled by that. "No, Pete told me."

"Pete?" I asked.

"Like Mr. Middleton, he too saw the creature up close." The professor nodded, as if agreeing with himself.

I didn't know what to think of that. Pete had made a joke about the werewolf with us. Was he just trying to suck up to the professor? Everyone knew Professor Giles was a bit nuts about mythical creatures, even going so far as to insist they were real.

"I confess, I'm not entirely surprised we encountered a werewolf," the professor continued, proving my point. "The whole reason for the trip was to attempt to connect to the magic behind the myths of the mound builders, and though we know little about the prehistoric society that built the mound, the ability to shift into an animal does come up in a lot of Native American lore."

"I thought the purpose of the trip was to verify the lunar alignment of the mound," I reminded him.

"Clearly, there was some lunar influence—since a werewolf was involved." The professor chuckled. "Why did you ask about the police?"

"A detective visited us," I answered, then went on to tell him about the video. "This wolf appears to be a New Magic shifter," I finished. "We need to find out who he is."

The professor had grown less and less giddy as I told my tale. "Why do we need to do that?"

"Because this New Magic shifter obviously followed us and attacked," Conor said, the exasperation evident in his tone.

Professor Giles studied him. "You don't believe at all, do you?"

Conor sighed. "Believe what, Professor?"

"The entire premise of my class: that the old myths can come to life—if you only believe."

Conor huffed. "Look. I believe magic is real, but it's something a person is born to. You can't just believe it into being."

Professor Giles chuckled and got to his feet. "Oh ye of little faith." He gave me a wink that made me uneasy. Had I been that agreeable in class, or did he know my true nature?

"I can prove it to you." He walked to the door and took down the battered duster he wore no matter what the season.

"Where are we going?" Conor asked.

Professor Giles pulled open the door and walked out of his office without another word.

Conor looked over, his expression so puzzled it was almost comical.

I shrugged. "I suppose it wouldn't hurt to see what he has to show us."

"The last time he showed us something, I got bit by a werewolf."

I grunted. Conor had a point.

Chapter 4

I CAN'T SAY what I expected, but it wasn't a visit to a dry cleaners just off campus.

"What are we doing here?" Conor frowned at the dark-brown awning over the front door with the words Brownie Cleaners in large white letters. I hoped the owner's last name was Brownie, but I had a feeling that wouldn't be the case.

Professor Giles gave us a mysterious smile and pulled open the door, leading the way inside. He'd refused to answer any of our questions on the walk over. This destination didn't clear up the situation.

"I'm dropping this class," Conor muttered to me as we followed.

"Good afternoon, Professor," the woman behind the counter greeted him with a broad smile. "What can we do for you?"

"Is Gordon in?" the professor asked. "I have a couple of students I'd like to introduce." He waved a hand in our direction.

The woman's smile didn't falter. "Yes, of course. He's in the back."

"Thank you." The professor gestured for us to follow him around the counter and through a swinging door.

I had never been in the back room of a dry cleaners, but it was about what I expected. The unadorned space held several large washing machines, dryers, and one oddly shaped unit that I assumed was the dry-cleaning machine. There were also ironing boards and presses, wheeled hampers, and racks of clothes in clear plastic garment bags. But where I expected several employees in what appeared to be a thriving business, there was just one man.

The man hurried over, and like the woman out front, greeted the professor warmly. Apparently, this was Gordon.

Intent on the conversation between the two men, I was surprised when Conor nudged me. When I looked up, he nodded toward one of the ironing boards, his eyes a little wide.

Looking where he indicated, I was surprised to see an iron sliding back and forth across the shirt draped over the board. No one was manning the iron, at least, no one visible.

Professor Giles chuckled. "I see you've spotted Gordon's help."

"Uh." I couldn't come up with anything more intelligent to say.

Gordon stepped forward, introducing himself as Gordon McAllister before exchanging a handshake with Conor and me. "I assume you are both prospects for the professor's graduate course?"

From what I understood, the professor had a very select graduate-studies program. I knew little about it since it wasn't my field, but I'd overheard several of the students in our class express an interest in it.

"Every student is a prospect," the professor answered.

Gordon chuckled. "True."

"So. Your help?" I reminded Gordon.

"Brownies, just like the sign says." A wide grin creased his face.

I glanced back at the iron, but it was no longer moving.

"They get a bit shy when I have company," Gordon added, no doubt aware of what had caught my notice.

"Brownies," Conor repeated. "As in the Scottish household spirit?"

"The very ones," Gordon agreed in what seemed to be his usual good humor. "My great grandpa, who grew up in Scotland, used to tell me stories of the family's brownies—whom he believed followed him to America. He insisted I leave offerings for them on the hearth at night, but it wasn't until Professor Giles opened my eyes that I saw them for the first time."

"I didn't see anything moving that iron," Conor said, skepticism heavy in his tone. Not that I blamed him. I could buy a little telekinesis, but brownies? There was magic in the world, yes, but no mythological creatures.

"Like I said, they tend to be shy around strangers," Gordon answered with another chuckle. "Hey, Moff, Berry," he abruptly called out, causing both Conor and me to jump. "Show yourselves, lads."

A familiar charge of static made the hairs on my arms stand up, and I instinctively knew it came from Gordon, but before I could fully analyze the situation, a pair of old men shimmered into view. One stood near the iron, while the other sat on a stool beside a laundry hamper.

I described them as old men, but on closer inspection, I realized they weren't human at all. They were small of stature, maybe four feet tall, but I had the impression they were fully grown. Their wrinkled skin was a shade of brown I'd never seen on a human being, though I couldn't articulate what made it so different. But it was their dark eyes that really unsettled me.

Conor gasped and the pair vanished once more—along with the static that stood my hair on end.

Everything had happened so fast, it wasn't until that moment that I realized what I'd been feeling. New Magic. I wasn't an Element. I couldn't tell if someone was magical just by getting close to them, but I could sense it in use. Like me, Gordon was New Magic. As for the rest, I still didn't believe that mythological creatures existed. Which meant his brownies were his own creation.

I walked toward the ironing board.

"Miss Terrell?" the professor prompted.

"That's amazing," I said, putting a little extra awe in my tone at the same time I *felt* my surrounding. "Can you make him appear again?"

"Well, I don't make him do anything," Gordon answered with

that characteristic chuckle. "But I can ask. Moff, lad? The lady would like to see you."

Once again, the small brown fellow shimmered into view. I was much closer this time, and I was paying attention. The wash of magic was distinctive.

Mott lifted his head, and those beady black eyes met mine. Though I'd only just met the man, I was certain that it was Gordon who stared back at me—or some aspect of him. What was this thing? I didn't buy that magic could be sentient, so I assumed this was a piece of Gordon himself. Some kind of construct.

It was unnerving, but not evil or anything like that. It was just… a shadow of its creator.

"Nice to meet you, Moff." I was so tempted to touch my own magic just to see what Gordon would do. He hadn't pulled the wool over my eyes as he had the professor's.

To my amusement, the brownie dipped his head at my greeting, then in a burst of static, vanished once more.

Fighting back a laugh, I faced the others. Conor still frowned, but there was a question in his eyes as they met mine. Gordon grinned like a proud papa—which was an accurate description. But the professor watched me through narrowed eyes like he suspected something. I had no idea what that meant.

"That was astonishing," I told Gordon, walking back to the men. "And you say Professor Giles helped you *see* them?"

"Yes," Gordon quickly agreed. "And in case, you're wondering, I haven't a magical bone in my body. But I have always believed—at least, on some level—that the lore is real. What Professor Giles taught me just helped me embrace it." There was an earnestness to Gordon's words. If I didn't know differently, I would never suspect he was lying.

"If you're considering his graduate program, I highly recommend it," Gordon continued. "I know those who don't understand scoff at a graduate degree in such an obscure field, but my successful business is a testament to how far it can take you."

"I see that."

"Thank you, Gordon," the professor spoke up. "But I believe we've kept you long enough from your work."

"It was no problem. Always glad to help." Another proud smile creased his face.

Annoyed that he thought himself so smart, I offered my hand. "Yes, thanks for the tour."

The moment Gordon pressed his palm to mine, I touched my own magic, though I did nothing with it.

"Whoa, shock." Gordon pulled back his hand with a laugh. "Sorry. I just pulled some fleece out of the drier before you arrived." He touched the metal cage of a nearby laundry hamper, then offered his hand to me. "Try again."

Stunned, I simply shook his hand—without the magic.

He offered me a happy smile before exchanging a shake with Conor, then the professor.

Could it be that he didn't know he was magical? Was he creating these *brownies* subconsciously? No way. That had to be some amazingly complicated magic.

Mind awhirl, I was lost in my own thoughts as the professor bid Gordon, then the woman at the counter, farewell and led us outside.

"You see?" The professor stopped on the sidewalk beneath the Brownie Cleaners awning.

"I saw something," Conor agreed. "I'm still trying to puzzle out what."

"Miss Terrell?" the professor prompted. He was still watching me with something like suspicion.

"I'm with Conor. I can't get my mind around what I just saw."

The suspicion faded, and Professor Giles gave us a smug smile. "You'll come around. I'm sure you will."

"Okay, let's say I do," Conor said. "That doesn't change the fact that we need to find the guy who bit me. Whether he's just some nut magic user, or as you believe, a mythical werewolf, he's still hurting people and needs to be stopped."

"Or helped," I added, inspired by what I just saw. "He might not understand what's happening to him. Not to mention, the police are looking for him."

The professor's forehead wrinkled as we spoke, giving me the impression that he hadn't considered all the problems this werewolf could cause. He'd been more focused on proving he existed.

"If he's the guy in the video," I continued, "he's either connected to someone in our class, or he's a member of our class."

"We can rule out Pete, Rick, and Kristie since they were all bitten," Conor said. Apparently, Rick was the guy with the injured shoulder.

"But we probably should include those who didn't go on the field trip since they knew where we were," I added, then turned to the professor. "Can you get us their addresses or phone numbers?"

"I'm not permitted to give you that information."

I started to speak, but Professor Giles raised a hand, silencing me.

"I know what to do. Leave it to me." He turned and walked off without another word.

I glanced over, meeting Conor's gaze.

"What the hell is he going to do?" Conor whispered, though the professor had started across the street and probably couldn't hear him anyway. "Buy some silver bullets?"

"I hope he isn't going to shoot anyone. A bullet being silver wouldn't be any more lethal," I answered. "This werewolf is New Magic. He's neither contagious, nor does the moon influence his shapeshifting. Magic is real, but mythological creatures are not."

"And what we just saw?" Conor waved a hand toward the cleaners.

"Gordon McAllister is New Magic. Those *brownies* were his own creation."

"Are you serious?" Conor started to face the building we'd just left, then abruptly turned to me. "Wait. I thought you said that only an Element could recognize another magic user."

"Just by being near them. But the magical can feel another using their magic. Well, I assume. I don't know if that's universally true."

"The brownie. That's why you moved closer."

"Yes."

Conor frowned, looking up at the building once more. "So this whole thing was just a trick. What are they playing at?"

"I'm not so sure it was a trick. I could be wrong, but I don't think Gordon realizes that he's controlling it. As for the professor, he might genuinely believe what he teaches."

"If you believe in something strongly enough, it becomes real," Conor paraphrased the professor's philosophy. "Of course if he believes *that* strongly enough, the concept becomes real."

I groaned. "Stop. You're making my head hurt."

Conor smiled but sobered as his attention returned to Brownie Cleaners. "It bothers me that the professor insisted on taking care of this himself—like he was trying to hide something."

"But what…" my voice trailed off as I came to another conclusion.

"He knows who this werewolf is," Conor voiced what I now suspected.

"Or he thinks he does."

"We should follow him." Conor didn't wait for a response before heading after the professor. It seemed the *we* part of his statement was optional.

That thought had no sooner crossed my mind than he stopped and looked back at me. "You coming?"

I had so many questions. What did he intend to do if the professor led us to the shifter? As a wolf, the guy had already proven to be quicker than we were. Was Conor depending on my magic to save the day? Did that mean he accepted my magical nature? And what happened when he learned everything?

Not ready to face any of those answers, I closed the distance between us. "I'm coming."

Chapter 5

WE FOLLOWED the professor back to his office, then spent the rest of the afternoon watching the front door from a bench across the street. Unable to sit still, Conor circled the building from time to time, but the only other exit emptied into a parking lot, and the professor didn't own a car. He'd told the class as much when opting for school transportation rather than having us each drive to Serpent Mound.

On one of his trips, Conor was gone a little longer than usual. I'd been just about to call him when he returned with a couple of hotdogs and drinks from the stand on the corner.

"I was starving," he confessed, sitting down beside me. "Of course, I did just wake up." He offered a sheepish look.

"You realize that if a shifter bit you, rabies are no longer a concern."

"True." Conor handed me a hotdog. "Hope you like sauce. I asked them to hold the mustard and onions since I didn't know what you liked."

"I like it all, but I'd rather not taste onions all evening."

"Because it might scare off the werewolf?"

I laughed. "That's garlic and vampires."

"Right. Do you think the professor believes in vampires as well?"

"Probably."

"But isn't that Old Magic? Vampires are dead."

"Old Magic isn't defined as a magic dealing with the dead. It has that reputation because the local Old Magic users are necromancers. By definition, Old Magic is just a magic that has always been here."

"What if this shifter is Old Magic? The werewolf legend has always been here, right?"

"It has, but curses and contagious magic are myths. Still, this shifter could be a variant of Old Magic. I won't know until he uses his magic around me."

"Hm. Well, for the record, I'm glad you're not Old Magic." He took a big bite of his hotdog, putting a momentary end to our conversation.

Conor still seemed a bit confused by the whole magical classification thing, but he'd basically just said he didn't mind my being magical. Smiling, I turned my attention to my own meal.

THE SUN WAS low in the sky by the time the professor finally left his office for the evening. When he walked to a nearby pub, we thought for certain that he'd gone to meet the werewolf, but instead, he dined alone. After his meal, he spent another hour sipping a beer and watching the soccer game on the TV over the bar.

We'd taken a table in the coffee shop across the street, so the wait wasn't terrible. Though the shop was too busy to engage in any deep conversations. Not to mention, Conor remained focused on the pub's front door.

"Finally," he muttered when Professor Giles stepped outside. "If he goes home and calls it a night, I'm going to be really frustrated," Conor continued as we left the shop.

"You didn't enjoy sipping a latte and hanging out with me?"

He glanced over, looking a bit surprised.

"I'm teasing," I said before he was forced to come up with an excuse.

"Under different circumstances, it would have been an enjoyable evening. Though I would have preferred a beer. I've had so much caffeine that even my hair has the jitters."

"I'm with you," I admitted, pleased way more than I should be by his enjoyable evening comment. "I should have gotten a water instead of that last latte."

"Aside from overdosing on the caffeine, we're pretty good at this stakeout stuff. If our chosen careers don't pan out, we'd make good cops."

"Or stalkers."

He sputtered as he tried to laugh quietly. "You're going to make me blow our cover."

Fortunately, the professor didn't even glance in our direction. He strolled along with an indifferent, casual stride, seemingly unaware that we followed him. He rounded a building, and we momentarily lost sight of him until Conor spied him cutting across an open area dotted with large trees.

As we watched, he slowed his pace, looking around. I thought he might be heading for the trio of benches surrounded by a hedge, but he stopped and whirled to face a large tree before he got that far. An instant later, a man stepped out of the tree's shadow.

"Is he about to be robbed?" Conor whispered.

Even in the low light, I could see the professor smile as he greeted the man. Unfortunately, the newcomer's back was to us, so I couldn't see his face.

"No," I answered. "They know each other. I think this meeting was prearranged."

"Why didn't they meet in the pub?"

"Hey, I manipulate moon beams, I don't read minds."

Conor smiled, though he kept his eyes on the two men. "Do you think that's the werewolf?"

"It's possible. Let's circle around behind that hedge. We should be able to get close enough to eavesdrop."

Conor agreed, and we quickly backtracked, working our way

around the perimeter of the grassy area until we could slip behind the hedge unobserved.

The area wasn't well lit, and even darker behind the hedge. We hadn't gone five feet when Conor tripped over a large stick. It got tangled between his ankles, and he fell to his knees with a soft curse. Fortunately, we weren't close enough to the professor and his friend for them to hear.

"Are you okay?" I said, fighting a smile.

Conor climbed to his feet and, still grumbling under his breath, dusted his knees. "I'm fine." He took a step, and his foot came down atop the same stick. It rolled out from beneath him, but I caught his arm before he fell again.

"Maybe I should lead."

"Why?" He still sounded angry, but I knew it wasn't directed at me.

"I can see better in the dark than you. It's part of my moon goddess superpower."

It wasn't so dark that I couldn't see his smile.

"Very well, my lady." He gestured at the area ahead of us, indicating that I should lead the way. "Please guide the helpless mortal through the darkness." He offered his hand.

I frowned, not understanding, then I realized that he wanted me to literally take his hand and guide him. Uncertain, I pressed my palm to his, and he gripped my hand, twining his fingers with mine.

"You're not going to smite me for being so forward, are you?" he asked. His tone was teasing, but the wrinkle on his forehead suggested uncertainty. Did he fear he'd overstepped himself?

"I do make allowances for mere mortals."

His forehead smoothed, and he gave my hand a squeeze. "Good to know."

Glad he couldn't see my blush, I started forward, pulling him after me. Even if this guy didn't prove to be the werewolf, I didn't think this evening had ended that badly.

Conor fell silent as we worked our way along the hedge. I thought he was just being cautious until he released my hand and a soft thump followed. I glanced over my shoulder and saw him sitting at the base of the hedge. I was about to tease him for tripping again when he rubbed both hands over his face.

"You okay?" I whispered, kneeling beside him.

"I don't know. I feel...odd."

"Odd?"

"Like I did last night."

"I told you to see a doctor." I sighed. "Sit tight while I eavesdrop, then we'll take you home."

"I'll be fine. Just give me a minute."

"Catch up when you're able." I patted his shoulder, then rose to my feet. I wasn't going to waste time arguing.

Hurrying along the hedge, I crouched down and peeked around the end. I was a bit alarmed to find that Professor Giles and his friend had moved closer to my position, but they were intent on their conversation and unlikely to notice me.

"That hardly matters," a male voice said. "What can the police do?"

"When this detective realizes his theory is true, he'll turn the case over to the PIA," Professor Giles said, an urgency to his tone.

"But this is what you wanted," the other answered, a pleading note in his voice. "You can now prove that your theory is real."

"His voice sounds familiar," Conor said in a winded whisper. I jumped at the sound of his voice, not realizing he had moved closer.

"But you can't control it, Pete," Professor Giles insisted.

I glanced over at Conor, meeting his wide eyes in the low light. Was the other man our classmate?

Carefully, I leaned around the hedge. As if my need to verify his identity controlled his actions, he abruptly turned enough for me to make out his face in the dimness. It *was* our Pete. But discovering his identity took a back seat to my fear that he'd turned because he'd heard me.

I held my breath, not daring to move as he fully faced my direction, but to my relief, he only gazed up at the sky.

"Crap. The moon's about to rise," Pete said. "We need to go."

"I'm not sure—"

"I told you I can control it, Professor," Pete cut in. "Come on."

He turned and headed for the sidewalk opposite my position, moving at a brisk walk that was almost a jog.

Professor Giles hesitated just a moment, then hurried after him.

"What are they doing?" Conor whispered.

"Leaving." The pair had reached the sidewalk and hurried on.

"We should follow." Conor pushed himself up, but didn't make it to his feet before flopping onto his backside with a grunt.

Alarmed, I rushed over to his side. "No, we're going to the nearest urgent care. You're definitely having a reaction."

"But we need to follow Pete and Giles," Conor insisted. "Where were they headed?"

"North, but that doesn't matter. We know the identity of the werewolf. That was the whole point of following the professor." I pushed back Conor's auburn hair to rest my hand on his forehead. His hair was damp and his skin warm.

"I think the fever came back," he admitted, then unzipped his hoodie and shrugged it off.

"Can you walk? At least to the curb?" I could call a taxi.

"Yeah." His actions belied his words as he leaned against the hedge behind him. "Just give me a minute."

I had no choice but to agree. At about six-two and close to two hundred pounds, he was far too big for me to carry.

Anxious, I rose to my feet and paced along the hedge. Pete and the professor were no longer in sight. Had the circumstances been different, I would have loved to follow them, but Conor needed me now.

I walked back to him and saw that his eyes were closed. Bending down, I felt his forehead once more. Was it hotter?

"Just a minute," he muttered.

I straightened with a sigh and pulled out my phone. Who could I call to help get Conor to urgent care? I'd prefer not to call an ambulance if I could avoid it.

Though my eyes were focused on my phone, I felt the moon rise above the horizon. The calm serenity of the soft blue light soothed me as I slid my finger over my phone screen, scrolling through my contacts. Who could—

Conor gasped, and I looked over—just in time to see a brilliant flash of light envelop him.

I jumped back, lifting an arm to shield my face, while at the time, I recognized the familiar burst of energy. New Magic. Were we under attack?

Heart in my throat, I whirled to face the perpetrator, but there was no one there. Even Conor was gone. In his place stood a big russet-furred wolf, wearing Conor's clothes.

Chapter 6

I STARED at the wolf who stared back at me. Even with just a fraction of the moon visible above the horizon, I had no trouble seeing that the wolf's eyes were green.

"Conor?" I whispered.

The sound of my voice seemed to break him out of his shock—or whatever emotion he was experiencing. He whirled away, stepping out of his sneakers and low socks. Twisting and shaking, he managed to discard the jeans, then he bolted.

"Conor!" I shouted, watching the big russet wolf—still clad in boxer briefs and a T-shirt—disappear around the end of the hedge.

Stunned, I just stood there and stared after him. It felt like a full minute passed, but it was probably only a matter of seconds before I shook my head and tried to collect my scattered wits.

"Not possible," I whispered, staring at the scattered clothing. But what was possible and what wasn't didn't matter at the moment. I had to get Conor back.

He was out of sight by the time I ran out from behind the hedge. I tried to follow the general direction he'd been heading, but it was a guess on my part. Had he put any thought into his flight?

Could he think? What if he was little more than an animal? The first busy street he encountered could be his last.

I ran nearly a full block and was about to backtrack when I spotted fabric hanging from a line of closely spaced evergreen shrubs along the edge of a building. Moving closer, I saw that it was a pair of boxer briefs. My suspicions were confirmed when I spotted the T-shirt Conor had been wearing a little farther down the line of shrubs. He must have used the stiff branches to wiggle out of the clothes. Perhaps he wasn't just an animal.

Confident that I was heading in the right direction, I broke into a run. Unfortunately, Conor had no other clothes to shed, but I continued to watch my surroundings and called his name frequently.

I searched several streets and alleyways until a stitch in my side slowed me to a fast walk. This was no good. I was never going to find him. Perhaps I should return to his place and wait. I should also go back and collect his jeans and jacket. No doubt his wallet, keys, and phone were still in the pockets.

Still debating on my next move, I rounded the corner and stopped with a gasp. Red and blue lights bounced off the houses ahead of me. Had there been an accident? Oh God, maybe he had failed to watch for traffic while crossing the street.

Side stitch be damned, I broke into a run, racing to the large two-story house that seemed to be the center of the commotion. But as I drew closer, I realized that everyone seemed to be staring at the house. I'd think house fire, but there was no smoke or fire truck. Then I spied a crowd of pajama-clad college girls gathered on the front lawn and noticed the Greek letter over the front door. It was a sorority house.

I doubted that Conor had caused the commotion, but the girls might have seen him run by. It wouldn't hurt to ask. Skirting an ambulance and a police car, I walked over to join them.

"What happened?" I asked, noting the way several were staring at the house with wide, teary eyes.

"It was horrible," a girl in the rainbow-print PJs answered. "This huge dog got in the house and started chasing people."

My stomach dropped. "A huge dog?" Oh my God, maybe Conor was to blame. He and I were only friends, but I felt a bit... discouraged that he'd chosen to run through a sorority house.

"It looked like a wolf to me," the other girl answered, her hair tucked beneath a shower cap. Judging by the faint chemical smell, I suspected she must have been coloring her hair.

"Whatever it was, it had to be rabid," Rainbow PJs said. "It was acting crazy."

"Crazy?" Had Conor entered the house by mistake, gotten turned around, then panicked? "What do you mean?" I asked.

"It knocked Trish down the stairs, then jumped through the dining room window," Shower Cap explained. "Betty cut her foot on the glass."

"There was blood everywhere," Rainbow added.

"How did a wolf get in the house?" I asked.

"No clue," Rainbow answered with a shrug.

"Someone said it came out of Kristie's room," Shower Cap offered. "But I wouldn't know how it got in there. We have a no-pets policy."

I stilled. "Kristie? I have a classmate with that name. Is she taking a class with Professor Giles?"

"Yes. She had the craziest experience at Serpent Mound last night. Were you there?"

"I was." I let the girl rattle on about how Kristie was bitten and had to spend most of the night in an emergency room—just like Conor.

"Where is Kristie?" I asked.

The two girls looked around, then shrugged. It seemed neither had seen her since she'd gone to her room earlier this evening. She'd claimed to be feeling sick.

My pulse was racing, but I forced myself to remain calm—at least, outwardly—and gather all the information I could. "Any idea of where this wolf went?"

"Witnesses claim she headed north across campus," a male voice said from behind me.

"Oh, are you—" I turned, and the words died in my mouth. The speaker was Detective Brody.

"Nice to see you again, Miss Terrell," Detective Brody greeted me. "Could I have a word?"

I agreed, and after thanking the girls for their help, I walked away with him.

"You were saying?" he prompted once we were alone.

"Um, I was just going to ask how certain you were that the wolf was female," I said, struggling to keep my panic in check. Though I wasn't entirely certain if it was caused by the situation or Brody's presence.

"A witness claimed it had a pink bow tied around its neck."

Dear God. Had it really been Kristie? That meant—

"I'm surprised to see you here," Brody cut in to my frantic thoughts. "Once again, I find you at the home of a person who was attacked during your field trip yesterday. A girl that no one can seem to find at the moment."

My heart thumped in my ears. Did he suspect? Should I tell him what I knew? I didn't want him to dig too deep into my past, but did I dare keep anything from someone who knew as much as Detective Brody?

I took a breath and looked the detective in the eye. "Since we last spoke, things have gotten a bit,"—I struggled to find a way to describe the last few hours—"stark raving mad."

The corner of Brody's mouth quirked upward with a hint of a smile. "Go on."

"I might have discovered the identity of your shifter, but I'm beginning to doubt whether he's New Magic."

"Why's that?"

I gripped my hands, trying to keep my anxiety in check. "It appears that the people this werewolf bit have become werewolves themselves."

Brody didn't appear all that surprised. Had he already put two and two together? "I didn't think such a thing was possible."

"Neither did I—until I witnessed it."

"Conor?"

"Yes, and it seems, Kristie." I waved a hand toward the sorority house.

"Are you certain that neither of them was a shifter before they were bitten?" Brody asked, watching me closely. I hoped he was just eager to hear my answer.

"I'm certain about Conor, but I don't know Kristie that well. All I can say is that this magic appears to be contagious."

"In that case, we need to find them. Quickly."

I took a breath to agree, but a uniformed policeman hurried up to us before I could respond.

"Detective," the man addressed Brody.

"What is it, Officer?"

"There's been another animal sighting. Apparently, this big dog ran across Martin Luther King Drive and caused a minor accident. You think it's our animal?"

Was it Kristie or Conor? He had been headed in the same general direction. North. Huh, just like Pete and Professor Giles. What if—

"Would you like to join me, Miss Terrell," Brody asked.

"I…"

"Come on." He turned and hurried toward the street.

I watched Brody go, not sure why he wanted me to come along. Did he have more questions for me, or was he suspicious of me for some reason? If I wasn't so worried about Conor, I'd be tempted to refuse.

Brody pulled open the driver's door on a late-model sedan parked along the street, then looked back at me. "Want to ride shotgun?" He offered an encouraging smile, as if aware of my internal debate. Maybe it was time to throw caution to the wind. I was probably going to need Brody's help.

"Do you have a shotgun?" I asked, checking for traffic before I circled around to the passenger side.

"In the trunk," Brody surprised me with his answer. "Here's hoping we don't need it."

"Let's hope." I slid into the front seat, reassessing the situation.

Conor wasn't only in danger of hurting others, he could be in danger himself.

I HADN'T REALIZED it until we reached the site of the accident, but there was an excellent location for a pack of newly transformed werewolves to hide just north of campus. Burnet Woods, a ninety-acre park and accompanying lake, was a popular hiking destination. The thickly wooded area deeper in the park was an oddly secluded location in the middle of the bustling city of Cincinnati. So it didn't come as a surprise when Brody learned that the dog who had caused the accident was seen running off into Burnet Woods.

We left the car where Brody had parked it and set off on foot. This was going to be like finding a needle in a haystack. It surprised me that Brody didn't call for help to search the park.

"My colleagues would think me mad to waste valuable resources hunting a stray dog," Brody explained when I asked. "If we need help, I'll have to call the PIA."

I swallowed. The last thing I wanted was to involve the Paranormal Investigation Agency.

"You said you might know the identity of the shifter in the security footage?" Brody prompted as we left the grassy area behind and followed a trail into the forest.

"I don't know his last name, but his first name is Pete. He's one of my classmates."

"Pete Anderson? He was one of the bitten ones at Serpent Mound."

"He must have staged that."

"To hide the fact that he was the werewolf?"

I shrugged. "Seems logical."

We didn't have much choice but to follow this trail through the trees, and regardless of whether Conor or Kristie had been the one who caused the accident, both would likely have headed this way.

"And you don't think this werewolf situation is New Magic?" Brody asked.

For a moment, I was a bit alarmed that he had asked me such a question, then I realized I'd suggested as much while telling him about all this back at Kristie's house. Still, I didn't want to give away that I had an inside track to that knowledge.

"New Magic isn't supposed to be contagious, right?" I asked.

"Good point. Maybe if we can bring in one of these were-wolves, His Grace can take a look."

His Grace, the Lord of Flames. I didn't know why the Elements had ended up with such goofy titles. I guess it went with the archaic name of their magic. But the reason didn't matter. All I knew was that I wanted nothing to do with the Fire Element who led the New Magic community here in Cincinnati. Of course, I didn't have to be present when Brody introduced this werewolf to the Flame Lord. I just hoped Conor wasn't the wolf Brody captured.

"Wait," I said as a new concern surfaced. "How do you intend to capture these werewolves?"

"Oh, um, I figured you could convince them," Brody didn't sound all that certain. "You're their friend, right?"

Anyone else, and I'd accuse him of knowing what I could do, but clearly, that wasn't the case here. Otherwise, Brody would have said something.

"I hope you're right," I whispered, leading Brody deeper into the woods.

THE PARK WAS WELL MAINTAINED with cleared trails and stone steps on the steeper parts. There were even streetlights where the trail met the road or at picnic areas, but I didn't think such public areas— even if it was closing in on midnight—would attract our elusive werewolves.

"There," Brody said, pointing to a trail head on the far side of the paved road that wound through the park.

I looked where he pointed and spotted what appeared to be a pink scarf hanging from a low branch. On closer inspection, we discovered that's exactly what it was.

"You think this is the pink bow the witness described the wolf wearing?" I asked, running the shear fabric between my hands.

"I think that's a very strong possibility. We're on the right trail."

"Literally," I said, starting forward.

Brody chuckled and fell in behind me. He seemed content to let me lead. He'd also been fine with my suggestion to forego flashlights. It made me a little uneasy that Brody might know my secret, but wouldn't he have said something? Of course, I was probably being paranoid.

However, I was glad to have him at my back. The forest around us was dark since the trees blocked most of the moonlight. Had I been alone, I would have been tempted to pull a few moon beams closer for comfort.

It came as a relief when we emerged in a small, moonlit clearing a few minutes later, but my relief was short-lived. The clearing was occupied.

Brody gripped my shoulder, pulling me to a stop, though it was unnecessary. I had stumbled to a halt on my own, my attention on the lone man standing in the center of the clearing.

"Professor Giles?" I whispered.

He glanced over at us, his eyes wide, but I didn't think it was surprise over our appearance. I suspected it had more to do with the six wolves who surrounded him.

Six pairs of eyes settled on us, and one large wolf with blue eyes stepped forward. I felt certain this was the same wolf who attacked Conor and me at Serpent Mound. Pete.

"Selena?" Brody whispered. There was an urgency to his tone, but I didn't know what he wanted.

"Don't," Professor Giles said, lifting his hands as if he was the one surrendering. Did he realize that Brody was armed? "Don't hurt them. It's a curse."

I wanted to tell him that this was some form of New Magic and that the old myths didn't apply, but to do that, I'd have to admit how I knew.

I studied the other wolves, but I didn't see one with a russet coat or green eyes. Had Conor's appearance changed as he adapted to this new form, or had he not joined the pack?

Pete took another step closer, then another. He lifted his lips and gave me a soft growl. I suspected he remembered what I did at Serpent Mound. Did he realize I could do more than just scare him off? Did I dare attempt that now—in front of Brody?

Earlier, Brody had suggested that I could talk to these werewolves and appeal to their human halves. But aside from Conor, I didn't know any of these people well. Still, it was better than revealing myself.

"Pete, please," I said, meeting the big wolf's eyes. "We're not here to hurt you."

He lifted his lips in a silent snarl and paced closer.

"Magic should be a gift, not a curse." I believed that, I really did, even though it seemed I'd used mine to create my own personal curse. But my issues weren't the problem at the moment. "This is Detective Brody. He's here to help. I'm here to help."

Pete's answering growl suggested that he wasn't buying what I was trying to sell.

"Please let us help you?" I spread my hands, hoping to show that I was no threat. "We can—"

"Selena!" Brody shouted as Pete sprang.

I didn't look over, but I knew Brody had pulled his gun. If his intent was to stop Pete, he wasn't quick enough. The big wolf slammed into my chest and took me to the ground before I could do any more than brace myself for impact.

I grunted as he landed on top of me, but managed to press my hands to his upper chest as he reached for my throat. It didn't seem that Pete intended to give me a nip as he had Kristie. He intended to take me out.

He lunged, his jaws snapping closed right before my nose. Something like a growl escaped between my clenched teeth as I struggled to hold him back.

Suddenly, Pete was knocked aside by a collision hard enough to get a yelp from him.

I thought Professor Giles had found a stout stick to bat him off me, but when I pushed up on one elbow. I saw a big red wolf standing over Pete.

"Conor," I whispered.

Unfortunately, Pete wasn't intimidated. He sprang to his feet and faced Conor with a vicious snarl.

"Here." Brody had moved to my side and, slipping a hand beneath my arm, helped me up.

I didn't comment, my focus on the two wolves that were now circling, challenging each other.

Hyperaware of Brody standing beside me, I once again vacillated about whether to use my magic to take control of the situation. If Conor got hurt—

Conor lunged at that moment, moving with an eerie grace that belied the fact that this was the first time he'd ever fought on four legs. He either closed so fast or the move was so unexpected that he appeared to take Pete completely by surprise. In the blink of an eye, Conor took him to the ground and closed his jaws over the other wolf's throat.

"Stop him!" Professor Giles shouted. Did he expect Brody to shoot Conor?

I couldn't let that happen. "Conor, don't—"

My voice was drowned out as Brody fired his gun. I gasped and spun to face Brody, then released the breath I'd drawn when I saw that his weapon was pointed toward the heavens.

"The next shot won't be in the air," Brody said into the silence.

Whether it was my command, Brody's threat, or just the act of being knocked out of his frenzied state, Conor seemed to come back to himself—or as much as he could in this form. He released Pete and stepped back, his tongue sliding across his lips and teeth as if he'd gotten a mouth full of fur.

Suddenly, a flash of light lit up our surroundings.

I blinked my eyes, struggling to recover from the flash blindness, and discovered that a wolf no longer lay at our feet. It was a naked man, bleeding heavily from the throat.

"No!" Professor Giles dropped his knees beside Pete. He shrugged off his duster, then his sweater followed. "Hang on, Pete."

He pressed the fabric to Pete's throat, using it as a compress. "Remember, werewolves heal quickly. They're only weak to moonlight and silver, the metal that represents the moon."

I thought this an odd time for one of the professor's lectures, but maybe it was just his way of calming himself.

Brody had his phone to his ear, calling for help.

I lifted my eyes to the other wolves, who were watching all this in silence. I didn't see any that looked ready to attack. Most had their ears down and tails tucked, their body language expressing uncertainty, or even fear. Odd.

As for Conor, he was watching Professor Giles attend Pete.

"Conor?" I whispered.

He looked up, his eyes meeting mine. Abruptly, he turned and ran for the trees. The movement seemed to break the other wolves from their paralysis, and they also turned and fled.

"Wait," Brody shouted after them, but they were gone.

Chapter 7

I STOOD WITH DETECTIVE BRODY, watching the ambulance pull away. Professor Giles had decided to ride along with Pete to the hospital, though the EMTs had seemed confident that Pete's injuries weren't life threatening. That came as a real surprise after I'd witnessed how the blood had gushed from Pete's throat. Had the professor been right about a werewolf's rapid healing? Despite everything I'd seen, I still couldn't get my mind around the fact that this magic appeared to act just like the old myths.

"Sounds like you won't need to arrest Conor for murder," I said, now that Brody and I were alone.

"I saw what happened. He was defending you."

I crossed my arms, not wanting to be reminded of that. Had I taken control of the situation, Conor wouldn't have needed to act.

"Besides," Brody continued, "we don't know if their human half is fully aware of their actions. I'll give his Grace a call when the hour is more appropriate and have him take a look at Pete. That should narrow down what we're dealing with, magically. Of course, I'll probably be off the case at that point. My superiors will turn this over to the PIA."

My stomach sank. "The PIA?"

Brody's eyes met mine. "But if you need my help, don't hesitate to call." Once again, I got that sense that he knew a lot more than he revealed. A new thought popped into my head. Could the detective be magical?

"Thank you." I offered my hand.

The moment his palm pressed to mine, I touched my magic, just as I'd done with Gordon at Brownie Cleaners. But this time, there was no static shock. Brody merely held my gaze.

"My pleasure," Brody replied to my expression of gratitude. A brief squeeze, and he released my hand. "Do you need a ride home?"

"No, I'm good." My heart thumped in my ears as I bid him farewell. What the hell had I been thinking? If Brody had been magical, I would have given myself away—after I'd just sacrificed Conor to keep my secret safe.

I DIDN'T GO HOME as I'd led Brody to believe. Instead, I went to Conor's place—after collecting his jacket and jeans from the behind the hedge where we'd first spotted Pete and Professor Giles. I had planned to use his keys to let myself in, but changed my mind.

Gazing up at the moon, I noted its distance from the horizon. If Conor's change was really tied to the moon, he wouldn't become human until the moon set a few hours from now. That was, if he could change back at all.

A surge of adrenaline coursed through me. There were legends in which the werewolf remained a wolf for years, if not forever.

"That won't happen," I whispered. After all, Pete clearly changed back. I'd seen him in human form twice since he attacked us at Serpent Mound. Not that I truly believed this was a mythical werewolf curse. I knew in my heart that this was New Magic. I'd felt Conor change.

Sitting down on Conor's front stoop, I decided to wait. He'd come home eventually.

I DIDN'T KNOW when I dozed off, but the brush of something cool and wet across my cheek woke me. Opening my eyes, I found myself staring into the face of a large red wolf.

Straightening with a gasp, I scooted away until my back thumped against Conor's front door.

The wolf stepped back, his head and tail lowering as if in shame.

"Conor. Sorry." I pressed a hand to my chest, aware of my heart pounding inside. "You startled me."

He lifted his head, looking...hopeful. I sighed in relief. Yes, there was still a lot of the man I knew in the animal before me.

"I have your things, including your keys." I rose to my feet and picked up his jacket and jeans. "I'll let us in."

He just watched me without blinking. Maybe that was his way of saying, *get on with it.*

"Okay," I muttered and turned to the door. It took a few tries to find the right key, but the moment I had the door open, Conor pushed past me and slipped inside. I followed and closed the door behind me.

"Can you change back?" I asked.

He turned to face me. Dear God, he was a big wolf. Though maybe it was just because he didn't belong in this setting.

The thought that Conor didn't belong in his own apartment struck a chord, and my heart clenched in my chest.

"Is it the moon?" I asked. "Is it holding you in this form?"

He held my gaze, but without the ability to speak, he couldn't answer.

I rubbed the back of my neck. Should I try something or just wait for the sun to rise? What if he didn't change when the moon sank below the horizon? My ability rose and set with the moon. If I didn't do something now, we'd have to wait until this evening to try again.

But I needed Conor in human form if I was going to have any

chance of understanding what had happened to him. I couldn't gamble with whether he *might* become human when the moon set.

Reaching out, I pulled in the last rays of the setting moon, and cool, blue light flooded Conor's living room. I wanted to close my eyes and revel in the joy that always filled me along with the moonlight, but a soft whine filled the quiet.

Conor had tucked his tail and dropped into a crouch.

"Don't be afraid." I knelt in front of him, a few feet away, and offered my hand. "Moonlight isn't to be feared." Even by a werewolf.

His eyes rose to mine, silver light reflecting in those green depths. Slowly, he took a step toward me, then another, until his cool nose brushed my palm.

I smiled, remembering the way he'd held my hand as I led him through the dark. This was just like that, but now, I was leading him back to his proper form.

"This isn't who you are," I whispered, aware of how the calm serenity of the moonlight had seeped into my voice.

Conor lifted his head, gazing up at me. I needed to be careful. Very careful. But the werewolf was a creature controlled by moonlight, so it shouldn't take much. Hopefully, my magic wouldn't even touch Conor the man.

"Change," I commanded, the cool clear tone of my voice ringing in the quiet room.

A flash of light enveloped the wolf, but I had expected it and was only aware of the brightness through my eyelids. When I opened my eyes a moment later, Conor knelt on the carpet before me.

"Welcome back," I whispered. If I'd known him better—or if he hadn't been completely naked—I would have hugged him.

I released the moonlight, and the silver light left in a rush, plunging the room into darkness. A brief pause, then the dim, natural moonlight once again seeped in around the edges of the curtains.

Conor doubled over, his forehead coming to rest against my

knees where I still knelt before him. "Oh God," his whispered, his voice rough.

"It's all right." I rubbed a hand over his tousled auburn hair.

"Is it?" he asked in the same broken whisper.

I released a silent breath. He hadn't gone along with my reassurance. He didn't believe me with blind devotion. The wolf had protected the man from my true power. I bit my lip as I struggled to hold in the swell of emotion the relief brought.

When I didn't answer, Conor lifted his head to look me in the eye.

I choked on a sob when I saw the dampness in his eyes. Like me, he was battling his own emotional response. Please let it be his *own* response.

"Leena?" he whispered. "Are you okay?"

"No, not me. What are *you* feeling?"

His brow wrinkled as he considered my question, then he bowed his head. "Fear, shame, but also"—he lifted his head to look me in the eye once more—"gratitude."

"Could you unpack that a little?"

The briefest of smiles flitted across his face, but he sobered as he took a deep breath. "Fear because I couldn't control any of that and it terrifies me that it might happen again."

"It won't," I whispered.

He studied me for one long moment, then continued. "Shame because I killed a man." His voice dropped to a whisper.

"No. Pete will be fine. He just needed some stitches. They probably won't even admit him. Though the Flame Lord might take him in for questioning."

Conor's eyebrows climbed his forehead. "The Flame Lord?"

"Problems for later. Gratitude?"

"That you are willing to use the magic that shames you to save me."

I choked on another sob. "No. I nearly let you kill a man because I was too afraid to reveal what I was in front of Detective Brody."

"Because you're not registered."

"That's not the reason." My pulse raced with the realization that I couldn't turn back now. I was really going to do this. I was going to tell him the truth. "I have a criminal record," I admitted.

The expression that silence is loud seems like an oxymoron, but it is so true. My ears were ringing from it.

"A criminal record?" Conor asked, breaking the painful silence.

How I longed to take my confession back. What was I doing? All I wanted was a hug and some understanding. Instead, I was going to push him away.

Unable to sit still, I rose to my feet and paced to the window. Pushing aside the curtain, I stared out at the fading moonlight. "After my parents died, I went down a dark path."

I toyed with the edge of the sheer curtain and forced myself to continue. "I fell in with the wrong crowd, and to make a long story short, I ended up leading a gang who periodically knocked off convenience stores. Most thieves rob by moonlight, we robbed *with* moonlight." I shook my head. I'd been so young and so stupid.

"Ultimately, we got caught. I got off with community service, and since I was only sixteen, my records were sealed. But someone like Detective Brody, who works closely with the PIA might have heard of me."

"The PIA?" Conor's voice came from the other side of the room, though I hadn't heard him move.

I released a breath, hoping he didn't hear how it shook. "I lied about fearing them because I wasn't registered. I just didn't want to tell you I'm a magical ex-con."

A soft snort carried to me, and I turned to see Conor standing by the coffee table. He'd found a pair of gym shorts somewhere and pulled them on.

"Hardly an ex-con," he said before I could speak. "You made some mistakes, regretted them, and have moved on with your life."

"Would you be so accepting if Pete had died?"

Conor looked away.

"I'm not talking about your actions. I'm referring to mine. I could have stopped you, but I was too selfish. To keep my secrets, I did nothing."

"How could you have stopped me? I know what you can do. A flash of moonlight wouldn't have frightened me away."

"Didn't you feel what I did a few minutes ago? I commanded you to change."

Conor cocked his head as he studied me, a faint frown creasing his forehead. I tensed, waiting for understanding to dawn on his features. When he realized that I could make him do what I wanted by—

He abruptly smiled. "You thought you *commanded* me to change?"

"Of course. I told you to change and you did."

"That's not what happened at all."

It was my turn to frown, though I didn't do the head cock.

"You showed me the way back to myself, and I was able to break free."

"Wait a minute. Are you saying that something actively held you in the wolf form?"

"Yes, after it forced me to take that form in the first place."

"What forced you?"

"Moonlight."

I cleared my throat. "That's not—"

"Possible? You witnessed it." Conor's brow wrinkled as he seemed to struggle to explain.

"I witnessed New Magic."

He lifted his hands and let them fall. "All I know is that the moment the moon rose, I was infected with an unshakeable certainty that werewolves were real, that I had been bitten by one, and that moonlight would free the wolf that was now trapped within me."

"And you changed," I whispered.

"I was helpless to stop it."

"What happened next? How did you know to go to Burnet Woods where the others were?"

"Honestly, I don't remember the journey. The first thing I remember was hearing someone shout your name, then the snarls." He shook his head, and it was clear he didn't like those memories.

"Never have I felt such rage, or…" He hesitated, then continued in a whisper, "Blood lust."

"How did you know to go home?" I asked to relieve him of further remembrances of his fight with Pete.

"I instinctively knew the moonlight was fading and that I would be forced to return to human form. Oddly, I didn't want that. At least, not until I found you waiting for me."

"I reminded you of your lost humanity," I suggested.

He shrugged, looking uncomfortable. "Yeah."

"But how did I help you change back?" I asked, struggling to make sense of his crazy tale.

"You calmed me. The serenity of your voice, the beauty of your face glowing like—" He stopped and even in the low light, I could see his blush. "You get the idea. It was like you took the place of the cold, blue light controlling me. You became my moon." He shrugged. "I don't know how else to explain it."

I stared at him. "That still sounds like I moon dazed you."

"Moon dazed?"

I sighed. I was going to have to tell him everything. "You once asked if I can do more than glow." I forced myself to hold his gaze and not pace away. "The answer is yes, I can. But I have no control over how it affects people. All become mesmerized by the light as long as I hold it. That's how I used it to rob those stores. I held the cashier in my power while my gang cleared out the register." I grimaced, hating to share any of this.

"I get that you used if for nefarious purposes, but what does that have to do with me?"

"Sometimes, the mesmerism remains. Most people shake off the effect rather quickly, but some remained moon dazed for days." My voice dropped to a whisper as I continued, "And there was one guy that I'd been forced to hold much longer than any other." I swallowed. "I heard he went mad."

Conor studied me and I tensed, awaiting the worst.

Abruptly, he smiled. "I'm neither mad nor mesmerized. Well, no more than I normally am around you." A hint of color appeared in his cheeks, and he hurried on. "You saved me *from* the madness."

I didn't know what to say to that. To any of that.

"Maybe those who suffered side effects were weak minded to begin with." A glint of amusement danced in his eyes as he continued, "They were mere mortals unable to handle the power of a goddess."

"Conor," I complained.

"Actually, there might be something to that." He grew serious as he continued, "Maybe your ability only works safely on the magical —or those that believe they are." His eyes held mine, his expression intense. "You have to help the other werewolves."

"I– I can't. I mean…" How did I refuse without sounding like an ass? "It's dangerous."

"It worked on me. I'm sure it will work on them. You need to break this curse."

Raking a hand through my hair, I struggled to find some way to refuse. Although, I did have a legitimate excuse at the moment. It would give me more time. "I can't now, because—"

"The moon has set." His voice dropped to a whisper, and he turned his face toward the west, though there was no window on that wall.

The way he turned and looked gave me a chill. "Did you just assume—"

"No." He faced me once more, his eyes wide. "I just know."

"The curse isn't broken."

"I don't think that's it," he said, his soft tone full of wonder. "I think I felt it through you." He reached up to touch my cheek.

I caught his wrist and pushed his hand away. "You *are* still moon dazed. You need to sleep this off." Without waiting for his response, I turned and walked to the door.

"Leena."

I stopped and looked back. "I'll return before moonrise." Or send someone in my stead. Like Brody or the PIA.

Ashamed of those thoughts, I pulled open the door and hurried away.

Chapter 8

I HALF EXPECTED Conor to follow me, but he let me go. I returned to my apartment and, after a hot shower, fell into bed. Even though I'd been up all night, I couldn't get to sleep. Or rather, I couldn't stay asleep. In my dreams, I was either chased by werewolves who wanted to eat me—or adore me.

It was close to noon when I gave up all pretense of sleeping and got dressed. Maybe I'd take a walk, or grab a coffee. Though I doubted anything would take my mind off my problems.

"And it shouldn't," I muttered. Running away wouldn't solve anything. I knew that and knew it well. If I was honest, I was still running. I'd made lots of new acquaintances over the last five years, but I wasn't close to anyone. I didn't have a best friend, and if I dated anyone, I broke it off after only a date or two. Now, I was running from Conor. Was it really because he needed to sleep off the mesmerism?

Then there was the problem with the other werewolves. Was I truly the best solution to that? Maybe this problem was bigger than I could handle. Perhaps I should contact Brody and ultimately, the PIA. They dealt with magical problems all the time. Maybe they had a better solution.

I took a deep breath and released it. I couldn't believe I was actually considering working with the PIA, but before I took that crazy step, I needed to discuss it with Conor. It would certainly get him some unwanted attention.

Retrieving my jacket, I stopped at the door and looked back at my spartan accommodations. Unlike Conor's snug, tastefully decorated apartment, mine felt cold and temporary. There was nothing here that meant anything to me. I could pick up and leave at a moment's notice.

"That needs to change," I told myself.

With new determination, I pulled open my front door and stepped out into the sunlight of a new day.

MY DETERMINATION FADED the closer I got to Conor's place. By the time I reached his apartment, I wanted nothing more than to turn and run the other way. But I stuck to my resolve and rapped my knuckles against his door.

Stuffing my hands in my pockets, I turned to glance across the street, looking at nothing in particular. When a good thirty seconds had passed, I lifted my hand to knock again, but hesitated. What if he was asleep? He'd been up all night as well—running on all fours for most of it—and unlike me, he wasn't plagued by guilt.

Or was I just using this as an excuse?

I pulled back my hand, but the door opened before my knuckles brushed the surface. Conor stood on the threshold, wearing a different pair of shorts and a faintly wrinkled T-shirt.

"I'm sorry. You were sleeping."

"Just dozing." He stepped back and held the door, inviting me to enter.

I stepped past him, crossing into the living room, and stopped at the edge of the couch, but I didn't sit down.

Conor closed the door, the snap of the latch loud in the silence. How did I begin? Did I—

"Before you say anything," Conor cut in, "I need to tell you something."

I faced him, puzzled by the request. I was the one with the issues. What could he possibly have to say?

He looked down and rubbed his palms against his hips as if nervous. Now, I was growing uneasy.

"I can't explain the moon thing," he began, "but I can clear the air about the whole mesmerized, moon dazed thing."

"Conor, I—"

"Please let me finish before I chicken out."

I stared at him, not sure what to make of that, but he just looked away, rubbing his palms against his shorts once more. What on earth could have him this unsettled?

"The thing is, I can't be...moon dazed because you only showed me your power two nights ago, and I've been, well, mesmerized by you for much longer than that." He spared me a quick glance, then looked away again. "As soon as Professor Giles handed out that crazy syllabus, I was going to drop the class. Then you took the seat beside me and asked if I'd tried the *drink me* potion. At that point, I was hopelessly hooked."

He looked up, an uncertain expression on his face.

"So you're saying it was the *Alice in Wonderland* quote and not the magic that won you over."

He offered an uncertain smile. "That's what I'm saying."

"Huh. Who knew?" My cheeks were burning, but I also couldn't fight the grin. Oh my God, he was attracted to me?

"So, um, you believe me—that I'm not moon dazed?"

"I should probably apologize. It just scared me. I overreacted."

"No. I get it." He fell silent.

The silence stretched, and I struggled to find something to say.

"Great. Now it's going to be awkward between us," he muttered.

"No, I'm glad you told me. If it makes things less awkward, I'm, um...attracted to you, too." The heat in my cheeks had never left, but that didn't stop them from bursting into full blaze again.

"Yeah?" His warm green eyes locked with my own.

"Yeah."

He watched me a moment, then reached up to touch my warm cheek.

My heart pounded in my ears, but I did nothing to stop him when he leaned down to kiss me. I didn't know if it was the kiss, or just the whirlwind of events over the last two days, but any attempt at higher cognitive function was no longer possible.

When he finally let me up for air, I just stared into his eyes, trying to pull my scattered wits together. This was so crazy. Two days ago, I thought he hated all things magical and that there would be no chance for us.

"You're really going to smite me now." His tone was teasing, but a wrinkle of concern creased his brow.

"Well, I'll probably need your help saving a pack of werewolves. Can I smite you later?"

His brows rose. "You'll help them?"

"I'll try."

"What's the plan?"

"We need to find the others, but Kristie's address is the only one I know."

Conor groaned. "Professor Giles."

"Afraid so. Hopefully, he'll be more helpful this time."

"Hopefully. I can't wait until this is over." The corner of his mouth crooked, his lips still flushed from our kiss.

I looked up from his very nice mouth. "Why are you smiling?"

"I'm just looking forward to my smiting." He wiggled his eyebrows.

So relieved that all was right between us, I threw back my head and laughed.

Professor Giles hung up his phone and looked across his desk at Conor and me. "Rick understands and will meet us tonight, before the moon rises."

I nodded, then glanced over to give Conor a grin. He returned the smile, though he didn't look as excited about our success as I thought he should. Perhaps he was still annoyed that he had to deal with the professor.

"It's such a relief that they understand what happened to them," I said.

"Of course they understand," Professor Giles answered, a hint of pride in his voice. "They're all my students."

The professor had already gotten the identity of the other three victims from Pete—who, according to the professor, had been surprisingly willing to cooperate. All three victims proved to be current or former students of the professor's Magic in Myth curriculum.

"Odd that Pete only chose to go after students in your classes," Conor said. "Does he have some conflict with you?"

"Pete believed he was sharing his gift with like-minded individuals." Professor Giles answered.

Conor lifted an eyebrow.

"Obviously, you just got in the way when he went after Miss Terrell," the professor added, his tone cool. He cleared his throat and turned to me. "Now, how is it that you plan to break this curse? Did you find something in the lore?"

"Not exactly," I admitted, debating what to say.

Professor Giles abruptly nodded. "Moonlight. Pete told me you wield the power of Selene."

My pulse jumped. Pete had told Professor Giles?

I glanced over at Conor, but he just shrugged. I guess it didn't matter if I let the professor in on my secret. I didn't have to admit to my criminal past.

"I'm New Magic," I admitted. "With it, I—"

"I don't believe in New Magic," Professor Giles cut me off.

For a moment, I just stared at him. "You don't believe I'm New Magic, or you don't believe in the phenomena in general?"

"It seems you haven't been paying attention in class." He smiled as he said it, his tone teasing. "Or perhaps you were so steeped in your own misguided beliefs that you couldn't comprehend what I was saying."

Clearly, he believed everything he was teaching.

"This New Magic, as everyone calls it, has always been with us," the professor continued his lecture. "I don't know what has happened to make us suddenly aware of it on such a large scale, but it is nothing new. Though in the past, it was viewed as it truly was: a gift from the gods. It surprises me that you haven't realized this."

A chill crawled up my spine as he studied me.

"I will say that our concept of gods and goddesses has become a bit skewed over the millennia," Professor Giles continued, lapsing into his familiar lecturing tone. "They were not all powerful immortals living in the clouds. That was only the perception of those who weren't part of their bloodline."

"Bloodline?"

"The magic of the gods is hereditary. Even today's New Magic recognizes that magic runs in families."

"What about Pete?"

"There are also gifts—and curses."

I didn't know what to say to any of this, but did it even matter what the professor thought? All I needed from him was help gathering the others.

"And you're willing to help me break this curse?" I asked.

"She can do it," Conor spoke up. "She showed me the way back."

"She lit the path." Professor Giles grinned at his pun. "As for your question, Selena, of course I'll help. Haven't I already started things in motion?"

I smiled, though I wanted to roll my eyes at the lame pun. Getting to my feet, I thanked the professor for his help, repeating the time and place for tonight's meeting.

"You've got my number if you need to reach me," I reminded him.

"Of course," Professor Giles agreed. "I'll see you tonight."

"We can handle it," Conor said, zipping up his jacket. "You don't need to come."

"They're my students." Professor Giles smiled, then gave me a wink. "I wouldn't miss it for the world."

Yeah, the guy was a few bubbles short of plumb, but at least he cared.

SINCE I COULDN'T USE my magic until the moon rose, Conor and I spent the afternoon at the zoo. It wasn't far from campus—just north of Burnet Woods—making it convenient. Despite the fact that I was going to have to display my talents to six people who were more or less strangers, I was able to relax and enjoy the day. We visited all the animal displays, though Conor spent a bit longer studying the wolves—despite my teasing.

Once the zoo closed, we walked to a nearby pub for dinner and ended up playing pool. Conor was pretty good, though I held my own, winning as much as I lost. All too soon, it was time to head out to a secret meeting with a pack of werewolves.

Professor Giles had insisted we meet in Burnet Woods. His reason was that most of his students didn't have transportation and he couldn't get a school van on such short notice. He did, however, choose a different spot to meet in the spacious ninety-acre park.

"You okay?" Conor asked as we crossed the street and started into the park itself.

"A little nervous," I admitted.

Conor took my hand. "You'll do fine."

Something must have shown on my face because he pulled me to a stop. "Leena?"

"What if what happened with you was a fluke? What if the others end up worshipping me—or go mad," I finished in a whisper.

"That won't happen."

"How can you know that?"

"Because they're all just like me. What you did for me will work for them."

"But—"

"More than that, I believe in you. And as Professor Giles taught us, if you believe hard enough, you can make it a reality."

I smiled despite my misgivings. But then, I'd discovered that Conor was good at making me smile.

"I think the professor is delusional," I admitted.

"First you call me a fool, and now I'm delusional," Conor teased, referencing our banter on the lookout tower at Serpent Mound.

At the time, I'd been so afraid I'd insulted him, but now I laughed. "If the shoe fits…"

He tried to look annoyed by the insult, but it faded quickly as he reached up to cup my cheek. "I'm serious, Leena. I have complete faith in you." Even in the low light, I could see the warmness in his eyes. "You were my light in the darkness."

He leaned in for another kiss but pulled away far too soon. "The moon will rise soon," he reminded me.

I hoped he hadn't sensed it, but I didn't ask. "You're right. Now stop distracting me. I've got work to do."

～

WE ARRIVED at the small clearing the professor had selected shortly before moonrise. It surprised me that we were the first to arrive. We were only about ten minutes early.

"Are we in the right place?" I asked Conor. "The moon will be up soon." I released a breath, aware of how it shook.

Conor still held my hand in his, and he gave me a reassuring squeeze though he kept his focus on our surroundings, watching for the others.

Another five minutes ticked past. The moon would be rising at any moment.

"Something isn't right," I insisted. "They should be here."

"But we are here," a new voice said.

I turned with a gasp and watched a robed figure walk out of the shadows. He stopped a few feet away and pushed back his hood, revealing Pete's smiling face.

Conor released my hand and moved forward. "I wondered if you would show."

"Of course."

Conor's eyes narrowed as he studied the other man. "Did you intentionally infect me and the others?"

"How much control did you have when you nearly ripped out my throat?"

Conor's frown deepened. "I—"

Pete lifted a hand, silencing him. "There's no need to explain. But as for your infection question, you know it doesn't have to be a curse. It can be a gift. Right, Professor."

"That's right, Pete." Professor Giles left the shadows of the trees and walked over to join us.

I took a breath, ready to demand they tell me what was going on when the moonlight enveloped us. The moon had risen.

With a flash of light, Pete became the wolf, but to my immense relief, Conor did not.

Professor Giles stared at Conor, his mouth dropping open in surprise before seeming to gather himself. "You are powerful, Selene." The words were whispered in awe.

I didn't get to revel in my success as Pete sprang toward Conor. I knew from their first confrontation at Serpent Mound that Conor was no match for Pete in wolf form.

I reached out to the moon, but at the last second, Pete veered around Conor. Surprised by the move, I hesitated, and it cost me. Pete changed course, and in a single bound, he was on me. Before I could do more than gasp, he sank his teeth into my right leg, just above the knee.

With a cry of surprise, I fell back, landing hard on my butt in the leaves.

Pete had released his grip on my leg when I fell and now stood over me. But rather than growl or snarl, he looked up at Professor Giles, as if he'd attacked me to please the professor.

"Hey!" Conor shouted.

Pete spun to face him. The move so fast it startled me, but he didn't immediately attack as I expected.

"How about a rematch?" Conor cast aside his jacket and toed off his shoes. What the hell was he doing?

Pete snarled and took a step closer.

"Are you sure that's wise?" Conor asked as he pulled off his T-shirt and dropped it beside his jacket. "This time, I will rip out your throat."

As if his threat had summoned them, six other wolves materialized out of the shadows one by one. None attacked, but all watched with interest.

Was Conor just buying me time, waiting for the other wolves to arrive so I could end this? I pushed myself to my feet, but before I could reach for moonlight, Conor shoved down his jeans, and in a flash of light, he too was a wolf.

This time, my mouth dropped open.

"Interesting," Professor Giles said, admiration in his tone.

"Interesting?" I demanded. "What's going on?"

Professor Giles pulled his gaze from Conor to focus on me. "I tried to show you the way. To explain that this New Magic propaganda is just lies and hot air, but you wouldn't listen." He offered a soft smile, his kind eyes sympathetic.

Vicious growls carried to us, and I glanced over at Conor and Pete. As they had last night, they were circling, each looking for an opening.

"Though I've told Pete not to force the truth on those who aren't ready for it," Professor Giles continued, "I'm afraid I had to make an exception in your case."

I faced him once more. "Are you saying you lured me out here so Pete could bite me?"

"I'm sorry I had to do this, but I couldn't allow you to spread your madness."

A chill crawled up my spine. He knew what my magic could do?

Snarls pulled my attention back to the wolves, and I saw Conor and Pete close in on each other, teeth flashing in the moonlight. It was hard to judge with the quickness of the attack, but Conor might be bigger and faster. Yet it wouldn't matter if Conor won. The other wolves moved closer, a couple laying back their lips and snarling.

I was fairly certain the others had a connection to Pete, the original werewolf. After all, they'd all been drawn to him last night. Whether they truly controlled the compulsion was immaterial. Conor was in danger.

Out of time, I reached for the moon—and nothing happened.

Chapter 9

"WHAT THE HELL?" I whispered. "Why doesn't the moonlight obey me?"

"Because you are now a servant of the moon. Or rather, the natural world of magic." The professor gave me a sad shake of his head. "I hope you can now see that New Magic is just an illusion."

I took a step back, and pain shot through my leg. Bending, I gripped the injury, aware of the warm blood that had dampened my jeans, just above my knee. "Because Pete bit me?" I demanded. "Shouldn't I be a werewolf?"

"I've observed that it requires about twenty-four hours to take full effect. You know the legends. Your paper was one of the best in class."

A yelp came from the wolves, and I instinctively knew it was Conor. I turned in time to watch one of the periphery wolves release his back leg. Had it managed to hamstring him? I couldn't tell. He barely had a chance to limp away before Pete was on him again.

Shit. What was I going to do? How could I stop this? It shouldn't be possible that Pete's curse could override my magic and take the moon from me, but maybe *I* didn't have to stop this.

"Professor." I struggled to hide my true feelings from the delusional nut. "This isn't right. Please ask them to stop. They'll listen to you."

"But Mr. Middleton is a heretic. He took their magic and twisted it. They recognize that."

"So you're just going to let them kill him?"

"Miss Terrell—"

I reached out to grip his wrist, to implore him, but the moment my skin brushed his, a bolt of static-like energy cracked between us. I pulled back with a gasp.

Professor Giles chuckled and rubbed his wrist. "I suspect it's that fleece jacket you're wearing. I've never been a fan of the stuff." He tugged the collar of his worn duster, straightening it.

I was no longer listening. It wasn't my jacket. I'd felt that kind of shock—when I touched Gordon. Professor Giles was New Magic. And since I wasn't holding my magic, he must be using his.

"What are you doing?" I demanded.

"Hmm?" Professor Giles had been watching the fight, but now glanced back at me.

"What kind of magic do you possess?"

He appeared genuinely puzzled by the question, then abruptly laughed. "None, I'm afraid. It seems I can only inspire belief in others. Ironic, isn't it?"

"You can drop the bullshit."

His forehead wrinkled as he studied me, and I thought he might confess, then he offered another sad shake of his head. "I like you, Selena. I hope one day you too will see the true magic of the world —even if I had to ask Pete to initially force the truth on you."

I just stared at him. Could it be that he didn't know what he was doing? And what exactly was that? Making other people magical?

No, that wasn't right. He gave other people the power to make their beliefs a reality. That was clearly what had happened with Gordon. He had believed that brownies existed, and the professor had given him the ability to make it real. Apparently, Pete believed in werewolves.

But mythical werewolves were contagious, and once Pete

became one, he was able to spread the magic. Which reinforced the professor's theory that belief in the mythical was what made it real in the past, and could make it a reality once more.

I remembered Conor's joke that if the professor believed his own rhetoric strongly enough, it would become real. It looked like Conor had nailed it.

Conor yelped. The others were now taking turns harrying him, which gave Pete a break. Conor wouldn't get the opportunity to rip out his throat as he promised. Not that I truly wanted Conor to kill the other man, but seven on one wasn't fair.

Conor tried to avoid the two wolves who charged him, but his back leg buckled, and he dropped to his stomach. The fall actually spared him as one wolf's jaws snapped closed where he had been.

With no other options, I grabbed a stick from the underbrush and ran toward the wolves.

My weapon of choice was overly long and still had a few leaves clinging to a pair of thin twigs on the far end. But I didn't let that stop me. I swung it with all my might at the wolf closing with Conor. Focused on dealing Conor a damaging bite, the wolf didn't even see me coming. I smacked him full in the face and sent him stumbling.

"Back off!" I lifted my weapon and positioned myself over Conor. If they wanted him, they had to go through me.

Several snarls answered my declaration, but they didn't charge me in mass as I expected.

I thought the professor might say something, but he just watched me with a disappointed, yet accepting expression on his face.

A deep growl came from the wolves. Pete moved toward me, teeth bared and blood lust in his eyes.

Bright light, like a camera flash, came from behind me, and an instant later, a hand wrapped around my calf. "Leena." Conor's grip tightened on my leg. "What are you waiting for?"

"I'm afraid the professor got the drop on me," I answered. "He used his stooge to take the moonlight from me."

"What?" Conor didn't have any idea what I was talking about, of course.

"Pete," I clarified. "The professor's self-styled werewolf."

The werewolf in question snarled but, to my surprise, didn't immediately attack.

"Professor Giles is New Magic," I said. "He made Pete what he is." I held the wolf's blue eyes, willing him to see the truth in my statement.

"Pete was bitten by a wolf beneath the full moon," Professor Giles said, moving closer. "He even put himself in that position to prove that the legends were true." He gave Pete the wolf a fond smile. "You could learn a thing or two about bravery from him, Miss Terrell. But perhaps you'll understand once you join their ranks."

Conor's hand slid up over my knee, finding the blood on my pants. "Leena?"

"The professor's talent is to make real the fables he believes—at least in those who fall for his rhetoric. He can then use those talents to infect his worldview on others. Pete's his pawn."

Apparently, Pete didn't like that description. He charged me, teeth bared and a vicious growl rumbling in his throat.

I swung my stick, but he was too close, and it was unwieldy. He ducked the blow, then whirled around and caught the branch in his teeth. Before I could regain my balance, he jerked it from my hands, pulling me off my feet in the process. I landed on my knees, now between him and Conor.

Pete dropped the branch, then lifted his lips, his eyes meeting mine.

Conor's arms came around me from behind.

I gripped his wrist. "I'm sorry," I whispered. "I can't feel the moonlight."

"Not possible." Conor spoke in a low growl, his mouth close to my ear. "You let him get in your head."

My breath caught and I looked up at Professor Giles. He watched the proceedings with a sad, but resigned expression. Was Conor right?

"He used Pete to infect you just like he did me," Conor continued. "But I saw through it because I believed in you." His arm tightened, hugging me briefly before he let go. "Believe in yourself."

Was that all I had to do? I rose to my feet to face Professor Giles and his wolves. My power had never left me. This was all just a trick. I reached for the moonlight—and felt nothing.

Even if my theory was correct that the professor was essentially unaware of what he was doing, he must have at least sensed something. Or I guess it could have been the stunned look on my face. Whatever it was, he smiled at my failure.

Pete paced toward me.

"I believe in you, Leena," Conor said. "How else could I control this." A flash of light, and he lunged past me, meeting Pete with a renewed frenzy.

Pulse racing, I stumbled back out of their path. Conor had broken out of Pete's—or rather, the professor's hold because he didn't believe. Not in his heart. He was able to see the professor's magic for what it was: an infection. Even Pete initially called it a curse.

But to break the curse, I had to *not* believe in the very thing that held me captive. Or maybe Conor had the right idea. All I had to do was believe in something else.

Me. Or more accurately, my magic.

Yeah, something that had been a source of shame for me since it had appeared a week after I lost my parents—like some kind of bad joke.

The vicious battle between Conor and Pete continued. Oddly, the other wolves backed off. Maybe it was his renewed fight, or they'd seen how he'd taken control of his magic.

Conor snarled and lunged, catching Pete by the shoulder. Pete's cry of pain sounded eerily human. I didn't want Conor hurt, but I also didn't want him to do something he'd regret. I remembered the tears in his eyes when he thought he'd killed Pete before.

"Focus," I whispered. Conor had taken command of his magic even though he hadn't been born to it. I was meant to be what I was. Dad had named me Selena after all.

Turning away from the fight, I found the professor watching me, worry etched on his features. He knew what I was.

I smiled and reached for moonlight, grasping those cool beams and pulling them to myself. The world beyond my glow darkened as I welcomed the exhilaration that filled me. I had been born to this.

"Stop." My voice carried the cool clarity of my power, washing away any opposition like moonlight washes away color.

Silence filled the clearing, but I didn't look to see what the wolves were doing. My gaze remained locked with the professor's. After all, he was the true source of this curse.

Trying not to think too deeply about what I did, I closed the distance between us.

"Professor Giles," I greeted him, smiling as I spoke, just as I'd smiled at those poor, unsuspecting mundanes behind their conve-nient-store counters. "This might have begun in innocence, but I saw your true nature when you showed your willingness to destroy those who did not conform to your ideals."

"My Lady," he gasped, and then to my complete shock, he dropped to his knees and began to grovel at my feet. "Please have mercy on me, Lady Selene."

I flinched at the address but held on to my resolve. "Withdraw your influence, Professor, and allow your students to find their own paths. Only then will I consider forgiving you."

He blubbered his gratitude, gushing his promises as he continued to genuflect at my feet.

Uncomfortable with this disturbing reminder of what my full power could do, I turned away. All the wolves were staring at us, then a series of bright flashes flickered around the clearing, consuming each wolf.

The clearing now rang with cries of surprise as the former were-wolves found themselves naked in a public park. Almost as one, they turned and fled into the trees, leaving only a single wolf standing in the blood-slicked leaves.

Conor the wolf looked over at me, his tongue rolling out in what I took for a grin.

"I hope they remember where they left their clothes," I said.

Conor swished his tail once, then abruptly laid back his ears and snarled.

Pulling the moonlight close, I spun to face whatever threat he'd spotted. To my surprise, I saw Detective Brody leave the shadows of the trees for the brighter light of the clearing. I was about to call a greeting when a second man followed. I'd never met him before, but I'd seen his face on TV many times.

Aware that Professor Giles was still proclaiming his undying devotion as he groveled at my feet, I released the moonlight and offered an uncertain smile to the Lord of Flames.

Chapter 10

"MISS TERRELL," Brody greeted me, his smile oddly smug. "I see you have everything in hand." He cast the Flame Lord a pointed look, then continued to me, "Just as I knew you would."

I opened my mouth and closed it. What?

"And last time you ended up in the hospital," the Flame Lord said to Brody. "Forgive me, but you don't always get it right." He looked more amused than angry, but he sobered as he faced me. "Miss Terrell is it?"

"Yes, Your Grace," I managed, surprised my voice didn't break. "Selena Terrell." I would have offered my hand, but I would have had to move closer, and I didn't trust my legs not to buckle.

"Selena is not the villain here." Conor's voice was accompanied by the rasp of a zipper. He stepped up beside me a moment later, clad only in his jeans, his chest and feet still bare. "He's your villain." Conor pointed at the professor, who didn't look up from his adoration of my shoes.

Dread wormed through my gut. Oh God, had I done it again? Had driven the professor mad?

"And you are?" the Flame Lord asked Conor. He didn't seem angry, but his cool watchfulness made me uneasy.

Conor stepped forward without hesitation and offered his hand. "Conor Middleton," he said as they exchanged a handshake. "I hope you'll excuse my forwardness, but I wanted to clear up any misunderstanding before it happened."

"Thank you." His Grace eyed Conor. "You're a shifter."

"Oh, um, yeah," Conor answered, clearly trying to hide his own shock. "You picked up on that through a handshake?"

"Your style of dress—though I am grateful for the pants. I don't always get that courtesy."

"Shifters tend to lose their clothes," Brody clarified, then turned to me. "So, the professor is my man?"

"Yes," I made myself speak up. "He has the ability to…make myths come to life."

Professor Giles lifted his head at that moment to stare up at me. Yeah, like make a moon goddess come to life.

I crossed my arms, trying to ignore the chill that gave me. "In truth, he may not have fully understood what he was doing," I added. "But he wasn't opposed to letting his werewolves take down Conor and me."

"His werewolves?" His Grace asked.

"The contagious ones I told you about," Brody spoke up. "Like Mr. Middleton here."

Conor looked up from pulling on his T-shirt.

"No. He's New Magic," His Grace insisted.

Conor caught my eye, looking a bit alarmed by that statement. Didn't he understand what had just happened?

"I can see there's a lot more to this story," His Grace continued. "Let's head over to the PIA offices, and you two can tell me all about it."

I stilled at the mention of the PIA, but there was nothing to be done about it now. Conor and I agreed while Brody snapped a pair of cuffs on the professor and helped him to his feet.

"My lady?" Professor Giles looked frightened.

"Go with Detective Brody," I told him. "Everything will fine."

The professor nodded, and Brody started him toward the path. That's when I realized the Flame Lord was watching me.

"He's just a little moon dazed," I explained. "I had to lay it on a little thick to break the spell he had on the others."

"Like those guys in the convenient stores?" His Grace asked.

I forgot to breathe.

"Miss Terrell?"

"Those records were supposed to be sealed," I whispered.

"I'm sure they are, but I still remember."

I swallowed. "I was young and stupid. I don't do things like that anymore. I didn't want to do it tonight, but I didn't have a choice. I hope the professor doesn't go mad."

"Go mad?"

"Like the old guy from the store on Tenth Street," I whispered. If His Grace knew my record he must know about—

"Barry Howard suffered from mental illness. Whatever you did wore off in twenty-four hours, but the medical attention ended up getting him some help." His Grace smiled. "So in the end, you helped him."

I pressed a hand to my chest. "I did?"

Conor stepped up beside me and rested a hand on the small of my back as if aware that my legs had turned to jelly.

"I'm sure Professor Giles will be fine," His Grace added. "Well, I'm sure he'll suffer no lasting effects from your magic."

I exhaled the breath I'd been holding, hoping no one noticed how much it shook. "Thank you, Your Grace."

He gave me a kind smile, then glanced at Conor. "Now that I don't have to worry about your buddy mooning me, let's go."

My relief left me giddy, and I laughed far more than the quip warranted.

Conor just rolled his eyes. "Well, that's different," he whispered as we followed His Grace. "Normally, it's your moon we have to worry about."

I elbowed him. "Careful. I still owe you a smiting."

Conor chuckled. "Looking forward to it."

∾

BRODY PARKED his car at the curb outside my apartment but didn't shut off the engine. "I want to thank you both for your help with this case." He glanced over at me in the passenger seat, then at Conor in the back seat. "I had a feeling you'd be instrumental in solving it."

"A feeling?" I asked. "Well, I have a feeling there's more than meets the eye where you're concerned." I arched an eyebrow. Having just survived a meeting with not only the Flame Lord, but the director of the regional PIA office, I was feeling a bit brazen.

Conor unlatched his seatbelt and scooted forward to rest his elbow on the back of my seat. "Leena's right. Are you magical, Detective?"

Brody glanced between us, a faint smile on his face. "No, I'm not." His blue eyes returned to me. "But you already knew that. You checked."

"How did you—" I began.

"He's Old Magic," Conor said.

"No. I really have no magic at all." Brody took a deep breath as if steeling himself for what came next. "I'm a seer."

Stunned, it took me a moment to find my voice. "They exist?" I'd heard rumors, but never believed that such an ability was real.

"You can see the future?" Conor asked.

Brody lifted a hand, silencing any further questions. "Before you accuse me of lying, or playing you, please know that this ability is nothing more than random, often nonsensical, visions and intuition. My first vision was of a snake frightening off a wolf in the moonlight."

"Serpent Mound," Conor said.

"Yeah, it's obvious in hindsight." Brody rolled his eyes, but grew serious as he continued. "I hope you both can forgive me for keeping my ability to myself, but people treat you differently when they think you can see the future."

"Leena said something very similar when I first learned she was magical."

"I guess you're about to learn that lesson first hand, Mr. Middleton."

"It's Conor. And yeah, I guess so." Conor's eyes met mine.

"Well, not to cut this little tell-all short, but I need to go," Brody said. "Tomorrow looks like another busy day, and it seems I can expect a late night." He frowned and continued to himself. "Though I didn't realize she was in town."

"Way to go, Detective," Conor said. "I guess the seer thing isn't all bad."

I didn't miss the faint blush that colored Brody's cheeks.

"It's nothing like that," Brody said quickly. "She's a necromancer and the late night has something to do with a grave. I just hope there aren't any zombies." Brody made a face.

Laughing, Conor and I thanked him for the ride and climbed from the car, letting him drive off toward whatever zombie-filled adventure was on his horizon.

Conor walked me to my door and waited while I unlocked it. He'd insisted on seeing me safely inside before walking back to his place.

Door unlocked, I turned to face him, meeting his fair eyes in the moonlight. "I still can't believe you're magical," I said softly, though there was no one around to hear us. It was almost two in the morning after all.

"To be honest, I haven't come to terms with it either. But the Flame Lord confirmed it, so…" He shrugged.

The whole situation was so bizarre. I didn't fully understand how it had come to be, but Conor's awareness that the source of his shifting came from New Magic enabled him to keep the ability. Unlike the others who truly believed it was the curse of a mythical werewolf that caused them to shift. And now that I had broken that curse, their ability was gone. Well, that's what we assumed.

Either way, it seemed Professor Giles was right. It was all about what you believed—though it was the professor himself who had somehow given his students an initial magical push. Conor and I planned to visit the other werewolves to make certain they were all mundanes once more.

"Are you disappointed?" I asked. After all, Conor had been rather disparaging of magic early in our acquaintance.

"No." He appeared puzzled by my question. "Why would I be? It's a rush."

I smiled. "Yeah, it is. Can I expect to see you running around campus in furry form?"

"Not during the day." His hands settled on my hips, and he pulled me closer. "I need my moon to shift, remember?"

I looked up into his eyes, a bit stunned. Perhaps he hadn't fully escaped the professor's magic. He still believed in the myth—just with a few alterations.

"Leena?"

"Are you saying you need me to make your magic work?"

He smiled at that. "A werewolf needs his moon."

When I didn't return his smile, he sobered. "Is that okay? I would have asked you to be my moon, but I can't change that now."

"Are you sure you're not moon dazed?"

"Oh, I'm sure am, but not in the way you fear." His warm gaze held mine. "This has much more to do with the heart than some lunar magic."

Whoa. Was he saying—

"But if I could ask," he continued, watching me closely, "*would* you be my moon?"

The enormity of his question hit me. He wasn't just asking me to be his girlfriend or anything so…mundane. He was asking me to embrace my magic, a magic I had always associated with shame, and be his guide, his partner, on a new journey. A journey of the heart. But the most shocking aspect of all of this was how quickly I had my answer.

I slid my arms around his shoulders, reaching for the moonlight as I pulled both it and him closer. "I'll be your moon," I whispered, watching my silver light dance in his green eyes.

"I'd howl with joy," he answered in the same soft voice, "but I'd rather kiss you."

Tightening my arms around his neck, I pressed my lips to his and kissed him back.

Thanks for reading A Myth in Moonlight. Looking for more in the same story universe? Begin your adventure with the highly rated Final Formula Series. (And learn the reason behind the Flame Lord's teasing comments to Conor.) The first book, The Final Formula, is free everywhere my books are sold.

https://beccaandre.com/the-final-formula-series/

Also, be sure to sign up for my newsletter and gain access to exclusive content—including a Detective Brody novella.

https://beccaandre.com/newsletter/